HIS CINDERELLA NEXT DOOR

CARA COLTER

THE BABY THAT BINDS THEM

STELLA BAGWELL

MILLS & BOON

First Published in Great Britain 2021
by Mills & Boon, an imprint of HarperCollins*Publishers* Ltd
1 London Bridge Street, London, SE1 9GF

www.harpercollins.co.uk

HarperCollins*Publishers*
1st Floor, Watermarque Building,
Ringsend Road, Dublin 4, Ireland

His Cinderella Next Door © 2021 Cara Colter
The Baby That Binds Them © 2021 Stella Bagwell

ISBN: 978-0-263-29977-9

0521

HIS CINDERELLA
NEXT DOOR

CARA COLTER

Cara Colter shares her life in beautiful British Columbia, Canada, with her husband, nine horses and one small Pomeranian with a large attitude. She loves to hear from readers, and you can learn more about her and contact her through Facebook.

After writing more than one hundred books for Mills & Boon, **Stella Bagwell** still finds it exciting to create new stories and bring her characters to life. She loves all things Western and has been married to her own real cowboy for forty-four years. Living on the south Texas coast, she also enjoys being outdoors and helping her husband care for the horses, cats and dog that call their small ranch home. The couple has one son, who teaches high school mathematics and is also an athletic director. Stella loves hearing from readers. They can contact her at stellabagwell@gmail.com

CHAPTER ONE

Come.

MOLLY BENTWELL CLOSED her eyes. How could a single word evoke so much feeling? The word removed her—thankfully and completely—from the chaos all around her.

Her small Frankfurt flat currently looked as though it had been burglarized. Boxes were stacked haphazardly. Clothes were strewn on the floor. There were bright empty squares on the walls, where the paint had not faded, where not so long ago all the pictures had hung.

She was getting ready to move, again. She wasn't quite sure where. Paris was too expensive. Ditto for London.

It didn't really matter where, though. Moving was an excellent antidote for pain.

She closed her eyes against the fresh wave of hurt that hit her. Ralphie was gone. Even now, eight months, one week and two days later, it seemed impossible.

He had been the one constant in her life. He had been the one it was safe to love. Every single day, no matter where her photography had taken her, he had been her touchstone. She would check the time differences and it didn't matter if it was the middle of the night where she was, if it was eight in the morning where he was, she called.

And the sun came out in her world when she heard his voice. When he told her news of Georgie, the cat he'd inherited from her.

The first thing Molly had done, in every single destination she had arrived at, was take a photograph of some special thing like an alligator, an elephant, a flower or a tree. Mostly she emailed them, and Ralphie would reply to the email with a picture of the cat that was beloved to both of them.

Now, the message she had grown up with—that love was the most dangerous thing of all—had been reinforced in the most terrible way.

She opened her eyes, and that single word jumped out of the email in front of her again.

Come.

The word filled her with longing to be with him. Oscar Clark, Ralphie's brother, the only other person in the world who would totally get the sharp ache of this never-ending pain.

Oscar. Truck, she'd called him the first day they'd met, in kindergarten. She'd been reading since she was four, and she had picked the word *car* out of his carefully printed name on his bright yellow sunshine-shaped tag.

"Truck is a better name," she'd informed him, full of the officiousness of being the only one in the kindergarten class who already knew how to read. "My daddy says he would never own a car. Never."

And so, Truck it was.

As it turned out, Oscar lived on the estate next to the ramshackle farm that Molly and her father, Jimmy, used as a home base when Jimmy wasn't working on a film as one of the most sought-after stuntmen in the industry.

Her mother, who had died when Molly was very young, was a vague memory of good smells and soft words read from a large picture book. Her mother was also Jimmy's cautionary tale to his daughter about the dangers of love.

"Beware of love," he'd tell her, made melancholy by a few drinks. "It is hiding daggers in its magical cloak."

And he'd been right. Because she had loved him, her father—and all of his magic and chaos—madly, and still felt the dagger of that loss in her heart daily.

Now, Ralphie.

And now, Oscar, asking her to come. She was aware of wanting what he promised—comfort, commiseration—with a yearning that was both compelling and frightening.

She thought, again, of that first day of school. Standing there, in the classroom, Molly had already been aware she was different than the other children, and not because she was the only one who knew how to read. The girls were in pretty dresses and had ribbons in their curled locks. All the children had a shiny fresh-scrubbed look about them. Nobody else's father was there.

Molly was in bib overalls, with a rip in one knee and a brand new white T-shirt, with which she had been inordinately pleased. Her dad had clumsily contained her unruly mop of curly hair into a braid so tight it felt as if her skin were being stretched. She had bathed last night, but on the way to school, her hand firmly in her father's—terrified of this strange institution she was being turned over to—she had seen a frog. And had to have it.

Her dad had helped her catch it and put it in his pocket for her to have later because, according to him, frogs weren't allowed in school. This astonishing declaration intensified Molly's feeling of being sent to some kind of joyless dungeon, like the ones princesses in fairy tales so often ended up in.

Molly and her father presented themselves to the kindergarten teacher thirty minutes late, and with smudges of mud puddle on their faces and hands. Her new T-shirt was nowhere near white anymore.

Halfway through that torturous first morning, the frog had decided to announce his escape from her father's pocket with giant hops down the row between the desks, croaking loudly, and relieving the pure tedium of learning the words for colors, which Molly already knew.

Miss Michaels jumped on her chair in an astounding show of hysteria. The girls in the class, apparently looking to Miss Michaels for what Molly already considered somewhat dubious leadership, began to scream.

The boys abandoned their seats and took after the frog, creating pandemonium. Soon, the classroom floor was littered with papers and books, pencils and crayons, one overturned desk and a broken chair.

He'd emerged with the frog—that boy with the big glasses and the sun-shaped name tag that said *Oscar* on it—and held it to his chest, protectively, away from the other boys. Truck had held that frog with tenderness that won Molly's young heart.

If she were a princess confined to a dungeon, he was the prince who would rescue her.

They had been friends ever since. Oscar was quiet, smart, steady, the class geek, even in kindergarten, and Molly was the bold one, the rambunctious one, the one who was always either in trouble or looking for it.

And then there had been his brother, Ralphie, the third member of their circle. Her throat closed as she remembered his laughter, and she felt a sting behind her eyes.

Eight months, one week and two days. How was Oscar surviving the loss?

Come.

Even now, a world away, six years from the last time she had seen him, Molly could feel the longing for the comfort of his presence, the steadiness of him, the feeling of being safe and cared about, liked exactly as she was.

Those feelings crowded out a sense of danger that had entered their relationship unexpectedly. When her prince had kissed her, making them both aware of each other in a new way.

A way that had made her understand love had a dimension to it that was as terrifying as her father had so dourly warned her all those years.

Looking at Oscar's invitation now, Molly was aware all those feelings he evoked in her—not to mention the added dimension—should be the exact thing she should run away from right now.

But life had stolen her strength. Molly let her eyes drop to the temptation of the next line.

I've broken up with Cynthia. Why don't you come to Vancouver for a few days? My place is huge. We could just hang out and have some fun, and do what best friends do, which is help each other through a rough time. I don't know how I'm going to handle Ralphie's birthday.

Just like that, she could picture Oscar, the way he had been when she last saw him, tall and lanky, like a puppy who had not yet grown into its feet. That shock of dark hair—*the perfect mad scientist doo*, she used to call it affectionately—falling down over one eye. Oblivious to peer pressure—you could afford that when you were born a Clark—he was always dressed as if his clothes were an absent-minded afterthought. She had seen him have on shorts in the winter, or different colored socks. Occasionally, his shoes didn't match, either. Sometimes his shirts were inside out.

When one of those popular girls—why did they always have such mean eyes—had tried to mock him for that inside-out shirt, he had looked down at himself with surprised interest and said, ever so mildly, "In Belize, they would say I am hunting witches."

Who knew that kind of thing? Oscar, that's who.

Six years since she had seen him. She felt the ache of missing him. But after her father's death, life had changed so quickly, her world had been upended so fast. She'd learned the hard way about love's daggers. And her feelings for Oscar… Molly frowned. She didn't want to think of that anymore.

As much as she had embraced keeping in touch with Ralphie, she had kept things deliberately at a distance with Oscar.

They sent each other the odd email, he always called her on her birthday, and she always called him on his, they exchanged Christmas gifts each year, the funnier the better. She usually added to his beloved, and ever so nerdy, science T-shirt collection, and he usually found her the worst photographs imaginable and had them elaborately framed.

Those photographs always hung in places of honor wherever she lived. Now, she'd taken them off the walls in preparation for her latest move.

She looked back to Oscar's email.

I need to do something for Ralphie. His birthday would be a good time, but I don't know what to do. I'm lost.

She had always counted on Oscar to be unchanging; she had relied on his steadiness. He was lost? It seemed unimaginable.

But she felt lost, too, ever since he had called her to tell her Ralphie had died. She had planned to go home for the service, but it turned out Mrs. Clark, Ralphie and Oscar's mother, had decided against a service. But how did they arrive at closure without that important marking place? Without holding some occasion to celebrate Ralphie's too-short life?

Molly let her eyes drop to the final line of the email.

I need you.

She had always needed Oscar—even from afar, his steadiness was there, in the background—but had he ever needed her before?

Come.

It felt as if she were a sailor on a boat that had been tossed about by a stormy sea and suddenly, by way of Oscar's unexpected invitation, she had spotted a lighthouse.

She clicked on the attachment that Oscar had sent with the email.

Molly wasn't sure what she was expecting. A recent picture of him, perhaps?

Her jaw fell. It was a first-class ticket to Vancouver from Frankfurt. It had her name on it and tomorrow's date.

She stared at it.

She couldn't possibly go. But why not? The move could wait. She hadn't given notice, yet. She was undecided exactly where to go, anyway.

Maybe being around Oscar's steadiness would help her crystalize her own plans for the future.

Ever since she was a child, she had traveled on short notice, and as a photographer, the pattern continued. In fact, she was scheduled to go to Africa at the beginning of next week, so it was not as if her passport was not up to date. She was an absolute expert at throwing a few essentials into the carry-on bag that she prided herself on being able to live out of—anywhere—for a week, or even two.

She glanced around at the mess of unresolved issues in her apartment.

She thought of Oscar—Truck. The warmth in his eyes, the easiness of his smile, his calm way of being in the world.

She thought of them needing each other to say a proper goodbye to Ralphie.

She sent a text to her contact in Africa. Molly hesitated, took a deep breath, hesitated for a few more seconds, then pushed print on the airline ticket on her screen. Only after she'd printed it, did she notice there was no return flight information.

Molly was a woman who did scary things for a living. She was a woman who welcomed the charge of the elephant, and who would eagerly hang from her knees from the tallest branch of a tree if it meant getting the picture perfect.

So why did the airline ticket, with no return, being spit out by her printer, feel like one of the scariest adventures she would ever embark on?

CHAPTER TWO

"Truck!"

Hearing the name only Molly had ever called him coming through the throngs at Vancouver International Airport, did a funny thing in the region of Oscar's heart. Since his brother had died, it felt as if his heart were a stone in the center of his chest. He didn't want it fluttering back to life.

It was so much easier to feel nothing at all. But if he had wanted to feel nothing at all, why ask Molly, the person who made him feel everything so intensely, to come?

Because she had navigated the sea of grief over her father. Because she had loved Ralphie as dearly as he. There was a hope she would know what to do.

And under that, it was a bit of a test for him. He was a scientist. He enjoyed tests. He needed to prove theories. And his theory—since the death of his brother and the end of his engagement—was that relationships sucked, and that he would not be having another one.

No, he would remain single. He would hike high mountains and explore the world on his own. No one could show you how to turn life into an adventure more quickly than Molly could.

That, and he was pretty sure she was the only person in the world who understood what he was feeling for Ralphie.

And it was that mutual love of Ralphie that made it so he could not hold himself back. He didn't walk to her. He ran. He scooped her up, and her weight felt familiar to him, featherlight, and yet there was that supple strength as she wrapped her arms around his neck. Her fragrance denied nine hours or more of travel, and was intensely familiar, sharp and sweet at the same time, like high-mountain huckleberries. It made him want to bury his nose in her hair.

Instead, he swung her around until her laughter—and his—rang out, joyous.

Finally, he set her down, inspected her closely. The laughter still lightened her features. Her hair had always been the most remarkable color—like maple syrup in a glass jar, with the sun shining through it. Her hair was shorter than he ever remembered it being, but if cutting it had been an attempt to tame those crazy curls, it had failed. Half of them corkscrewed wildly around her face, and the other half were smooshed to one side.

The darkness of her freckles over her snub of a nose, the faint golden tone of her skin, spoke of a life outdoors, and her eyes were still as green as the lushness of a mountain meadow in spring.

And her lips—those cute little bow lips—were as plump and inviting as a field-grown strawberry. Still, he wasn't going to look at them for too long. Even though it had been six years, he remembered the taste of them, the surge of energy that had gone through him that nothing and no one else in his life had ever replicated.

So, really, he had a mission here that would not be advanced by the study of her lips.

Molly and he were going to say goodbye to his brother together.

Just seeing her again, he was acutely and deliciously aware of how much this friendship meant to him.

"How can you look just the same?" he asked her. "You were eighteen years old the last time I saw you!"

"It was probably the same outfit," she said wryly.

He regarded her: the khakis, the wrinkle-free green shirt that made her eyes look greener, though he was sure that was unintentional.

"I'm pretty sure it *is* the same outfit," he said thoughtfully, and was rewarded with her laugh.

He didn't add that she looked as good—better—in that casual outfit than most women would look in an evening gown.

"You know how I like to shop. Once I find something that works, I just get ten of it. Though sometimes…"

Her voice drifted away, and she looked faintly embarrassed.

"Sometimes, what?"

"I'm just tired."

"No, what?"

She seemed to consider. "I guess sometimes I wonder what it would be like to be a real girl. You know, with a wardrobe that had a dress in it. Like I say, I'm just tired."

He couldn't miss the tiny bit of wistfulness in her voice. It was true that being raised by a single dad she had probably missed many of the feminine touches in her upbringing that her mother would have provided. She had always seemed so secure in herself, that it had never occurred to him before that she might have secretly longed for what other girls took for granted.

He made a note to himself and filed it away.

Molly cocked her head at him and studied him solemnly. "You've changed. A lot."

He lifted an eyebrow. "In what way?"

"You're sophisticated. I think your haircut might be better than mine. No worn high-top running shoes that don't match. I guess I was hoping for a T-shirt that would make me laugh."

"I've got a great new one. It says, Scientists Do it with Energy."

Her blush actually deepened, and he felt a sudden need to change the subject. What had made him say that? The last thing he needed to be thinking about when he was with Molly was *that*. Particularly since he was taking her home.

He wondered, a little too late, if he had thought this thing through enough. The truth was, he hadn't thought it through at all. Molly had always brought out an impulsiveness in Oscar that he usually did not indulge. She had also always been a disruptive force in his ordered life.

"Let's head to the baggage claim."

"I've got it all here. My legacy from Dad, pack quick and tight."

He looked at the medium-sized bag hanging from her shoulder. Even as it underscored his sense that she had not changed—how many women could pack everything they needed for a trip in an overnight bag—he thought he heard a touch of wistfulness again.

From the size of the bag, it looked like her visit wasn't going to be extended. He'd left the ticket open, so she could book her return at her convenience. She was, just as her father had been, a rolling stone. No surprise there.

"I have enough to last me for a while. I didn't actually book a return flight yet. I thought we'd just see how it goes," she said, as though reading his mind.

The part of Oscar that liked order—that needed to know exactly how many groceries to buy, and made reservations weeks or months in advance—cringed at that. But another part of him didn't. Because even though she seemed unchanged, she was right.

He was changed.

He knew, as he had not known before, that efforts to control things, to put them in order, were largely an illusion. The world did what it wanted.

And he was aware he had changed in another way, and that way seemed to involve an acute awareness of her.

"It's probably half cameras," Oscar said, focusing on her bag instead of her.

"I have my travel wardrobe down to an art," she said. She cocked his head at him, and that familiar smile teased her lips. "Or would that be science?"

"Let me take it, at least."

For a moment, she looked as if she might argue, fiercely independent even about such a small thing as surrendering her bag. But then she shrugged it off and gave it to him. There was an odd look on her face. What was it? Could she possibly enjoy being looked after somewhat guiltily?

"I'm looking forward to hearing about some of your travels," Oscar said. And he meant it. Molly Bentwell had always had a way of finding an adventure.

But a little voice in his head insisted on reminding him that she had gone on to have her adventures *without him*.

She had left what they had shared together with the most perfunctory of goodbyes.

This is what he needed in his newly single life: deep friendships, uncomplicated by other agendas. That feeling of being supported and seen, without the complication of other, well, feelings.

Feelings. Pesky things to his scientific mind. Complicated and rife with consequences that couldn't be predicted.

It was raining hard when he held open the door for her. Without thinking about it, he shrugged off his jacket and put it around her shoulders.

For just a moment, that look of familiar stubbornness crossed her face, but then she relaxed and snuggled into the coat.

"Ah, Galahad," she said. "My prince."

"Galahad wasn't a prince," he said. "He was a knight."

"Trust you to know that," she teased him.

If ever there were a woman who made him want to play the part of a knight in shining armor, or a prince riding in to the rescue, it was Molly.

Thankfully, Oscar thought, his pragmatic nature, and the loss of his brother, made him immune to the charms of fairy tales. Plus, she was the woman least likely to ever play the role of anyone's princess.

Outside the airport, Molly paused at Oscar's vehicle. "But it's not a truck," she said.

Oscar shook his head. This was one of the things he remembered best about Molly Bentwell.

He came from a world where every status of wealth and success and accomplishment was collected and displayed, as if that said who you were in the world.

But Molly had always dug deeper, required more.

"The only girl in the world who would look at a sports car of this caliber and say *that*," he replied dryly.

"It's not that it isn't gorgeous, it's just not what I expected," she said.

He stowed their things and held the door for her, then he got in the car. He couldn't help but show off just a little bit. The car was exquisite in its power and ability to maneuver in and out of choked traffic. The windshield wipers slapped at the rain, and inside it felt cozy and oddly intimate as her scent took over the small area.

"Humph," she said, unimpressed, and apparently not feeling the intimacy at all, thank goodness. "If you can drive a car like this, you could easily drive a truck in this traffic."

"Molly, I don't have any use for a truck."

"Humph."

"What do you drive?"

"I don't have a car. But if I did—"

"It would be a truck," he said, wryly. "You haven't changed your opinion on that since kindergarten."

And then they were both laughing, a familiar ease flowing into place between them. He felt as if he had last spent time with her yesterday, not six years ago. And yet, it had been six years and now there were so many blanks that needed to be filled in.

"How did you end up in Frankfurt, this time?"

"I know it seems weird, what with there not being a wild animal in sight, but it's central, it has a great airport and flights are cheap. Africa would be a couple of days travel from Canada and Asia even longer. So I can get to most of the wild places that are left in the world in pretty short order from where I live. And the biggest market for my photos is European, so it just makes sense."

All the places had made sense, Oscar thought, and yet she never stayed in any of them. She had moved at least six times in the six years since she had been away and he knew it was only a matter of time before she moved again.

She confirmed this by saying, "I'm thinking of moving."

"Again?"

She lifted a slender shoulder and yawned. "I'm feeling restless."

He was pretty sure what she was feeling was pain, pure and simple, just like he was. Could he say to her, *Oh, Molly, there are some things you can't run away from*?

It seemed too personal, the six years of separation yawning between them.

"What time is it, here?"

"Nine p.m. Are you going to have jet lag?"

"No, the secret is to get into your new time zone as quickly as possible. So, it's five a.m. in Frankfurt. I'm just getting up! I'll be good for a few hours. Did you have a plan for tonight?"

"I do," he said. "It's a surprise."

CHAPTER THREE

MOLLY SLID OSCAR a glance. As if the way he looked wasn't surprising enough!

"I have a surprise for you, too," she said. "But it's a secret. Don't even try to pry it out of me."

"One cinnamon bun, and you'd talk."

"No fair using the secret weapon." The truth was she wanted to tell him, to share her excitement. But no, for once in her life she would keep a secret from him. So far, she had two confirmations and a tentative venue to celebrate the beautiful life that had been Ralphie's. But things could still fall apart, so she would say nothing about it and totally surprise Oscar with it, if it all came together.

She considered the fact that Oscar has planned a surprise for her tonight. Everything about him seemed to be a surprise: the new suave look, the sleek car, her awareness of him. His jacket, settled around Molly's shoulders, was deeply comforting in a way that had little to do with its protection from the damp.

The frog had remained a prince, but now he looked like one, too. She slid him another look, taking in the changes. He had filled out substantially, his youthful skinniness giving way to a broadness of shoulder and a depth of chest it had never occurred to Molly that he would achieve. He'd always been tall, but with the stick-like long legs of a crane. Now, she could see the large muscle of his thigh being molded by the fabric of dark denim. The jacket draped around her shoulders was expensive and in taking it off he had revealed a crisp white dress shirt, open at the throat. He had on a leather belt that matched the buff of his brown leather shoes.

The sophisticated haircut showed off the lines of his face: the wide intelligent forehead, the straight nose, the extraordinary cheekbones, the full sensual lips.

Lips she had tasted. Kissed. In that one moment that had changed everything.

Had she come here thinking she could put that behind her? That they could just be the best of friends again? Sitting in the tight confines of his car, she just wasn't sure about that, especially since he had matured so exquisitely. The sharp angles of his face had filled in, making him handsome in that extraordinary way that turned heads and elicited smiles from strangers.

At the airport, when she had first caught sight of him, a well-dressed woman—she had had a moment of envy for just how well-dressed the other woman was—had looked at him with interest, bumped him "accidentally" and apologized. How endearing that he'd acknowledged the woman with the briefest nod, hardly glancing up from his phone.

Everything about Oscar—his looks, his clothing, his impeccable grooming, the way he was standing—made him look sophisticated and confident, the man least likely to send an email that said he needed someone.

He had started a company while he was still in university. When she had asked about it, in their infrequent emails, and even more infrequent phone calls, he'd said it was fun and it was doing okay.

What exactly had he said his company was doing?
Saving the world, one piece of garbage at a time, he'd told
her. Recycling. *So* Oscar. And also, so Oscar to down-
play his success.

It was obvious, from the car and from the clothing,
that he was *very* successful. Nothing in his offhand job
description had prepared her for this.

But that was what he came from. Wealth. Stability.
Success.

That was what his mother had reminded her all those
years ago. That Molly and Oscar came from different
worlds and that Molly had no hope of ever fitting into his.

Nastily, his mother, having witnessed their kiss, in-
sinuated Molly might use her body to try to wheedle her
way into the Clark world.

*I won't allow you to trap him with a tawdry pregnancy,
and you don't seem suited to raise a child, period, let
alone on your own.*

Molly remembered her words now, feeling that same
horrendous shame she had felt at the time.

So nearly everything about him was a surprise except
the fact he had a plan, which he always did. And except for
the fact he was still *Galahad*: the perfect knight, always
known for his courage, gentleness, courtesy and chivalry.

Oscar to a T, in other words.

Molly had always made it clear that she was the
woman least in need of rescuing. She could look after
herself, thank you very much.

And yet his eyes and his smile were so much as she
remembered them, and gave her the same feeling. A delicious sense of being at home with someone, comfortable
with them, safe, able to relax her defenses.

But the new look and the new physique didn't feel safe
at all. Instead, they felt faintly dangerous.

Somehow, she had thought his apartment, a glass-and-steel condo building located close to the ocean, would be more "scientist geek" in its decor: a few experiments on the go, an absent-minded jacket tossed by the door, interesting books scattered about, maybe a gerbil or two in a cage.

But when they took the elevator up, it opened to a corridor with only one front door—his. His space, to her photographer's eye, looked ready for a photo op for Houzz, the home renovation website. Nothing was out of place. Everything was new, and clean, and shiny. The decor, the space, like his clothing and his car, were exquisitely sophisticated, and reflected a level of success she had not known about.

As she surrendered the jacket, Molly reminded herself, this was what he came from. He had grown up in a home very much like this one, beautiful, but faintly impersonal, like the very best of hotel rooms.

She was aware he was watching her.

"What's that look on your face?" he asked quietly.

"It's just not what I expected."

"In what way?"

"It doesn't look like anyone lives here!"

"It doesn't?" he said, looking around with a frown.

"Where are the books about all the millions of things that interest you at any given time? *The Sex Life of Geckos, Secrets of the Volcanoes, Beyond Black Holes.* Where's all that?"

"I'll have to put *The Sex Life of Geckos* on my reading list," he teased her.

Molly hoped it wasn't a Freudian slip that she had mentioned any kind of sex life to him. She decided to deflect.

"Where's the milkshake maker? The popcorn machine? The T-shirt collection? The socks on the floor?"

To her great relief, Oscar tossed the damp jacket carelessly on the couch.

"It probably looked more like that before. When Cynthia and I got engaged, I gave her free rein of the place. I didn't care what it looked like, and she did. And then, as it turned out, she never moved in anyway."

"I'm sorry, Truck." Why would she feel relieved that Cynthia had never lived here?

He lifted a shoulder, but his eyes were sad as they came to rest on her, and then moved away.

"Plus, the housekeeper was here today. I wanted it to look nice for you. She loves to hide my stuff. I'm not sure why she puts away all the appliances. It's not handy."

He wanted it to look nice *for her*. Somehow, that simple statement made her feel a little more relaxed in the opulent space. She looked around. It was very open. The far end of it was completely taken up with a bank of floor-to-ceiling windows that gave an incredible view of the rain-washed nighttime Vancouver skyline, and the ocean beyond that.

Then a movement caught the corner of her eye. Her mouth fell open.

"That's not—"

"One and the same," he said, watching her.

She fell to her knees. The cat marched over to her, and began to meow loudly.

"Protesting your long absence," Oscar said dryly.

"Georgie," she crooned, opening her arms. The cat climbed into them and she buried her face in his fur. He was, as he always had been, the world's ugliest cat. His gray fur was too long in some places, and too short in others. He had a permanent scowl on his face and a tail shaped like a question mark.

But his purr made up for all of his defects. "I can't

believe you have him," she whispered. "I wanted to ask, but I think I was scared of the answer. I think your mom only tolerated him for Ralphie. I recall she was furious when I gave him the cat. Apparently there was supposed to be a long consultation process."

At the time, it had seemed like a small—but still sweet—revenge that Mrs. Clark was going to have to tolerate the cat, not quite managing to get rid of everything about Molly.

"I had to track him down to a shelter."

There was something in his tone that suggested he had had words with his mother.

"Thank you," she said softly, "Especially since I don't remember you caring much for him, either."

Oscar. Even though he had never cared for this cat, he was *that* guy. The one you could count on to be decent, no matter what.

"That's not entirely accurate. He hated me. In fact, he hated anyone who wasn't you. Or Ralphie."

Still, Molly had to fight back tears. "But you love him now?" she asked.

Oscar laughed. "That's a little too strong. We tolerate each other."

"And he's with you for good?"

"Of course. He's part of Ralphie. And you."

He acted as if he'd admitted something he hadn't meant to, and went on quickly, "Besides, I'd miss the old guy glaring balefully at me if I don't buy the right brand of cat food. Stalking after me, demanding kitty treats."

With the cat still in her arms, she got to her feet. She felt vulnerable in a way she had not felt since her father died.

Cared about in a way, she realized sadly, she had not

felt in about the same length of time. Her hard-earned independence suddenly felt exhausting.

"Is that a pool out there?" she asked as a diversion from the uncomfortable feelings clawing at her throat. It was a pretty good diversion: beautiful, the infinity edge made it look like water was cascading off the side of the building.

"Yeah, and a hot tub."

"Like a common pool and hot tub for the whole building?"

"No," he said. "It belongs to this unit."

His level of arrival took away the sense of coming home that the cat had given her. Georgie still in her arms, purring deeply, she went over and looked at the pool, its turquoise waters twinkling under soft patio lights. The hot tub was separated from the pool by a stone ledge, a waterfall cascading between the two.

"I didn't bring a bathing suit," she said regretfully.

"None required."

She whirled and looked at him, wide-eyed. He gave her a teasing grin. She focused on the living room, feeling a hint of that delicious danger in the air between them.

"Most people who come aren't expecting the pool. I keep a selection of suits in the cabana."

"Oh," she said, pretending grave interest in the room to keep him from seeing her blush. Why was he making her blush so much? They had known each other forever!

Deep distressed leather couches faced each other across a rug that she knew from her travels was Turkish and probably very expensive. At the other end of the room was a sleek kitchen, all stainless steel and granite. An island the approximate size of a billiards table faced the living room.

"This looks like something out of a movie set," she

said. Again, it was the not-lived-in look and she found it faintly distressing.

"Which movie?"

"Obviously not *Little House on the Prairie*."

"That wasn't a movie, Mary Ellen."

"You're mixing it up with *The Waltons*. And not like that, either. More like something out of James Bond."

Oscar laughed. "Double-O-Seven at your service."

That was almost worse than picturing him as Galahad!

Still, his laugh reminded her what he was to her, that she didn't need to feel uncomfortable or intimidated by him. She turned back to the room and caught a glimpse of large framed photos on the walls going up a wide hallway. She went and looked at them.

They were hung, and lit, as beautifully as if they were in a gallery.

"They're all mine," she whispered.

He came and stood beside her. "This one's my favorite," he said. Though who the figure in the photo was would not be distinguishable to most people looking at it, they both knew it was a self-portrait of her taken on a timer. She was sitting on a rock ledge, her feet dangling into space, gazing off to the distant peaks.

"Why would this be your favorite?" she asked. "Truck, you're terrified of heights."

"You look so relaxed, despite the fact a sneeze could send you to certain death. I see such strength in it. Independence. Gratitude. Almost every time I look at it, I see something else. It's a great photo, Molly."

She felt the smart of tears, again. Oscar had always had this gift. He saw in her things that others missed, or perhaps things she kept deliberately hidden.

"But every time I look at it, I do think, *how is it she's not scared?*"

She looked at the picture. "You know how some parents come down hard on lying or beating up your brother or stealing cookies before supper? My dad detested fear. It just wasn't tolerated in his world. Some people say, *go big or go home*, but he said, *go bold or go home*. He approved of taking chances, being a daredevil, being courageous. The words I never heard from him were, *be careful*. I think I'm a better person for it."

"You are the bravest person I know."

Well, she thought, except in matters of the heart, where maybe *real* bravery was required. She walked down the wall of photos and stopped at one. This time the tears did come. "This one is my favorite of all time," she whispered, not trusting her voice.

It was true. She had traveled the world, won awards, her photographs were in countless distinguished personal and gallery collections, but this photo, which she had never published, that no one had a print of other than Truck, and her, was her favorite.

Ironically, it was a portrait. She had started seriously taking photos when she was sixteen. She had been accompanying her father on a trip to Africa, where he had been working on a movie. It had been one of his longest jobs he'd ever had and they'd been in Africa for over a year.

He had loved her action shots, and her wildlife shots, but had always been more lukewarm about landscapes and portraits. She wasn't sure whether it was just that she had a natural talent for those things or whether it was because she had adored her father's approval, but she focused her career almost entirely on wildlife now.

But this photo was a black-and-white, a headshot, of Ralphie. He had had Down syndrome and it had been taken right after he was awarded his participant medal in the Special World Games.

Across the bottom of it, scrawled in his childish printing, was Ralphie's motto for life: *Go for it.*

"I love it, too," Oscar said quietly, and his hand came to rest on her shaking shoulders. "It reminds me of such a great time—our senior year, after you got back from Africa, when you and I were assistant coaches on his team."

"I remember it being difficult at times but so worth it," she said with affection through the tears.

"I think it may have been the happiest time of my whole life," Oscar said quietly.

She absorbed that. Here was a man who had achieved phenomenal success and yet that time with his brother remained his happiest.

And hers, now that she thought about it. The cat's purr deepened as if it were satisfied that she had recognized a basic truth.

"And you captured it," Oscar said. "You captured our moment in time. Because the look on his face says it all. What I love best about the photo is it doesn't even show the medal, and yet the triumph is so evident. That's how I felt about his life. The joy of him overshadowed everything else. He triumphed over incredible challenges. I miss him so much."

He handed her a hankie. So Oscar! Who else would have a beautiful linen hankie available for moments like this?

Molly dabbed at her eyes. She hated crying. It was weak. "I would have come if there had been a service."

"I know. It wasn't my choice to make."

Molly heard a trace of anger in his voice that reflected her own. His mother had made the choices, of course, as was a parent's right. But it had only under-scored Molly's uncomfortable feeling that Ralphie had disrupted the perfect picture Mrs. Clark wanted of her family to show the world.

Instead of the service, Mrs. Clark's choice had been to put Ralphie's name on a swim pavilion being constructed in his honor. It was a huge gesture but, to Molly, as a way to commemorate Ralphie's life, it lacked heart.

"Ever since you mentioned it, I've been mulling over an idea to honor him," Molly said.

"Have you come up with something?"

"I think so. But that's my secret. Will you trust me with it?"

The relief on his face reminded her of why she had come. For once, Oscar needed her, and it felt of grave importance to be able to do this for him.

"Of course," he said quietly. "He loved you so much, Molly. He treasured every postcard and every photo you ever sent him. After you would video chat with him, he would call me and give me the highlights. And all I would hear is how Molly had seen an elephant. A real elephant. A real elephant with a baby. A real elephant with a baby in Africa."

The tears came again, and Oscar's arms folded around her, squishing Georgie deeper into her breast. Oscar smelled so good. He felt so strong. She wanted to melt into that embrace and let him hold her forever.

But forever was not in her vocabulary and never had been. And she certainly wasn't going to risk one of the most important things in her world—her friendship with this man—by changing anything about their relation-ship now.

Even though it felt so tempting here in the circle of his arms, feeling the steady beat of his heart under the softness of her cheek, inhaling the intoxicating clean man scent of him. She could not make herself push away.

It was Georgie's howl of protest that made them let go of each other. She gave Oscar a watery smile.

"You know it isn't like me to be teary. I think I might be more jet-lagged than I thought. Can you show me where to freshen up?"

"Sure, I'll show you your room."

"How should I dress for the surprise?"

He laughed, and again his laughter deepened her sense of being comfortable—even giving in to tears—in this space that was so posh.

"The surprise is here, so anything you want from pajamas to an evening gown."

"Yeah," she said wryly. "I packed that. An evening gown. I think my Versace. And my pearls."

The strangest thing was, ever so briefly, she wished she did have a Versace and pearls, just to try it, just to see...

"Pajamas it is."

"How do you know I don't have pajamas that would make you completely uncomfortable if I trotted out in them?" she demanded.

He looked at her. He smiled. "Because you haven't changed a bit."

"Hey! Do I have to remind you I've become a high commodity item in the photography world?"

"That doesn't mean you've changed," he said, with soft certainty. "That means others have been allowed to see what I always saw."

CHAPTER FOUR

SHEESH! MOLLY FELT as if Oscar was going to make her cry again if he kept it up. But he deliberately changed to a lighter tone of voice.

"I bet Molly Bentwell, world's most-sought-after photographer, still wears boy bottoms in some shade of plaid and a T-shirt for pajamas."

It was true. She wore the same kind of pajamas she had always worn. Why had she become predictable, when he had not? Why did she suddenly long for something a little more delicate, more feminine? She'd like to see a look of shock—and maybe appreciation—on his face.

He knew what kind of pajamas Molly wore because he used to call at her window, and she would climb out of it, and they would lay on her roof in the dark of night.

He would name all the constellations. He could tell her how many light years away Mars—that little red speck in the sky—was. He could explain dark holes and the big bang theory with such ease.

Good grief. A pajama party with her best friend. She didn't know if she was disappointed in the surprise or thrilled by it. Or faintly frightened. Because it might be true that she had not changed all that much.

But he had.

Oscar had no remnants of the boy he had once been

remaining in him. He was 100 percent potent and powerful man.

"What are you wearing?" she asked him. "Your pajamas?"

He lifted his eyebrow at her in a way that stole her breath—and suggested he didn't wear pajamas!

He carried her bag down a wide hallway and set it, with extra care, inside a bedroom door. The fact that he remembered her cameras were in there reminded her of why he was that guy—the one who could be counted on to always do the right thing, in big ways and small.

She shut the door behind her and put the cat on the bed. Georgie curled up, and made it seem a bit more relaxed, almost homey, thank goodness. Because the room was gorgeous: deep luxurious carpet, the bed covered in layers of soft gray fabrics, the walls papered in a subtly patterned silk, a wall-to-ceiling window looking over the glorious city and ocean view. It had all the personality of a hotel room, which made her wonder about Cynthia.

Which was none of her business!

It had its own bathroom, and Molly dragged her bag in and tossed off her travel-rumpled clothes. Gratefully, she got into the shower.

When she got out, she was sorry she had thrown only her normal travel kit into her bag, not that anything she had left at home was that exciting, either. What was it about Oscar that was making her want to explore a different side of herself?

She laid out everything she had brought with her: one pair of stretchy black pants that could look formal in a pinch. One tailored white shirt. One tailored striped shirt. One pair of ballet-style shoes. The khakis she had just taken off, which she would rinse out tonight. Three

T-shirts. A pair of casual shoes. Enough comfortable underwear for three days before she'd have to start washing it. A sturdy pair of light boots that would go well
with the khakis. One pair of pajamas: no surprise, plaid
bottoms and any one of the T-shirts she had brought.

Molly considered the stretchy black pants and the
white shirt, but they really weren't any more alluring
than her pajamas.

Alluring? With Truck? She put on her pajamas, and
she put them on hastily.

She took a deep breath and walked out of her room.
The cat woke from his snooze, jumped off the bed and
followed her, as always, dog-like in his devotion.

Oscar was in the kitchen. Now it looked as if someone lived here. He had a variety of ingredients spread out
around him. He was in a black chef's apron and chopping
something with a sharp knife with amazing speed and
comfort. Molly lived a life of fast food, grabbing bites
to eat when she had time.

Seeing Oscar so at home in his amazing kitchen should
have been sweet and made her feel more comfortable.
Instead, she found it disconcertingly sexy.

"You look like a professional chef," she said.

"And you put on your pajamas. I'm glad. I want you
to be comfortable."

He didn't tease her that he'd been right about her pajama selection, just grinned at her, and it made everything, including her choice of what to wear, seem just
right.

"This is the surprise," he said, pleased. "I cook. Are
you impressed?"

"I guess that will depend how good you are at it," she
teased him.

"Oh, I'm good. It goes surprisingly well with a science

background. It *is* science, really. Pellegrino Artusi recognized that in 1891."

Who dropped names from 1891? Oscar. *Her Truck.*

"Can I do something?" she asked.

"No, tonight I'm looking after you."

I'm looking after you. It felt like a weakness to enjoy those words so much.

"What are we having?" She went and glanced at what he was preparing. She laughed. "Hamburgers, Chef Oscar?"

"I'm saving the big culinary reveal for tomorrow. Tonight, I tried to think what you might miss about home. I decided a person could only eat so much bratwurst and spaetzle before they started craving a big one hundred percent Canadian beef burger. I'm going to grill for you."

There it was again. *For you.* His thoughtfulness was in such sharp contrast to every man she had ever tried to have a relationship with that Molly felt faintly squishy inside.

Weak.

She tried to kid it away. "I'm a vegetarian," she announced.

He glanced at her. And saw right through her. "Nice try. Here. You can do one thing. Grab that platter and bring it outside."

"It's raining out."

"It's always raining here," Oscar said. "I've designed the patio to accommodate it."

He filled his own arms with platters and led the way outside. He held open the door for her, and Molly passed through it. Georgie just managed to squeak through, with an indignant meow, before Oscar slid the door shut again.

From inside, Molly had been able to see the pool and hot tub. Now, she saw the outdoor area extended far beyond what was visible from the living room window. Oscar flicked a light and the area was softly illuminated from several sources, including strings of small round bulbs, and a chandelier at the center of the pavilion. Unlike the inside space, there was something about this one that felt warm and cozy and welcoming.

She stood for a moment with her mouth open.

"Don't get wet," he said. "Follow Georgie."

The cat obviously had no intention of getting wet. Tail up, he marched over to the outdoor pavilion. Under that large structure was a full stainless steel kitchen that included a huge grill, a fridge and a bar. Beside the food-prep area was furniture like she had never seen. A dining table, with deeply padded chairs, cushioned in tropical lime green leaf pattern, invited people to sit and seemed to promise lively conversation.

He could host a dinner party for at least a dozen people out here! Oscar hosted dinner parties?

There was a huge sectional sofa, and again it was a surprising pop of lime green on the accent cushions that made it seem like the unexpected would happen here. But the most astonishing piece of furniture was a suspended basket chair. Shaped like a teardrop, it looked something like a bird cage with the door taken off. Inside was a nest, created by a huge cushion in that same shade of lime. It was definitely a snuggle spot for two people!

Oscar was watching her. She was drawn to the chair.

"I've never seen anything like this."

Georgie jumped up and made himself at home.

"Try it," Oscar invited her, setting down his platters and walking over to take hers from her. "Hop in."

Molly gave herself over to the chair.

"Oh," she said. Georgie shifted to accommodate her.

The chair enveloped her, and swung gently. The cat found his way to her tummy. "It's amazing."

Oscar grinned and bowed. "This is what I do. This is my recycling business."

"Sorry? I'm not following you."

He had a pair of barbecue tongs in his hand. He gestured around—the pagoda, the beautiful furniture inside of it, the chair she was sitting in.

"I recycle waste into this. My company is called Current Ocean. We started with plastics from the ocean, making small items, like necklaces, bracelets and earrings. But we've expanded since. We use a lot of tires now, too. The outdoor furniture has become our major product. It's all completely weatherproof."

"It's incredible." No wonder this space was so warm and welcoming. Unlike this inside space, this was pure Oscar. He had created all of it. She loved that he glowed under her approval.

"Our motto," Oscar told her, "is *making problems into solutions.*"

She almost blurted out that she needed him in her personal life, but what problems did she have? Professionally, her every dream had come true. But personally? She couldn't seem to stay in one place. She couldn't seem to sustain a relationship. She sometimes had this secret longing to be girlie: to get her nails done, to wear high heels, to buy a gorgeous dress, and she fought it off as if it were the worst kind of betrayal of everything she had learned growing up.

He turned and busied himself with the food as she swung gently, watching him, and feeling faintly guilty about it.

"I'm not used to being a lady of leisure. Do you need help?" she asked, as she watched him fire up the grill.

"I told you, I'm looking after you tonight. You've been traveling all day. Relax. Any preferences for music?"

"Metal," she said.

"What kind of vegetarian listens to metal? Hey, Siri, play my list."

Just like that, the space filled with music. The first piece was classical guitar.

Once she would have known what he listened to. The guitar music was the most pleasant of surprises, and so perfect with the setting.

After the first few minutes, she allowed herself to enjoy the sense of being looked after. In her pajamas, snuggled up with the cat, watching Oscar work his magic at the grill, Molly let the incredible smells envelop her and listened to the rain patter on the roof mingling with the selection of music that ranged from flute solos to soft rock and pop.

"Did you drift off?"

Molly opened her eyes, startled. "I didn't think so. I was just so relaxed." She didn't add it had been a long, long time since she had felt that way. Her life always seemed to hum with a fine tension, with the potential for catastrophe to unfold unexpectedly.

It was such a treat to experience this kind of serenity.

"Dinner's ready."

"I'll get up."

"No, you won't. Just shift over. Get rid of the cat."

She saw now Oscar had two plates. She tried to push the cat off, but with a miffed expression, he just moved to the bottom of the cushion.

The chair swung gently as Oscar joined her. It held them both easily, but tightly, touching the full length of their bodies, shoulder to thigh. The feeling of serenity was edged out slightly by the awareness of him—his strength, his scent, his closeness.

He passed a plate to her. She bit into her hamburger. "Ambrosia," she decided. "And no tomatoes."

"Did you think I'd forget you don't like tomatoes?"

It was a lovely reminder of just how well they knew each other. She didn't like tomatoes. He didn't like pickles. She liked hot sauce. He liked mayo.

But now, seeing him in his lush surroundings, there was a whole part of him she didn't know about, and she wanted to fill in the blanks.

"Tell me more about your business," she invited him.

It turned out Oscar had been earning a degree in chemical engineering, but it was a beach holiday in Thailand where he had first started mulling over the idea of turning plastic, harvested from polluted oceans, into usable objects.

As always, when he talked about science, he became very animated. Over the next years, while still a student, he had tried experiments that succeeded and just as many that failed, but he had finally come up with a formula where he could turn a small amount of plastic into a usable product at a decent price. He had started by making a small necklace.

But it was when he was approached by a furniture designer that things went big. The designer had connections, and with Oscar's business background from his family, Current Ocean exploded. Their products were now in demand around the world.

"I still like being in the lab the best," he admitted. "And as we've grown more successful, I've been able to pull back from the parts I don't like more and more. Cynthia liked the glamorous part of starting an exciting new company: schmoozing, getting invited to important events, but I just didn't care. It was one of many differences between us."

"What happened between you and Cynthia?" Molly realized it was way too personal. Sharing the chair had lulled her into thinking they were best friends, confidants, just as they had been most of their lives. But six years separated them, and a lot of life had passed under the bridge since then.

He hesitated, and then said, his voice low, "You know how you said the apartment looked like no one lived there?"

She nodded.

"The relationship felt the same way. It looked so perfect and felt so..." His voice drifted off. "Don't get me wrong. She's a really great person. We've remained friends. We just discovered we weren't right for each other."

It was so like Oscar to remain friends with an ex. He was such a decent person. But it sounded as if Cynthia had been, too. Why did Molly want to hate her?

"I knew she must be a good person," she said grudgingly. "Ralphie mentioned her sometimes. He liked her."

Something tightened marginally around Oscar's mouth. "That's enough about me. What happened to your last relationship? A musician, right?"

"I suck at relationships," she said, trying to sound breezy, not a hint of finding-someone-else's-panties-under-her-bed in the tone. "It's my lifestyle. I'm never around."

That had been Werner's excuse, too. As if it were somehow her fault he had strayed.

And maybe it had been. Not so much because of life-style but because of fear. Fear that she didn't have what it took to make things work out. That she always held part of herself back because love was, as her father had always said, the biggest pain of all.

Look at how she had felt when she left Oscar to go to photography school. Bereft. Between leaving him and losing her father in such a short period of time, she hadn't eaten or slept properly for months. Only the work removed her from the pain, and she had poured herself into it. People thought she had talent, but what she had was a single-minded focus driven by the need to escape the fact she was so alone in the world.

"Are you lonely?" he asked her quietly, always able to read her so accurately.

It was too personal, just like her asking him about Cynthia.

"I don't feel lonely when I work—which is almost always—I feel alive." Sometimes it was the *only* time she felt fully alive, but she didn't feel ready to surrender that truth to Oscar.

"You take some big chances to get those photos," he said quietly. "Is that what makes you feel alive? The adrenaline rush of surviving?"

"I *like* being death-defying," she said stubbornly. "It's in my blood."

Did she feel Oscar shudder ever so slightly beside her?

"I hear a *but* there."

Shoot. She'd never been able to hide her truth from him. She tried, anyway. "No, you don't."

"Yes, I do."

He was her best friend. Was he still? It felt like it. She was shocked that she wanted to tell someone.

"Sometimes I look at a normal couple in the park with a Golden Retriever and a baby on a blanket and I itch to capture that baby with my camera, instead of a pride of lions lunching on a gazelle or a hippo crushing a canoe in his jaws."

"So, do that," he said, as if it were the easiest choice in the world.

"You know what babies lead to?"

"Is this a trick question? I know what leads to babies."

She could feel herself blush. She gave him a little warning nudge with her fist. There were certain conversations that were not going to be safe for them. What led to babies was going to be one of those.

"Weddings," she said, glumly. "Babies lead to weddings."

"Um, I think you might have that backward. I thought weddings led to babies. As hopelessly old-fashioned as that makes me."

She shot him a look. She *loved* that about him. That he was hopelessly old-fashioned, a traditional kind of guy. Honorable. Decent.

"Photography," she said. "Baby photos lead to wedding photos. I've already had several requests. I *hate* wedding photos."

"But you'd like to do baby photos," he said, too astute, as always.

She was silent for a long time. "Can you keep a secret?"

"You've always been able to tell me your secrets," he reminded her.

"I've regretted it, too."

"You have not!"

"Remember the time I told you I had a crush on Vincent Marcello?"

"We were thirteen!"

"Aha! So, you do remember."

"Okay, yes I do."

"And then a week after I confided in you, he asked

me if I wanted to go to a movie with him. I always wondered if that was a coincidence."

"I don't recall the details."

"Did you tell him?"

"Of course not. I might have hinted that if he asked you out, you'd say yes. That wasn't giving away your secret. It was using something I knew about you to make your dreams come true."

"He might have asked me out on his own."

"I doubt that. All the guys were scared to ask you out."

"How come? My dad?"

"Well, maybe that, a bit, but mostly you'd beaten them all at arm wrestles."

"Anyway, all your efforts did not make my dreams come true," Molly said. "He turned out not to be a white knight."

"Thirteen is a little early to want to be whisked off on a white charger, anyway."

"He tried to kiss me in the theater without my permission. I blacked his eye."

Oscar chuckled softly. "And sealed your dating fate for the rest of your school years."

"I never really believed in that white-knight stuff, anyway."

"But you wanted to," Oscar said softly.

This was the problem with being with a person who knew you so well, knew you better, sometimes, than you knew yourself. This was the problem with someone knowing your secrets and wanting to help your dreams come true.

"Well," Molly said, after an uncomfortable silence between them, "I'm even more jaundiced now than Vincent Marcello left me."

"I know," Oscar said, quietly, his voice threaded

through with sympathy. "But there's been some winners along the way, hasn't there?"

"I'm having a nice night. I don't want to talk about it."

"Okay, let's get back to your secret, then."

She hesitated. "I think I'd like to do more portraits," she admitted.

He actually chuckled. "That's the big secret?"

But that was only part of it. The other part she would never tell him because she could barely admit it to herself. Seeing families, wanting to photograph them, to capture what they had, seemed to be about some secret yearning in herself. A yearning for belonging. For warmth. For hope. That secret was, well, terrifying.

The fact that she longed for the thing her father had detested the most—normalcy—felt like some kind of betrayal.

"That's it," she said. "That's the big secret."

"Have to say I don't get it. Who would pick taking a picture of a baby instead of standing in front of a charging bull elephant, having it blow snot in your face?" he teased her.

"The elephant snot thing was only once."

"It was Ralphie's favorite story from you," he told her, with a smile.

"You don't get it," she said dismissively. "I love the challenge of getting a great shot. Anybody with a bubble blower and a teddy bear can get a great shot of a baby."

CHAPTER FIVE

THE PROBLEM, OSCAR THOUGHT, with Molly in her pajamas, nestled under his arm, the rain pattering on the pagoda roof, the soft music and the cat at their feet, was not that he didn't get it.

The problem was that he got it completely.

He'd always gotten it.

This was a part of Molly that she did not show the world. Despite that image she loved—the fearless photographer facing down the charging elephant—Molly yearned for all the things everyone yearned for. Family. Connection. Children.

But she saw those yearnings as a weakness. As things to be kept secret.

He got up and got them both a glass of wine, then returned to the chair. It was, as it had always been, just so easy to be with Molly. Their conversation roamed easily between old friends and new interests, current events and the hometown changes.

But there was a new element there, too. An element he had introduced, six years ago, the last time he had seen her.

He'd kissed her.

Thoroughly.

And it was not the kind of thing a man just put out

of his head, especially with her fitting so comfortably against him again now.

Like they were two pieces of a puzzle made to fit together precisely.

The chill of the rainy night began to gather around them, but instead of suggesting they go in, he went and got a blanket, and lit the ethanol fireplace. He refilled their wine glasses and came back to the chair.

He covered them both with the blanket.

"It reminds me of the old days," she said, "sitting on the roof outside my bedroom window together. We used to talk until our voices were hoarse. Remember?"

Of course, he remembered.

And that's what they did again now. They talked until their voices were hoarse, and they couldn't keep their eyes open another second, and then they fell asleep, cocooned from the world, not just by the chair but by each other.

Her breathing had grown deep and steady, when suddenly she jerked. And then she sat up.

"Oh, geez," she said, "I've forgotten to check my messages. I'm waiting for a really important call."

Oscar felt the disappointment of this moment coming to an end. Of her other world infringing. But he recognized, ultimately, it was for the best.

"It's late here, anyway," he said, getting up from the chair, and reaching out a hand to help her. "I was getting ready to turn in."

That wasn't true. He had been getting ready to stay up all night—or to fall asleep in the big chair with her. Whatever happened.

But that was over now. Molly let go of his hand as soon as she was out of the chair and scrambled through the rain to the door. The cat gave him a look that said, *See? She's mine*, and then jumped off the chair and followed her.

Oscar gathered the dishes and food, double-checked that the barbecue was off and went into the apartment.

Molly was sprawled on the couch inside, going through her phone with an intense look on her face. She looked somehow right in his space, bringing it the thing it had never had, and that she had sensed it was lacking right away.

Life.

As he watched, the scowl left her face. She beamed down at the screen. The look on her face—anticipation, delight—made him wonder who she had just heard from. Was it a man that brought that look to her face? She had just extradited herself from one of her horrible choices. Surely, she wasn't already—

None of his business, he told himself firmly. It was probably work. Work was, by her own admission, the thing that made her feel alive. He was aware he wanted other things to make her feel alive, but that made him look at her lips.

And recall feeling as alive as he had ever felt. But that was about him. Because whatever she had felt that night they had kissed had been part of what had driven her away.

Friends. They were just friends. Despite his niggling awareness of her—or maybe because of it—it was his responsibility to keep it that way.

She looked up at him. The glow from whatever she had seen on that phone still showing on her face.

"Thank you for a wonderful night, Oscar." She got up off the couch, came and stood before him, reached up on her tiptoes and pecked his cheek. "I've got some stuff I have to look after."

And then she was gone. Her bedroom door clicked shut behind her.

Oscar resisted the impulse to lay his fingers across his cheek where her lips had touched. He went to his room, shut the door, shucked off his clothes and slid between the sheets. On second thought, he could not imagine being in the same apartment with her and having no clothes on.

Annoyed with himself, he got up and rummaged through a drawer until he found something that resembled pajama bottoms. Something like what she would wear.

He got back into bed, contemplating the strange, irrational restlessness he felt. Nothing had happened, really. They'd had dinner, visited, fallen asleep. The cat had thrown him over for her, completely, and Molly had shared a few harmless secrets.

Nothing had happened.

And yet it felt as if a wind were picking up, tossing a few items of his life around. Really, wasn't that restless feeling the first warning that a tornado was about to strike?

She was, Oscar reminded himself firmly, his oldest friend. They had known each other since they were five years old.

He knew her better than he knew any other living soul on earth.

And yet, when he thought of that long-ago moment, when their lips had touched, he was aware something had changed between them that could not be put back the way it was before.

In some ways, Molly felt like a stranger to him now. Like he didn't know her at all anymore.

Yes, it felt like there was a tornado coming. He would just have to make sure to batten down the hatches. And avoid the worst of the storm.

He was glad he had a nice safe bike ride planned for tomorrow.

Oscar was shaken out of his spiraling thoughts by a muffled sound. It was her phone ringing. He willed her to ignore it. He willed her to be glaring at it.

But no, she answered.

Oscar was ashamed to strain his ears, listening. Breathless.

Hello, James.

Oscar pulled the pillow over his head. And then, even more ashamed of himself, took it off and listened some more. Just long enough to hear her laugh and say something about how she never wore dresses. Which was true.

Except now, if he was hearing correctly, she was promising to wear one for James. He put in his ear buds. He told himself he was not jealous. There was no way he was jealous. He was feeling protective of her, that was all. She did have a tendency to jump into things with both feet. In Molly's world, regret was for later.

He was up early the next morning and felt as if he had not slept a wink. Grumpily, he threw a robe over his pajama bottoms and padded out to the kitchen.

Molly appeared a few minutes later, looking annoyingly giddy, as if she had experienced a fantastic sleep.

"Look," she said gleefully, pointing at him, "matching pajamas."

"Huh," he said.

"I thought—" She stopped herself in the nick of time. She was blushing, though. It pleased him in some wicked way that she was blushing, thinking of him naked while she was planning on wearing a dress for James.

"You look tired," she said to him.

"Do I? I'm not a morning person."

She cocked her head at him as if her lie detector was beeping.

"I'm not sure what we should get up to today," he said. "I was planning a bike ride, but look at the weather."

Molly went and looked out the window. "I love bike riding in the rain," she said.

"You would," he said.

An hour later, he found himself in a little store close to Stanley Park, waiting while Molly tried on raincoats.

And galoshes.

"I wonder if they have this in any other color than yellow?" she said, wrinkling her nose at the coat. "I don't like yellow."

"Who doesn't like a whole color?" he asked her, still feeling unreasonably crabby with her, especially with her standing there looking so utterly adorable.

"Who doesn't like a whole time of day?" she shot back. "'When you arise in the morning, think of what a precious privilege it is to be alive, to breathe, to think, to enjoy, to love.' That's Marcus Aurelius."

"'Yellow,'" he shot back, "'excites a warm and agreeable impression… The eye is gladdened, the heart expanded and cheered, a glow seems at once to breathe toward us.' That's von Goethe."

She considered. "My Aurelius trumps your von Goethe."

"How come you get to decide that?"

And then they were laughing at how quickly this old game had come back to them and Oscar felt some tension he had been holding in himself slide away. She bought the yellow jacket and the rubber boots.

Molly had awoken in the morning to find several more messages on her phone. Her plans were coming together so well for Ralphie's memorial event that she felt nearly giddy with it.

Or maybe that was a lie to herself. All that giddiness could be from spending a lovely evening cuddled up with Truck… She went out into the apartment, trying to tell herself she wasn't feeling what she was feeling.

But she'd felt excited to see him.

However, it was quickly apparent that he didn't share her feelings. Oscar was downright grumpy. He said he wasn't a morning person, but she didn't remember that about him. If she didn't know better, she'd guess he had a hangover.

He was making coffee, and had a selection of pastries out for breakfast. He had on a very posh robe, like the kind you got in expensive hotels, and he looked very sleep mussed and sexy. His stubble had thickened overnight and it was quite a roguish look. She had felt a funny little desire to touch his face and see what it felt like.

She was aware he didn't look as giddy as she felt. But after they had the little quote battle, whatever tension had been there seemed to ease off.

Molly was thrilled to find, because of the rain, they had the famed Stanley Park seawall mostly to themselves. With Oscar slightly behind her, she aimed at a puddle. She hit it full force and the water sprayed out behind her. She looked over her shoulder and laughed gleefully at his expression when the water sprayed him.

That old competitiveness leaped up between them and he raced by her. She tried to slow down, but wasn't quick enough. He shifted in front of her and she saw the puddle he was aiming for way too late for her to avoid it.

"Bombs away," he shouted, and a wave of muddy water cascaded over her.

"Oh, yeah? Watch this." She tried to pull out to pass

him. He blocked her. She tried the other side. He blocked her again. She finally managed to squeeze beside him, and they raced side by side, like two Thoroughbreds heading for the finish line. Their breathless shouts of laughter filled the air. She saw a jogger coming. One of them was going to have to move or they'd be playing chicken with the poor jogger.

As she had known he would, Oscar—ever the gentleman—reluctantly swung in behind her. She looked for a puddle. She chortled with glee when she saw the one coming. It was enormous. A lake! He was going to get soaked to the skin.

She aimed right for it. She peddled hard and lifted her feet high in the air as the water grabbed her tires. She glanced behind her.

Oscar had stopped, and was leaning on his handlebars, grinning. She realized she shouldn't have looked back. The handlebars wobbled in the deep water. The tire wallowed. The bike abruptly slowed and veered left.

Her pant legs snagged on the bike as it started to fall over. She came off with an ungracious plop and the bike fell on top of her. She heard a tearing sound, and then the water closed over her head.

She emerged from the puddle laughing, sputtering and spitting out water, to find Oscar had abandoned his bike and was kneeling, heedless of the water, in the puddle beside her.

"Are you okay?"

She looked at the concern on his face. His glasses were covered in water from mud puddles and the rain. He hadn't shaved this morning, and little droplets of water clung to his stubble.

Something in her went very weak. She *wanted* him to pick her up, and carry her over to the grass, and tenderly touch the place on her ankle where it hurt. And she wanted to touch that damned attractive stubble!

Instead, she splashed him, got out of the puddle and raced for her bike.

"Hey," he called after her, "just an FYI, you're showing the whole world your panties."

CHAPTER SIX

IT HAD BEEN such a long and wonderful day. They had spent most of it on the bikes, exploring Stanley Park, playful and then sedate. Oscar had given Molly his jacket to tie around her exposed behind. When she'd objected, he had said he couldn't get any wetter, which was certainly true. Finally, soaked to shivering, they had headed back to his place.

Despite her jet-lag strategy, Molly had come out of the shower and told herself she would just lie down for a minute. When she woke up, she could hear Oscar in the kitchen, and something already smelled good.

Because of the ripped pants, she had only two choices left to wear, so she went with the stretchy black pants and white shirt tonight instead of her pajamas.

"Come on over," Oscar said, when she came down the hall. "I have a job for you."

He was freshly showered and changed. He was wearing the chef's apron over his clothes again, and she noticed he had shaved, finally. She wanted to touch his freshly shaven face the same way she had wanted to touch his stubble.

"A job for me?" she said, joining him at the island, ordering herself to focus on the task at hand. Unfortunately, the fresh scent that came off him was heady and masculine, and as good as whatever was cooking in the oven. And even more distracting.

"Oh, Truck," she warned him, "you know my culinary skill runs to boiling an egg, right?"

"Right," he said. "I've already taken that under consideration."

"Chefs are notoriously bad-tempered and temperamental," she informed him.

"This, to the man who rescued you from the mud puddle," he said, aghast. "Who gave you his jacket to prevent your derriere from becoming public knowledge, who tried three different ice-cream places before we found one with licorice flavor."

"Okay, okay."

"Having said that—" he wagged his knife at her "—do exactly as I tell you, and nothing else."

"Yes, Chef," she said with pretend meekness, and they both laughed at the impossibility of her ever being meek.

He held out an apron, and he slipped it over her head, and she turned and let him tie it behind her back.

His hands brushed the small of her back. His breath touched the nape of her neck. It was strangely and sumptuously intimate.

Molly didn't think of Truck like this! Except that she had been, all day, starting with his stubble.

"What are you making?" she asked, turning quickly to look at the counter top.

"A dish I looked up on the internet. It's called How to Impress a Girl."

"That doesn't sound very scientific." She gulped when she realized what he had said. "Are you trying to impress me?"

"I don't have to, do I?"

"No, of course not." She recovered quickly. "But I can see it's a good idea for you to practice. For when you do. Want to impress a girl, that is."

How wrong was it to have the dangerous wish that she were that girl? Today had been so much fun. What would it be like to have a life like that?

"That's going to be never," he said, firmly. "I've decided I'm forever single."

"Me, too," she said.

"Ha."

"What does that mean?"

"It doesn't take a psychology major to figure out there's something behind that secret longing to take baby pictures."

Her mouth opened. Then snapped shut. Sometimes that was the problem with having a best friend. They saw things too clearly.

"Here," he said, deftly changing the subject. "Open the pomegranate."

"Who cooks with a pomegranate?" Molly groused, looking at the hard pinkish cylinder-shaped fruit he had placed in her hand.

"We're not cooking with it. It's going in the salad." Oscar put a small sharp paring knife in front of her.

She glared at the pomegranate, the knife and him. "I don't know how to open a pomegranate."

It was an unexpected reminder that this was his world: where people knew how to open pomegranates. She bet his mother knew how. And Cynthia.

"For Pete's sake, Molly, it's not a test of your worthiness. We're supposed to have fun."

Again, that reminder that Oscar knew her so well, and could see things others missed. Despite professional recognition, she still sometimes felt like that girl who was not good enough.

"Anyone who can take photos like you does not have to be a domestic diva," Oscar told her firmly, fishing his phone out from under that sexy apron. "It's not rocket science. Here. Look it up."

"Domestic diva-ing?"

"Pomegranate opening!" He was busy finely chopping herbs and the rich aroma of rosemary joined the other scents in the air.

She found his phone in her hands. His screen saver was her photo of Ralphie.

"Hey," she said, scrolling through his phone. "Did you know every pomegranate is supposed to have exactly six hundred and thirteen seeds? Wow. It's biblical or something. We should count them."

"Even I am not that scientific of a scientist," he said. "Are you done opening that thing yet?"

He was grating cheese.

"The pomegranate," she continued, "is revered for its beauty, flowers and fruit. It symbolizes sanctity, fertility and abundance."

Thankfully, he turned from her just then, placing a tray of bread rolls with cheese and rosemary sprinkled on them in the oven. She couldn't possibly be blushing because she had said the word *fertility* in his presence!

"Were you and Cynthia going to have kids?" she asked.

"Did you know you have the attention span of a gnat?" he growled at her, coming to stand behind her, and looking over her shoulder at the pomegranate.

"You're being very disapproving," she said. "I knew I wouldn't like you with a chef's temperament!"

"In my defense, I'd like to eat sometime before midnight."

"Okay, okay." She watched a two-minute video on sectioning a pomegranate. In the video, the correctly sectioned fruit fell open like a flower, and then the seeds could be easily scooped from it. "Were you?"

"Wanting to eat before midnight?" he asked dryly.

"Wanting to have children."

"Were you and your latest?" he shot back.

"I asked first." She held her breath and cut into the pomegranate. Bright red juice sprayed out of it, splattering on the cuff of her white shirt.

"Yeah," he said gruffly. We planned on having kids someday."

Oscar—her Truck—had contemplated having a child with a woman…who was not her. Molly and Oscar were *friends.* She hadn't even seen him for six years. She knew he had been engaged. So why did it feel, oddly, like a betrayal?

Probably because being here with him made him so *real* for her, all over again, as if six years hadn't separated them.

"Were you?" he asked. He had moved away. His tone was casual, but he wasn't looking at her. "Going to have a child? Some day? Does longing to take baby pictures mean something?"

What could she say to that? *I don't pick the kind of men anyone sane would ever have children with. On purpose. Because your mother told me I didn't seem suited to raise a child.*

She slid him a look. He was looking at her now, reading her face for the clues that only he would see. And she did not want him to see this one: Oscar was the kind of man a woman picked if she wanted to have children.

Infinitely stable. Mature enough to put the needs of another human being ahead of his own.

He was the kind of guy you wanted in your baby pictures.

Not that she ever wanted to think about Oscar like that.

"My lifestyle doesn't give itself to having children," she said carefully. "I can't even keep a plant alive. I even abandoned poor Georgie."

"Not really abandoned. Ralphie loved him as much as you did. I always thought I'd have kids," he said softly. "Until Ralphie died. Something changed in me. Cynthia saw it."

Molly looked at him. Nothing had changed in him. Oscar had always been *that* guy. The one with deep loyalties. The one who wanted to protect everything he loved. The one who was stable. The one who had an instinct for the right thing. It told her more about Cynthia than about him, that his betrothed had not understood his struggle with the death of his brother, the depth of his grief, the unending sea that would be his sorrow. How could anyone know him and not know he would take the death of someone he loved as an affront to his need for order and control and predictability?

"She didn't deserve you," she said simply.

He lifted a shoulder. "There was something missing, even before Ralphie died. She knew it. I knew it. We just couldn't put our finger on it."

Passion, Molly thought, and was stunned at herself. She didn't really know anything about Cynthia.

Except that she'd seen a picture or two of her, in her designer clothes, and diamond tennis bracelets, her perfect makeup and hair. She'd seen this apartment.

"Ah, look, Molly, you've gone and massacred the pomegranate."

She looked down. The pomegranate was in a messy heap in front of her. The bright ruby red juice had not only stained the cuff of her shirt but also her hands and the countertop. The precious little seeds—that stood for fertility—were mashed in with the pulp in a pretty much unsalvageable mess.

For some reason, the destruction of the pomegranate—or maybe the fact Oscar had not been loved passionately, the way he deserved to be loved—made her want to cry.

"I've ruined my shirt," she said, her voice wobbly. She didn't like wobbliness, and she was miffed at herself that she was experiencing quite a bit of it since landing in Vancouver.

However, if it had to come out, she was glad it was with him. She was pretty sure Oscar was the only person in the whole world she ever trusted with this side of herself. Not the fearless photographer, but the side that wobbled every now and then.

He was looking at her so intently. As if he knew darn well it wasn't about a shirt. She realized she had missed seeing his eyes: the intensity of his gaze, the intelligence, the compassion.

"We'll get you a new one," he said, going along with her claim it was about the shirt. "There's some of the best shopping in the world here."

Normally, she would have reminded him she hated shopping. But suddenly, she *wanted* to shop. To find something new. Maybe to let loose a side of herself she had never dared explore.

"Okay," she said.

"Well, that was the surprise answer," he said with a grin.

That grin—lopsided, boyish, charming—drew her back to their simple days together, filled with friendship and laughter. Days when maybe she had dared to hold the secret hope—even as she proclaimed her independence, her utter lack of *need*—that she would have a normal life and a normal family, despite the fact she had not been raised to see that as a worthy goal.

Don't fall into the trap of security, her father had always instructed her. *Adventure is the elixir of life.*

And fall into the trap she hadn't. And yet the pursuit of adventure had left her feeling strangely empty sometimes. And that emptiness seemed more acute standing here with Oscar in his kitchen, smashing a pomegranate.

"Hey," he said, gently, the one who could always read her, the one who there was no hiding any of her secrets from, "we're supposed to be having fun."

It was too intense. She saw him too clearly. He saw her too clearly. The six years separating them made it uncomfortable in ways it had not been before. Before they had been kids. Now they weren't. It added a sharply unexpected dimension to their relationship.

Molly did what she always did when she felt exposed. She pulled out her devil-may-care reckless persona.

"Oh, yeah?" she said. She took her dripping pomegranate-juice-stained hand, and made a swipe for his face.

He ducked out of the way. "Um," he said, reluctant laughter tickling across the beautiful firm line of his mouth, "maybe *I* should define *fun.*"

"You? Define *fun*?" She scooped up some of the mash and reddened her hands even further. "No, I think I'll define *fun.*"

He read her intent and dashed away from her. He put the sofa between him and her. "Molly, squishing pomegranate into someone's face isn't fun."

"I think it might be. I won't know until I try it."

* * *

Molly leaped over the back of the sofa. Oscar had expected her to try to come around it, but Molly was not one to do the expected.

He had seen the truth on her face for that split second.

She wanted to have children. She didn't trust herself to have children.

This was what was behind that "secret"—that she liked photographing babies.

And this was her way of trying to keep him from her truth. He vowed he would get back to it later. That's what friends did. They helped each other with truth. She had seen his instantly, hadn't she? That the death of his brother had exposed the weaknesses in his relationship with Cynthia.

And so, they would help each other outrun that truth until the time was right to tackle it. Oscar sprinted away from the threat of her little red-stained hands.

He felt laughter rise in him. He realized it had been a long time since he'd had a day like today: laughter, right in the bottom of his belly, rising to the surface, like bubbles rising in champagne, rolling out of him, chasing everything else away.

He circled, just out of her reach, back to the counter and doused his own hands in the massacred pomegranate.

"I'm armed," he warned her.

"Good. I couldn't have a fair fight with an unarmed man."

"You'll ruin your shirt completely."

"It's already ruined."

"No, I think we could save—"

She lunged at him. He shouted with laughter. They chased each other around the kitchen island and in and out of the living room furniture. He knocked over a lamp, and the vibration on the floor knocked one of the pictures on the wall crooked. The cat jumped off his favored chair, yowled once, protesting, then hightailed it down the hall. Oscar and Molly chased each other until they were both breathless with the sheer merriment of being silly.

"Stop," he finally said, pulling a dining chair in her path to try to slow her down. "I'm going to get a noise complaint letter from the condo association."

"Aw, that's a shame." She pushed past the chair. It toppled over with a crash. "You'll lose your gold star."

"No, seriously," he said, turning so he could face her.

"So long, Resident of the Month Award," she said, undeterred, charging toward him with her red mash hands.

He moved swiftly backward. "The neighbors are going to complain. This is not the kind of place where people stampede about like a herd of elephants."

He felt the hassock hit the back of his knees. He fell backward over it.

Chortling wildly, she was on top of him, squishing pomegranate into his face, until he could feel the juice running toward his ears. He retaliated, wiping his hand from her jaw to her cheekbone, and across her nose. It left a wide welt of red.

She snickered, then threw back her head and let loose a warrior howl that matched her face paint.

He shouted with laughter, condo association be damned.

And then he became very aware that she was on top of him. Her every curve was molded to him, the heavy chef's apron providing scant protection of his sudden, disconcerting awareness of her. Her scent—wild huckleberries on a sun-drenched day—filled his senses. The light from the kitchen shone behind her, illuminating her curls, each strand spun in gold. Her freckles were scattered across her nose like a mad toss of fairy dust had landed on her.

Oscar's laughter died abruptly. So did Molly's.

The air between them became charged with an electrical current.

CHAPTER SEVEN

MOLLY TOUCHED OSCAR'S FACE, not playfully now, but ever so gently, exploring. Then, she trailed her red finger, a pomegranate aril clinging to it, over his lip. His tongue, of its own volition, darted out of his mouth and took that seed from her finger.

The charge between them intensified, hissing and snapping like a storm-broken electrical wire on the ground.

The current held Molly and Oscar prisoner in its field. Oscar found himself helpless to resist the force that pulled him closer to her. He reached up, slowly, deliberately, and put his juice-drenched hand to her lips.

Everything intensified. The color of her eyes. The sensations along his skin. The sounds of both of them breathing. The delicate heave of her chest.

Molly's tongue flicked out, pink, soft, moist. She tasted the juice that clung to his skin, a hummingbird tasting nectar. He watched her eyes darken to a shade of green he had seen only once before, in a mossy and shaded dark corner of a forest.

And maybe once before that, even. After her father had died, and their lips had found each other in a moment so exquisite and so tortured it had burned a permanent etching in his brain.

He should have learned a lesson from that. He had felt things he had never felt before. But Molly had disappeared from his life as quickly as mist burned off by a hot sun, leaving him with a sense that the kiss had ruined everything.

Taken the most important thing in his life from him.

And yet, here it was again, the most delicate form of torture he had ever endured. Her lips, as soft as velvet, as plump as a ripe strawberry, on his hand, a gentle nuzzle that sizzled. Her eyes, wide and smoky, on his face.

He held his breath. Was she going to taste the pomegranate juice on his face, as well as his hand, with those delicate, exquisite lips? She leaned in toward him. He leaned toward her, pulled on a cord of desire that had been there for a long time between them. Invisible. But no less powerful for that.

Could it be different this time?

Was he willing to take that risk?

Did he have any choice?

The fire alarm shrieked at the same time he realized the burning smell was not his own heart going up in smoke.

They snapped apart from each other. She leaped up. He leaped up. The cat raced by them and hid under the sofa.

Despite the possibility the place was burning to the ground around them, they stood frozen, staring at each other. She should have looked hilarious, with her curls gone crazy around her clown-stained face. She looked anything but.

He whirled away from her. He had totally forgotten about sticking those bread rolls in the oven.

He must be forgetful these days. Because he had also totally forgotten the consequences of their last kiss. But he'd been lucky, this time. Fate had intervened before he ruined everything again.

He should have been more grateful than he was at the dark smoke that curled out of the oven door and hung wispily around the ceiling.

While he dashed to the oven and took the charred remains of the bread out, she grabbed a tea towel and stood under the smoke detector, fanning wildly at it until, with a final indignant whimper, it gave up.

"Eviction," he told her solemnly, "is imminent."

"But where will we live?" she asked, just as solemnly.

We. It seemed, for one insane moment, it wouldn't matter where he lived if she were with him. Molly could turn a cardboard box under a bridge into a grand adventure.

He turned deliberately from her and pulled the remains of the other item from the stove. She came and stood beside him.

"What was that?"

"A soufflé," he said. "Cheese. My first attempt."

"Maybe we could salvage it."

The soufflé took that moment to collapse completely in on itself.

"It reminds me of a building imploding," she offered, and then after a moment's consideration, "we could still eat it."

"It'll taste like smoke."

"We could pretend we're camping."

All of it an adventure, with her. Even the things that didn't go right. Maybe especially the things that didn't go right.

"It's pretty much my fault," she said. "It was the wrong time to start a pomegranate war. I can see that now."

She tried to look contrite, but her red-stained face

made it very hard to take her seriously. His face probably looked just about the same.

"There's a right time to start a pomegranate war?" he asked her.

"Oh, sure," she said. "There's a little spec of—"

She reached out to his lip. He caught her hand. They had literally been saved by the bell—or the alarm, as the case may be—and she could undo that with a single touch.

Wordlessly, he looked down at her. He wanted to lick every drop of that pomegranate juice off her face. He wanted her laughter-filled eyes to darken to that mossy shade of green again.

But he resisted all temptation, except one. He picked her up, his arms under her shoulders and her thighs, cradling her slight form against him. Her curls tickled his chin.

She didn't resist, either, but wrapped her arms around his neck. She sighed against him, and her breath whispered hot across his chest.

He had the unfortunate sensation of being a warrior with his plundered bride. Molly seemed to have surrendered to whatever might happen next. He could not allow himself to even contemplate the options.

There was only one option. They both needed some cooling off. He strode across the living room and slid open the sliding glass door to the deck with his foot. He took three long steps through the driving rain and across the smooth surface of the Italian-marble-tiled patio and leaped into the pool with her in his arms.

The water closed around them, cool and delicious. Just yesterday, he had not been the guy who would be leaping, fully clothed, into his pool, with a woman in his arms.

"You know what I like about you?" he asked, when

they had both surfaced and were shaking drops of red-stained water from themselves.

"Everything?" she suggested, impertinent, despite the fact she was choking on laughter and water in about equal parts.

"Besides that."

"What?"

"Nothing ever goes as planned."

"Oh."

"Should we order pizza for dinner?"

"After we've had a swim," Molly said. "The water is glorious."

She tilted back her head and caught raindrops on her tongue. The tongue that had touched his hand.

"I can't swim in these clothes, though."

"I have suits—"

"Don't be silly, Truck."

A little late *now* for her to be telling him not to be silly.

"You've already seen my undies today. Plus, we've been swimming together in our underwear since we were kids."

She slid out of the apron and tossed it. Next came her wet blouse. She inspected the sleeve mournfully, then tossed the blouse on the deck and shucked off her trousers. They joined the blouse in a sodden heap on the deck.

This was not quite the same as glimpsing her panties through torn pants this morning. It was very evident to him, seeing her in her underwear now, that they were not kids anymore.

"Take off your pants," she invited him.

Nothing ever goes as planned, Oscar thought dryly. Not that he had ever planned her extending that particular invitation to him, but if she had, he would have hoped the circumstances might be different.

"Are you being shy?" she laughed. "I've seen your tighty-whities lots of times."

It was true. They'd always done this. Raised by her father, she'd never had the long list of dos and don'ts that most of the girls—and then women—in his acquaintance had had. There was nothing suggestive about her leaving her clothes behind if they became inconvenient. Molly had always prided herself on being one of the guys. She had never thought a single thing of stripping down to her underwear when their adventures had led them to the discovery of an unexpected swimming hole.

Not only would she strip down, Oscar remembered fondly, but she'd be the first one in the water, even in the spring, when you practically had to break the ice off of it to get in. And the tire swing hanging from a tree branch was never enough for her. No, she had to climb up the tree, to the top branch, as high as she could go, and swan dive into the water below. It was nerve-racking to watch her, even when you knew her stuntman father had been teaching her his crazy art at the same time she was learning to walk.

It occurred to Oscar that if he had thought he was lessening the danger between them by plunging them into the waters of his pool, he had made a serious miscalculation.

Molly was wearing underwear as utilitarian as the khakis she'd arrived at the airport in. He had seen bathing suits far more revealing than her black sports bra and her high-waisted white panties.

And yet her sliding through the water, effortless, strong, near naked, felt like one of the sexiest things he'd ever seen. And really more than his battered defenses could take. This new complication made him able to resist the temptation to be drawn back into the carefree world they had once shared—and the temptation to show her he no longer wore tighty-whities—and he hauled himself out of the pool.

"Towels are over there in the cabana when you need one. I'll go see about that pizza."

He needed a friend more than a lover, he told himself sternly. And the loss of his brother should make him very wary about loving Molly beyond the way he already did.

A woman who embraced danger was a poor match for a man who had learned the hard lesson that loving someone did not protect you from the loss of them.

It only made that loss, when it came, so much worse.

Molly floated in Oscar's pool, on her back, the rain splashing down on her face. As always, Truck was the reasonable one. He sensed the danger building between them and he'd walked away.

She, on the other hand, truly her father's daughter, never walked away from danger. She was invigorated by it. Exhilarated.

And the danger between her and Oscar had been as real as any she had ever felt, and she had experienced—and invited—many dangers in the quest for the perfect photograph.

In the quest to feel exactly what she was feeling right now.

Alive.

After a while, the pure joy of being alive lost some of its luster. Molly moved to the hot tub. She looked into the condo, craning her neck, but it looked dark. She did not see Oscar.

She waited, hoping he would see that moment of danger between them had passed and come back out.

But he didn't.

Finally, relaxed and tired despite the fact it was daytime in Germany, she got out of the pool and wrapped herself in a towel. On the way across the deck, she noticed raised planter boxes that she had not seen the night before.

There were neat rows of herbs growing in dark soil. Each was neatly labeled, all capitals, in his precise printing. *Basil. Oregano. Rosemary. Thyme. Mint. Parsley.* Beside the herbs, two cherry tomato plants grew vigorously.

He was that guy. The guy you could rely on. He always had been. The guy who could keep plants alive. Thank goodness he had pulled away tonight, before she had given in to that thing that could wreck what he represented to her: the only stability she'd ever known.

She padded back into the opulent apartment.

It appeared to be empty, a night-light shining above the range. The space was deeply silent. She crossed the open space to that granite and stainless steel marvel that was his kitchen. It was obvious Truck had gone to bed. He had left pizza out for her on the island. It was still in the box it had come in. He had also managed to salvage some of the pomegranate and left her a small salad.

She opened the pizza box and saw he hadn't even eaten. She was starving. She wolfed down the salad, grabbed a slice of pizza, then went and stood in front of the picture of Ralphie to eat it.

She felt the ache of missing him. What a good brother Oscar had been to Ralphie. His enjoyment of his brother had been so genuine. If he was playing football, Ralphie was included in some way on the team. If they went to a movie, Ralphie came along. Oscar, seemingly without effort, had made Ralphie part of everything. And it was Ralphie's joy in that inclusion that had made so many of the times they had spent together shine.

Oscar. The rarest of men. Decent. Honorable. Selfless. She had all those things to thank for the fact she was sitting here eating cold pizza alone. He, sensibly, had kept them both safe from the danger of that passionate current that had leaped up between them.

Oscar had concluded, just as she had moments ago, that to give in to that passion could destroy their most valuable asset.

Their friendship.

Given that he was saving them both, why did she feel faintly resentful? Restless? Irritable with him?

Jet lag was making her unreasonable, Molly decided. She ate the last of her pizza crust and checked her phone.

Thankfully, some things were going according to plan. She made her way to her bedroom, showered off the pool water, and then she put on her plaid pajama bottoms and her T-shirt. She fell into the luxury of a very expensive bed, the crisp sheets announcing their thread count by feeling like silk against her tired body.

She told herself she probably would not sleep.

But she was asleep almost instantly.

CHAPTER EIGHT

OSCAR WOKE UP EARLY. Outside his window, he could see the rain had lifted and it was going to be a perfect summer day in Vancouver.

His space was silent, but that did not change the fact he was very *aware* that Molly was in it with him. On the other side of this wall. Curled up in bed, in her boy pajamas, her curls probably all squished to her head from sleeping on them wet.

For his own self-preservation, he'd abandoned her last night, and now as he lay there, contemplating her close proximity on the other side of the wall, he also contemplated the possibility of continuing with a strategy of avoidance.

But *he'd* invited *her*.

They were best friends. He'd known her since kindergarten. He probably knew her as well as any other person in his world. It was a sorry way for a friend to behave, to want to give her a ticket to go home as soon as possible.

How could he have forgotten how Molly complicated everything? She would definitely complicate his deliberately simple world.

And those complications seemed to be intensifying since the last time he'd seen her.

That wasn't quite true. It was the last time he'd seen

her that had complicated everything. He could still—six years later—conjure the taste of her mouth, the dazed look in her eyes, the hammering of his heart, the wanting…

So easily triggered again, last night.

"Suck it up, buddy," he muttered to himself. He reviewed today's agenda. Shopping.

Molly had always been the quintessential tomboy. It was actually one of the things he loved—he stopped himself and edited that to *liked*—about her. She was unpretentious. Real. Molly in jeans with a rip in the knee and a too-large shirt knotted at her waist was more gorgeous than any model or movie star he'd ever seen.

She hated shopping, so today should be a cinch. In and out in thirty minutes.

He got out of bed. Though he normally would have just thrown a robe over his nakedness to go out to the kitchen, it now felt imperative that he be fully clothed around Molly at all times. See? Already, two minutes into the day, a complication in his simple routine.

Because normally, he would wander out to the kitchen, have a coffee, maybe flip through the news on his phone before showering and dressing.

Geez, he told himself, it's not that big a deal to change a habit temporarily.

It was only when he went to the kitchen, passing the photo of Ralphie, that an awareness—other than of his disrupted routines and Molly in his space—hit him.

It was the first time in eight months, one week and four days that he had not woken up with his first thought being of Ralphie. It was the first time he had woken up without the odd feeling of being crushed by the empty space that his brother's death had left in him.

Yesterday was the first time he had laughed like that. Let go like that. And it suddenly felt like a few complications were a small price to pay to be out from under the burden of this grief, even briefly.

Friends, he said to himself, like a vow that could not be broken. *We're just friends and it is going to stay that way.*

And here she came, his friend, just as he'd imagined—in those plaid pajama bottoms that were too big for her, and a plain white T-shirt that was also three sizes too large. Her feet were bare and her toenails, peeking out from under the too-long legs of the pajamas, were a shade of neon pink that was startling. Her hair was flattened to her head in some places and springing wildly away from it in others. There was a little print from the sheet tattooed across her cheek.

"Morning," she said, and yawned and stretched, way up high. Despite the fact the T-shirt was too large, it slipped up to show him the taut line of her belly. "You went to bed early."

"Uh—"

"You didn't even say goodnight."

"I didn't?" he said, raising his eyebrows, as if he were surprised.

"I hope you're not becoming a dull boy, Truck."

He hoped not, too, but sadly he thought of how the small change to his morning routine had grated on him. It reeked of dull, didn't it?

If he had not made and taken the *just friends* vow, he could take it as a challenge. And unfortunately, he could easily think of a way to prove to her he was not dull, right now.

"Early to bed, early to rise," he said, evenly.

"What's your plan for us for the day?"

She was trusting him to be predictable. Dull. And suddenly everything he did have planned seemed exactly that, dull.

"I was thinking a bit of sightseeing." The Vancouver Aquarium and the VanDusen Botanical Garden had been on his agenda today. Maybe the gondolas at Grouse Mountain, depending how time went.

"That sounds wonderful," she said, as if it weren't dull at all. "Should we get the shopping out of the way first?"

Out of the way. Hard not to love—correction: *like*—that about her.

She sighed. "Between the loss of the pants yesterday and the stains on the shirt last night, I could use a few things." She hesitated. She looked almost shy. "I need a dress."

James, he remembered sourly.

"It's not like you to need a dress," he said carefully.

She scrunched up her nose. "I know. I hope you'll help me pick the right one."

That was just the reminder he needed—that while he struggled, Molly was managing to still be *just friends* with him. Was he really going to help her buy a dress to wear for another guy?

"What's the occasion?" he asked, careful in his tone.

"A party. I'll be hopeless at picking that out. You'll help?"

Just what every guy wanted: to help a woman pick something to wear for another guy. Would it be evil to help her pick something ugly?

"What's the party for?" he asked, casually, as if it were about helping her with the right dress choice and not prying into her relationship with James.

"O-oh," she stammered. "It's…um…a birthday party."

She had always been a terrible liar. Still no mention of James, the one she had promised to wear a dress for.

"What kind of a birthday party?" he pressed.

"A birthday party is a birthday party!" She said this

a bit aggressively, because he suspected she didn't have an answer ready.

"Is it a child's birthday party? Or an adult's birthday party?"

The deer-trapped-in-the-headlights look let him know there was no birthday party.

"Both!" she cried.

"Okay. How far away is it? Because currently, your choices might be limited by the color of your toenails."

She looked at her toenails, then tried to tuck them inside her pajama legs, as if the wild color revealed something of herself she didn't want revealed.

"It's soon," she said. "I could remove the color."

"It's cute, though."

She blushed. Who blushed over the color of their toenails?

Complicated, Oscar thought with a sigh. She could cavort around the swimming pool in her underwear without a trace of self-consciousness, but try to hide her feet as if they were revealing some big secret about her.

He thought about that for a second. Her toenails were bright pink. What would that say about a person?

Feminine.

And passionate.

Molly's two most guarded secrets.

A friend would let her know it was okay to let those secrets out, that really, being a girl didn't have to be a cause for alarm.

Even if there was another *friend* involved.

Molly hated shopping. Dreaded it, actually. And yet her emails this morning confirmed that her plan was coming together for the celebration of Ralphie, and she would need something to wear other than what she had brought.

She'd promised James a dress, which, given her plan, was silly.

But really, the sillier—the more fun—the better.

Besides, walking down the busy downtown Vancouver street with Oscar at her side, the familiar dread she felt around shopping didn't seem to be there. She felt incredibly light, connected to him, ready for whatever the day held.

She hadn't felt like this for a long time. The swim last night—or maybe chasing him through the apartment before that—had awakened her senses, and they remained awake.

Of course, having one of the world's most handsome men making you a coffee for the second morning in a row—coffee that a barista would have been proud of—might have had something to do with that. And the fact he'd noticed the color of her toenails.

It was those things and more. It was just *being* with him.

Again, today, the geeky scientist of her memory had been banished. The man walking beside her was loose-limbed and confident. He was like a magazine cover model with his crisp haircut and perfect features. Unlike some men, who got paunchy and pallid as they settled into their desk jobs, Oscar radiated fitness and good health, getting better as he matured.

If he were a model, his look today would be "summer casual for the successful guy." He was wearing a light blue pressed shirt, untucked, tan cotton pants, canvas loafers with no socks. Sunglasses hid his eyes from her and completed that film-star look.

And yet, despite the fact his appearance was so sophisticated now, there was a solidness, presence and inner strength about Oscar that was the same as it had always been. It seemed to quiet her chaos. She was so aware of how lucky she was to have this man for her friend.

Don't wreck it, she warned herself, again.

"Let's try this one," Oscar said, holding open a door to a shop. She looked up at the sign over the door.

"Seriously? Elite? I think they have the snooty salesladies."

"Who are you kidding? What would you know about Elite? You've never bought anything but Everest Outdoor in your adult life."

"You've barely seen me in my adult life."

"That's true."

"Which means you're reading the label on my pants," she teased him, "and it's creepy. These slacks are their office-to-cocktails line, by the way."

"As quick-drying as their outdoor line!" he said. "I remember those pants being soaked last night."

"I know," she said. "It's a miracle! Hang them over the shower rod, dry by morning."

"Imagine Everest Outdoor being able to cover all your shopping needs. And probably from a catalogue, too."

"I also shop at Crockett and Davey for Women now. Less expensive. More durable."

"How's their dress selection?" His mouth lifted at the corner. "Durable?"

"I bet they could deliver overnight," she said hesitating at the door.

"I don't think they'll have suitable party dresses." He slipped off his sunglasses and turned the full force of those suede brown eyes on her. "Besides, you can't show off those toenails in hiking boots."

She looked down at her feet. "They're not exactly hiking boots. They're comfortable!"

"And durable," he guessed dryly.

"Yes!" Why was she defending her footwear? And what kind of weakness was it that suddenly she *wanted* to show off her toenails?

"When's the last time you bought a dress?"

She lifted a shoulder.

"High school graduation," he guessed. "I remember that dress."

"So do I. It wasn't like anything any of the other girls were wearing."

"It wasn't?" he said, genuinely baffled. "I don't remember that."

"Well, I do and not fondly. It was too long, even with ridiculous shoes. Didn't I rip it before the night was over?"

He laughed. "Pretty sure you did. It wasn't really made for climbing trees."

"But I wanted to get that shot, looking down through the branches at the graduating class."

"Is that really the last dress you bought?" he asked.

"No. But to be honest, I don't have good taste in *girl* clothes. I'm counting on you to steer me in the right direction!"

He rolled his eyes. "I'm probably the wrong person to trust with this. I don't mind the..." he looked at her, searched for a word "...the girl Indiana Jones look."

"Really?" Coming from him, it felt like one of the nicest compliments ever.

"Really," he said, reminding her of why they had been best friends for so long. "But if you're going to give up that look, this is probably the place to do it."

The snooty saleslady zeroed in on them and came across the store like a battleship plowing through rough waters. If her look at Molly's best slacks—okay, maybe they were sporting a rather obvious crease where they had hung over the towel bar—and her T-shirt was faintly disparaging, all Oscar got was the brilliant smile.

"How may I help?" Her name tag said Barbara Kay.

Molly waivered. Her eyes were adjusting to the change in light from coming inside. The shop looked very expensive, with mood lighting and antique furniture scattered artfully about. Her sense of adventure abandoned her. She wanted the safety of same old, same old. She wasn't going to shop for dresses with Truck. What momentary madness had made her agree to that?

"What have you got in travel clothes?" she asked.

"Travel clothes?"

"You know, wrinkle-free? You can crumple them in a ball, throw them in your suitcase and put them on right away when you unpack?"

"Like what you have on?" The old battleship looked horrified and made no attempt to hide it.

"No," Oscar said smoothly. "We're looking for a special occasion dress."

"I'd be happy to help. Formal? Informal? Cocktail? Business?"

"I'm getting a headache," Molly said.

"Gorgeous," Oscar said, easily. "The perfect summer dress. In a brilliant color. Fun. Flirty."

"I'm not going to be flirting with anyone," Molly warned him in a dark undertone.

Something crossed his face. Surprise? Relief? Was he hoping she wasn't going to be flirting with him, then?

CHAPTER NINE

NOTE TO SELF, Molly thought, a little glumly. Truck did not want her flirting with him. Why would that bother her? It was so darned *wise*. Didn't he ever get sick of being the wise one?

"I don't like those kind of dresses," she told him. "The flirty kind."

"How would you know?" he shot back. To the saleslady, he said, "Please show us what you have."

"Here are summer casuals," Barbara Kay said, leading the way. "Let me know if I can help you find any sizes. When you're ready, I'll be happy show you the fitting rooms." She beamed at Molly before backing away.

The dresses were not squished together on racks, but displayed as if they were art pieces. Still, there appeared to be way too many to choose from. Molly turned over a price tag. "My headache is getting worse," she said mournfully.

"Why don't you pick three, and I'll pick three?" Oscar said. "How hard can it be?"

Reluctantly, Molly played along and went over to the "small" section of the circular rack closest to her. She flicked through them and chose one. She held it up.

"Navy is always practical," she said.

"It doesn't exactly sing *party*."

She gave him a mutinous look, held onto it and made her second choice. "And this one is good. A nice length to it."

He stared at the selection she held out to him. "What exactly do you mean by a *nice* length?"

"I won't be showing my panties to strangers if the wind comes up?"

"It's an outdoor party, then?"

"Yes."

"What would you say that color is?" he asked, carefully, focusing on the dress and not her frown.

"Beige? Leaning toward rusty brown?"

"I was going to suggest cat puke. Remember when you found Georgie in that hay barn?"

"He was so skinny," she said, smiling despite herself. "And scared."

"It took you a week to lure him out of hiding with cat food. And then, once he started eating, he wouldn't stop. He ate and ate and ate and then…that color. All over my shoes."

"Okay, okay, I'm putting it back, even though it's a perfectly respectable color that would go with anything."

"Except a party. Ralphie loved it when you wore bright colors," Oscar reminded her.

Suddenly, she remembered what all this was for. Had he figured out the party wasn't a birthday party at all, but a celebration to remember Ralphie? Was that why he'd mentioned his brother?

She looked at him closely. She didn't think so, but it changed the texture of the shopping trip, and erased her reluctance. It suddenly didn't feel as if they were in a high-end store, where she didn't belong. It felt as if that other world, the one they had shared, swam around her and held her up.

"Okay, okay, for Ralphie." It was truer than he knew. She chose the brightest colored dress off the rack and held it up for his inspection.

"That's better," he said. He called for Barbara, who must have been hovering close by. "We're ready for the fitting room."

"I've only picked two dresses," Molly said.

"Three, if you include the cat puke one."

"But I put it back."

"Clearly that's enough. I'll pick the rest."

"You're being very bossy."

"Because it's evident this is a topic you know nothing about. That's why you invited me, remember? I know. It's the blind leading the blind, but I'm willing to give it a shot."

Molly would have liked to complain, but she snapped her mouth shut. It was hard to argue with that. And it was a weakness, but she was just a little bit curious what Truck would think looked good on her.

"Think of it like princess boot camp," he suggested mildly.

"I've always been a better pirate!"

"You've always been a great pirate," he agreed, the affection rough in his voice, "but it's good to experiment."

"This from the guy who once blew up his mother's basement *experimenting.*"

He ignored her and made his way along the rack of dresses. How was it possible he looked so darn comfortable sorting through the racks? It did a funny thing to her heart, seeing that strong confident guy so intent on picking just the right thing for her.

Far more intent than she was herself!

"You are so lucky," Barbara said, acting like her new best friend, now that she had caught a whiff of a sale.

"How many men want to shop with their girlfriends? How enjoyable for you!"

She opened her mouth to say she wasn't his girlfriend, but Barbara tucked her in a fitting room and shut the door.

It was, after all, *literally* true. Molly was a girl and she was Oscar's friend. And the saleslady was right. Why not just enjoy this? A treat. A break from her ordinary life. An opportunity to explore a side of herself that she didn't let out very often. An opportunity to be cared about. Looked after. And then she would surprise him with her gift—a tribute to Ralphie—before she left.

"Especially a man like him," Barbara cooed, through the door. "On the ooh-la-la scale, I'd say he's a perfect ten."

Molly thought of Oscar, the perfect ten, going through the racks, that look of intense concentration on his face she knew so well from when he was conducting science experiments. He'd already admitted that's what this was to him, some kind of experiment.

And that's what she should treat it as, too. An experiment. A new kind of adventure. Fun. Allowing herself to be pampered a little bit. To indulge that inner girl that she'd always been a little bit curious about. And wary of.

If there was anyone she could trust with this experiment, it was him, who genuinely thought she looked great when she didn't dress up at all.

Princess boot camp.

Good grief. The very thought brought a giggle to her lips. And Molly Bentwell, pirate, did not giggle!

By the time Oscar arrived in the mirrored area outside the fitting rooms, Molly had on the navy dress. It was a narrow shirtdress style and she was looking at it, over her shoulder, in the full-length mirror. She noticed he seemed to have quite a few dresses draped over his arms.

"I don't want to be here all day," she warned him.

He hung his choices on a hook outside the door of the only fitting room that was obviously occupied.

"Why? You have better things to do?"

"Ah, you know, ships to plunder, booty to be captured."

Something in his expression shifted ever so slightly at the word *booty*. She suddenly remembered it had several meanings that had nothing to do with pirates.

"We've already decided you're good enough at being a pirate. This is princess camp."

"Just a sec, I'll flounce and look pretty." She did her best to flounce. She blinked her eyes at him.

Oscar made a face. "A bit of work to do there. That dress looks great on you, but it's not what I would call a party dress. It failed the flouncing test."

She considered that a mark in its favor, even for a party dress. "I think it's flattering. It makes me look very slender."

"You are slender. You'd have to fill your pockets with potatoes to not look slender. It looks like a guy's shirt. Against all odds, you've found the Crockett and Davey line of dresses. In Elite. The only time a woman should be wearing a guy's shirt—"

He stopped, suddenly uncomfortable.

"No, do tell," she purred, enjoying his discomfort. But then she thought of that. Of what it would feel like to be wearing his shirt, and what circumstances that might happen in. She changed the subject. Rapidly.

"The color is nice."

"I thought we agreed something to go with your toenails."

Had they agreed to that? She thought that was a bit of an overstatement. Still, she liked the way he looked at her toes, and remembered he'd called them cute. "It's silly to match a dress to toenails."

"Let's be frivolous," he suggested.

"You couldn't be frivolous if your life depended on it."

"Your bra strap is showing."

She tried to wrench it under the dress.

"That won't work. It's too wide. It's the wrong thing for that dress. Probably for any dress."

Molly felt her face getting very hot. "I invited you to help me find a dress, not discuss my underwear."

"If you had spinach stuck to your front tooth, I'd tell you. That's what friends do."

"My bra is like spinach stuck to my front tooth?"

"Figuratively," he said, and then laughed that Oscar laugh that made her love him, even when he was being annoying. "Figuratively? Get it? We're talking about your figure—"

"Okay, I got it," she said, faking far more irritability than she felt. "It's not funny if you have to explain it."

"Okay, let me explain this—your bra strap is showing, because it's too wide for that neckline." He regarded her thoughtfully. "Is that, like, a running bra?"

"It's like a none-of-your-business bra."

Undeterred, he leaned in and squinted at her bra strap. For an electrifying moment, Molly thought he was going to touch it. But no, he stepped back.

"It looks like something a woman weight lifter would wear at the Olympics."

Despite her protest, despite the fact the new electrical element was there, Molly found herself *loving* this interchange, bickering back and forth with Oscar. What a remarkable thing it was to have a friend who could be so honest with you, and who you could be so honest with.

Well, maybe not totally honest. She didn't really want

him to know that the mere thought of his hand brushing her shoulder caused an electrical current to pulse through her.

"Barbara, can you…" He looked around. "Oh, never mind. I'll find one myself."

"Find one what yourself?" she squeaked.

"A bra. For you."

"You are not going to get a bra for me!"

"I am."

"It's not manly."

"I'm secure enough in my masculinity to handle it."

That was true. Oscar seemed a man so certain of himself that nothing could rattle him.

"You don't even know my size." Molly realized this was a bit of a retreat from a flat-out no.

He did, too. He grinned wickedly at her. "I bet I can guess."

"I bet you can't."

"You're on. Winner buys lunch."

She scowled at him, though she felt like laughing at the thought of her absent-minded scientist, Truck, sorting through women's underwear.

"Okay, since it's an outdoor party and the wind might come up, grab me some pantaloons, too." She might as well make the surrender complete. Did that mean she thought someone was going to see them?

"Pirates wear pantaloons. Princesses wear…"

"Ha! You have no idea what princesses wear."

"We'll see," he said. "I'm a man up for a challenge."

Truck wasn't, Molly realized, a little breathlessly, that absent-minded scientist anymore. He was a man who looked like he might know his way around women's underthings, which was a new and rather frightening light to see him in.

Frightening and thrilling, the two things hard for her to separate, as always. She bet he was good at kissing. Really good at it. Not that awkward boy who had comforted her, with his lips, shortly after her father's funeral.

Even then, it had been a wonder. To taste him in that way. To add that dimension to all the other dimensions of their relationship. She could have fallen toward that, what she had tasted on his lips that night, and it would have been like falling through a night sky, studded with stars.

Her eyes found his lips.

"What are you thinking about?" he asked, quietly. "Because either you still have pomegranate stains on your face, or you're blushing."

"I'm thinking about bras," she told him. "A topic I am not accustomed to discussing with members of the opposite sex. But since we are having this unfortunate discussion, no underwires!"

From inside the change room came the clear *ping* of an incoming message on her phone.

"Could you turn that thing off?" he asked, annoyed.

It was hard to annoy Oscar, but it was also proving very hard to plan an event on short notice.

"I can't, sorry. I, uh…have something going on."

He raised his eyebrows at her. "Are you going to tell him you're shopping for pretty dresses and underthings with a man?"

"Tell who that?"

"Whoever's texting you."

"It's probably work-related."

"Uh-huh."

Molly squinted at him. Was Oscar jealous? Of course, he wasn't. He was just annoyed at her lack of techy etiquette.

"I can clearly see you don't need an underwire."

She folded her arms over the part of herself he could clearly see. It was his turn to blush ever so slightly.

"And no lace."

"Come on. It's pretty. Every princess should—"

"No. It's scratchy. And no—"

He took a step toward her. He looked down at her in a way that increased that breathless sensation. "That's enough rules, Mollie-Ollie. Trust me."

When he used that old nickname, a familiar little smile tickled across his lips. Had that smile ever made her want to kiss him before? Had it ever made her think of falling through a night sky, studded with stars?

That's what was making this dangerous! It wasn't two kids catching lightning bugs in jars on a hot summer night.

It was two adults discussing something only intimate partners should be discussing.

CHAPTER TEN

"I'LL PROBABLY REGRET trusting you with my lingerie choices," Molly muttered in an attempt to hide the hard hammering of her heart from him.

"I bet you won't," Oscar said, his voice a bone-melting growl.

Molly went back into the fitting room. She looked in the full-length mirror. There was nothing wrong with this dress! It went fine with her coloring. It was a good practical dress. One that could take you to meet a new client, or out for a drink. It might be okay on a short flight, or to do a really tame photo shoot.

He was right, though. It wasn't any kind of a party dress. Suddenly, seeing it through his eyes, she saw it was boring, just like he'd said, and she couldn't wait to get it off. And once she had it off, she looked at her underwear with a newly critical eye, too.

She suddenly couldn't wait to cover that up. She put on her second choice for a dress. It was horrible. She had picked it only for the bright colors, but it was a two-layered dress. It consisted of a straight white sheath in a flimsy fabric she thought might be chiffon. The sheath was circled with layers of polka-dot-patterned ruffles, the polka dots all different sizes and every color of the rainbow. It seemed a bit like a child's party dress. She was going to take it back off, but decided it would be way more fun to pretend she liked it for Oscar.

Molly came back out of the fitting room just as he was coming back, his hands—unselfconsciously—full of frilly things. Frilly things in light pinks and sweet lavenders, brilliant whites and jet-blacks. She should have mentioned she liked only two colors for underwear, white and black.

She could feel a blush rising in her cheeks, again.

Oscar saw her like that? Like a woman who could wear those kinds of things?

"Look at this dress," she gushed. "Isn't it great?"

He skidded to a halt in front of her. "I like it."

"What?" She looked at him closely. Was he pranking her prank? "This is possibly the worst dress I've ever seen."

"It matches the toenails."

She squinted down at her feet. "I don't think it does. I think it may have every color on the spectrum, except that one."

"It's got a lot of movement," he said, approvingly.

She put her hands over her head and did a little hula move, her hips swiveling, the dress swishing around her. "I think it might be moving because it's possessed. By the ugliness demon."

"If you don't like it, don't buy it. But I think it's fun and perfect for a party."

"Ralphie would have loved the colors," she said softly, surprised by how suddenly serious she felt.

She realized, too late, maybe she had touched a tender spot, the one he didn't want touched.

But Oscar cocked his head and looked at it a different way. He smiled. "You're right. He would have. On the other hand, I don't think anyone would have placed Ralphie—or me—in charge of wardrobe selection."

She swung around playfully, in a circle, and the dress floated and flicked in the air around her.

His smile deepened. "You know, I think maybe you were right. The dress is horrible, and yet you carry it with a certain panache that makes me like it."

She spun around again, and the dress swirled around her, its abundance of ruffles rising and falling like feathers on a bird.

"That definitely would have been Ralphie's choice," Oscar said. He went quiet for a moment and gave his head a bit of a shake.

"What?"

"You know, today I've mentioned him several times, and I just realized, I haven't felt as if I would fall to my knees with grief."

"Truck," she said softly, "remember those overalls he loved so much? They drove your mother to distraction. She couldn't wait for them to wear out."

"I seem to remember, as soon as they did fall apart, you bought him another pair."

"Part of why your mother hated me."

"My mother didn't hate you," he said.

Oh, Truck, you have no idea.

"It's true, she didn't get you. Or your dad. You both thumbed your noses at the very convention she had adhered to so religiously her whole life. It threatened her."

Molly had never thought of his mother in that light. Mrs. Clark was so cool and so contained. Threatened by her? Not as scornful of her as she had appeared, but threatened?

"I think, after Ralphie was born, her sense that she could control the world was snatched from her. It made her redouble her efforts."

She heard both sympathy—and the faintest aggravation—in his voice.

"Your dad—and you—challenged her view of the world. I think she was afraid I would like your world better than hers."

Threatened that Molly would draw her son away from her world? It presented that long-ago conversation in a different light.

"Did you?" she whispered.

"Oh, yeah."

That simple statement changed everything. And so did the wisps of smoke and spiderwebs that he held in his hands. He thrust them at her. He was actually blushing, which was totally endearing. "One of these will fit. And then I win the bet."

"If they are all different sizes here, you're guessing. You didn't really win the bet," she said triumphantly as she turned away from him.

"Here, wait, let me move these." He took the armload of dresses he'd hung outside the fitting room door and put them inside. He brushed against her and her every nerve felt as if it stood on end.

Had Oscar felt it, too? That electrifying jolt? Because he stopped, looked at her, then quickly backed out of the tiny space and closed the door behind him.

She sorted through the underwear, more self-conscious because he had selected it. They were all so delicate, so beautiful, so feminine. Somehow the fact he had chosen them made it feel as if each piece were burning her hands.

She finally chose a bra, a confection of spiderwebs and butterfly wings, slipped off her old one and put on the new one. Then she found the matching pair of briefs.

When she turned and looked at herself in the mirror, it

felt as if she had slipped off one skin and put on another. She could feel herself going very still as she looked at her reflection in the mirror.

She looked *sexy*. She felt sexy.

It was just the fabric, Molly told herself. She was unused to delicate silks up against her skin.

She quickly took the top outfit off the choices Oscar had hung for her. It was a pale pink blouse, nearly as wispy as the bra, in its construction. The dark ruby skirt seemed very structured—not an improvement over the navy shirtwaist—but in fact, it was made of a stretch material that hugged her, and made her slender frame look delicately curvy.

"Pink is not my color," she called through the door.

"Tell your toes."

"Did you pick this just to match my toenails?"

"Yup."

She assessed the result in the mirror. It wasn't just an improvement; there was that sense, again, of having slipped out of her skin, of being brand new.

The skirt was really just a background piece for the blouse, which was gorgeous. It was sheer, gauzy, semitransparent. It felt as if she were wearing fog, and the silhouette of her new underwear peeked through, subtle, sensual.

"It's not really me," she called.

"Okay," he said. "Just pick the last one, and let's go."

"I didn't like the last one," she reminded him.

"I thought it grew on you? Show me this one. Let's compare. That would be the scientific thing to do."

Only he would think dress shopping could be turned into a science.

She didn't want to. She wanted to. Good grief! She was a woman who often placed herself in harm's way to get a photo—she couldn't possibly be scared to show Oscar this outfit, could she?

Taking a deep breath, Molly the princess stepped out of the fitting room.

Oscar gave Molly a grin, so slow, so loaded with frank male appreciation, that it felt physical, as if he had touched her, as if she were turning to butter, melting on a hot griddle.

"Nice toes," he said. He didn't even glance at her toes.

"It's not really me," she repeated.

"Isn't it?" he asked softly.

And in the way he said it, she saw a different her, the one she tried to keep as hidden as her pink toenails.

"You look beautiful," he said. "But then, you always look beautiful."

Beautiful. The fact that he found her beautiful— this man that she could trust for his absolute honesty— hummed along her skin.

"Could you find me some shoes that might go with it?" she asked, deliberately breaking the intensity of what was going on between them.

After that, it felt genuinely fun putting on her princess persona. For him. But mostly for herself. Molly embraced the role she was playing.

"What is it with men and stilettos?" she asked with fake chagrin as she waltzed out in the shoes he had found.

Oscar had exquisite taste—she had to give him that. The shoes added a subtle layer of sophistication to each outfit she tried on. And a not-so-subtle layer of pure—

"Sexy. They're sexy as hell," he growled.

She gulped at the spark in his eye when he said that.

Every dress he had chosen was different, and yet each seemed to celebrate her shape, each moved her closer to embracing her feminine side. Every time she modeled one for him, and saw the approval in his eyes, her confidence grew.

She was actually a little sad when she came to the last dress. She took it off its hanger, and even before she pulled it over her head, the fabric spoke to her fingertips. It had to be silk. It floated down around her. Except for the new underwear, Molly had never had a fabric touching her make her feel quite so exquisitely feminine.

"I'm not a yellow person," she called to him, turning slowly to stare at herself in the mirror.

"You said that yesterday. Remember von Goethe!"

"It has roses all over it. Like as big as cabbages."

"But they're pink," he called back, "remember our theme?"

"It's very loud. I don't like to call attention to myself."

"It's an experiment," he reminded her.

Her protests faded away. In all the other dresses, as beautiful and sexy as they had been, she had felt like a girl playing dress-up in her mother's clothes.

This dress made her feel as if, until this very moment, she had been a woman playing dress-up in a girl's clothes.

The dress was gorgeous, summery, fun. And yet, underneath all the summery fun of the color and the extra-big flowers, was an extraordinary fit that celebrated womanhood. It was sleeveless and, minus the thick strap of her regular underwear sticking out, it made her arms look lean and tanned and lovely.

The neckline was a deep V, much more plunging than anything she had ever worn. But, with the new underwear, it showed the snowy swell of her breast to sweet advantage. The waist was belted and the skirt flowed out from it, wide, wispy and full of movement. It ended at mid-thigh—way too short—but the way it swished around her legs made it an utter temptation.

One she had to resist!

"I'm going to take it off," she called through the door. She felt ridiculously shy, as if she didn't know who this person looking back at her through the mirror was.

"Okay. I'm getting hungry, anyway. You owe me lunch."

Suddenly, even though it felt as if it would take all the courage she had, Molly wanted to see this stranger who stood before her in the mirror through Oscar's eyes. She stepped out of the change room.

Oscar was silent. She watched his Adam's apple slide up and down the column of his throat as he swallowed. Then, he let out a low appreciative whistle. There was no smile this time. He met her eyes. "Now why wouldn't you want to call attention to yourself?" he chided her.

She lifted a shoulder.

"Don't tell me," he said softly, "that I didn't win this bet."

Had he won? Oscar asked himself. It was obvious everything he had chosen fit her perfectly, as if in his mind's eye, at some level of pure male instinct, he *knew*. He knew every sweet gentle curve of her.

But sharing this experience with her had created a deep and abiding awareness of the hunger in him that had nothing to do with friendship.

He had just made everything more complicated. But the look on her face—kind of a shy delight in herself—made it worth it.

Even as it called for him to be stronger than he had ever been before.

"Which one should I get?" she asked him.

"Get all of them."

"No."

"I'll buy them if you're worried about the cost. I want to get all of them, for you."

Most women would have loved that. Not Molly, of course.

"Uh-uh. I'm not the poor kid who hangs out with the rich kid anymore."

"I never thought of you as poor."

"Our house was practically falling down. My dad was employed sporadically. I never had the stuff the other kids had."

"You had such panache I don't think anyone—including me, really—ever thought of you as not having. You had things the rest of us didn't have. World travel experience. You met movie stars. And once you started taking photos, you seemed the furthest thing from poor. Rich in ways most people will never be."

This was Oscar: he could take the thing she felt the worst about, and somehow weave magic into it.

"You thought of me as poor," she challenged him. "You were always trying to buy me things."

"You never let me buy stuff for you," he reminded her sourly. "Stupidly, stubbornly proud. Sometimes at my expense. I *wanted* to see *Episode VII, The Force Awakens*, and you wouldn't go."

Speaking of the force awakening, he felt like a powerful force was awakening right now. In him. And in her.

"You could have gone with someone else."

"I did. I took Ralphie. But I wanted to see it with you." Then again, he would have probably been watching her changing facial expressions instead of the movie. He would have lived it vicariously through her reactions to each of the scenes.

That was how dangerous she was, he reminded himself. She could distract the world's biggest nerd from a science fiction classic.

She could distract him—a guy who considered himself very goal-oriented—from his goal.

A force awakening wasn't necessarily a good thing.

"When you're poor," she told him, "that's all you have. Your pride. Your sense of honor. You cling to it like you've found a log to ride down a swollen stream. I couldn't let you buy things for me."

"As would any guy who was completely besotted with a girl?"

Molly went very still. She looked at him with wide eyes. He realized he had said something that was as secret to him as her pink toenails were to her.

"You weren't!"

"Yeah, I kind of was. I mean not when we were five, obviously, and probably not even when we were twelve. It was when you came back from Africa that you seemed like this exotic, mature stranger. You had a style and a strength about you that took my breath away."

But, he reminded himself, when he had acted on that, she had rejected him. She had practically moved to a different planet. This wasn't how he'd pictured addressing this—in the middle of a women's clothing store—but he realized he had always wanted to address it.

"Then your dad died, and I kissed you. And my timing was the worst ever. I never got a chance to apologize for it. You were just gone."

He didn't know how far to take this. The truth was, he had not known how he was going to survive his world without her. She had been the fresh air blowing into a stuffy room. She had been the sunshine on gray days. His world without her had turned so bleak.

He felt wide open, and he didn't like it one bit. There was some unknown named James lurking in the background.

"Hey," he said, his tone forced in his own ears, coming across as flippant, "why don't I buy you the dresses to make up for it?"

"There is nothing to make up for," she said. "Nothing. I didn't go because you kissed me, Truck. I went because you were inviting me into a world I couldn't belong in. Not ever."

"That's not true." Somehow, this conversation had gone seriously off the rails. Things tended to not go as planned with Molly. Why hadn't he remembered that?

A lighthearted excursion to buy her a party dress turned into this: him making a mess of apologizing to her for something she had probably nearly forgotten.

"It is true. I can't fit into your world, Truck. Even the offer to buy the dresses shows that. Every one of these dresses requires a different set of shoes. It gets complicated. And I'd never get it all in my bag."

What kind of woman thought about being practical when it came to buying dresses? Though he was aware she was giving him a deeper message. And it was very true: around Molly, it got complicated.

"You could buy a new suitcase."

"See? It just becomes more and more stuff. I don't need all this stuff. I travel light, Truck."

Ah, yes, there was the hidden message in all of her photos, the one that he thought he might be the only one that could see it. The reminder of what kind of woman Molly Bentwell was. She traveled alone. And she traveled light.

That's why she had left after he kissed her. It required more of her than she could give. Or maybe more of her than she wanted to.

CHAPTER ELEVEN

"Rejected again," Oscar said casually, as if there was no sting at all to Molly's words that she traveled alone and traveled light.

"Don't say that."

He lifted a shoulder.

"You may buy me one outfit," she said, a little desperately, as if that could heal what she had hurt in him. That was one of the problems between them. It didn't matter what words you said. There was a deeper meaning.

"One," Molly said, holding up one finger, as if he might miss the point if she didn't. "But I'm buying the shoes. Which dress?"

It was obvious to him which dress. The yellow with the roses had been spectacular on her. "You choose," he said. "Surprise me."

She tilted her head at him and nodded. "Okay."

He tried to smile, but somehow he didn't feel like it. Somehow, it felt like whatever dress she chose was going to have a secret message.

Complicated.

Because then he remembered she wasn't buying the dress to surprise him. In fact, as he stood at the cash register paying for a dress that she wouldn't show him, it occurred to him he had just bought her a dress to go to a party with James!

As the transaction completed, her phone rang. She fished it out of her pocket and glanced at it.

"Oh," she said, "I've got to take this."

Speak of the devil, he thought, as he watched her walk away, needing privacy, apparently, a little smile on her face that made Oscar achingly aware how little he now knew about her new world.

Whoever that was, she'd been pleased.

"And just for your information," she said, when she came back, "I didn't really lose the bet because the sizes of stuff you brought for me to try on were all over the map."

Was she beaming like that because she hadn't really lost the bet? He wanted to ask her who had been on the phone, but it seemed way too "teenage boy."

"But the right size was in there." Oscar made himself follow her conversational lead.

She tilted her head at him and tapped her lips thoughtfully with her finger. He really wished she wouldn't do that.

"I guess we could call it a partial win for you," she decided.

"What's that mean?" he asked, his grumpiness not all pretend. "Partial lunch?"

"Lunch, but nothing fancy. Do you have a favorite food truck?"

Somehow, he had the feeling she would think he was a complete dud if he admitted he had never eaten at a food truck.

"Not really," he said.

"After lunch, let's *do* something."

It seemed to Oscar they had been doing something, almost nonstop since her arrival. He suspected she wanted to put awkward conversations behind them. Who could blame her?

"I'm picking this afternoon's activity," Molly announced.

"And what can I look forward to?"

"A zip line, I hope."

That should, indeed, be a conversation killer. "Molly, have mercy, you know I'm afraid of heights."

She chortled happily. "We'll call it pirate school."

With her parcels wrapped up like she were carrying state secrets, they walked to a place where several food trucks congregated each day. Molly ordered the Zombie Special from Hong Bong. It claimed to be a fusion of Asian and West Coast culinary influences.

He ordered a plain burger from a nice plain-looking truck called Mike's.

They found a little park, and even though there was a very respectable-looking bench there, vacant, Molly threw herself down on the grass, belly first, legs crossed up behind her, propped up on her elbows.

He could see why Molly and dresses weren't necessarily a good match.

He eased himself down on the grass, gingerly, keeping a sharp eye out for any sign a dog might have enjoyed the spot before them.

"Want a bite?" she asked him, opening her food box and eyeing the contents with a certain rapturous delight.

The temptation to take food off the same fork she had used was countered by the appearance of the food: a mishmash of mushrooms, sprouts and unidentifiable items. He shook his head and unwrapped his burger.

"Delicious," she proclaimed. "How's yours?"

The aroma of hers was drifting up to him. It smelled delectable. His burger was predictable.

Which was what he liked…normally.

"You're not eating very much," she said, looking at her own overflowing plate a bit guiltily.

Less to chuck up if the zip-line experience went as badly as he suspected it was going to. Not that he was going to admit that to her.

Which brought him to her plan for the afternoon's activities.

"About zip-lining," he said.

"Yes, I'm on it." Eating with one hand, she thumbed through her phone with the other. "Here's one. A two-hour tour. Is this close to here?"

She turned her phone to him.

"Unfortunately," he muttered.

"Oh," she read enthusiastically, "Zip lines reach speeds of eighty kilometers an hour and can be up to two hundred feet above the ground."

"Molly, you know I hate heights."

"Yes, I know. But I did something I don't really care for this morning."

"But it was your idea. Plus, I'm *actually* afraid of heights. You can see the difference between dislike and fear."

"You live on the fortieth floor of an apartment building!"

"You haven't noticed how I avoid the railing around the deck?"

She got that stubborn look on her face. He loved that stubborn look, though it almost always foreshadowed trouble. For him.

"I did something I didn't like, and I enjoyed it," Molly said.

"You did?"

"Very much," she said. "So can't you try something you think you don't like? Please?"

Oscar had never been able to resist her saying *please* like that. He guessed they were going zip-lining. He finished his burger and stretched out on the grass.

Despite the looming threat of an afternoon suspended on a flimsy wire two hundred feet above the ground, despite some mystery guy named James, Oscar was aware of feeling happy.

That she had enjoyed shopping. That they were together. That the discussion of the kiss seemed to be behind them.

She put her phone away—apparently, her choice for a suitable zip-lining experience was made—and finished every bite of her food. Then she stretched out beside him. Her shoulder was touching his, and her hair was tickling the side of his neck.

Some women didn't need to wear a gorgeous dress to make a man so intensely aware of her that it felt as if his skin were tingling.

They stared up at the clouds drifting across a perfect sky. She tilted her head and looked at him. The grass was making her eyes look greener, and her lips seemed puffy.

"Penny for the thought," she said.

Who is James? "We don't have pennies in Canada anymore."

Molly gave him a smack on the arm. "A nickel, then. Sheesh. Inflation."

He couldn't very well tell her that he was feeling stupidly jealous. And that even though the discussion of the kiss had gone quite badly, it seemed as if he had not learned one thing from it. Because he wanted to kiss her. To see if it could go differently this time.

And he wasn't admitting that to her. Not even for a measly nickel. Probably not for a million dollars.

"I feel really alive," Oscar hedged. It was not quite a lie. It was just not the full truth. "As if I can feel every blade of grass digging into my back, the sun on my face, the birds chattering. There's a hum, like the energy is rising from the earth."

"That doesn't sound very scientific," Molly teased him.

"I think it's probably a well-documented phenomenon, how everybody feels before they die."

She snorted. "You aren't going to die zip-lining. Besides, I haven't managed to kill you, yet. Truck?"

"Yeah?"

"Don't let me go to sleep. It'll wreck my whole jet-lag-avoidance program."

"I don't know. Sleep sounds like a great strategy for my whole zip-line-avoidance program."

She laughed.

He loved that sound. His feeling of drowsy happiness intensified. So long since he had felt this way.

Since Ralphie had died.

No, a voice inside him said. *Way before that.*

Since he had woken up one morning and Molly was no longer a part of his world.

Her phone started ringing, *again.* It was an annoying sound like the buzzing of a bee. She pulled it out, a little too eagerly.

"Hello?"

No doubt about it. She sounded breathless with excitement. He opened his eyes to squint at her—he hoped she registered the disapproval—but she just lifted her shoulder apologetically, and then walked away.

So she could speak in private. *Again.*

Thank God he hadn't confessed her lips were a temptation to him.

When she came back, she looked happy.

"Sorry, I have to cancel zip-lining this afternoon. Something has come up that I have to look after. Can I meet you back at your place in a couple of hours?"

Oscar digested that. She was abandoning him. She had been in the city less than forty-eight hours. She was going to go off on her own? Or was she meeting James?

"Can you take my dress home for me?"

Why did that feel like a relief? That whatever she was planning, she didn't need the dress. Still, she was in a strange place. She didn't know her way around Vancouver.

But Molly had been in strange places all over the world. She'd been in way more strange places than he had.

"What's up?" he asked, trying to keep his voice casual, the very same tone he would use if one of his guy friends announced a change in plan.

"It's something to do with work," she said.

She wouldn't meet his eyes. She was *lying* to him. The same as she had about the party she needed the dress for.

She'd always been the most horrible of liars. Why would she lie?

He was aware he felt worried. And protective.

But Molly wasn't the eighteen-year-old girl she had been when she walked out of his life. She was an adult woman and feeling as if he *knew* her so deeply could be the greatest of illusions.

What if her ex had realized what he was losing, and had followed her around the world, and was begging her to come back?

Oscar tried to decipher the look on her face when she'd seen who was calling. Definitely pleased.

Another feeling overrode both the sense of being worried about her and the sense of wanting to protect her.

Anger. He was angry that Molly was here to see him and she was now dumping him to spend time with someone else.

He thought that over.

How could he possibly be mad that he *wasn't* going zip-lining?

Logically, he knew that after the way he felt about choosing underwear for her, and watching her come into some dangerous new part of herself in those dresses, that anger was the best possible thing he could be feeling right now.

A protection, like armor.

But for once in his life, Oscar found absolutely no comfort in logic.

CHAPTER TWELVE

HOURS LATER, WHEN Molly let herself back into the apartment, it was quiet. Really quiet, as if Oscar weren't there. But when she went down the hallway to her room, she saw his bedroom door was closed. It was silent but a light shone out from underneath it.

She paused outside it. Should she knock and tell him she was back?

She had a feeling he knew she was back and she was nervous about disturbing him. That was brand new.

Being nervous around Truck.

But she was hugging a little nugget of information to herself: he'd said he was besotted with her.

Mind you, that was a long time ago.

And all the same obstacles were in place, weren't they? Still, that admission made her feel edgy, and excited and frightened.

Because she had also been besotted with him.

What did all this mean right now? It was all so new it made her nervous.

But his anger was also brand new. It had been very clear when she had left him in the park this afternoon that he had been angry.

Once she revealed to him the reason she had abandoned him today, it would make everything okay. She knew it would. For all the exciting things she had done in her life, this felt the most thrilling.

Doing something for him. Something great for him.

But, meanwhile, she had to digest this new thing: Truck, on the heels of admitting he'd once been besotted with her, was angry.

With her.

Of course, she had seen him angry with other people. Not often. He was a man extraordinarily slow to anger. But when Molly had seen him angry, it was usually around Ralphie. He had never been able to tolerate any kind of meanness toward Ralphie. Even curiosity, people staring at his brother, sometimes made him angry.

"I can understand little kids staring at him," he'd told her once. "But their parents? I'd like to go over there and knock their heads together."

That anger transformed him. It showed an innate power in him that he did not unveil very often. But when he did, he became a warrior, that man who was willing to lay down his life in the protection of those he cared about.

But this was a strange thing to have him angry with her. She had hoped to come back, and maybe try cooking together again. A swim in the pool. Maybe they could discuss the besottedness a little more. Maybe, she could expand on not fitting into his world, and why she felt that way…

Instead, there was note saying the pizza was in the fridge for her.

Cold pizza. Alone. Again.

It was so much smarter than what had transpired between them last night. And yet, she felt robbed. Sad in a way she had rarely felt sad, that Truck was a breath away from her, and apparently they were not speaking.

There was also the secret to consider. If she spent time with him tonight, would she be able to keep all this bubbling excitement to herself, or would she spill the beans?

So cold pizza and an early night it was.

When Molly got up in the morning, she had a text from Oscar saying he'd gone to the office.

She felt a moment's panic. Was he going to wreck everything? She sent him a text back.

I thought we were going to hang out together.

There was a long pause before he answered.

That's what I thought, too.

Can you set aside the afternoon for me? It's important.

Not if it involves zip-lining.

It doesn't. I promise.

What does it involve?

It's a secret.

It seemed like a long time dragged by before he answered.

Okay, I'll be back by noon.

Molly set down her phone, nearly trembling with relief. Her eyes flew to the clock. Noon! So much still to do.

* * *

Oscar, always punctual, came through the door at a few minutes before noon. He stopped and stared at her.

"That's the dress you chose?" he asked. He looked like he didn't want to smile at her, but he did anyway.

Molly did a pirouette for him. The polka-dot ruffles swished around her.

"You know only you could wear a dress like that, with those boots, and somehow look as if you are setting a trend, not posing as a hillbilly, circa 1935."

"You know me," she said. "An on-trend kinda girl."

"I'm not sure I do know you," he said, and she could tell a bit of that anger was still there.

"Come on, we have to go."

Shaking his head, he followed her out the door.

"We're going to this address," she said, showing him the address on her phone. She could feel the anticipation building.

"I don't recognize that address."

"Can you put it in your GPS?"

He complied and they wove away from downtown Vancouver and out into the suburbs. And then they left the suburbs behind.

Finally, they came to what appeared to be an empty lot behind a chain-link gate that hung open on its hinges.

"Look," he said, impatiently, "you better start explaining. This is the kind of place shady deals go down."

"Trust me."

He looked insultingly uncertain about that. Then he squinted at the sign that hung crookedly from the fence. "Mad Mudder's? Where are we? And why?"

"You'll see," she said. She'd found her way here yesterday and despite the look of the place, it was going to be perfect.

They pulled up to a small shed. A man came out. Thankfully, he looked crisp and professional in a matching khaki shirt and pressed slacks.

"Molly," he said, "It's nice to see you again."

Oscar slid her a look out of the corner of his eye before taking the hand that was being extended to him.

"I'm Tracy Johnson."

Then he stepped back and regarded her with a frown. "Did you bring something else to wear? I told you yesterday, it's a pretty extreme experience."

"Yesterday," Oscar said, looking at her quizzically. "This is where you were yesterday? What exactly is this place?"

"You didn't tell him?" Tracy asked.

"It's a surprise," she said.

"Oh. Well, welcome to Mad Mudder's team-building experience."

Oscar shot her a look. "This is in some way preferable to zip-lining?" he grumbled.

"Where's everyone else?" Tracy asked.

"Everyone else?" Oscar asked, just as another vehicle came down the road and turned into the rutted driveway. It was a seven-passenger van. The windows were tinted.

Molly did not look at the van. She could not take her eyes off Oscar's face as the side door slid opened. He shot her a quizzical look. She realized she was trembling with excitement.

"I didn't do it right on Ralphie's birthday," she whispered. "I thought the actual day should be quieter. More reflective."

The van stopped. The door slid open. And one by one, they came out. The three remaining members of Ralphie's Special World Games relay swim team, and their coach, Mrs. Treadwell.

Oscar turned to her, understanding dawning in his face.

"What is this?" he whispered.

"Our celebration of life. For Ralphie."

His eyes rested on her face, and what she saw there stopped her heart.

"It's good to see James again," he said quietly. "I heard you mention his name on the phone, but I never put two and two together. It's so good to see them all. Fred. Kate. Mrs. Treadwell."

But it felt as if the one he was really seeing was her, Molly, and what was in his gaze was enough to stop her heart. Unless she was mistaken, Oscar was still as besotted with her as he had ever been.

Or perhaps she just saw the pure love in his face. Not just for her, but for all of them.

But maybe, just maybe, there was a special place in his heart for her. For having, somehow, someway, gotten this just right. The way a best friend should.

He smiled at her, and the warmth of that smile felt as if it could carry her through frozen days and winter nights and storms of all kinds.

And then he was engulfed in the team. From her phone calls to set this up, Molly had found out that, like her, Oscar had kept in touch with the members of his brother's old swim team. As per the rules, each participant was only allowed to compete twice in the Special World Games, so the team had not been together for a number of years.

The time gap only served to make the reunion more poignant for all of them, but Oscar was definitely the star of the show. His brother's teammates were surrounding him, touching him, hugging him, calling his name. Molly knew they loved her, and she would get her turn, but he was first for them, the man who had been the big brother to them all for the years that Ralphie had been part of the Special World Games team.

Truck had often said to her one of Ralphie's gifts to him was that how people interacted with Ralphie showed him who they really were.

This was also true of watching him with the old team. Watching him at the center of all that affection Molly could see, so clearly, who Oscar really was, and who he had always been.

Strong. Reliable. Decent.

It was a beautiful chaos. Hugs. Tears. Shouts. High fives and ruffled hair and secret handshakes. Oscar knew all the secret handshakes.

He was a man with such a good heart.

They turned from Oscar then and swarmed around her. She was engulfed in all that love, but it was Oscar's smile that was at the center of a heart that felt filled to overflowing. It was a smile that put the stars out at night and drew the sun from the darkness in the morning.

"Ralphie," Oscar said, turning to Molly, finally, his arms thrown over the shoulders of Ralphie's friends, Fred and James, his eyes just ever so faintly misted, "would have loved that dress. Thank you for choosing it for him."

Truck got it. He got it so completely, that it felt as if her heart were going to burst with happiness.

Finally, Tracy blew a whistle and held up his hand. "Okay, so you people have to divide up into two teams. And then you have to get through that obstacle course. You have to figure it out together. The first team through wins, and there is a very special prize for them. They get to throw the other team in the mud pit at the end."

This announcement was met with roars of approval.

"How do we pick teams?" Mrs. Treadwell asked.

"That's part of the exercise," Tracy told them. "You have two minutes."

"I want to be on Oscar's team," Fred shouted.

They were all jumping up and down with excitement. They all wanted to be on Truck's team.

Molly saw something she had never seen on Oscar's face before: panic. No matter how the teams were divided up, someone's feelings were going to get hurt. He was the sun that they all wanted to rotate around. Including her.

"One minute," Tracy called.

Mrs. Treadwell cleared her throat.

"I think it should be the four of us—me, Fred, James and Kate against Miss Bentwell and Mr. Clark. We haven't trained together for some time, but we've already worked as a team. Frankly, I think we'll kick some butt."

CHAPTER THIRTEEN

THERE WAS PANDEMONIUM after the butt-kicking pronouncement. Mrs. Treadwell's team solidified instantly, high-fiving, and calling happy jeers at their opponents.

But Molly felt something go very still in her. She and Truck as a team. Working together.

"Name your team," Tracy called. "Thirty seconds."

"Down Under," Mrs. Treadwell called.

"Truck Stop," Molly suggested.

Tracy provided coveralls: blue for Down Under and orange for Molly and Truck, but Molly refused hers.

"You'll ruin that dress," Truck told her, gamely putting on the coveralls.

"For a good cause!"

"You can't wait to wreck that dress," he guessed, laughing.

"You're so right. And you'd better hope the sheriff doesn't show up, because you look like an escaped convict," she said. Then she flicked up the edge of the skirt. She had shorts on underneath. He threw back his head and laughed even harder, and right then she knew it was going to be wonderful to be a team.

They were allowed to inspect the two identical courses that ran side by side.

There were smaller obstacles, but Oscar and Molly

quickly identified the four tough ones: crossing a very narrow log; a rope swing over water; a huge straight wall; and a crawl under strands of barbed wire. There were all kinds of rules about finishing obstacles together, as a team, that increased the level of the challenge.

At the very end of the course, with a little more glee than might have been strictly necessary, Tracy showed them the mud pit that the losers would be thrown in.

"Throwin' you in the mud," Fred called joyously to Oscar.

"Throwin' you in the mud," Oscar called back.

"Do you think we should let them win?" she whispered.

"They would hate that. Besides, it's not in your blood."

And then the starting whistle blew, and he proved that was true. Oscar was fiercely competitive. Having grown up with a disabled brother, he knew there would be no worse insult than "letting" the other team win.

She was fiercely competitive, too. Often, that competitiveness had come out between them, and so it was invigorating to switch channels and to work as a team.

And it was delightfully astonishing how quickly they became one mind, how they played seamlessly together.

It was glorious to see Oscar in this element, both his enormous physical strength and his brain power being put to good use. After some trial and error, they put the first two obstacles behind them.

But a new obstacle between them was not being conquered at all, instead it was growing in size and intensity and their inability to navigate it. The obstacle course had obviously been designed for teams of four.

With just the two of them, they quickly realized getting through most of these challenges as quickly and as efficiently as possible was going to require that they practically be glued together.

There was laughter. And heated discussion. Evaluation of the other team's progress.

And underneath all that, something else brewed and sizzled, growing white-hot. He piggybacked her across the log. They clung together on the rope swing. They fell off on their first attempt, and now, soaked, the physical awareness between them intensified.

Molly was drunk on the heat of his skin. The beat of his heart. The play of his muscles through the thin fabric of the dress.

She was drunk on the fact that once he had been besotted with her. And it seemed as if he might still be.

The electricity between them translated into energy. It looked as if Truck Stop was going to smash the opponents. But then they came to the wall.

It simply was not a two-person challenge.

Oscar somehow managed to scale to the top. He hung over it on his belly, reaching out his hands to her, but no matter how hard she ran, and no matter how high she jumped, she couldn't reach his outstretched hands.

He turned over and slid back down the wall. He crouched down.

"Get on my shoulders."

She scrambled on. She could feel the simple strength of him as he lifted her up. She stretched as high as she could. No dice.

"They're gaining on us," she cried. As she watched, dismayed, Down Under came to their own wall. They stood around it, chatting, and then quickly formed a human pyramid. And then they were over it and gone, out of sight, their shrieks at victory in sight in the air.

She stretched higher. She stood on one foot, trying to just get that little bit more height… She wobbled.

He tried to stabilize her but it was too late. She was falling off his shoulders.

And then she was in his arms.

Blinking at him. His strength closed around her. The obstacle course, and the yells of the opposing team, faded.

It felt as if it were just she and Oscar in all the world.

"Should we finish what we started all those years ago?" he growled.

"Yes," she whispered.

His lips were dropping over hers.

He was tasting her. She was tasting him. It was exquisite.

But just like last time, the timing was terrible. The place was all wrong. There couldn't be a less romantic setting in all the world.

And yet there was no denying what was unfolding inside of her.

She had waited her whole life for this exact moment.

To finish what she had started. With Oscar. With her Truck.

She was aware she had wandered aimlessly in the desert since she had left him. Nothing had ever filled the hole that had been left. Not her successes. Not her relationships. Not her moves from one city to another.

She could see so clearly now that each of those things had just been an attempt to outrun the hole in her heart.

The hole that only he could fill.

She sighed into him. She surrendered into this moment, which felt as if she had waited her whole life for.

Homecoming.

And then it was over, as quickly as it had begun. Molly found herself unceremoniously set on her feet.

She opened her eyes and looked at him. He nodded over her shoulder, and she turned around.

The whole Down Under team was staring at them.

"Were you kissing?" Kate asked.

"Um, sort of," Oscar said.

Kate cocked her head at him. "How do you *sort of* kiss?" she asked, guilelessly.

Molly looked up at him. He was blushing.

"Uh, Molly was on my shoulders, trying to get over the wall and she fell. I was just, um, making sure she was all right."

"Like her lips were all right?" Katie asked dubiously.

"Like a get-better kiss," Fred told Kate officiously.

"Yes!" Oscar said, "Just like that. Have you guys finished the course?"

"No, we're waiting for you."

"You're going to win. We can't get over the wall," Oscar said. "It's not a challenge for two people."

"It wouldn't be fair to win like that," James said. "It would kind of be like cheating, because we have four."

Molly looked at Oscar. She could see the emotion in his face.

Because this was grace. A Ralphie moment if ever there was one: the generosity of it; the pureness of heart; the inability to put competition above decency. Love trumped all.

"Here," Fred said. "We'll help you."

And so the pyramid was reformed, and Oscar was put on the top of the wall to help haul people over.

None of them ran to the next obstacle, barbed wire. They ambled over to it, and helped each other get through it.

Even with help, Molly's flimsy dress got ripped to tatters. Everything underneath it did, too, the shorts not quite providing the protection and privacy she had hoped for!

She thought Oscar might try to remove himself from the intensity of what had just happened between them, but no.

In a voice only for her, filled with the sensuality of smoke and fog drifting in a forest, he growled, "I see you wore the pink."

She knew that stolen kiss was not the end of it. A beginning. It felt as if she were standing at the edge of a cliff.

With no rope and no parachute.

"Well," Tracy said, "I have to say I've never seen one unfold quite like that before. Who's the winner, and who goes in the pit?"

Fred looked at him with baffled innocence. "We're all the winners," he said, as if that was the most obvious thing in the world.

And then they raced to the edge of the mud pit, and one by one they took each other's hands, until all six of them stood there.

"On the count of three," Oscar said.

Screaming with laughter, holding tight to each other's hands, at the count of three they all yelled, "*Go for it*," and then they leaped.

Mid-air, Molly realized this simple truth: a hand to hold was the rope, and love was the parachute.

"Everybody's coming to my place," Oscar announced, after they had all hosed off. "Pool and hot tub. What do you guys want for dinner?"

"Pizza," they yelled in unison.

"Are you okay with pizza one more time?" he asked Molly.

"It's not a soufflé kind of crowd," she told him, laughing.

The Down Under team clambered back in the van, which would follow his car back to the city.

"I'm going to wreck your car," Molly said, getting in gingerly. "Truck! You'll never get it clean."

No, he probably wouldn't. And, given the mud on everyone, his apartment was probably never going to be pristine again, either.

None of it mattered.

"You did all of this?" he said, turning on the heater when she shivered. "For me?"

"For me, too."

"So, getting everybody here, booking plane tickets—"

"Hotels, the van, the venue. There were a few times I just wasn't sure if I could pull it off, but it turned out pretty good, huh?"

He contemplated that. *Pretty good?*

"Molly," he said softly, "I have never received a gift like that one. It was exactly right. Perfect from beginning to end."

Including, he thought, a bit uneasily, that kiss.

And her pink underwear.

And a sense of the future stretching ahead of them, unknown. It was like that broken electrical cord on the ground, again. Sparking.

Electricity, tamed, could be a good thing. It could provide light and warmth and comfort and convenience.

He glanced over at her. She had mud on her face. Her hair was plastered to her head. Her clothing was soaked and clinging to her. Her pink bra was peeking through what was left of that dress.

Awareness of her shivered through him. Right now, she looked more beautiful than she had looked in that yellow dress and the stilettos. In fact, Oscar was not sure he had ever seen a woman as gorgeous as Molly.

Electricity, untamed, could be a bad thing. A single spark could burn a whole forest down.

CHAPTER FOURTEEN

UNTIL MOLLY HAD arrived Oscar had never considered that his apartment was missing something. Cynthia had insisted on hiring a designer and each—expensive—decision had enhanced an already beautiful space. His home was perfectly decorated *and* functional, not just pillows and poof.

The kitchen—with its double ovens, built-in coffee maker, wine cooler, stand mixer—would have made a professional chef happy.

In the living room, a seventy-five-inch television hid behind a piece of canvas wall art that rolled out of sight at the push of a button.

The pool, and spa, the exquisite outdoor entertaining area furnished with all of his own creations, was outside the door. The views were jaw-dropping.

The space quietly proclaimed arrival. It had everything a man could ever dream he wanted.

But right now, Oscar's apartment had never looked so bad. There were towels on the floor and draped over the leather sectional. Half-eaten slices of pizza seemed to be everywhere. White square boxes, grease-stained, with leftovers in them, were scattered about randomly.

A soda had overturned, and despite Molly's and Mrs. Treadwell's frantic efforts to sponge it up, there was a dark stain on a carpet that Oscar knew to be worth more money than his vehicle.

So, his apartment had never looked so bad. And it had never felt so good. He had called it home before, but it had not felt that way until now, filled to overflowing with Ralphie's friends. They were jumping in and out of the pool and hot tub, running around outside, coming into the apartment, dripping water on the floor. Oscar knew, with sudden clarity, exactly what ingredient had been missing from a space filled with spectacular things and stuff.

Life.

Molly had been right. Before it had been a movie set. Now, with Molly at its center, it teemed with life and his gaze kept seeking her out.

She had made a great ceremony of tossing out the dress when they got back to his apartment. Then, she had found the ugliest bathing suit in his guest collection—leaving the nicest one for Katie—and led the charge to the pool. Now she was in her pajamas, two cameras around her neck, her feet bare, working unusual angles to get those great shots she was famous for. If that meant standing on the granite kitchen island, or crawling under the coffee table, or straddling the back of the sofa, that's what she did.

Finally, things seemed to be winding down. Bathing suits were fluttering from the balcony railing—strictly against condo rules—and Fred and James and Molly were sprawled out on the carpet on the floor. Kate and Mrs. Treadwell were on the sofa. Oscar was in his easy chair. Even Georgie, who made a point of hating people, could not stay away from the love in the room. He had crept in and found a place on James's lap.

Oscar did not know how much he had waited for this moment, until it happened.

"Remember how he loved Uranus?" Fred asked quietly.

The Uranus stories started. They all had one. They could all remember a time Ralphie had cornered some unsuspecting stranger and begun an earnest discussion of his favorite planet.

Of course, his love for all things Uranus had only deepened when he discovered people thought he was saying *your anus.*

By the time each of them had shared a story, they were all howling with laughter. The floodgates had opened and they told stories about Ralphie deep into the night. Some of them made them laugh and some of them made them cry.

Mrs. Treadwell fell asleep on the couch. So did Katie. Molly brought out blankets and pillows. At one in the morning, Mrs. Treadwell woke up and declared the party over. Between the obstacle course, the pool party and stuffing themselves with pizza and soda, everyone was so exhausted they didn't even protest the party's end. The van was called to bring them back to their hotel.

At the door, there were tears and hugs and kisses and promises.

And then the door whispered shut, and something else happened that Oscar was not aware he had waited for, until it happened.

He and Molly were alone.

Molly went back into the living room and looked in one of the pizza boxes. She picked up a very dead looking piece of pizza, plumped up one of the pillows, sank down on the sofa, pulled a blanket over herself and took a bite.

"That's going to—"

"Anchovy," she declared with a blissful sigh before he could finish his sentence. She was pretty sure, Oscar being Oscar, he planned to warn her the pizza was going to be cold, not to mention have a potential food poisoning hazard.

It was nice to have someone care about such things. "Should we watch a movie?"

"Aren't you exhausted?" Oscar asked her.

"Sorry, no. It's almost lunchtime in Frankfurt. Are you exhausted?"

"Yeah. No movies for me tonight."

"Go to bed, then."

So silly to be so happy that he didn't go to bed. Instead, he came over to the couch and said, "Scoot over. I'm too happy to go to sleep."

She pulled back the blanket, inviting him in, and he climbed in behind her. She leaned on him, munching her pizza. Maybe it was the pleasant exhaustion that enveloped him, but he touched her hair.

She didn't protest. In fact, she leaned deep into his fingers, like a cat who wanted to be stroked.

"Best day ever?" she asked him.

"Without a doubt."

"What happened between you and Cynthia?"

"Why end the best day ever with *that*?" he asked back.

"It just seems like the time of night and the kind of day that encourages confidences," she informed him.

"That's true. The long day has lulled me into a state of languor that makes me want to tell you my whole life story, except you already know that."

"So, fill me in on the bits I've missed out on." She nestled deeper into the solidness of him behind her.

"Something was missing with Cynthia and me. I'm

not even sure I knew what it was until tonight when I saw my apartment filled with laughter. And light. And love. Everything with Cynthia looked so good, but…" His voice trailed away.

"Just like your house that you grew up in. I see that in a different light since you mentioned when your mom's control issues started."

"I don't know that they started with Ralphie. But I think that made them worse."

"Everything was just so perfect. Like a stage set. Coming from my place—Dad's motorcycle parts on the kitchen counter—I loved it. And maybe even envied it, a bit. And was afraid of it, too. It had an unspoken look-but-don't-touch vibe. Looking back, it lacked…er…soul. Except for you. And Ralphie."

"I think I knew it couldn't work with Cynthia even before Ralphie died. We were planning the wedding—*she* was planning the wedding, I should say—and I was going along, because she was doing a fantastic job and didn't really need much input from me."

"But?"

"I had one request, which I considered nonnegotiable. I told her Ralphie was going to be my best man."

Molly twisted to look at him. "She said no?" she whispered.

"She didn't say no. It was just the look on her face. Something in me quit right then, though it wasn't until after he died that I realized how badly it had unsettled me, how much of a wedge it had put in the relationship. That look haunted me. I guess, I had always thought he would come live with us, one day. After Mom and Dad couldn't look after him anymore. But that look…"

"How could he *not* have been your best man?" Molly asked, chagrined.

"Well, no doubt he would have blurted out *Uranus* at exactly the wrong moment."

"But that would have been the best part," Molly said.

"Yeah," he agreed softly, "I think it would have been."

"How come he died? I've been scared to ask this—"

"Don't ever be scared to ask me anything."

"I just didn't want to hurt you if you didn't want to talk about it."

"I like talking to you about it," he said softly, as if that came as a surprise to him. "It makes me feel not quite so alone with the grief."

"Me, too," she said. "Eight months, one week and six days."

His arms tightened around her. Did his lips touch her hair?

"When you called to tell me," Molly said softly, "you said he just went to sleep one night and didn't wake up. He was only twenty."

"His heart stopped."

"All those years of swimming," she offered pensively, "and he never seemed to have a health problem."

"It went undetected, though lots of people with Down syndrome have heart problems. Fifty years ago, it was rare for someone to make it past twenty-five, now their life expectancy can be in their sixties. They think it's partly because they used to be unfairly institutionalized. They do better at home, surrounded by family."

"Of course, they do better at home. Sheesh!"

Someday, it would have been Oscar's home. Where Cynthia would not have welcomed Ralphie. She knew it wasn't fair to hate someone you had never met, but Molly didn't let that stop her hating Cynthia just then.

"Ralphie had such a good heart, spiritually, if not

physically. I guess I took it for granted that he was always going to be part of my world," Oscar said softly.

"I'm so sorry, Oscar."

He smiled sadly. "I like to think his great big heart just outgrew his body."

They sat with that for a bit, quiet, comfortable with each other's sorrow.

"What happened between you and your latest?" His finger was wrapping one of her curls, unwrapping and then wrapping it again. She wished he would kiss her head again, so she could be certain that he had.

"I found panties under the bed. Not mine. Maybe that's why I'm sensitive to underwear discussions."

"You deserve so much better," he said quietly.

"You, too."

"I meant in the underwear department," he said.

And then they were both laughing again.

"Maybe you deserve better in that department, too," she said. "How would I know? I haven't seen them, yet."

Yet?

Thankfully, Oscar didn't pick up on her Freudian slip. In fact, Molly could feel the spaces between his breaths get longer, and his finger remained in her curls, but he wasn't playing with them anymore. The rise of his chest was steady and strong.

A man with a heart every bit as big as his brother's had been.

Feeling as safe, as secure as she had ever felt, Molly let her eyes close. Sleep enveloped her.

When she woke up, she had a sore neck. She glanced at her watch. She was turned around despite herself. She had only slept a few hours. It was 6:00 a.m.

Still, sleep deprivation aside, she had a good feeling.

A delicious feeling. Oscar was still behind her, propped up on the couch cushions, his arms wrapped around her midriff, his breath stirring her neck. The scent coming off him was heavenly, utterly male, clean, sensual.

He was going to have a sore neck, too. She should wake him up. But first, she had to look her fill of him, take in the sleep-mussed hair, the lines of his face, the masculine bow of slightly parted lips.

Had she ever noticed before how long and thick his lashes were? They were sweeping the high plain of his perfect cheekbones. His stubble had thickened, dark and roguish around the line of his lips. She wanted to touch it.

And his lips.

"Hey," Molly said, softly, before she did something stupid. "Hey, *sonya*, wake up."

His eyes opened slowly. He took her in with grave surprise. His arms tightened around her waist.

"I love it when you speak Russian to me," he said, his voice a drowsy growl.

"*Sonya* means sleepyhead. Sorry, nothing sexy. You should get up and go to your own bed before you have a permanent kink in your neck."

He ignored her suggestion. "Should you and I discuss kinks? Probably not. Aw, hell, let's throw caution to the wind. Do you know anything sexy?"

She went very still. The temptation to touch the stubble on his face grew.

At the look on her face, he grinned and amended hastily, "In Russian?"

Probably better not to play with fire. "Nope, sorry."

"Ha. Could you hand me my phone? It's on the side table there."

Molly felt disappointed. One of those kind of guys, then. The first thing they did in the morning was check their phone. Well, you probably didn't get to an apartment like this by not being on top of things at your business.

He looked at his phone. He yawned. He tapped. He scrolled. Then he typed something in. Answering texts already.

CHAPTER FIFTEEN

"EVERYTHING IS AT our fingertips these days. I'm looking
up something sexy. In Russian."

So Oscar wasn't opening texts from the office. It suddenly felt as if they were playing, but somehow an inno-
cent game had transformed into a very dangerous one.
Russian roulette.

But she could not bring herself to stop it, even though
her heart was pounding, and she wanted to touch his
stubble more than ever.

She nodded. Oh, sure. Why not see if it was loaded?

"You be Ursula," he said. "I'll be Dimitri."

"I don't like my name."

"Choose, then."

"Anastasia."

He raised his eyebrows as if she had said something
deliberately wicked.

It was just like in the old days, when the playfulness
leaped up between them as naturally as breathing. Only
this had a different thrilling element to it, as if they were
walking a tightrope between the young people they had
once been and the adults they now were.

In a low voice, definitely sexy, Oscar/Dimitri spoke
into his phone. "You have the most beautiful eyes I've
ever seen."

The phone translated, and spoke Russian to them.

"The voice is a little mechanical," Molly said. Molly was the girl who never giggled, but Anastasia didn't have that problem. "I think it scares me a bit."

"Scares you? That won't do. Here let me try to say it myself." He listened carefully to the mechanical Russian voice. He gave her a look worthy of a Cossack warrior who had galloped a white stallion across an endless steppe just to see her, and then he said the phrase. Not that she was any kind of expert in Russian, but to her his accent seemed pretty good. Not that it mattered. The tone of his voice, husky, intense, commanding, was dreamy.

"I think I'm going to swoon." Anastasia was free to say things Molly never would. And Anastasia was only partly kidding.

"Here, Ana, you try it."

She looked at the phone he handed to her. She took a deep breath. She took a risk. She looked at him. "I want to touch your stubble," she whispered into the phone, her voice hoarse.

The mechanical male voice spat it out.

"That was creepy," Oscar said, pretending horror.

She repeated what she'd heard, working the accent, blinking her lashes at him, making a little pout with her mouth. His eyes darkened. He touched his stubble. Her eyes followed his hand, yearning.

"Okay," he said, his voice a croak. "Whatever you want to touch is fine with me."

Even before the phone spat out the garbled translation, Molly, freed of her inhibitions by Anastasia, was reaching for his face.

Her fingertips scraped the rough surface of his stubble. And then her palm slid down his cheeks, cupped his chin. She closed her eyes, just letting the sensation of it sink in, the beautiful intimacy of it all. And then her fingertips trailed upward…

He stopped her hand. He held it, and held her gaze. Without saying a word, Oscar was asking her a question.

Was she sure she wanted it to go there?

Molly nodded, ever so slightly. "*Da*." She remembered the Russian word for *yes* from her childhood.

But then Anastasia gathered her cloak around herself and faded away. Dimitri galloped off into the sunset.

Just like that, it was so real. It was Molly and it was Oscar.

"I have to tell you something," he said hoarsely. "About Cynthia."

Now?

"It wasn't about Ralphie. Not really. It was about you."

"Me?" she whispered.

"You turned my life upside down. When you left. So suddenly. Cynthia, in a way, represented everything I'd ever known. She was safe and she was predictable, and I retreated to that. But I never stopped missing the way you made me feel. Feeling like *this*—on fire with life— is what was missing."

Molly felt the fire he was talking about. She let him guide her hand to his lips. He touched her fingertips to his mouth. She explored the warmth, the softness, the texture. Ever so slowly, like a cowboy working with a wild colt, being ever so careful not to startle with the quick, unexpected move, he drew her fingertip of her index into his mouth.

His eyes never leaving her face, his tongue tangled around it. He drew gently on it, pulling it deeper into the soft cavern of his mouth.

No translation was needed for the jolt that shot through her, white-hot. No translation was needed for the delectable weakness she felt. No translation was needed for the all-consuming hunger that licked at her as surely as his tongue had.

And no translation was needed for what happened next, either.

Oscar groaned with such helpless need, with such pent-up wanting, that Molly felt herself melt further into the thing she hated most: weakness. She felt her bone and her sinew turn to putty.

Part of her tried to warn her this was Oscar. This was her best friend. She could not risk this friendship. She had to think about tomorrow, about the future, about consequences.

But another part of her wanted only this moment with all its seductive and enchanting power.

She didn't want to be brave anymore. She wanted to surrender, to fight no more.

She acknowledged the part of her that gave up wanted something, and maybe had always wanted it. It was one of those hidden longings that became more powerful when you unleashed it.

This is what Molly wanted: something more complex than friendship, more layered, as multifaceted as a diamond.

It suddenly felt, not as if this was wrong, but as if this was the most right thing that had ever happened to her.

As if a hole inside of her made itself apparent, and with that knowledge of its existence came the knowledge that only Oscar could fill it.

Molly had a deep sense that if she did not explore this thing unfolding between them, she would spend the rest of her life—and possibly beyond, into eternity—carrying the emptiness. Feeling the void of not having known Oscar completely.

She fell toward him with the inevitability of a leaf falling to the ground in autumn.

He stood up off the couch, taking her with him, in the cradle of his arms. Carrying her easily, as if she weighed no more than a feather, he went down the hallway to his bedroom, nudged open the door with his foot, crossed the room and laid her across his huge bed.

She sank into the incredible softness of it.

Oscar stood, motionless, looking down at her with a heated gaze. As Molly watched, his hands moved to the buttons of his shirt. A smile tickled across his lips as he tormented her with slowness, flicking one button open, pausing, and then doing the next one.

Each open button revealed him to her.

She had just spent an evening with him in the swimming pool. She knew what he looked like. She had hardly been able to take her eyes off him.

But this was different.

Totally different.

Because this was a giving of himself to her and only her. This was Oscar, declaring silently, with actions rather than words, what he was about to unveil would belong to her.

Completely.

To touch. To explore. To discover. To know.

He finished with the buttons. He peeled off the shirt.

He stood there, in the half dark, holding the shirt loosely in his hand. Golden morning light was beginning to spill through the windows, gilding the broadness of his shoulder, the depth of his chest, the perfect cut of pectoral mounds, the pronounced line of his triceps, that kiss-worthy hollow at the base of his neck.

He let her look, and then Oscar let go of the shirt and it whispered to the floor. He moved to his slacks, a flick of a powerful wrist dispensing with the snap, his hand gliding down the fly. Slowly—so slowly—he slid off the pants, revealing the narrowness of his waist, the jut of his hips, the dent of his belly button, the arrow of dark hair leading her eye downward.

"You don't wear tighty-whities anymore," she squeaked.

He didn't smile. He didn't allow her to distract from the intensity of what he was revealing to her.

Instead, he bent, sliding the legs of the slacks off one at a time. He straightened and stepped out of the puddle of his discarded clothing. Her eyes trailed down the length of his legs. She shivered from the pure power of his masculine form. She looked back to his face, to see his eyes had never left her.

A smile tilted his mouth—a smile that knew what he was doing to her, that he relished it—when she licked her lips.

She could stand it no more. She held out her arms to him. With a groan of need and desire, he surrendered into them.

"Are you—"

She stopped his words with her mouth. The time for talking was done.

Oscar woke up to the sound of rain, the promise of sunshine early this morning gone, as was so often the case in this coastal city. He looked at the clock.

Had he ever slept until noon? It felt luxurious to be nestled deep into the goose down comforter, rain hammering on the windows. It felt glorious to have Molly beside him.

He got up on his elbow and looked at the woman sleeping on her side in a tangle of sheets. One arm was under the pillow, and one leg straddled the pure white squares of the comforter.

His bold and beautiful Molly.

But she had not given him that side of herself last night.

She had honored him with the other side. The hidden side. The side that sometimes he felt only he knew about, that part of her that was sweetly vulnerable, that didn't trust easily, that waited for the other shoe to drop.

The Molly that was so tender, and so sensitive. The Molly that was fragile, not strong. The Molly who might be filled with doubts this morning.

He was aware he did not want her to have a single doubt.

He tossed on a robe and tiptoed out of the room. He made coffee, and he checked on her. She was still sleeping deeply. So much for her jet-lag strategy, he thought wryly.

He didn't want her to wake up if he slipped out to get a few things, so he called the florist and the bakery. He was not sure it had ever been quite so satisfying to have enough money to do anything you wanted, to buy the contents of an entire florist shop, to order hot croissants delivered immediately.

All Oscar wanted to do was sweep that girl right off her feet.

By the time she woke, he had filled every available space in that bedroom with flowers. He had coffee and croissants on a tray for her.

Molly waking up was the cutest thing. A stir, a lapse, another stir. A blink. A stretch of one hand out from under the pillow, that slender leg finding its way back underneath the covers.

Finally, an eye opened. And then the other one.

He grinned at her.

What he saw in her face was not a single doubt.

She took him in slowly, and with wonder that made his heart go still.

"Did I die and go to heaven?" she asked huskily.

Had he made her that happy?

She set him straight. "What is that scent in here?"

Oh, so that was what was heavenly. He made a sweeping gesture to the flower-filled room.

She got up on her elbows. "What the heck?" she asked, looking around the room.

"I didn't want you to think the rain was depressing." He spoke the words into his phone. The message was re-delivered to her. In Spanish.

"Depressing?" she said, her voice throaty, "It sounds like the perfect kind of day to stay in bed."

He said something really naughty into his phone. It was translated. She blushed. She laughed. She held back the covers for him. He climbed into bed with her.

"A perfect day for a trip around the world," Oscar whispered in Molly's ear, taking advantage of his close proximity to give it a little nibble. "We'll start with Spain and see how far we get."

"Okay," she agreed. "You be Bruno, I'll be Isabella."

"I don't like Bruno," he said.

"Okay, choose."

"Angelo," he said.

"Perfect. My angel." She took his phone from him. And spoke into it. He was pretty sure he blushed. Before he laughed. And then the laughter died.

When night fell, it was still raining. They had made it to Iceland, sitting in his hot tub, faces held up to the rain, pretending it was the Blue Lagoon. Bjorn and Hallveig were murmuring Icelandic endearments to each other and trying not to get the phone wet.

They fell into bed, finally, exhausted.

"It's the first day I haven't thought of Ralphie," Oscar realized, loving the feel of her head on his chest, her hair springy and wild under his fingers. "Until now. And it's weird because it's his birthday tomorrow."

"Eight months and two weeks," she said, softly, always knowing the right thing to say. "Do you feel guilty that you didn't think of him until now?"

He thought about that.

"No, his whole life was about love. He celebrated it like no one else."

There. He'd said it. Love.

He slid her a look. She didn't appear to be getting ready to run. If anything, she snuggled into him more closely.

"You're right," Molly said. "I feel like he'd be happy, as if all the pieces of the puzzle are finally in place. We couldn't give him a better birthday gift than this. Living so fully."

"That's what I think, too. That he's dancing around Uranus, beside himself with joy."

"Oh," she said happily. "We only went around the world today. Should we tackle the universe tomorrow?"

CHAPTER SIXTEEN

OSCAR FELT AS if he had been holding his breath without knowing it.

But she was the one who had mentioned tomorrow. Molly would still be here tomorrow. He allowed himself to breathe. He recognized a fear in himself, left over from their past.

He was afraid he would wake up, and without warning, she would be gone. Last time a mere kiss had driven her away. This time it had gone so much further than that.

He realized he had to address the fear.

"Why did you go?" he asked. And what he really meant was, *Will you go again?*

"I felt as if I didn't have any choice," she said, suddenly somber. "My dad had died and the farm sold. I didn't have a home anymore. I had no place to go."

He wanted to say, *I would have looked after you.* But they had both been fresh out of high school. What hope would he have had of looking after her? Still, it hurt him deeply that she had carried the double burdens—the loss of her father and suddenly being without a home—by herself.

"Photography school was suddenly an option. It hadn't been before. Even though I wanted it, I don't think Dad and I could have scraped together the money.

The scholarship I got solved the problem of not having a home, and it gave me one dream to cling to, while another was gone."

"Why didn't you come to me?" he said hoarsely. "Why didn't you talk to me about it?"

"If I talked to you, I wouldn't have been strong enough to go, Truck." She hesitated for a long time.

He got up on his elbow, and saw that tears were slithering down her cheeks. He touched one. "What?" he whispered.

"You were the dream I gave up."

"The whole time I was growing up, you were solid. We moved. You stayed. We had adventures. You had routines. You were the one reliable thing. My touchstone.

"I used to think it was your mother buying the farm that made me leave, but now I'm not so sure. I'm afraid of love, Truck. Terrified of it.

"And you kissed me that night, but you, my touchstone, were already moving on. You were going to university in the fall. You had plans and ambitions, and I had few prospects. I didn't want to hold you back."

Something in him went very, very still. It wasn't that she had used the word *love* in the context of him, though he knew he would return to that later.

"My mother bought your farm?"

Her eyes went every wide. She swiped at a tear sliding down her face. "I thought you knew that," she whispered.

Oscar felt something he had rarely felt in his entire life. It was pure fury.

His mother had forced Molly's hand while she was still reeling from the death of her father. His mother had ripped Molly from his world. His mother had played on her insecurities about love.

Even those words *I didn't want to hold you back* sounded more like something his mother would say than Molly.

He remembered, suddenly, the fury deepening, that his mother had walked in on the tail end of that kiss with Molly.

And he remembered, now, that she had never once mentioned it to him.

Come to think of it, hadn't he been astonished by that? That his normally meddlesome mother had not commented on that kiss she had interrupted?

At the time, he had thought she was being sensitive, to the circumstances, to Molly's loss, to his need to comfort her.

Now, he saw it more clearly. He had said to Molly, once before, that his mother was threatened by her. The thing was, he had not realized, until this very moment, just how threatened. His mother had never once mentioned to him that she had purchased that farm. He had gone to university shortly after, so he hadn't really paid attention to what happened to the property next door to his childhood home.

Molly sensed his fury. "Don't be mad."

"I'm not mad at you."

"It's understandable from a mother's point of view," she said. "She didn't approve of me. I was the one who led you astray. Good grief, I got you arrested!"

"We swam in the public pool in the middle of the night and got caught. That's hardly a felony."

"You broke your arm because of me."

"It wasn't *because* of you."

"Uh-huh. As if you would have ever decided to jump on the back of one of Knapp's horses if I weren't around."

"Please, don't defend her," he said wearily. "And don't

ever do this to yourself in my presence. Make it as if you were, or are somehow, less than the Clarks. You were more than all of us put together. Do you get that? Everything you have and achieved, you did with your own guts and gumption. That's what terrified my mother. That you could be so *much.* So real. So bold. So generous. So strong. So free. And all of that came straight from inside of you. That's real power, and she knew it."

His tone softened. "And I know it. I've always known it. I see you, Molly Bentwell, I see you completely. I always have, and I always will."

She was crying really hard now. "Thank you," she whispered. "Thank you."

He took her in his arms and held her. And then, when her tears had stopped, he kissed her.

And then she kissed him back.

And then they were lost in that place where all pain was erased, and all the past, and only this moment, in all its glory, remained.

A long time later, Molly slept, and Oscar got up, and went over to the window.

Tomorrow would have been Ralphie's birthday. That's why she had come. Now, would she go? She hadn't mentioned leaving. But she hadn't mentioned staying, either.

He was not a man accustomed to being uncertain. But he was aware of feeling uncertain about this. It wasn't really about her departure date.

It was about whether or not they were feeling the same thing.

The truth tickled along his spine, and then seemed to explode, like Fourth of July fireworks inside his head.

He loved her. He didn't want to. Love involved losses and he was still reeling from Ralphie's sudden death.

Plus, Molly had already taught him about love and loss. But he had never known her reasons for leaving before. Knowing deepened what he was feeling. A quiet truth made itself known to him. It wasn't as if he had fallen in love with Molly over the last few days. It was more like he had realized he had never fallen out of love with her.

This, then, was the biggest risk of all. To love someone, even when that journey was fraught with unknown perils and unnamed dangers.

But it felt as if before he took the greatest risk of all—declaring his love to Molly—he had something else he had to look after.

With one more glance at the woman who slept in his bed—and filled his heart to overflowing—he left the room.

He went out on the deck. He didn't want Molly to overhear this call.

But, to his frustration, he only got her voice mail. "This is Amanda Clark. You know the drill. After the beep."

"I need to talk to you, *now*." He hung up the phone.

Molly watched as Oscar listened carefully to the briefing at Zippity-Do-Da. It was like listening to the attendant go through the safety instructions before you took off on your flight. No one did it!

They had decided to do this on Ralphie's birthday. Tonight, they would go out for dinner. She had purchased the yellow dress for the occasion.

This would be good to get his mind off things. He had been carrying an undercurrent of anger since she had told him about his mother.

She looked at Oscar's familiar features, his brow furrowed in concentration. Even with that underlying current of anger, she could not look at him without feeling that rush of warmth and delight.

"Any questions?" their guide, Basil, asked.

Oscar had scientific questions. About friction. Speed. Physics. Pull. Cable strength. Regularity of cable testing. Platform testing.

She tugged at his arm. "I'm sure it's safe, Oscar."

"For your benefit, I'm going to satisfy myself."

He was the one afraid of heights, and yet he was worried about her safety. *So* endearing.

"Okay," Basil said, when he had finally managed to answer all of Oscar's questions, "if any of the following apply to you, you are not allowed to ride…"

"Please, God," Oscar murmured.

"Under five feet tall—"

"Damn."

"Heart problems—"

"Double damn."

"Pregnancy."

"I am not getting out of this, am I?" Oscar made a comical face. Normally, she would have laughed, but this time…

"Recent flu symptoms."

"How recent?"

Again, normally she would have laughed.

"Inertia. Inebriation." Basil was obviously taking his cue from Oscar and being funny now, practically reading from a medical textbook. Of course, as long as it was delaying the moment of truth—clip onto cable—Oscar was going to play along.

Typically, she might have prodded the whole process along. But suddenly nothing felt normal. Because Molly had stopped at one word.

Pregnancy.

Good grief. She was an adult woman. A responsible woman. A woman who could absolutely not afford a pregnancy at this point in her career.

She had packed pills. She was 100 percent certain of that. She'd been supposed to start a new pack... What day? She didn't always take the "reminder" pills, just kept track of when she was supposed to start again. The travel, the jet lag—let's be honest, the drugging ecstasy of being with Oscar—might have made her careless.

Had definitely made her careless. She had not taken a pill since she arrived here, of that she was certain.

Was it really possible she had not taken a single precaution? Was it really possible that she had been so swept up in the moment that *that* had completely slipped her mind?

CHAPTER SEVENTEEN

"HEY," OSCAR CALLED to Molly. "Hey, Uranus to Earth. What's up? You're a million miles away. It's important you pay attention."

It seemed to her both of them had not been paying the least bit of attention to what was important.

He was the science guy. You'd think he could have asked that simple question about basic biology.

But then she thought of the first time, their first night together.

He had started to ask something.

Are you—

In the heat of the moment, she had assumed he was going to say *are you sure?* Or *are you ready for this?*

But, thinking about it now, both those things had been obvious, hadn't they?

No, he'd been asking her, *are you protected?* And he'd taken her fevered response to him as a *yes* to that question.

Still, there was no need to panic. What were the chances? Probably infinitesimal. There was no sense letting it spoil this incredible time they were having together. She'd missed a few days. No biggie. She'd take one as soon as she got back to the apartment. And every day thereafter.

"Are you okay?" Oscar asked.

He had come very close to her. He was looking at her with grave concern. No one in her entire life had ever been this sensitive to her, this in tune, this caring.

"Just having a little case of nerves," she said.

He didn't tease her. He didn't say she was letting him down, and that he expected her to be the brave one. He didn't ask her where her customary boldness was.

He did what no one had ever done in her whole life. Except him.

He accepted her exactly where she was at. That was a gift she had not even been able to give herself. Instead, she was always pushing. Always proving.

He leaned in very close to her. He laid his forehead against hers. He, the guy who was terrified of heights, said quietly, for her ears only, "I got you."

She closed her eyes.

Oscar.

He'd have her back. He'd keep her safe, no matter what. It occurred to her that this man was the epitome of courage.

There was no courage, really, in doing things you had absolutely no fear of.

"I'll go first," he said. "I'll test it and make sure it's okay. And then you can follow me."

A few days ago, she would have protested that. She would have pushed her way to the front. She would have leaped first.

But now, she relaxed into this new feeling of being taken care of. Protected. Kept safe.

He turned to her just before he launched. He kissed her. Thoroughly. And then he turned and jumped.

Not with fear. There was no tension whatsoever in him. That anger that had bristled around him thankfully, and finally, appeared to be gone. After a moment, his laughter rang out, joyous, bold, off the canyon walls.

And then, at Basil's signal, Molly launched, too. And it felt as if her life—soaring through the air with the exhilarating freedom of a bird—was an exact reflection of what was going on in her heart.

Right there, right then, she knew the truth.

It was a truth that had always been there.

Like a huge Sitka spruce tree, shrouded in fog, always there, even when you couldn't see it.

And then the sun came out and burned the fog away and it stood there so majestic a person could feel foolish for having let the fog make the tree seem as if it had been an illusion.

If anything in her had been holding back, it let go now.

Her heart raced toward the man who stood on that platform in the trees, waiting to catch her.

Oscar stood out on his deck, right at the balcony, not afraid of heights at all anymore. He was annoyed that his mother still had not gotten back to him. Had she heard the anger underlying his message?

He had deeper concerns now, concerns that felt more pressing and more urgent.

He and Molly had come back from zip-lining and she had modeled her new dress for him, the one she would wear out tonight for Ralphie's birthday. He'd reserved a table at the most exclusive restaurant in Vancouver. It could take months to get a reservation, but he'd managed to pull a few strings.

It occurred to him that they had ridden bikes, eaten at food trucks, zip-lined, played in the mud and eaten pizza. All things she was comfortable with.

But they hadn't done anything fancy yet, and he was

eager to explore this world with her, too. Fine restaurants. Live theater. Concerts. Charity galas. Travels. Trips.

Thoughts of the worlds they had yet to explore had then been erased from his mind, as by turns shy and confident, bold and bashful, Molly had modeled all of her other new purchases.

Until one thing led to another, and no world seemed more important than the world of two that they were in.

But then, ever so casually, just before she napped, Molly had mentioned she was going to need a bigger suitcase.

Which meant, despite it all, she was still planning on leaving.

Before Molly had arrived, it had felt to Oscar like he might never laugh again. And yet now the laughter came frequently and easily.

They had always known each other.

But now they knew each other deeply.

He could finish her sentences. She could guess his thoughts. They were unraveling the beautiful mystery of giving each other pleasure.

In that area, it felt as if they had just discovered the tip of the iceberg. It felt as if a lifetime would not be enough.

They had skirted the issue of her departure, as if hiding from it could prevent it from coming.

Now, she was talking about suitcases. He stared out at the Vancouver skyline, and it struck him like a bolt of lightning.

It was so simple. She was asking him about suitcases because he had not invited her to stay.

Invited her to stay?

That felt all wrong. Disrespectful. Without honor. As much as he wanted to have her here, he realized *this* was not what he wanted.

It was fun, yes. And exciting, definitely. Having Molly with him had turned his life into an unbelievable adventure in the seeming blink of an eye.

And yet, somehow, it wasn't sitting right with him. It had the tawdry feeling of an affair.

Oscar realized he had to show her, despite all the fun, he wasn't just playing around. He was playing for keeps.

He wanted to marry her. And the sooner the better. He wanted to spend the rest of his life with her. Thanks to his mother, they'd already lost six years.

He could almost hear his brother's voice—familiar, full of conviction—saying *go for it*.

Oscar didn't want to lose another minute.

He glanced at his watch. The stores would still be open. He could dash down now, before she woke up, and get her a ring.

He could propose to her tonight. After dinner. With her in the yellow dress.

He had to keep himself from whooping with joy and letting that whole city know what was going on with him.

Molly woke up and stretched, content. Oscar wasn't beside her, and for a moment she felt abandoned. She loved waking up with him at her side.

Still, Georgie had taken his place and having the cat in her lover's bed with her gave her an exquisite feeling of domestic contentment.

Molly realized in her whole life she might have never felt this: simple contentment. At ease with where she was. Whole in some way she had never been before. The restlessness seemed to have evaporated in her. The need to prove anything was gone. She lay there just feeling the delicious warmth of feeling accepted.

Not just by Oscar.

But by herself.

Then, she glanced at the clock, and frowned.

She was really turned around. It was afternoon, nearly four o'clock. She didn't sleep in the afternoon.

It was jet lag, she told herself.

But another part of her whispered that maybe she was...

She leaped from the bed and threw on the shirt Oscar had taken off earlier. She'd take that pill, right now.

She did up the buttons on his shirt, loving how it felt on her, how it touched her thigh, and reminded her of the differences in their sizes, how perfectly their differences melded together, made them fit together.

The shirt smelled of him, and it increased that sense of belonging here and to each other.

Hadn't he even said that?

It seemed so long ago. On their first shopping excursion. There was only one time a woman should wear a man's shirt.

And this, she realized, with a sigh, was that time.

"Oscar?"

She padded out of his bedroom. The apartment was empty. She found her purse, tossed on the couch—*as if she lived here*—and picked through it for the pills. She realized, when she found them, and confirmed that she had missed starting again on the appointed day, that she didn't know a very important fact. If you were pregnant, and then resumed taking pills, could it harm the baby?

Baby.

The very thought made her go weak with longing.

She thought of that couple with their baby and Golden Retriever that she had seen on the picnic blanket that long-ago day.

To have a baby with the man you loved...

But fear rocketed through her. It would be so wrong. Backward. Oscar was a traditional kind of guy. He had even said it, and recently. He felt weddings should come before babies.

If she were pregnant, Oscar was *that* guy. The one you could trust to do the right thing.

She frowned. Did she want to be with Oscar because he was doing the right thing? She realized she was making all kinds of assumptions because of what had unfolded over the last few days.

But neither of them had said it.

The words were missing.

The *feeling* was there, Molly told herself firmly. She *knew* him.

But caring about someone and being their best friend was quite different than a declaration of love. Waking up with a sensation of belonging and completion was not a substitute for the kind of commitment that was needed to bring a new life into the world.

Molly nearly jumped out of her skin when the doorbell rang. Somehow, this apartment had felt like a small oasis, disconnected from the rest of the world. She hadn't even known it had a doorbell. The building was so secure. Somehow, she didn't think the girl guides were allowed in to go door-to-door with cookies.

She got up and tiptoed to the door and put her eye to the peephole.

Molly felt the thing she so rarely felt in her life. She swung back from the door, then told herself it couldn't be, and made herself look out the peephole again.

No, no doubt about it. It was Oscar's mother— perfectly coiffed, in a coral Chanel suit, her face suspiciously wrinkle-free—standing outside the door. Mrs. Clark rang the bell again.

"Yoo-hoo, darling," she called quietly. "I know why you called. I knew you wouldn't want to be alone today."

Molly shrank against the wall beside the door, not even daring to breathe. After her last encounter with Mrs. Clark six years ago, she didn't want Oscar's mother to see her here, and she particularly did not want to be caught running around Oscar's apartment in one of his shirts and nothing else.

She closed her eyes. A sound forced them open. *Please,* she whispered inwardly, *don't be what I think it is.*

Which was a key being inserted in the door. But under her horrified gaze, Molly watched as the lock turned.

CHAPTER EIGHTEEN

THE DOOR SQUEAKED OPEN, and Mrs. Clark swept into the room in a cloud of perfume. Georgie, who had been sleeping on the couch, startled awake, glared at the intruder and then, with an indignant yowl—Molly was not sure if it was recognition—leaped from the couch and marched from the room, tail in the air.

Mrs. Clark watched the cat with naked dislike and then saw Molly, still tucked against the wall beside the door. Her mouth formed a perfect, surprised O. But her surprise didn't last very long. Her eyes narrowed.

"Molly Bentwell," she said, managing to load Molly's name with enough disapproval that Molly cringed inwardly, though she let nothing—she hoped—show outwardly.

"Mrs. Clark," she said evenly.

"I thought you were half a world away," Mrs. Clark said, disparagingly. "Taking pictures of monkeys, or something."

A whole career dismissed in one hateful sentence.

"I do wildlife photography," Molly said, keeping her tone level, despite the fact she was seeing red. "It's a little more complex than taking pictures of monkeys."

Mrs. Clark waved a hand, as if a fly had landed on

her nose. "Really, it's exactly the kind of work I always expected you would find."

How was she making a perfectly respectable profession seem as if it were somehow lacking respectability?

Of course, respectability in Mrs. Clarks's world would be very narrowly defined.

"Can I ask what you are doing trotting around my son's apartment in an outfit like that?"

There was her narrow definition of respectable, right there. Molly could feel her cheeks burning. How dare Mrs. Clark cast the situation with Oscar in that light? As if it were cheap, and impulsive and base?

And yet, by appearances alone, would it not seem as if Mrs. Clark were correct.?

"Always the train wreck, Molly," Mrs. Clark said, with a sad shake of her head. "Hardly a week went by without you leading my poor Oscar on some kind of misguided escapade. Police, arrests, hospital visits, mischief reports from school. We just aren't the kind of people who enjoy that kind of activity and attention."

We.

With Molly Bentwell on one side of the great divide, and the Clarks on the other. All the Clarks. Did it hurt so much because there was truth in it?

"I'd ask again you what you're doing here," Mrs. Clark said, her gaze sweeping Molly, "but now it's perfectly obvious. You've started up right where you left off, it would appear. Why would you horn in to our family at a time like this, though? Especially today. It's unbelievably cheap and insensitive to insert yourself in our pain over Ralph. Of course, I wouldn't expect *you* to know some events are sacred within families."

"What does that mean?" Molly asked, even though she knew she was going to be sorry she had.

Mrs. Clark sighed. "I'm not without sympathy for you, Molly, I'm really not. I mean your father..." Her voice drifted off. "You really were like a child raised by a wolf. It's no wonder you have so few skills. It's no wonder you look at what we have and would go to any length to get it."

"My father did the best he knew how," she said tersely.

"Of course he did, dear," Mrs. Clark said, her soothing tone belying her total insincerity.

"I remember my childhood with extreme affection."

"What child wouldn't? The lack of rules, no structure, bad behavior *encouraged*. Your father thought it was hilarious when the two of you were arrested."

"For breaking into a swimming pool, after hours," Molly reminded her.

"One thing does lead to another."

"But it didn't."

"Oh, I don't know. Then he broke his arm. Riding horses he did not have permission to ride."

Who saw adolescent hijinks through this lens?

"I did not horn in on your grief for Ralphie. Oscar invited me here."

In fact, she could see that one line of his email. *Come.* She wanted to cling to it, as if it were a lifeline.

"Don't you know when someone is merely being polite?"

Suddenly, Molly saw there was no sense trying to convince Mrs. Clark of her worthiness. That boat had sailed a long time ago. It was not helped by the fact she was now standing barefoot in front of her lover's mother in a state of undress.

"I'll just go get dressed," she said woodenly.

When she reappeared a few minutes later, she was

caught up short as she entered the living room. Mrs. Clark was sitting on the sofa.

And she had Molly's phone in her hand.

Her mouth was twisted in a sneer of complete contempt. "Your search engine was open," she said. "It seems you were researching pregnancy."

"It's extraordinarily rude to snoop through other people's phones," Molly said.

Mrs. Clark appeared unchastised. "It's just as I feared all those years ago. You were intent on trapping him then, and you are intent on trapping him now."

There was, of course, the desire to explain, the need to be respected, and accepted. She loved Oscar. Naturally, she wanted the approval of his mother.

But she could see in those hardened features that was the one thing she would never get from Mrs. Clark.

"What will it cost me this time?" his mother said with a sigh.

To get rid of her.

It would be insulting, except that Molly had allowed herself to be bought all those years ago. And now, she *had* risked a pregnancy, the very thing she felt she had been falsely accused of.

Maybe there was the awful possibility Mrs. Clark saw her more clearly than she saw herself.

Her *need* for everything Oscar offered. Stability. Security. Protection. Acceptance. Love.

But Mrs. Clark already saw that Molly would never fit in his world. Never. That would be the price for him if he accepted her love.

And now, because she might be pregnant, she would never know. She had been reckless, careless, just like her father... Everything that this woman sitting before her despised.

She would never know if Oscar would have turned his back on his world for love of her.

Or if he would have done it only because there might be a baby.

Either way, she could not ask that kind of sacrifice of him. She loved him. And she didn't want him to have to give up anything, let alone the respect and acceptance of his whole world, because of her.

Without a word, Molly went and held out her hand. Mrs. Clark placed the phone in it.

"It won't cost you anything to get rid of me," Molly said quietly. "I don't want anything to do with you or from you. I find it funny that you think I would want anything you have. I always felt sorry for Oscar and Ralph, being part of your soulless world that always had to look so good. And that always felt so bad."

"You felt sorry for my children?" Mrs. Clark said, something satisfyingly shrill in her voice. "Why, you little…upstart."

Allowing herself the satisfaction of that tiny victory, Molly went back to her room and packed her bag. She put only the things in it she had come with. Assuming his mother would be in the guest room, she carefully made the bed, and took everything else. She went into his room and stuffed it way in the back of his closet.

This time together with Oscar was going to be hard enough to get over without reminding herself of him every time she put on her underwear.

It would only serve to remind her, too, of who she had become when she was with him.

Georgie was in the middle of his bed. Molly went and sank down just briefly, held her cat to her, and felt the deep purr calm her and give her the strength she needed. She set the cat down.

She would not cry. She would be the girl her father had always wanted her to be: proud, fierce, independent.

Bentwells were not sissies.

Not even if their hearts were breaking in two.

Putting her bag over her shoulder, she took a deep breath, and put her chin up. She sailed out through the living room and out the door without a single glance back at Mrs. Clark.

Oscar burst back into his apartment. It had taken longer than he expected to find the ring. He wanted it to be perfect.

And for Molly, that would mean nothing garish. Nothing too large. Nothing ostentatious. It had taken him three jewelry stores until he had found exactly the right one, a beautiful simple band, with a single small solitaire, multifaceted and brilliant—just like Molly—winking at its center.

Tonight, after dinner, he would ask her. He went over it in his mind. In the restaurant? Maybe he could have the ring hidden in a dessert dish, or a rose. Or would she'd like it better if, as they were walking home, hand in hand, he just fell down on one knee? And after she said yes, they'd come back here to the apartment, and he'd show her how to dance. Maybe on the deck, beside the pool, under the stars.

It could give new meaning to dancing with the stars. He couldn't wait to make her laugh by saying that to her.

"Molly!" He stopped in the doorway. Some strange fragrance tickled his nostrils. For a moment, he thought, *I know that scent.* Definitely not Molly…but his desire to see her made him dismiss anything that was not her.

"Molly!"

His voice rang back at him. Surely she wasn't still

sleeping? He went into his bedroom. The bed was rumpled, and the cat was there, but Molly wasn't. He raced to her room. Empty. The bed was neatly made. She clearly hadn't slept in it for a while. He cocked his head, listening for the shower. Nothing.

He raced through the apartment and out to the pool.

But Molly wasn't anywhere. He went back to the spare bedroom. It struck him, suddenly, that it felt empty. He didn't see her bag. He went and opened a bureau drawer. Empty.

Where was Molly? It felt as if that was all that mattered to him. He took out his cell phone and texted her.

Maybe he hadn't been abandoned. There was probably an explanation. She had gone to get something to surprise him tonight, just as he had her.

And she took her travel bag with her to do it? a cynical voice inside of him said.

It hit him then, and it hit him hard.

It was his brother's birthday. Molly was gone. He didn't think he could get through the next hours, days and weeks carrying the burden of the loss.

CHAPTER NINETEEN

MOLLY SAT IN the airport lounge, waiting for a flight. The pings started coming on her phone, fast and furious.

All of the messages were from Oscar.

Where are you? What happened? What's going on?

Obviously, there was no point in honesty here. She couldn't exactly say *your mother thinks I'm a tramp, and that I'm trying to entrap him. And I might be pregnant, so maybe she's right.*

She could discern the frantic worry in each of his messages, so she texted back.

So sorry to leave on such short notice. I've had some business things come up that I have to look after. It was urgent.

Are you kidding me? No goodbye? Just out the door?

You know me…a little lacking in social graces. Don't get me wrong, I had a glorious time.

It's his birthday.

For a moment, weakness nearly doubled her over. It

was Ralphie's birthday. They *had* to be together. That had been the plan, all along.

Her father had been right. His entire life he had scorned plans.

And this was why. They went awry. Tentatively, she responded.

Your mother suggested I was intruding on a private family moment.

He didn't answer and her phone began to ring instantly. She suddenly felt weary, emotionally wrung out.

Just like last time, his mother had given her an excuse to do what she wanted to do, anyway. Run from the terrible complexities, the potential for pain, of loving someone the way she loved Oscar.

Her phone began ringing again and then went to voice mail.

Oops, there's my plane. Till next time.

She shut off her phone. She laid her head on the back of the chair. And she wept. And when she was done, she wiped her eyes, blew her nose and vowed that was it.

It was not as if she had not done this before. Left him when it felt as if it would tear her in two to do it.

And if her father had given her a gift, it was this one: she was tough, and she was resilient. She could outrun anything if she had to.

She filled the days that followed by moving. Moving was always an excellent antidote for pain. Changing countries made it even more complex. She threw a dart at a map.

Oslo, Norway.

Why not? What did it matter? Her father would have approved.

The pregnancy test came back negative, but warned her it could give a false negative if she took it too early.

She went on assignment in Africa. No nausea, no headaches, no exhaustion, despite moving and jet lag.

She took the test again, still negative.

Her new neighbors in Oslo had a baby. She took photos of it. Their friends wanted a session. And then their friends wanted a session. And then *their* friends wondered if she would think about doing a wedding...

Her period came.

Molly didn't feel relieved. Not at all. Her sense of loss and grief intensified.

She started canceling assignments to do baby pictures. She thought the babies might be a trigger, but in fact, she loved immersing herself in baby smiles, and baby fat, and baby toys, and baby smells.

Slowly, it dawned on her that while leaving Oscar had broken her in two, something about those days with him had made her better.

When she looked at her work, Molly saw a new dimension to it. Something in her was more open than it ever had been, and it showed in her photos.

They were warmer, kinder, softer.

Somehow, she was capturing a light in people that she had never captured before. She was digging deeper.

Even though she had walked away from love, the irony was that she felt as if she was on intimate terms with love for the first time.

It was when she was not working that the memories would hit.

Oscar in his chef's apron. Oscar with pomegranate on

his face. Oscar covered in mud. Oscar riding a bike, leaping off a zip line, lying in the grass beside her.

But that was the place she could not go.

Oscar lying beside her.

That was what she missed the most. Her world had gone from wholly complete to wholly empty, from total bliss to total despair.

In the blink of an eye.

She learned to distract herself at the first twinge of a memory. She could watch a movie, as long as it wasn't a romantic one. Hockey games were great. So was playing word games on her phone, or watching talent shows. She could chat online about photography.

She could make it okay. She could make life bearable.

As long as she did not think of his eyes.

His smile.

His deep voice whispering in her ear.

His lips on her hair.

And on her lips.

And on her...

Damn. She was crying again. The strong one, the resilient one, a hot mess of emotion. It seemed totally unfair to be this emotional, without the pregnancy.

A knock came on the door. Everything in Molly froze. Maybe he had come. But why would he? She had run out on him, not once, but twice. In his heart, he probably knew, just as his mother did, that he was better off without her.

So, who then?

She got up and looked out her peephole. It felt like déjà vu. Mrs. Clark was standing outside her door. For a moment, Molly considered not answering it. What had Oscar's mother ever brought her other than pain?

But there was something about her that was not the same. Her hair was disheveled. Her makeup was smudged.

What if something had happened to Oscar?

Molly flung open the door.

"Oh, Molly, thank goodness. It's been so hard to find you." His mother—his self-contained, controlled mother—burst into tears.

"What's wrong? Is Oscar okay?"

"N-n-n-o-o-o," she wailed. "I've lost both my sons."

"He's—?"

"No, no, he's not dead. But he might as well be."

Molly's heart went into her throat. She fought down the pure panic she was feeling, ushered her in and set her on her sofa. Her heart was beating out of her chest.

"Mrs. Clark, please tell me why you have come around the world to find me. And please tell me Oscar is okay."

"I've come around the world to find you because I couldn't very well ask Oscar for your phone number. And, anyway, I needed to speak to you in person. I need you to understand and I wasn't sure I could convey that on the phone."

"Understand?" Molly whispered, still trying to fight down panic.

"He's not okay. He won't even speak to me now. He's not going into the office. I sent Cynthia to check on him. He wouldn't let her in, but she said he looked horrible! His place was a catastrophe. She could see it behind him, even though he was blocking the door.

"It's all my fault. He won't forgive me. I pretended I hadn't been there when you left. I pretended I had just showed up.

"But he said he could smell my perfume. He *knew*. When I told him I felt you were unsuitable, Molly, he lost his mind. And then he told me he knew about the other time, too. About me buying your farm.

"I've never seen him like that. He was nasty. He said

my world had never brought him one moment's happiness. He said all the rules, looking a certain way, acting a certain way, getting a degree, achieving success, having anything money can buy, finding a woman who fits in that world—he said none of that had brought him one moment of happiness. He said it was all a complete illusion."

Mrs. Clark looked imploringly at Molly. "Do you think that's true? Not one moment's happiness?"

"Of course not," Molly said soothingly.

"He even accused me of not loving Ralphie. He said I had no idea what love was. That it wasn't about manipulating people to get them to meet your needs."

Mrs. Clark took a huge shuddering breath. "And he's right," she said. "Even when you were children, I saw the way he looked at you. The way you looked at him. You put out the sun in each other's worlds every morning and drew down the moon at night. I wasn't jealous. I wasn't. But…"

Her voice drifted away, and then came back stronger. "I wasn't jealous, but maybe scared. He was right about love. His father and I didn't have one of those warm, cozy relationships. I had my boys and they gave me a sense of purpose. They made my world feel justified and important. Oscar, in particular, was so bright, and had so much potential. It felt like a reflection on me.

"But I could feel him moving toward a different world. The one you held out. And I tried to stop it.

"Oh, Molly, I tried to stop my son's happiness to meet my own needs. He was right about me, wasn't he? Not that that matters. I don't matter. I've made my mistakes and I'll live with the consequences.

"But I don't want him to live with the consequences. To be unhappy forever because of what I've done. He won't come to you, Molly. He won't. Because he wants you to choose. He *needs* you to choose."

"Of course, I choose him," Molly said.

"He doesn't need you to choose him. He needs you to choose yourself."

And just like that, Molly saw the truth in what Mrs. Clark was saying. She needed to make the choice to overcome all of her insecurities. All of her fear. All of her self-doubts.

To rescue Oscar, she needed to be more than she had ever been before. What had passed as bravery before would not do for this assignment.

And she could not have a single reservation left about love. To save Oscar—and herself—she had to throw herself at the mercy of the most powerful force in the entire universe.

When Oscar woke up his mouth tasted gritty and his hair felt caked to his head. Someone was knocking at the door. He closed his eyes and willed himself back to sleep.

Except he heard the door open, the tap of footsteps coming down the hall.

He braced himself. Only two people had keys to his apartment. His mother and Cynthia. He did not want to see either of them.

But it wasn't either of them.

It was Molly, in travel clothes, her hair springing up on one side of her head and crushed on the other. She didn't have on a speck of makeup.

And he had never seen a woman look so beautiful.

Not that he could let her know. Ever.

He loved control and he had found the perfect way to control the whole world. And that was not to engage with it.

Molly was not going to threaten the thing that was most precious to him, ever again.

"What do you want?" he growled.

"I hope that smell isn't you," she said. "Poor Georgie. When's the last time you changed the litter?"

Maybe his world wasn't quite as controlled as he thought.

She marched over and opened his drapes. The light flooded in, hurting his eyes. She turned and looked at him. What he saw in her eyes—the softness, the understanding, the connection to him—could make a weaker man give up on control forever.

But he had been weak. He had given up on control. He had fallen for Molly when he knew better. It had not had the result he wanted. And he was still enough of a scientist not to do the same thing over and over again expecting different results.

"Why are you here?" he asked.

That traitor cat had found his way out from under a mess of blankets and meowed a greeting at her. She went and picked him up, and he snuggled against her, purring rapturously as if there were no abandonment to be forgiven.

"I came," she said softly, "because I couldn't stay away."

"Huh. You wouldn't have had to stay away if you hadn't left in the first place."

"Truck, I thought I was pregnant."

He sat straight up in bed. He was out of his fog in an instant, staring at her. "Are you?" he whispered.

"No. It's probably a good thing. Can you imagine me raising children?"

He could, actually.

"I can imagine you raising children," he told her. "I'm sorry you aren't pregnant."

CHAPTER TWENTY

MOLLY GAZED AT OSCAR—at the unshaven face, the rumpled hair, the sharpness of his cheekbones.

I'm sorry you aren't pregnant.

"Isn't that lucky for all of us?" Molly said. "Me *not* having a baby?"

She kept out of her voice how she had wept when she had seen the *negative* flash across the little screen.

It wasn't until that moment that she'd realized how totally selfish she could be—if she couldn't have Oscar, she had wanted his baby.

Even knowing she would be the world's most unlikely mother.

"Maybe we could talk about babies in a minute," he suggested, and Molly heard some tenderness in his tone that made her want to melt into him when she most needed to be strong. "I want to sort out the past, before we tackle the future."

The future. Her strength felt as if it abandoned her a little bit more.

"My mother told me it was her behind you leaving."

"I thought she was right, Oscar," Molly said quietly, marshalling what was left of her strength, after a long soul-searching trip. "That I couldn't fit into your world. That I'm just kind of a wild girl from the wrong side of the tracks—"

"Then why are you here?"

"Because I realized it wasn't really about her and whether she was right or wrong. It was about me. All my life, I've been rewarded for being brave, for taking chances. And yet, the greatest risk of all filled me with terror. I looked for any excuse to run from it. So, that's what I did. I used your mother as an excuse to run from what my heart was telling me."

"What was your heart telling you?" he asked. His voice was so gentle, so safe. She was coming home, finally, to her Truck. She was one truth away.

"It was telling me the only truth worth knowing. That I love you. Past. Present. Future. The possibility of a baby confused everything. Would you feel honor-bound to do the decent thing? It felt like a baby would remove *choice* from the equation."

"Choice," he said hoarsely. "Baby or no baby, I would never choose a world without you. Why would I want that? That hurts me. That you would know me so well— maybe better than anyone else on earth—and yet you would think that keeping the stuff in my world, all the trappings of success, would mean more than you... I would rather live under a bridge, in a cardboard box, with you, than live in a world without you. That's how alive you make me feel. How full to the top."

"There's so much I don't know," she warned him. "I don't know the rules everyone else plays by. You do. You had a place where the rules were clearly defined. A place where dinner was always ready at the same time. You had a place where if you got arrested, people were appalled rather than applauding. What can I give children? I can't even keep a plant alive. I don't know how to bake cookies. I tend to see a kitchen counter as a great place to store cameras and parts. I think a *great* supper is potato chips with a side of onion dip. I—"

Oscar stepped in close to her. The look in his eyes mesmerized her. He laid a finger across her lips.

"Stop it," he ordered her softly. "Did you come here thinking I would listen to your arguments and be convinced you're somehow wrong for me?"

"I just want you to know *exactly* what you are getting into."

"Oh, I already know exactly what I'm getting into. Do you think I don't know what you'd be like with a family? With children? I've watched you for years.

"I watched you with your dad. I saw your fierce loyalty to him. You loved him unconditionally, flaws and all. What a gift that would be to give children.

"And I watched you with Ralphie. Of all the people who knew him, you were the one always coaxing him to be himself, rewarding him for being himself, loving him for being himself.

"And the whole swim team—gathering them around you, making the hardest things fun, making them into a family, for each other, for you, for us.

"I've watched you with Georgie, ever since he was a little scared kitten, teaching him it was okay to trust, and okay to love.

"And most of all, Molly, I've watched you with me, taking my rigid thinking and bending it on its ear. Challenging me—to take risks, to press boundaries, to challenge truth, to be more than I ever was before."

He turned from her and took something off his bedside table. "I've been sleeping with this beside me. Tormenting me, but also giving me hope."

He came back to her.

"I can't live without you," he said. He went down on

one knee. "This isn't how I planned it, Molly, but I've always known, with you, things don't go as planned. Sometimes, they are so much better than anything I could have dreamed."

Her hands flew to her mouth and covered it as Oscar— her Truck—held out a velvet ring box.

He snapped open the lid.

"I bought this on Ralphie's birthday," he said softly. "I was going to propose that night, at dinner. I didn't want to waste another six years without you."

"Do you really feel as if those years were wasted?" she asked him through tears.

"Yes!"

"I feel so differently. I feel as if it showed me what I most needed to see—how empty a life without you would be. I think those six years might be what are making me brave enough to say yes, Truck."

"I haven't asked you yet!"

"Yes!" she said, again.

"Would you wait? I have the most romantic—"

"I'm not waiting," she said, "I don't regret the six years, but I'm not waiting one more minute."

And then she launched herself at him, and knocked him off his knee and they were on the floor with her on top of him, covering his face with kisses.

And Oscar was aware, for all of his planning, he could not have imagined a more romantic ending to his proposal than this one.

EPILOGUE

OSCAR COULD FEEL the faint pleasurable burn in his legs as he climbed the high hill. The baby, thankfully, had finally fallen asleep inside the kangaroo pouch Oscar had strapped to his chest.

Ralph—unlike his big sister, three-year-old Harriet—was a difficult baby.

"Can't we put him back?" Harriet had asked this morning, when the crankiness had started.

"Um, that would be a little painful for your mother," Oscar had said, and slid Molly a look. His wife. His partner. She seemed to grow more beautiful each day, even now with this fractious new edition intent on keeping the whole family from sleep.

"I'll take him for a walk," Oscar had volunteered. Being stuffed into the snuggly baby carrier seemed to be the only thing that soothed the crabby baby. Molly shot him a grateful look, and Harriet, having had quite enough of the baby brother, did not even volunteer to join him.

Now, the baby slept, finally, and Oscar found a rock and perched on it, taking in the spectacular view with wonder. He could hear Walter—a donkey Molly had rescued—braying incessantly, every bit as demanding as the new baby when it came to his feeding schedule.

Below him, looking like toys in a giant's game, was

his mother's property: the sweeping grounds, the white colonial style mansion, the sparkling waters of the pool, the clipped hedges, the rose garden, the trimmed lush pastures. Even from this height, it was evident everything was manicured, ordered into place.

And next to that was Molly's farm.

Their farm now, since Oscar had bought it back from his mother. This is where they came when they needed a break from everything. They could have gone and skied the Alps, or lounged on some of the best beaches in the world. They could have gone to Paris and explored little cafés and strolled the banks of the Seine. They could have gone on safari in Africa.

But no, more and more, they came here. And each time, it seemed they stayed a little longer and were a little more reluctant to head back to Vancouver.

From his vantage point, so high above it, Oscar could see Molly's childhood home had come a long way from what it had been. The house was looking good, painted white, the wraparound porch, with its deeply cushioned furniture, looking cool and inviting. Three small cozy cabins had been built, and dotted the wooded area behind the house. Molly was putting the pieces in place to host photography retreats, someday.

Still, for all the improvements, he could see the property needed a lot of work. The pasture was weed-filled. The fence was leaning haphazardly. The barn looked as if a good wind would take it down. A dead tree needed to be looked after.

Possibly a lifetime's worth of work. For some reason, that increased Oscar's sense of contentment.

Inch by inch, day by day, she was uncovering the true beauty of the house that had gone a bit to ruin over six years of being uninhabited. When Oscar had seen that the roof had leaked and rodents had gotten inside, he had thought maybe they should just tear it down and start again.

But, no, she saved things. Just like she had saved him.

She was showing what was underneath the water-damaged ceilings, what was underneath the peeling wall-paper and what was underneath the vinyl floors that had been curling at the corners. She had discovered shiplap and original hardwoods and custom tile work. The walls had hidden fireplaces and someone, sometime, had decided it was a good idea to cover up a stained glass window with a wall.

It seemed to Oscar that Molly worked the same magic on him as she was working on that house. Inch by inch, day by day, she was uncovering him, showing him what was underneath, revealing who he really was, *loving* what was underneath the layers he had built up over the years.

From the first day they had come back here, Molly had thrown open the doors to anyone who wanted to come. And so, on any given day, members of the old swim team might drop by—or the new one that swam now, in the swim pavilion named after his brother.

James lived in one of the little cottages behind the house, and acted as their caretaker when they weren't here. The neighbors came by, and old friends from school. The grill was fired up. The campfire was lit in the pit behind the house. Sometimes, guitars came out and the music and laughter and conversation went deep into the night.

They were forming a community.

That's what family really was.

As he watched, from his perch high up on the hill, Oscar saw Molly and Harriet come out of the house. Harriet was carrying a basket of carrots for Walter in one hand and skipping ahead of her mother. Today, she was wearing a pink princess dress and wielding a plastic pirate's sword in her other hand. Her hair was dark like his but her springy curls were just like her mother's and made attaching the toy tiara nearly impossible. It sat on her head crookedly.

Walter's braying increased in volume, hysteria and intensity when he spotted the little girl skipping toward him.

And then out of the corner of Oscar's eye, he saw his mother coming down the well-worn path between the two properties.

There was a spring in her step, as if she were moving eagerly toward all that chaos. Not that she would ever admit it. No, she would get there and complain about the noise the donkey made, and remove the crooked tiara, and run a disapproving hand through Harriet's tangled curls. She would get a pinched expression on her face when she noticed the flowerbeds were now almost completely taken over with weeds.

After his mother's treachery toward Molly, Oscar would have been just as happy to keep her at a distance.

But Molly wasn't having it.

She paved the way to forgiveness even as she came into herself, or maybe it was because she came into herself so completely that Molly was able to extend such grace to others.

After he had told his mother he and Molly were going to get married, Mrs. Clark had tried to take over the wedding.

"It can't be trusted to a girl who doesn't even know how to use the right fork," she'd said, and thrown herself into choosing guests and a posh venue that specialized in the weddings "of anybody who was anybody."

Gently and firmly, Molly, the girl who didn't even know how to use the right fork, had vetoed that. They had been married in that falling down barn right over there.

He still could not think of the merriment, the utter joy of that day, without smiling. Molly, the one who had *hated* dancing, had danced until dawn.

"Your poor mom," she had told him. "Something made her life that. So rigid, so bound by rules, so worried about what everything looks like. She's afraid of being real. But she's also very, very brave."

Slowly, he had watched Molly's love transform his mother.

Just as it transformed everything around her. She had started doing photo shoots here. With chickens and the donkey, with falling down fences, and overgrown pastures as the backdrop. Georgie loved to stalk out of the house and photobomb the sessions.

Celebrities had discovered her and flocked to her with their children, and always, she gave them what they wanted.

Her gift was capturing the perfect against the backdrop of imperfection. She captured the light inside of people.

And it didn't really matter if it was a celebrity shoot, or the new Special Games swim team, or a single mom with a new baby.

This was Molly's gift. She no longer had to face a charging elephant to get the perfect shot, or edge too close to the cliff, or hang from her knees from the tallest tree branch.

She no longer had to do those death-defying things to *feel.* She had faced a greater fear—that love would let her down—and she had won, and now she brought that out in others.

She found the love that lit people up from within. It didn't matter how deeply they had buried it, or how hard they tried to hide it.

She found it.

And for being the recipient of that, of Molly's spectacular gift, Oscar would be forever grateful.

Ralph, suddenly aware the walk had stopped, woke up with a roar. Oscar got to his feet, swaying back and forth with the baby.

It was time to go join whatever was going on down there today. Were they painting a picket fence, or weeding a garden, or taking a picnic into the woods?

The baby, Ralphie's namesake, often made Oscar feel as if his brother were close to him. Right now, it felt as though the wind had whispered to him in his brother's voice.

Go for it.

He said the words out loud.

It felt so good, he shouted them from the top of that hill, listened to them roll down the landscape around him.

Startled, the baby quieted, arched his back, and looked at his father as if he recognized something in him for the first time.

He gurgled. It sounded, well, approving.

Go for it.

It didn't mean win a medal, or make a million dollars. It meant embrace whatever the day put in front of you. Completely.

It meant, live well. Love well.

And as he headed back down the hill toward his farm, toward his family, that was exactly what Oscar intended to do.

* * * * *

THE BABY
THAT BINDS THEM

STELLA BAGWELL

To all the readers who have followed
my Men of the West stories down through the years.
Thank you from the bottom of my heart.

Chapter One

Prudence Keyes hated weddings. Especially the romantic kind such as the one she was currently attending. Love was radiating from the faces of the bride and groom, while many of the female guests seated throughout the church were shedding sentimental tears.

Prudence had tried to squeeze a few drops of moisture from her eyes, just for appearance's sake, but they'd stubbornly refused to surface. Which was hardly surprising, considering that she'd rather be in a dentist chair, suffering through a root canal procedure. Anything would be better than sitting here on this wooden pew with rows of candles flickering around the room, the sweet scent of peonies and roses filling the air, and the notes of a love song drifting from a piano.

Everything about the ceremony was a beautiful example of true, lasting love. Which made it an especially awful reminder of everything that Prudence lost so many years ago.

Oh, God, if only she could come up with some feasible excuse to avoid the reception, she silently bemoaned. But so far, she couldn't think up one good reason to miss what would probably be one of the largest and most elaborate parties to ever be thrown in Yavapai County. At least, not an excuse that her friend and personal secretary, Katherine Hollister, would accept.

The wedding of Maureen Hollister and Gil Hollister, brother to late Joel Hollister, had been months in the making. Family and friends were ecstatic that the widowed matriarch of the family and the man she loved were finally getting married. Everyone wanted to celebrate their happiness. If Prudence didn't join in, she was going to look like an ass. Along with hurting Katherine's feelings and those of the whole Hollister family.

The piano suddenly stopped and the officiating pastor opened his Bible in preparation to speak. Behind her, she could hear a few women sniffing, while on down the pew from her a man quietly cleared his throat. Prudence shifted her position on the bench and for no explainable reason, other than to relieve the stiffness in her neck, turned her head slightly and looked across the aisle to where more wedding guests were seated a few rows in front of her.

At that very moment, a man glanced over his shoulder and straight at Prudence. For a fraction of a second, a pair of dark hooded eyes met hers, and then his head turned forward and the contact was broken.

Her curiosity momentarily snared, she allowed her gaze to wander over the dark brown fabric stretched across the backs of his broad shoulders and the unruly waves of crisp black hair edging over the collar of his white shirt.

Who was *he*? A friend or distant relative of the Hollisters?

The minister suddenly instructed the wedding guests to bow their heads in prayer, and as Prudence complied, she pushed the questions from her mind.

Luke Crawford had attended a few big parties in his time, but none of them could compare to this massive shindig. Even knowing the enormity of Three Rivers Ranch and the magnitude of the Hollisters' wealth hadn't prepared him for a wedding reception of this magnitude. Luckily, the dry Arizona climate and the waning sunlight made the outdoor weather perfect for the hundreds of people scattered from the yard at the back of the ranch house all the way to where a fence blocked off access to the working ranch yard.

Driving over to the Fandango and sharing a beer

with the ranch hands was the sort of socializing Luke was accustomed to. Not mixing and mingling with wealthy men in tailored suits and women wearing designer dresses and diamonds big enough to blind a guy. But with the Hollister family being his new employer, he felt more than obliged to be standing here among the wedding guests, pretending to enjoy himself.

To Luke's far right, beneath a cluster of cotton-wood trees, dozens of long tables were loaded with an endless assortment of hors d'oeuvres and finger foods, while nearby, three portable bars were serving a variety of drinks, including French champagne. About fifty feet behind Luke, a live band played from a small stage, while couples packed an enormous portable dance floor.

So far, the music had been lively, ranging from country tunes to jazz to romantic standards. But Luke doubted the crowd was paying much attention to the wide variety or the excellence of the band. Ever since the reception had begun, the champagne bottles were being emptied almost as fast as they could be opened. And Luke was close to draining the last of his second round of the bubbly spirit.

Turning slightly, he peered longingly at the distant ranch yard where the horse barn sat directly behind the cattle barn and Blake's office building.

Too bad foaling season had come and gone. A mare nearing delivery would have given Luke a good reason to be at the barn instead of this wedding reception. What was all the celebrating about, anyway? Hell, he didn't even believe in marriage. At least, not for himself. He'd seen his father go through too much misery to want the same.

Grimacing at the thought, he decided it was high time to finish the contents in his glass and go in search of a third round when someone from behind barreled straight into him. The jolt was so hard it caused the liquid in the fluted glass to slosh over the edge and onto the snubbed toes of his cowboy boots.

Hell!

Barely managing to hold the word on his tongue, he turned to see the person who'd staggered into him.

Well, I'll be damned!

The thought raced through his head as he suddenly found himself face-to-face with *the* beautiful woman. The one he'd spotted briefly during the wedding ceremony.

"Oh, it's you!" she said.

Apparently, she remembered their eye contact at the church. But the surprised expression on her face wasn't enough to tell him whether she was annoyed or happy to encounter him again.

"I was sitting in front of you at the wedding—if that's what you mean," he told her.

As she carefully regarded him, a waiter passed close to Luke's right shoulder, and he used the opportunity to place his empty glass on the young man's tray.

"Yes. That's what I meant." She glanced awkwardly toward the crowd of dancers, then back to his face. "I—apologize for knocking into you. My heel must have caught on a rock or something. I hope I didn't hurt you."

Back at the church, he'd guessed her eyes to be blue. Now that she was a mere arm's length away, he could see the luminous orbs were a mixture of blue and green, like a tropical sea washing onto a bed of dark sand. Her dress was pale pink satin with tiny straps and a hem that stopped at the middle of her calves. If it hadn't been for the lacy shawl wrapped loosely around her shoulders, he would've mistaken the dress for a slip or nightgown. One thing was for sure, Luke decided—she looked as sexy as hell in it.

"I'm fine," he said wryly. "Although I'm not too sure about my boots now that they've had a champagne shower."

Her gaze dropped to his boots and he used the moment to take a survey of her lips. Small, but plush, they were painted a cherry-red color that stood out against her fair skin and light brown hair.

"Oh, your boots—I'm terribly sorry! I—"

The rest of her apology was abruptly halted as a woman in the crowd called out. "Pru! I've been looking for you!"

Glancing over his shoulder, Luke spotted Katherine Hollister emerging from a nearby group of guests and hurrying straight toward the two of them. The tall brunette was married to Blake, the eldest of the Hollister siblings, and also the general manager of

Three Rivers Ranch. Katherine was all smiles as she came to a stop next to Luke and the brown-haired beauty standing in front of him.

"I see you've met Pru already," she said to Luke.

"Uh—we've sort of met," Luke told Katherine, while darting an awkward glance at the woman. "We just had a bit of a collision."

"I'm afraid I've ruined this man's boots," Prudence told her. "And they're such nice ones, too."

"I'm sure he and his boots will survive." Glancing at Luke, Katherine gestured to Prudence. "Luke Crawford, meet Miss Prudence Keyes. And I didn't get the Miss part wrong. Pru is single."

"Kat, please!" Prudence muttered under her breath.

Questions were suddenly racing through Luke's brain. How could a woman who looked like her be unattached? Or perhaps she wasn't, he thought. Could be she had a partner that Katherine didn't know about.

Trying to push that disheartening thought aside, Luke extended his hand to the woman, and she promptly slid her palm alongside his.

"It's a pleasure, Miss Keyes."

Her hand felt so small and soft that he instinctively cradled it between both his hands rather than grip it with one.

"Nice to meet you, Mr. Crawford," she said to him. "And I am truly sorry for tripping into you. I'm only glad I didn't knock you down."

The husky note in her voice was especially sexy and a total contradiction to her soft, sweet features.

"Luke wrangles horses all day. He's used to handling twelve-hundred-pound horses. An itty-bitty thing like you couldn't knock him off his feet," Katherine explained, before she turned a smile on Luke. "Pru is superintendent for St. Francis Academy in Wickenburg. She also happens to be my boss."

"And dear friend," Prudence added.

"Definitely a dear friend," Katherine agreed, then inclined her head toward Luke. "Luke is our new assistant horse trainer. Can you believe Blake found a man brave enough to work that closely with Holt?"

Prudence looked straight at him and Luke wondered why he felt as if something had struck him between the eyes.

"It's hard to imagine," she said. "You must be a brave man. When it comes to his horses, I've heard that Holt is terribly particular."

"I was given that warning before I took the job," Luke admitted. "But Holt and I get along fine."

Katherine cast Prudence a coy wink. "That's because Luke is just as particular. And why the ranch is so lucky to have him."

From somewhere in the crowd behind them, Blake called to his wife. "Kat! Sorry to interrupt, but we have to go get the twins. The photographer wants a shot of all the grandchildren."

Katherine let out a good-natured groan. "Oh, this

is going to be fun! Two sets of twins, plus eight more kids. See you two later!"

She took off in a hurried stride, and as Luke turned his sole attention to Prudence Keyes, he realized he still had her hand pressed between his.

"Sorry. I'm sure you'd like your hand back." Hoping he didn't look as hayseed as he felt, he forced himself to release his hold on her.

"Well, I might need it eventually. To feed and clothe myself—things like that."

The faint tilt to the corners of her lips told Luke she was teasing. The notion surprised him. It also made him feel ridiculously happy.

"Yes. Those tasks are much easier with two hands," he impishly agreed, then asked, "How are you enjoying the reception?"

"It's quite a gathering." Her head swiveled as she took in the multiple groups of people standing nearby. All of whom appeared to be either laughing and talking, or eating and drinking. "Some of these people I've never met before."

"Like me?"

She smiled and Luke noticed how the expression momentarily sparked her eyes.

"Like you," she agreed. "Kat hasn't mentioned Three Rivers hiring a new horse trainer. But with school just getting back into the swing of things, we've been very busy. Have you been here long?"

"Six weeks. I'm living here on the ranch in a house down by the river. I think it was originally built years ago, for Maureen's mother. They tell me she passed on not long after she moved into it."

She nodded slightly. "I'm familiar with the place. Do you like living in such a secluded area?"

"It's perfect for me. I've always lived in the country. What about you?"

She let out a little laugh. "No, I'm a city girl. Originally from Palm Springs, California. But for the past thirteen years I've lived in Wickenburg. From big city to a small-town girl. That's me."

"You must like it," he said. "Thirteen years is a long time."

"Yes—I like it."

She let out a long breath that sounded something like a sigh and Luke figured he was probably boring her. In fact, if he wanted to be a real gentleman, he'd excuse himself and allow her to go on her way. But at this very moment he was so transfixed with her that his brain refused to accept the idea of giving up her company.

Grabbing at the first reason he could think of to delay their parting, he asked, "Have you tried the champagne yet?"

"I haven't had anything to drink or eat. To be honest, I was a bit late getting here. At the last minute, I realized my car needed gas to make the long trip out here to the ranch," she said, then with a self-deprecating shake of her head added, "Most schoolteachers are hopelessly disorganized, even though we're supposed to be the exact opposite. That's why I have Kat. She keeps everything perfectly straight for me."

"In that case, let's walk over to the bar," he suggested. "You can't be at a wedding reception and miss having champagne. Or would you rather go by the buffet tables first?"

"I'm really not hungry. Something to drink is all I need," she told him.

She turned in the direction of the bar and Luke gently caught her by the elbow. She paused and looked at him questioningly.

"Uh—I thought I'd better ask if you're meeting someone here at the reception. I wouldn't want to interrupt your plans."

"You mean like a date?" She shook her head. "I'm all alone."

"You aren't alone now." Grinning, he offered her his arm. "You might need something to hold on to. Just in case you trip again."

Laughing softly, she placed her dainty hand on his forearm and Luke suddenly felt like he was a foot taller. What in the heck was going on with him? Two glasses of champagne were hardly enough to give him a buzz.

"I'll try not to let that happen," she said.

He placed his free hand over the one she'd rested on his arm. "Don't worry. I'll keep a hold on you."

Prudence didn't allow any man to *hold* her. Not in any way, shape or form. Yet here she was walking through the reception crowd with Luke Crawford's hand resting warmly over hers.

No. The man's hand wasn't just warm, she mentally corrected herself. It was as hot as the Arizona sun in mid-July. Only this wasn't July. It was the beginning of September and the cool evening air was already drifting over the ranch yard. But it was hardly enough to chill the sparks of fire that seemed to be shooting from his hand and traveling all the way up her arm.

What was wrong with her, anyway? She should've already given Luke Crawford a polite goodbye and lost herself in the crowd. But she'd been stunned when she'd recognized his was the face her eyes had locked onto in the church. And then when he'd made a sandwich of her hand, she'd been so captivated she couldn't do much more than stammer out a few inane words.

As they walked along, she peeked at him from the corner of her eye. Just to see if he actually looked as good as he had a few minutes ago, or if the golden sunset was playing tricks with her eyesight.

Now that the wedding party had moved here to the ranch, he'd donned a black cowboy hat that rode low on his forehead and covered the top portion of his thick black hair. His angular face was dominated by amber-brown eyes hooded beneath black brows, while hard, masculine lips set over a stubborn dented chin. Like most men who worked outdoors in the Southwest, he was darkly tanned, but she had the feeling that part of his brown coloring came from Native American descent. The high slanted cheekbones and hawkish nose certainly hinted at the notion. In any case, the man was too sexy for his own good and definitely too sexy for her peace of mind.

"Here we are," he said as the two of them finally managed to work their way up to the bar. "Would you like champagne or something nonalcoholic?"

Being in his company was already causing her head to swim. She hardly needed alcohol to make the whirling sensation any worse. But Luke was right about one thing: a person could hardly attend a wedding reception without consuming a bit of champagne. Besides, if she was lucky, it would settle her jangled nerves and allow her to behave like a reserved woman, rather than a ditzy schoolgirl.

"I'll take champagne," she told him.

After the bartender promptly served them each a glass of the bubbly wine, Luke suggested they find a spot to sit and enjoy their drinks.

"I'm not sure my boots can take another soaking," he added with a wink.

Prudence laughed under her breath and was promptly taken aback by her carefree reaction. She didn't have this sort of playful exchange with men. Not since she'd discovered how easily a man could cheat and lie and then expect a woman to forgive him.

Those dark, sad days are long gone, Prudence.

For heaven's sake, you're at a wedding reception. Can't you at least pretend to be happy?

Pushing the annoying voice out of her head, she smiled up at him. "I'll be sure to watch my step."

"I see a spot over there beneath that tree." He inclined his head toward a large cottonwood not far from the rope barrier that separated the guests from the working ranch yard. "That is, if you don't mind sitting on a hay bale."

"Not at all. It's covered with a blanket."

As they began to work their way through the crowd, Prudence was acutely aware of his hand resting lightly against the small of her back and the faint scent of sage and evergreen drifting from his jacket. Compared to her five foot three inches, he towered over her, and she guessed him to be at least six foot one, or perhaps even more. And she didn't have to see him without his clothing to know that he was all long, lean muscle. But then, she'd probably never see Luke Crawford without clothing. Not in her lifetime.

Once they reached the tree, the guests were few and far between and the band was somewhat muted.

"Ahh. This is a little nicer for talking," he said. "I love music, but a lower decibel would make it better."

Nodding, she said, "There was a time Mom or Dad would come to the bedroom I shared with my sister and order us to turn down the volume on the radio. But that was years ago. And anyway, I don't think teenagers listen to a regular radio nowadays."

He laughed and Prudence decided the raspy tone was just as pleasant as his voice.

"I still listen to a regular radio," he admitted. "In the morning, that is, when I'm cooking my breakfast. To hear the ag market report. Ranchers like to hear what's happening in the market with livestock and crops. Especially hay and grain prices."

With an empty ring finger and no mention of a wife or children, it was fairly obvious the man wasn't married. She couldn't gauge his age exactly, but she'd guess it was several years younger than her. He was certainly at the age where most men were getting married and starting families. The notion had her wondering if he had a special lady tucked away somewhere, or even several ladies.

Damn it, Pru, why do you think all men are serial cheaters? Take the Hollister brothers, for example. None of them would ever cheat on their wives. Just because your ex was a no-account adulterer doesn't mean Luke Crawford is a womanizer.

Attending a wedding always affected Prudence in the worst kind of way. For days afterward, she'd be tormented with the nagging voice in her head, along with memories of her failed marriage. Images of Gavin's guilty face would flash through her mind. Along with all his whispered lies of how he'd love her forever.

Shoving mightily at the dark thoughts, she took a seat on the hay bale and waited for Luke to join her before she spoke.

"You sound much older than you look."

He chuckled. "Is that supposed to be a compliment?"

She smiled. "You can take it that way if you'd like. I only meant you seem wise for your age."

"I'm thirty-one. Not that young. I'm really not that wise, either," he added with a wry grin. "I just try to sound that way when I'm in the company of a pretty woman."

She bit back a sigh. "I'm thirty-nine."

The brow over his left eye arched upward. "You make it sound like a curse."

She very nearly laughed. "Did I? Well, I was trying to imagine how it would feel to be thirty-one again."

The smile on his face deepened and Prudence noticed that a faint dimple dented his right cheek. No doubt plenty of women had kissed that charming little crease.

Shocked that such a silly thought had entered her head, she quickly tilted the stemmed glass to her lips. The champagne was cold and fruity and fizzed on her tongue.

Maybe after a few more sips, she'd quit behaving like a fool and tell Mr. Crawford good-night. But why would she want to do that when he was being a gentleman and she was...? Well, just looking at him was like eating rich chocolate. A woman couldn't stop with just one piece.

"If you were my age you'd feel good—just like I do," he teased.

Smiling wanly, she said, "I get the impression you like working for the Hollisters."

He crossed his ankles out in front of him and Prudence found her gaze drawn to his long legs and how the fabric of his trousers molded to his thighs. No doubt spending long hours in the saddle kept them hard and lean. Unlike the bulky muscled athletic coaches at St. Francis.

"It's long hours and lots of work," he replied. "But it's a dream job. I couldn't be happier to be here at Three Rivers."

"Where were you working before you moved here?" she asked curiously, then shook her head. "I'm getting too personal."

He shrugged. "Not at all. For the past seven years I worked for the T Bar T. That's a ranch near Clovis, New Mexico. Before that I lived in Deaf Smith County in Texas. That's where I'm from originally."

She sipped more of the champagne and tried not to notice that his knee was only an inch or two from hers. "Oh, so you're originally a Texan migrating west."

"Trust me, this is as far west as I'm going," he replied. "To be honest, I took the job without knowing what this area of Arizona was really like. I was thrilled when it turned out to be beautiful."

When Prudence had first moved to Wickenburg, it had taken her a long time to appreciate the beauty of the surrounding area. She'd been too busy trying to mend a crushed heart and convincing herself that she could recover from being a fool. "Yes, it has a stark, wild beauty. I wouldn't live anywhere else," she said, then glanced at him. "I'm guessing that you've always liked horses."

He nodded. "My dad is a horse trainer. I learned everything from him. He learned the trade from his dad. Granddad was a full-blood Comanche and horses have always been a big part of the tribe's history. He was like a true horse whisperer."

"Does your grandfather still do that kind of work?"

"No. He passed on about ten years ago. Complications from diabetes. But Dad still trains for a large ranch near Canyon. That's a town just east of Deaf Smith County where we all used to live."

"We. You mean you and your family?"

He glanced out toward the milling crowd, then lifted his glass and drained most of the contents.

"Yeah. Me and my younger brother and our parents. We had a little ranch with enough acreage for Dad to raise a few horses. He sold the property some years back, though. The place never was the same after we lost Mom."

As he spoke, his features had become drawn, and though his remark had left her curious, Prudence was hesitant to ask him to explain what he meant by "lost." They were at a joyful party. Hardly the place to bring up a sad memory. Besides, she barely knew the man. His personal life was none of her business.

She was about to change the subject completely when he suddenly spoke.

"She died in a car accident. She and Dad were on their way home one night and the pickup truck he was driving lost control. It killed Mom instantly. She was only thirty-eight at the time. Dad ended up losing a leg just below the knee."

Prudence was not only shocked by his story; she was also stunned by how much it affected her. Luke must have gone through so much grief. Not only over losing his mother, but also with the trauma of his father losing part of a limb. "How tragic for you— for your whole family," she murmured. Then she offered on an encouraging note, "But if your father is still training horses, it sounds like he didn't let the loss of his leg keep him down."

He smiled and Prudence was relieved to see his happy mood returning.

"Dad is as tough as a boot. You'd never know he wears a prosthetic. I've always wanted to be the man he is, but I'm far from there yet."

Prudence wondered if he was talking about living up to his father's skill with horses, or simply the man himself.

"What about your brother?" she asked. "Is he in the horse business, too?"

Grinning now, he said, "It's in the Crawford blood,

I guess. Colt works for the same ranch where I worked before I moved here."

"Oh, I imagine he was sad to see you leave."

"Not really. He was happy to see me moving up the ladder, so to speak." He finished the last of his champagne, and with the empty glass pressed between both palms, he glanced at her. "You mentioned you have a sister. Is she anything like you?"

Prudence shot him an impish smile. "Not in the least. She's very pretty and bubbly and far more adventurous than me. She thinks her older sister is a stuffed shirt."

"Are you?" he asked.

Was she imagining it, or had his face dipped a tad closer to hers? It must have, she decided. A moment ago, she couldn't see the pores in his tanned skin or the brown flecks in his amber eyes. But she could see them now. Along with the faint vertical lines in his lips and the dark shadow of whiskers on his chin and jawline.

Suddenly, her heart couldn't make up its mind as to whether it wanted to stop completely or take off in a wild sprint. Either way, the erratic beats were drumming in her ears, sending out a warning signal to put some space between her and this mesmerizing man.

"Uh—not exactly. I'm just a careful person. It pays to be that way, you know."

She gulped down the rest of her champagne, then practically jumped to her feet. "I should be getting back to the party. Kat is probably wondering where I've gotten off to."

Rising along with her, he said, "With all the family and friends Katherine has, I doubt you'll see her the rest of the night."

He was probably right about Katherine being occupied with family and the multitude of other guests. Still, Prudence could see she'd be asking for trouble if she continued to hang around here in the twilight with Luke Crawford. She didn't know what it was about him, but he was doing something to her common sense. Like making her forget she had any.

She looked in the direction of the partygoers as she tried to come up with an excuse to shake his company. But nothing reasonable came to mind, and then his hand was suddenly folding around hers and she forgot all about being sensible.

"I think it's high time you and I go join the party and the music. Surely there's room enough for two more on the dance floor."

"You want to dance with me?"

He must have found the disbelief in her voice amusing, or maybe it was the shocked O that had formed on her lips. He gave a slight chuckle and asked, "Why not? You do know how, don't you?"

Lord, she couldn't remember the last time she'd taken anything close to a dance step. Not since Mr. Roberts, a science teacher, had tried to waltz her around the gymnasium floor during a faculty

Christmas party. And that had been more than three years ago.

"Sort of. I mean, I haven't done any dancing since college and I'm th—"

"Yes, I know—you're thirty-nine years old," he interrupted with a chuckle. "That means it's high time you got back into the swing of things."

He plucked the empty glass from her hand and placed it next to his on the hay bale, then tucked his arm around the back of her waist.

"Come on," he urged. "The night is just getting started."

Snugged in the crook of his arm, Prudence walked along at his side, and the closer they grew to the music and the sound of laughter, she was struck by a strange premonition that something more than the night was just getting started. Was it another heartache for her? Or a new beginning?

Chapter Two

Dancing. And with a schoolteacher, at that. What the hell was he thinking?

He was thinking like any red-blooded man when he saw a beautiful, unattached woman, Luke answered his self-imposed question. He wanted to enjoy her.

But this woman is different, Luke. She's the serious kind. She's the type that could wrap you around her finger before you realized she even had a hold on you. And then where would you be? Like your father? Tearing yourself to pieces just to keep a woman happy?

Shaking away the voice in his head, Luke glanced down at the woman in his arms. The top of her head barely reached the middle of his chest, while the rest of her felt so delicate he wondered if he was holding a wispy cloud instead of a real flesh-and-blood woman. But a cloud couldn't possibly be as warm as the smooth skin of her back, or curved so perfectly, he decided.

"I'm sure you can tell I'm rusty at this," she said as he guided her slowly around the edge of the dance floor. "Your toes will probably be blue tomorrow."

At this very moment, Luke didn't know if he had a pair of feet, much less toes. The moment he'd taken Prudence into his arms, his senses had shot into orbit, and if the dance went on much longer, he wasn't sure he'd be able to pull himself back to earth.

"You couldn't hurt my toes," he assured her. "You're as light as a feather."

She laughed lightly. "You'd be surprised if you saw my bathroom scales when I stepped on them. I'm more solid than I look." She glanced out at the crowd of dancers. "I missed seeing Gil and Maureen's first dance. Was it nice?"

Not as nice as this, Luke thought. How had he gotten so lucky? For the past week, he'd been dreading this whole damn wedding party. The Hollister men were all married and had wives on their arms, while nearly all the single cowboys on the ranch had girlfriends. He'd expected to feel like a little lost dogie. Instead, he couldn't remember the last time he'd enjoyed a woman's company as much as he was enjoying Prudence's.

He attempted to answer her question. "I'm sure you would've thought it was very nice. But I'm hardly the person to ask about such things. I'm about as romantic as a rock and I know nothing about dances at a wedding reception."

She chuckled. "Really? You seemed to be handling this one quite well."

Smiling, he dared to bend his head and breathe in the scent of her hair. It smelled like sweet gardenias, and the utterly feminine scent caused his mind to drift to places it ought not go. Like a soft bed with moonlight streaming through the windows and this woman wrapped tightly in his arms.

"Dancing is like riding a horse," he told her. "It's easy once you get into rhythm."

There was a long pause before she glanced up at him, and as Luke's gaze swept over her face, he thought he spotted an extra bit of color to her cheeks.

"I wouldn't know," she said stiffly. "About the horseback riding, I mean."

"You don't ride?"

She shook her head and he clicked his tongue with disapproval. "That's hard to imagine. Wickenburg is a cowboy town. Surely you could find a place to take lessons."

Her gaze roamed his face and Luke got the impression she was trying to figure out the motives for his questions. She might even be wondering why he was dancing with her. Frankly, he was wondering about those things, too. He had no idea why he'd taken one look at her and broken all his old rules about keeping a safe distance between himself and a beautiful woman.

"Absolutely. Kat has often invited me to come out here and ride with her. She's the clop-along-slowly kind of rider, which would be my style. She says Maureen would be glad to teach me. She's an excellent horsewoman. So is Holt's wife, Isabelle. In fact, she's also a trainer. But you probably already know all of that."

"I see Maureen riding every day. Don't tell anyone, but I figure she has more knowledge about horses than I'll ever have. As for Isabelle, Holt talks a lot about his wife. It's obvious he thinks she's mighty special."

Her lips took on a wry slant, but even that twisted expression couldn't dim Luke's fantasies about kissing them. Her mouth reminded him of a red Christmas bow. If he ever had the chance to untie it, he knew there'd be something delicious underneath.

"She is mighty special," she said. "Besides being a nice person, Isabelle is incredibly attractive and talented. She was totally on her own when she started building Blue Stallion Ranch. Can you imagine how much courage that would take?"

"Not to mention money," he said wryly.

Disappointment pointed the corners of her lips downward.

"Money can be found at any financial institution," she said. "But it can't replace human character. I can get money if I need it. But courage? I don't have Isa-belle's kind."

"Why not?" he asked. "You keep a whole school running. That requires plenty of education and know-how. A woman like you should have a truckload of confidence."

More pleased than she had a right to be, she asked, "Do you always flatter a woman while the two of you are dancing?"

"No. I'm not usually this talkative," he admitted, then chuckled. "You must be doing something to me."

Prudence could've told Luke that he was defi-nitely doing something to her, too. Exactly what that something was, or how it had happened, she could only guess. But the moment he'd taken her into his arms, she'd felt as though her feet were floating off the floor. And each time her gaze met his, she felt some sort of strange connection. As though it was meant for the two of them to find each other in this huge crowd of people.

The notion was ridiculous, she thought. Especially given the fact that she wasn't looking for a man for any reason.

"Tell me, Prudence. How is it that you happened to come to the reception without a date? There has to be a line of guys waiting at the door to ask you out."

Her short laugh was drier than the champagne being served. "I have single male friends. But they're all aware that I don't date, so none of them bother to ask."

A frown tugged his brows together. "Must be a bunch of cowards."

There was nothing amusing about her situation, but suddenly she was fighting to hold back a loud burst of laughter. "I don't enjoy turning them down," she explained. "And they don't like hearing it. It's that simple."

"Why don't you date?"

She was beginning to notice that whenever he asked her something, he didn't hem and haw—he threw the question straight at her. Oddly enough, she liked that about him. It made him seem more honest, somehow.

Trying to sound as casual as possible, she said, "I tried marriage once—a long time ago. After it ended in divorce, I decided I didn't want to go down that road again."

Although she wasn't looking at him directly, she could feel his gaze thoughtfully studying her face. Funny, but before tonight, it never bothered her to explain her ideas about dating. Now it all sounded rather silly.

You got that right, Pru. It is silly. Millions of women have experienced cheating husbands and divorces, and they haven't turned into paranoid recluses. Not the way you have.

Damn it, she wasn't paranoid or a recluse. She was

cautious and careful. There was a huge difference, she argued with the voice in her head.

"So, if dating isn't going to lead to marriage, you don't see any point in it?" Luke questioned. "Is that what you're saying, more or less?"

"More or less. And now you're probably thinking I'm neurotic or something equally bad. But honestly, my job keeps me so busy that I don't miss the headache of trying to keep a man happy."

"Whoa!" he exclaimed with a laugh.

Her eyes narrowed with speculation. "What does that mean?"

He grinned. "That you sound exactly like me. I decided I don't want the headache of trying to keep a woman happy. Not on a permanent basis. So there. We're so much alike it's scary."

In the past, she'd had men give her all kinds of lectures about how she needed a man in her life to make her fulfilled and happy. The smug speeches had only made her resent them more. Apparently, Luke Crawford was a different breed.

Smiling with relief, she unconsciously squeezed his hand. "I think you understand."

"You can't imagine how much I understand. Now, my father and brother don't get my way of thinking. They believe my mind is twisted. But I just laugh at them. I figure it's like this. In order to be happy, a person has to follow his own heart. Not do what somebody else thinks he should do."

For the past thirteen years, Prudence had been

trying to do just that—follow her own heart. But that was awfully hard to do whenever her heart felt so empty.

"Yes, I think you're right," she murmured.

He started to reply when the music suddenly stopped and their dance steps came to a halt.

Lowering her arm, but still holding on to her hand, he said, "I—uh—think we've gone through three songs. Would you like to go for another? Or are you getting hungry?"

They'd danced through three songs? And she hadn't even noticed? Oh, Lord, this wasn't like her. Not like her at all. If she didn't get away from this man and soon, she was going to drift off to fantasyland. Where anything might happen.

A blush stung her cheeks. "Oh. I hadn't realized we'd danced that long. I must've been concentrating on my steps."

Sure, Pru. Who are you kidding? You didn't know where you were stepping. After a few seconds in Luke's arms you didn't even know you were dancing. Have you suddenly decided you don't want to be without a man?

Slamming the door on the mocking voice in her head, she glanced around the crowd of dancers. Had anyone noticed how she'd been wrapped in the new horse trainer's arms for the past several minutes? It didn't matter, she thought. After tonight, she'd most likely never see the man again.

He continued to smile at her. "Good job. I don't think you missed a one."

"Thanks." She breathed deeply before smiling back at him. "I haven't eaten since early this morning. I should probably put something in my stomach other than champagne."

"I totally agree."

As the music started up again, he wrapped his hand tightly around hers and led her off the elevated dance floor.

After winding and wedging their way through a mass of guests, the two of them finally reached the buffet tables.

Presently, only a few stragglers were helping themselves to the fancy finger foods.

"Well, here's my man! How's it going, Luke?"

Pausing in the act of placing a stuffed shrimp onto her plate, Prudence glanced over to see that Holt had walked up behind Luke and rested a hand on the back of his shoulder.

Turning, Luke gave Holt's arm a playful swat, making it obvious to Prudence that the two men had already become close buddies.

Luke said, "This is some party, Holt. Your mother has done it up in style. I've never seen anything like it."

Holt chuckled. "All the Hollister women have been planning this thing for months. And I have to admit that so far it's gone off without a hitch." Spotting Prudence, he stepped over and gave her a brief hug. "Pru, how are you? I haven't seen you out here at the ranch in a while. Nice to see you."

"Prudence has been kind enough to dance with me." Luke spoke up.

Holt laughed. "Pru, you must be a brave woman. If Luke dances anything like he rides a horse, then you've had a rough go of it."

Knowing Holt was always the teaser, she said to him, "Luke isn't exactly king of the ballroom, but he'll do."

Holt laughed again, only louder this time, then lifted a squatty tumbler to his lips. When he caught her eyeing the dark contents, he shot her a coy grin.

"I never was much for champagne. Bless her heart, Jazelle is off work tonight so she can enjoy the reception with the rest of the family, but she personally fixed my bourbon and cola for me anyway. Nobody can do it like her."

Jazelle was the young blonde who'd worked as the Hollisters' housekeeper for many years. Her job also included being nanny to most of the small Hollister children.

Luke glanced thoughtfully at Holt. "I see Jazelle coming and going from your office. Looks like she's going to have a baby fairly soon."

"In November, I think. And so is my sister-in-law, Tessa, Joe's wife."

"They're going to have babies at the same time?" Luke asked.

"It's one of those happy coincidences," Holt explained. "You see, Connor Murphy is Jazelle's husband and also a Yavapai County deputy with my brother, Joe. The two men have been close friends and work partners for many years and have gone through lots of situations together. But this was one they didn't plan on—their wives became pregnant at the same time."

Shaking his head, Luke declared, "That's more than a coincidence. That's divine intervention."

From the corner of her eye, Prudence glanced at Luke's face. Did he ever think about having children of his own? Stupid question, she thought. The man wasn't planning on having a wife. And he hardly seemed the type who'd purposely choose to be a single father. No, he was just like her. He didn't want the hassle and heartache of a serious relationship.

She leveled a suggestive smile at Holt. "Are these pregnancies giving you and Isabelle any ideas?"

He laughed. "Isabelle always has baby ideas. Hell, we just now have Carter potty-trained. Why would I want to jump into the whole thing again?"

Prudence's smile turned knowing. "Yeah, why would you?"

Holt tossed back the last of his bourbon, then straightened the turquoise slide on his bolo tie. "Speaking of Isabelle, I promised her a few dances, so I'd better see if I can find her. See you two later. And, Luke," he added as he started walking off, "make sure you see to it that Pru doesn't get bored."

Prudence watched Holt disappear into the crowd

before she looked over to Luke and smiled. "Was your boss back in New Mexico anything like him?"

Laughing, Luke asked, "Are you serious? I've never met anyone like Holt. He's one of a kind. I've noticed something else about all the Hollisters. Their bond as a family goes deeper than most."

He was right. The Hollisters were such a tightly knit bunch that what affected one affected them all. They worked together, laughed and cried together, and shared their hopes and dreams as a group. That was the sort of marriage and family Prudence had wanted for herself. But it hadn't worked out that way.

"Prudence Keyes! I've found you!"

At the sound of the female voice, Prudence glanced around to see Camille Waggoner barreling straight at her.

She barely had time to place her plate on the table before the youngest Hollister sibling grabbed her up in a tight hug.

Luke watched the young redheaded woman wrap Prudence in a tight hug, and for the next ten minutes, he stood patiently to one side while the two friends caught up on all the family news and local happenings.

"Camille is the one who lives on Red Bluff, the Hollisters' second ranch. Right?" he said, after the woman had gone on her way.

Prudence picked up her plate and a fork. "That's right. Her husband is Matthew. He was the foreman here at Three Rivers for many years. Now he manages Red Bluff. Have you met him?"

"Yes, this morning before the wedding. He was down at the barns bright and early. Seems like a great guy," he told her. "After hearing him and Holt talk about Red Bluff, I'm looking forward to seeing the place and meeting TooTall, the foreman. They tell me the guy is a dandy horseman. And for Holt to give him such an endorsement, he has to be good."

"Camille tells me he has mystic powers, too. But that's another story." She motioned a hand toward his plate. "If you're finished filling your plate, let's find a place to sit before someone else comes along. Not that I don't like chatting, but at this rate, we'll never get to eat."

"We could go back to the hay bale," he suggested. "I doubt anyone else will mosey down that far."

"Okay. Lead the way."

Just as they stepped away from the table, a waiter passed by with a tray loaded with fresh champagne glasses. Luke plucked up two and winked at Prudence.

"To go with our food," he explained.

She let out a good-natured groan. "I'm going to have a headache in the morning."

"Don't think about the morning. Just enjoy tonight," he teased.

She had been enjoying it. Too much, Prudence thought. And that was the scary part.

* * *

After finishing their meals and doing a little more dancing, Prudence and Luke joined in the newly-weds' send-off. Gil and Maureen emerged from the house having changed into street clothes and waved goodbye to the crowd of well-wishers. After the rice had been thrown and the newlyweds had driven away, Prudence told herself she needed to call it a night and head home. But for reasons she didn't want to analyze, she couldn't make her mouth form the words. Instead, she'd allowed Luke to lead her back onto the dance floor.

Eventually, though, the crowd began to grow smaller, and the realization that the reception was coming to an end hit her like a brick.

"Everyone is starting to head home," she said. "I need to be going, too. I have a million things to do tomorrow before school on Monday."

He looked like he wanted to protest, but he simply nodded, and when the band paused at the end of the song, he led her off the dance floor.

"I'll walk you to your vehicle," he told her. "Where are you parked?"

"On the west side of the house. I wanted to make sure I wouldn't get hemmed in. But there's no need for you to walk that far," she reasoned.

"Nonsense. If I can dance, I can walk, can't I? Anyway, there might be a coyote out there and I'll need to chase him off for you."

In spite of the melancholy feeling that had settled

over her, she managed to chuckle. "A coyote coming near all this noise?"

"He smells food," he joked.

Smiling, she said, "Okay. I suppose I might need a protector."

With his arm around the back of her waist, he guided her away from the reception area, past the front of the house and finally through a maze of parked vehicles. As they walked, Prudence tried to keep her mind on anything and everything except the man at her side.

The night wind had turned even cooler and the scent of juniper drifted down from the mountains. Away from the endless strings of party lanterns, the stars had become visible in the black sky, while straight over their heads, a crescent moon illuminated the ground with silvery light.

"It's beautiful out here," she murmured. "Don't you think so?"

He glanced down at her. "Very beautiful. It makes my job even more of a joy."

Smiling faintly, she said, "Lucky you. Not to be cooped up in an office all day."

"Lucky you. Sitting in a comfortable office and not getting kicked, bitten, pawed or bucked off by a colt or filly," he told her.

"Put that way, I guess I am pretty fortunate," she said. Then, spotting her car, she pointed to a dark blue compact. "There's my car over there."

He glanced at her empty hands. "Where are

your keys? Did you forget your handbag back at the house?"

"I locked my bag in the car. It has a keyless entry."

He stood to one side while she punched the number sequence on the pads located beneath the door handle. After she heard the click of the locks lifting, she opened the door and turned back to him.

"Luke, I—"

"It's been—"

They spoke at the same time, causing them both to laugh.

"You go first," Luke insisted.

Silver moonlight etched his features against the darkness, and she knew for as long as she lived, she'd remember the way he looked at this very moment in his white shirt and with the green cabochon of his bolo tie pushed against his throat and the brim of his black hat partially shading his eyes. He was definitely one sexy man.

She swallowed at the nervous lump that had suddenly developed in her throat. "I was only going to say how much I've enjoyed this evening. You've made it very special for me."

"I was going to say how nice you've made this whole event for me." Stepping forward, he clasped her hand in his. "It's been a joy."

"For me, too." Her hoarse voice made her sound like she was coming down with a bout of laryngitis.

He lifted the back of her hand to his lips and she

wondered what was keeping her from swooning at his feet.

"Think of me sometime," he said gently.

Sometime? She had the terrible feeling her thoughts were going to be stuck on him for a long, long time to come.

"I will. And you be safe when you're breaking those young horses."

Smiling wanly, he released his hold on her hand. "Always."

After his one-word reply, silence fell between them. Yet Prudence hesitated about climbing into the car. A few more seconds might give him time to suggest they see each other again or, at least, ask for her cell number and promise to phone her. But the sensible side of her prayed he wouldn't do either. Where he was concerned, she was far too vulnerable.

She forced herself to take a step backward and away from him. "Well, good night, Luke. And good luck with your new job."

"Thanks. And you take care of yourself, Prudence."

Nodding, she hurriedly turned and slid into the seat of the car before she could change her mind and do something crazy. Like throw her arms around him and kiss him directly on the mouth.

"I will," she promised.

He shut the door for her, and after fastening the seat belt, she quickly started the engine. As she pulled away, he gave her a little smile and a simple wave.

Prudence waved back and then promptly felt a tear roll down her cheek.

Chapter Three

The following Monday, just before lunch break, Prudence hung up the telephone on her desk and punched the intercom button to Katherine's office.

"Yes, Pru?"

"Kat, I need those estimates for replacing the auditorium seats. And print up an extra set of them, would you? I need to present the whole issue to the board tonight."

"Give me two minutes," Katherine cheerfully replied.

Prudence disconnected the intercom and released a long sigh as she rested her head against the back of the leather executive chair.

This was not good, she thought. She'd believed

that diving back into work today would help rid her mind of Luke Crawford. But so far, his image was still swimming around in her head, shredding her focus.

How long was it going to take to forget the man? It needed to be soon, she decided. She had too much to do and too many important decisions to make to have her thinking interrupted by silly romantic daydreams.

And silly was exactly what it was, she thought crossly. Luke was a confirmed bachelor. She didn't want to be anything to him—or any other man, for that matter. So why was she wishing that Luke had kissed more than her hand? Why did she keep wondering what it would be like to be close to him? Like skin to skin and mouth to mouth.

Damn it all.

She was massaging her closed eyes with the tips of her fingers when she heard the tap of Katherine's heels entering the room.

Not wanting the woman to guess Prudence wasn't herself today, she quickly lowered her hands and leaned forward in the chair.

"I put them in a folder," Katherine said as she came to a halt in front of Prudence's desk. "And I added that projection cost for remodeling the cafeteria kitchen. You did mention you were going to bring that up at the meeting, too."

"Thanks, Kat. I'm glad you thought of it. The subject slipped my mind. I guess I've been too busy dreading the fight I'm going to have with the coaches over replacing the old sports equipment." She grimaced as she reached for the folder Katherine had placed on the corner of her desk. "In their minds, nothing should be approved over sports. Well, I have news for them—the arts count around here, too! When parents and other citizens of the town attend a musical recital or a play put on by the speech department, I don't want them sitting on lumpy seats. Or having their clothing snagged by exposed springs!"

"Oh, what's brought your claws out this morning? Did you miss breakfast? Or have you already had an ugly confrontation over the phone?"

Prudence sighed. "Sorry. I—uh—have a lot on my mind, and I guess it's all getting to me."

"No need to apologize. If you want to gripe, I'll go get my earplugs," Katherine joked. "I keep a pair in my desk."

Prudence looked at her and laughed. "Now that you're back to working five days a week, you have your plate overloaded, too. What with taking care of a teenage son and three-year-old twins, plus your husband, I honestly don't know how you do it."

"I have plenty of help at the ranch. And working here with you energizes me. When I get home in the evenings, I'm ready to do things with my family. It's all great."

Yes, it would be great, Prudence thought. That was the kind of life she'd planned for herself so long ago. Having a job that she loved, along with a family of her own.

"I'm glad that you're happy, Kat. Dear God, if anyone deserves it, you do. And don't worry about me. I'm fine. Really. Just a little tired."

Katherine's grin turned coy. "No doubt. If I'd danced as much as you and Luke did at the reception, it would take me a week to recuperate."

Prudence inwardly winced. She'd expected Katherine to bring up the subject of Luke. No doubt she and plenty of others at the reception had noticed how he and Prudence had practically lived on the dance floor.

"I'm not tired from all the dancing." Just tired of thinking about it and Luke. Weary of telling herself that she had to forget him, Prudence thought miserably.

Her expression rather smug, Katherine eased a hip onto the corner of Prudence's desk. "I don't think it's necessary to ask if you liked Luke. It's obvious that you enjoyed his company."

Prudence tried to keep her expression bland. "We had a nice evening together. He was a gentleman, danced like a dream and could converse in complete sentences."

"Ha! He should be able to form complete sentences. He has a bachelor's degree in agriculture business."

Prudence's brows arched with surprise. "He has

a college degree? He didn't say anything about it to me."

Katherine shook her head. "Luke is not the type to tout his accomplishments. He told Blake that he went to college mostly to please his father. But he says now he's glad he furthered his education."

Luke hadn't talked like a man with huge dreams. He hadn't mentioned a desire to own a big ranch of his own or make tons of money. Unlike Gavin, who'd constantly talked about becoming a wealthy football star, then dropped out of college the minute life had thrown him a curveball.

"I'm a bit surprised. I got the impression Luke would be happy as long as he had a horse and saddle and a comfortable place to lay his head."

"Blake is like that, too. He'd be thrilled just to be a regular ranch hand. But he's a man who could never shirk his responsibilities, and Lord knows he has more of those than any one person ought to have."

Prudence nodded. "You've heard me say this before, but I'll repeat it. You're very lucky to have found him."

Katherine's expression turned clever. "Blake and I crashed into each other on the sidewalk—that's how we got together, remember? Now you and Luke had a collision at the reception. I'm thinking it's fate at work."

Her spine as straight as a board, Prudence scooted to the edge of her chair. "Fate didn't make me stumble! Anyway, I never plan to see Luke again."

"What?"

She glanced at Katherine's stunned face. "Why are you surprised? Saturday night was a party— a celebration. Not the beginning of a lifelong romance."

Rolling her eyes, Katherine said, "Tell that to Maureen and Gil."

"Maureen and Gil are different. They were meant to be together. You and Blake were meant to be together. But I…" Bitterness suddenly rose in her throat, blocking the remainder of her words.

Katherine shot her a disgusted look. "Sorry, I forgot. Other women can have love and a happy marriage, but you can't."

Prudence snorted. "Kat, you must have guzzled a gallon of coffee this morning. Your imagination has gone off on a wild tangent. Luke was a nice dance partner, but he's a confirmed bachelor. And I'm—"

"Stubborn," Katherine interrupted. "Otherwise, you'd let yourself see that Luke is a good man."

Prudence picked up an ink pen and tapped the point on a scratch pad. "He probably is—a good man. But I'm not looking for a good one, or any other kind. Anyway, you're not thinking, Kat. I'm eight years older than Luke. Even if we had something going, it wouldn't last."

Expecting a lecture about being cynical, Prudence was surprised when the other woman simply laughed.

"Well, you know what's best for you, Pru." She

slipped off the corner of the desk and started out of the office, only to pause at the door. "By the way, I've secured your flight ticket to Reno and hotel reservations for Thursday through Saturday night. You should be arriving up there around five that evening. That should give you plenty of time to get settled before the teachers' seminar begins the next morning."

"Thanks, Kat. That's perfect."

Prudence watched her secretary disappear through the doorway. It wasn't like the woman to let go of something so easily. Her laughter must've meant she recognized the silliness of trying to pair her up with Luke Crawford.

Sighing, Prudence reached for the folder Katherine had left on the corner of her desk.

Her time with Luke Crawford was over and done with, she thought. She had to get on with important things. Like the board meeting tonight. She had to be prepared and focused in order to present her best argument for school expenditures. She couldn't be thinking about a horseman with brown eyes and a smile that had melted her bones.

The sorrel at the end of the lunge line was a beautiful specimen of horseflesh. His registered name was He's a Flyboy, but Luke and the other cowboys who worked the horse barn called him King. At two years old, he was already big-boned and heavily muscled. The white blaze down his face and four perfect stockings all the way to his knees made him what cowboys described as "loaded with chrome" and especially sought-after. Holt had decided to keep him a stallion, and most of the time stallions were a challenge to handle, much less train to any type of discipline. Only this horse was very special, and Luke already had him broke to the saddle and following hand and feet commands.

"You're a good boy, King," Luke said to the horse as he secured the animal to a nearby hitching rail. "And far smarter than your older brother. That's why you're going to eventually get a harem of mares and your brother is going to chase cows the rest of his life."

The stallion pointed his nose in the air and let out a nicker that closely resembled a laugh. At the same time, Holt came up to stand a few feet from Luke's left shoulder.

"I do believe King understood what you were telling him," Holt said with a chuckle.

"He's exceptionally smart and a joy to work with." Luke picked up a brush from a wooden crate and began to groom King's glistening coat. "Have you heard from Maureen and Gil yet? Guess they're lying on a Hawaiian beach about now."

Holt laughed. "Mom lying on the beach? I figure the newlyweds are visiting ranches around the islands. That's what Mom considers fun."

Luke pulled the brush through King's long mane. "I'll say one thing—the ranch yard feels empty without having them around."

"We're all missing them." Moving closer, Holt casually leaned a hip against the hitching rail as he watched Luke continue to groom the stallion. "Speaking of the newlyweds, I've been wondering what you thought about Prudence. Looked like you two hit it off at the wedding reception."

Although they hadn't known each other that long, Holt hadn't been shy about encouraging Luke to jump into the dating scene and find himself a special girl. Considering that Holt had been one of the biggest womanizers in both Yavapai and Maricopa Counties before he'd married Isabelle, Luke had taken the man's advice with a grain of salt. And he'd certainly not explained to Holt that he wasn't looking for a "special" girl.

Luke said, "It was nice having a pretty woman like her for a dance partner."

Holt regarded him with a keen eye and Luke hoped the man couldn't read his mind. Otherwise, he'd know that Luke had gone home from the reception with his head in the clouds. And he was still struggling to get his feet back on solid ground.

Holt's grin was knowing. "Hmm. Guess there weren't any other pretty single women at the reception willing to dance with you. But I was kinda occupied with all that was going on. I could've missed seeing you dancing with a different woman."

"You didn't," Luke said tightly. "I only danced with Prudence. But that doesn't mean a thing. I'll never see her again."

"Why the hell not?"

Luke grimaced. "Lots of reasons. Mainly because she's…uh, the serious sort."

Holt rolled his eyes. "What do you want? The silly sort?"

Holt didn't understand, Luke thought crossly, because he'd never had a mother like his. Paula had caused her own death and her husband to lose his leg. Holt, or any of the Hollister men, couldn't possibly understand how it had felt as a child to hear his mother screaming obscenities one minute, then singing a soft lullaby the next. She'd been like an unpredictable alcoholic, only there hadn't been a drop of alcohol around. She suffered from bipolar disease and mostly refused to stay on her meds.

Luke said, "Pru is the kind of woman a guy takes home to meet his parents. That's not for me, Holt." Lowering the brush, he glanced at his boss. Maybe if he had an ounce of Holt's self-confidence, he would already have a family of his own. As it was, he didn't even have the nerve to pull out his cell phone and call Prudence. Not that she'd given Luke her number. But he knew where she worked, and Katherine would give it to him. "Look, Holt, the way I see things, having a horse for company is much safer than having a woman."

Holt threw back his head and laughed. "Well, Isabelle wouldn't give you much argument there. She loves me, but there are times she just wants to be with her horses." His laughter sobered as he crossed his arms against his chest and continued to study Luke. "Don't worry. I'm not going to rib you any more about Prudence. I'll just say she's a very good person and leave it at that."

The relief Luke felt must have shown on his face because Holt suddenly laughed again and slapped a hand on his shoulder. "When you finish with King, come to my office," he said. "I want to show you some pics of a stallion I'm thinking about buying."

"Okay. I'll be there in a few minutes," he told Holt.

After Holt had walked away, Luke smoothed a blanket over King's back, then added a thick saddle pad. As he adjusted the equipment over the horse's withers and followed it with a saddle, he thought about Holt's parting words.

Yes, he had no doubts that Prudence was a very good person with a stable disposition. But that didn't mean she would be good for him. That didn't mean he should break all the rules he'd made for himself. Rules that would keep him from ever going through the hell and heartache his father had endured during his marriage to Luke's mother.

Still, Luke couldn't forget how it had hurt to tell Prudence goodbye. As he'd stood there looking at her in the moonlight, he'd had to fight like a madman to keep from pulling her into his arms, kissing her mouth and telling her that he wanted to see her again. That he *had* to see her again.

Somehow, he'd managed to keep those reckless

urges under control. But now he couldn't help but wonder what would have happened if he had kissed her. What would happen if he did see her again?

"Hey, Luke, I got the filly saddled. Want to see how she looks?"

The eager male voice interrupted Luke's thoughts and he looked over his shoulder to see that Farley, one of the grooms, had walked up behind him. Barely past twenty, the young man was an extremely hard worker and made no secret about idolizing Holt and Luke.

"Sure, Farley." He fastened the girth on King's saddle before walking with Farley to the opposite end of the huge horse barn. As they approached the black filly all tacked out in a worn ranch saddle, Luke asked, "Did she give you any trouble?"

"Shoot no!" Farley happily exclaimed. "I did everything like you told me to and she stood there like a perfect lady."

"That's great, Farley. You keep this up and it won't be long before Holt lets you work in the round pen."

Laughing sheepishly, the young man tugged on the brim of his cowboy hat. "That ain't gonna happen. Well—uh, maybe someday I'll get to move up. A man has to dream, don't he?"

A vision of Prudence's green-blue eyes and raspberry lips suddenly entered Luke's mind. Yes, a man had to dream, he thought. Even if he knew his dreams could never come true.

* * *

The sky was covered with dark clouds, and a cold wind was blowing steadily from the north when Prudence's flight to Reno landed late Thursday afternoon. By the time her taxi pulled alongside the curb in front of the downtown hotel where she'd be staying, a light rain had started to fall.

As she climbed out of the warm car and motioned for the bellhop to collect her bags, she shivered and wrapped her arms around herself to ward off the chill.

"I wasn't planning on Reno being this cold at this time of year," she said to the young man as they started toward the hotel entrance.

"September can be cold," he said cheerfully. "That's when our fall weather hits. You must be from out of town."

"Arizona," she told him. "Not far from Phoenix."

He flashed her a grin as the two of them passed through a pair of wide glass doors. "No wonder you're shivering, ma'am. You need a jacket."

Ma'am? The term sounded matronly. Did she look that old to this young man? Jeez, that ought to be more than enough to get her thoughts off Luke Crawford.

Inside the spacious lobby, Prudence crossed over to the reception desk where several clerks were attending to guests. She'd just finished the check-in process and was slipping the card that served as a key into her handbag when directly behind her, a male voice called out.

"Prudence! Is that you?"

Dear Lord, now she was doing more than thinking about the man. She was hearing his voice!

Certain that she must've misheard, she turned and stared in stunned disbelief at Luke Crawford. What in the world was he doing here? Reno was nearly eight hundred miles away from home!

"Luke! This is quite a surprise. What are you doing up here in Nevada?"

He laughed and she was struck by the difference in his appearance. At the wedding and reception, he'd been wearing a dark brown Western suit. Today he was dressed in blue jeans with a denim jacket over a green plaid shirt. A shiny round belt buckle sat at the middle of his waist, while a brown felt hat was tugged low on his forehead. His rugged masculinity jumped out at her like the cold wind had slapped her cheeks only minutes earlier.

"I'm wondering the same thing about you," he said.

Recognizing that she needed to move away from the reception counter to make room for the next person, Prudence motioned for Luke to join her at the spot where the bellhop was waiting with her bags.

Once they were standing face-to-face, Prudence couldn't stop smiling. Seeing him again was like being given a surprise birthday party. She was happy and shocked at the same time. "I'm here for a teachers' administration seminar," she told him. "What brings you all the way up here? Does Holt know you're missing from Three Rivers?"

He laughed. "Holt is the reason I'm here in Reno. He's sent me on a horse-buying mission. He wants to add a couple more stallions to his stables and I'm here to look a few over for him before he makes the deal."

"Hmm. That's impressive that he trusts you with such an important task."

Luke chuckled. "He either trusts me or wanted to get me out of his hair for a few days."

From the corner of her eye, she noticed the bellhop was still waiting patiently with her bags. "Excuse me for a moment, Luke. I need to deal with my bags." She pulled out a bill and handed it to the young man. "Sorry for keeping you waiting. Just forget the bags. I'll take them on up to my room."

He looked at her, then darted a curious glance at Luke. "Thanks," he told her. "But—it's my job and—"

Luke suddenly interrupted. "Don't worry about it," he assured the young man. "I'll make sure the lady's bags get to her room."

The bellhop darted a questioning look at Prudence and she nodded to convey she was agreeable with the situation.

"In that case, thanks to—uh—both of you."

He hurried away and Luke grabbed the handles on

both suitcases. "The elevators are right over here," he told Prudence.

The two of them crossed the hotel lobby. A spacious area furnished with leather couches and armchairs was decorated with artwork involving depictions of cowboys and miners during the silver rush days that had taken place more than a century and a half ago. On the far side of the room, several guests were seated near a huge rock fireplace where a crackling fire chased away the evening chill. Beyond the lounging area, a wall of plate glass revealed the cold rain dripping off the edge of the awning that sheltered the hotel entrance.

"Are you staying in this hotel, too?" she asked as they reached the doors of two separate elevators.

He punched the up button. "Yes. On the fourth floor," he answered. "What's your room number?"

What would be the odds of the two of them ending up in the same city, in the same hotel and on the same floor? Katherine would say it was fate at work. Prudence thought it was downright spooky.

"Room 403," she answered.

"I'm in 410. Just down the hallway. Crazy coincidence, isn't it?"

Her laugh sounded more like a nervous little moan. "I'll say."

The doors to the elevator slid open and she promptly stepped inside. Luke followed with her rolling bags and pressed the button for the fourth floor. No other guests entered the elevator before the door drew shut, and as the lift swooshed upward, Prudence stood hugging herself with her arms and wishing she'd worn something heavier than a white lacy blouse with sheer sleeves and a short black skirt with a slit on one side. She was freezing, and for some idiotic reason, she felt half-naked.

There was no reason she should be feeling so exposed to this man, she thought crossly. She was decently dressed. But something about the looks he'd been giving her was making her feel vulnerable.

One thing for certain—she needed to get a grip. She was a grown woman, perfectly capable of dealing with any man. Even one who looked like Luke Crawford.

Releasing an unsteady breath, she said, "Now that I know you're only a short distance down the hallway from me, I won't feel guilty about you dealing with my bags."

His chuckle was the same rich, wonderful sound she remembered from their time together at the reception. Since then, she'd thought a lot about his laugh and the way his white teeth had flashed against his brown skin. She'd thought a lot, too, about the way his hand had felt holding hers, the way his arm had curled around the back of her waist as though she'd belonged to him and him alone.

He said, "Stepping on and off an elevator with two little rolling bags is hardly a strain, Prudence."

The upward movement stopped and the doors of the elevator swished open. As they walked off,

Prudence asked, "How long have you been here in Reno?"

"Since around noon," he answered. "I drove as far as Beatty last night and finished the rest of the trip this morning."

"You drove? Why? Is Holt getting skimpy on business expenditures?"

Luke laughed. "Not hardly. Flying would have been cheaper than pulling a four-horse trailer behind a big diesel truck. See, if I buy horses, I need to haul them home."

Feeling a little silly, she said, "My ignorance about the ranching business is showing."

"And I don't know one thing about a teacher seminar," he admitted. "So that makes us even."

After a short walk, they reached her room, which was located on the left-hand side of the carpeted corridor. Prudence opened the door with the key card and motioned for him to enter ahead of her.

Glancing around, he asked, "Where do you want your bags?"

"Anywhere will be fine."

The room was nicely furnished with a king-size bed and matching dresser, a computer desk and chair, and a rather large TV. Across the outer wall, dark green drapes were half-drawn against the rainy sky.

He left the suitcases in front of the closet door, then walked to the other side of the room where the thermostat was located on the wall. "You need some heat in here," he said.

At some point during their journey from the lobby to her room, she'd stopped shivering, but that was probably due to Luke. Each time she looked at the man, heat flamed in her loins and shot all the way to her cheeks.

"It is rather chilly," she said.

Turning away from the thermostat, he gazed toward the plate-glass window. "Lucky you. You have a view of the Truckee River. My room is on the opposite side of the corridor. All I see is a busy street. Mind if I have a look?"

"Help yourself," she told him.

He walked over to the window, and unable to stop herself, Prudence slowly moved across the room to join him.

She said, "When my taxi pulled up in front of this beautiful old building, I noticed the river. I'll have to tell Katherine she did a super job choosing a place for me to stay."

"I've never been to Reno before," he said as he gazed down at the river. "Have you?"

"A few years ago. But I didn't stay in this part of town."

He glanced over at her and smiled, and Prudence's insides were doing more than flaming. They were melting to a quivering mass of goo.

He said, "Then you probably know all the fun places to visit."

Her smile was more like a snarl. "Fun? Sorry, Luke. That's rarely on my agenda."

He frowned. "That's downright shameful. Every-one needs to have fun. What's the use of working if you can't have fun in between?"

She pulled her shoulders back to such a rigid line that even a drill sergeant would've commended her posture.

"Food and shelter are necessities to survive. Fun isn't," she reasoned, while thinking he had no right to push his ideas about life onto her. If she wanted to always be serious and single and lonely, then that was her choice.

Shaking his head, he said, "Teachers always have a red pencil. Where's yours? I need to mark an *X* by your answer. The superintendent has flunked the course on making merry."

His nonsense had Prudence rolling her eyes. "Fun is for young people."

"What are you? A part of the geriatric crowd?" he goaded playfully.

Something made her move closer to him. Maybe it was the subtle hint of man that seemed to perme-ate the very air around him. Or perhaps she was drawn to the warmth she knew would be radiating from his body. Whatever it was, it was pulling at her from every direction.

"Downstairs, the bellhop called me *ma'am*," she said, as though that explained everything.

He laughed. "What was he supposed to call you? *Lady*, *dame*, *chick* or something a little edgier?"

Suddenly struck by how ridiculous she'd sounded, Prudence laughed with him.

"*Ma'am* caught me off guard, that's all. And compared to you, I am almost geriatric."

"Now you're really sounding silly. You must be suffering jet lag. What you need is a good dinner tonight. With a nice guy like me. How about it?"

Dinner with him? She'd been planning on never seeing the man again! Now here she was in a hotel room with him. Far, far away from anyone who knew them. How had this happened? And what would happen if she did go out with him?

Nothing will happen, Pru. You'll eat dinner. You'll thank the man for the meal and his company, and then you'll tell him good-night. He'll go to his room and you'll go to yours. There won't be one thing to worry about.

"I—uh, just got here. I haven't had time to think about dinner," she said as her mind continued to weigh the pros and cons of going out with this tall, dark horseman.

"What's there to decide? You have to eat something. Or maybe you have a can of sardines and a sleeve of crackers packed away in your suitcase. Saves money. But the sardines will stink up your room."

Smiling faintly, she said, "I'm beginning to think you're a little bit crazy."

He feigned a look of disappointment. "Oh, I thought you were going to say *persistent*."

Tilting her head to one side, she allowed her gaze to meander lazily over his face. "You're that, too. But to be honest, dinner might be relaxing. I've been going in a whirlwind since the alarm went off at four this morning."

He reached for her hand, and Prudence was helpless to resist as he pressed it between the two of his.

"I'm glad you've agreed to go." His expression suddenly turned serious as his gaze dropped to their linked hands. "You can't imagine how shocked I was when I spotted you standing there at the reception desk. I was pretty happy about it, too. I—uh—I've missed you."

The sincerity she heard in his voice caused her throat to grow so tight she could scarcely breathe.

Finally, she managed to say, "I didn't think you wanted to see me again."

"I didn't think you wanted to see me again." He echoed her words.

She struggled to push out the breath she'd fought so hard to pull in only seconds ago. "I thought it best not to."

"I thought the same thing."

Try as she might, she couldn't tear her eyes away from his face. "We both want to stay single and un-attached. But that doesn't mean we can't be friends."

His black brows lifted ever so slightly. "Friends. Is that what you want us to be?"

His hand tightened around hers while at the same time she saw a warm glimmer dancing in his amber-brown eyes. Whatever he was trying to convey to her was causing a tingling sensation to ripple down her spine.

"I don't know what else we could be," she murmured.

"There's one other thing. It's something I've been thinking about ever since we said goodbye at the reception."

Her heart was suddenly pounding. "What's that?"

Instead of answering with a word, his head suddenly lowered and his hard, masculine lips covered hers.

Initially, Prudence was too shocked to react. And then suddenly a plethora of sensations were pouring over her, urging her not to think, but to simply enjoy.

She opened her lips and he deepened the kiss just long enough for her to get a brief taste of his mouth and feel the tempting pleasure of being connected to him in such an intimate way.

Her senses began to swirl and her hands made a fluttered landing in the middle of his chest. And then it all ended as he quickly pulled his head back and stepped away from her.

"Is seven okay with you for dinner?" he asked in a low, husky voice.

Nothing about the kiss or his thoughts behind it. But she could wait for an explanation.

"Seven? Sure. I'll be ready," she told him and wondered if she sounded as loopy as she felt.

He let himself out of her room, and after Prudence regained her breath, she walked back over to the window and stared out at the river and the rain soaking the sidewalk below.

She was skidding across thin ice, Prudence thought. But for once in her life, she wasn't going to worry about the dangers. For the past thirteen years she'd tried to be wise. And what had all those careful decisions gotten her? Nothing but a cold, lonely bed and an empty heart.

Luke wanted her company and she wanted his. Could Katherine be right? Was fate trying to tell her that she finally deserved a little happiness in her life?

Chapter Four

Luke wiped the last remnants of shaving cream from his face and stared at his image in the bathroom mirror. It wasn't like him to be impulsive or reckless. Especially when it came to a woman. But grabbing Prudence by the shoulders and planting a kiss on her lips had been both those things and more. It was a miracle she hadn't shoved him away and ordered him to get lost.

But Prudence hadn't protested. Instead, she'd kissed him back like she'd enjoyed it. Like she'd welcome the notion of the two of them being more than friends.

Don't be stupid, Luke. Your lips weren't on hers long enough to determine what she was thinking or feeling. Reckless doesn't begin to describe the way you react whenever you're near Prudence. You go a little crazy. The section of your brain that deals with logic went haywire from the moment you met her, and since then, you've let your guard down. Not only that, you're allowing your daydreams to go beyond a few hours or even a few days. You've started thinking in long terms. And that's a mistake. One you can't keep making.

Disgusted with the negative voice in his head, Luke turned away from the mirror and reached for the pale gray shirt he'd draped over the doorknob. He wasn't going to let himself start analyzing his motives for kissing her or asking her to join him for dinner. And maybe he was a little crazy for thinking they could be lovers.

But hell, even a psychiatrist would tell him it was perfectly normal to feel desire for a beautiful woman and want to spend time with her. No, the way Luke saw things, running into Prudence here in Reno was sheer providence. And he planned to make the most of the opportunity. Not spend his waking moments worrying about future consequences.

After Luke finished dressing, he decided he had enough time to walk down to a florist shop located a few doors down from the hotel. After purchasing a single red rose, he hurried back to the hotel and managed to reach the door of Prudence's room with a couple of minutes to spare.

She immediately answered his knock, and Luke

was completely floored when she opened the door and smiled at him. He'd expected her to look prim and pretty. Not like an alluring siren with her long brown hair draped near one eye and glittery earrings dangling from her earlobes.

"Hello, again," she greeted him.

His gaze dropped to the sweet smile on her lips, and as he took in the moist red curves, he could almost taste them.

"Hello." He offered the rose to her. "For you."

The smile on her face deepened as she took the rose and lifted the half-opened bud toward her nostrils. "It's lovely, Luke. Thank you."

Feeling a bit foolish, he said, "I thought you might enjoy a flower in your room."

"I'll definitely enjoy the rose." She pushed the door wider and gestured for him to enter. "Won't you come in while I put it in some water?"

Luke stepped past her and walked to the middle of the room, where there were notable signs of her presence everywhere. Along with the familiar scent of her perfume lingering in the air, a pale blue bathrobe was lying across the foot of the bed; a hairbrush, can of spray and bottle of lotion stood on the dresser, while house slippers sat on the floor near the nightstand.

"It's warm in here now." He stated the obvious.

Laughing, she carried the rose into the bathroom. "After you left, I turned the thermostat even higher.

I think I've overdone it a bit. But I live in the desert. I'm acclimatized to the heat."

"I can tell," he said with a chuckle.

She emerged from the bathroom carrying the rose in a drinking glass filled with water. But his attention was hardly on the flower. The night of the reception, she'd looked beautiful in a sophisticated way. Tonight, she looked downright sexy in a copper-colored sweaterdress that clung to her curves and brown leather boots that molded to her calves and stopped just short of her knees.

He tried not to stare as she placed the rose on the nightstand, then crossed to the thermostat and adjusted the dial.

"Seventy-five. That's as low as I'll go." She turned to face him. "Were you planning to eat here in the hotel restaurant? If not, I'll need my jacket."

"Better get it. I made reservations at a restaurant on down the river walk. Judging from the reviews I read, it's supposed to be good. But if it turns out rotten, I'll take the blame."

"I'm so hungry I think I could eat baked cardboard," she said as she opened the closet and pulled out a short leather jacket that matched her boots.

Stepping forward, Luke took the garment from her and held it behind her so that she could slip her arms into the sleeves. Once he'd smoothed the soft leather over her shoulders, his hands lingered there, while his thoughts went much further. He wanted to move closer, until her back was pressed to his front and he could reach around and cup her firm little breasts in his palms. But he couldn't do that. If he did, and if she was so minded to let him, they'd never see a bite of food for the rest of the night.

Clearing his throat, he said, "I might be able to stomach a little cardboard if I had a juicy steak to go with it."

She laughed, and Luke decided this was definitely going to be a night to remember.

Fortunately, the rain stopped long enough for them to walk the short distance to the restaurant. It was a small brick-front building with canvas awnings covering the plate-glass windows and two brass-and-wooden doors for an entrance.

A young hostess with pale blond hair and bright pink lips met them at the entrance of the foyer and ushered them past several square linen-covered tables until they reached a quiet corner located near one of the windows.

Once they were comfortably seated, a waiter appeared almost instantly with menus and Luke ordered glasses of wine for the both of them. After the waiter left to fetch their drinks, Luke removed his hat and jacket and placed them in the empty chair to his left.

"I think I'll keep my jacket on until I get warmed up," she told him. "If I lived this far north it would probably kill me."

Amused, he said, "Good thing you didn't go any

farther than Wickenburg. What made you stop there, anyway? I can't imagine you were looking for a cowboy town to settle down in."

"That wasn't a part of my agenda. I was searching for jobs and ran across the position at St. Francis Academy. It was exactly what I was looking for, so I sent in my résumé, and the rest is history. As far as Wickenburg goes, it is a rodeo town and very different from Southern California. But I quickly fell in love with the place," she said, while thinking she'd never expected him to look this good tonight.

The soft overhead lighting glistened on the raven-black waves of his hair and softened the hard angles of his face. His gray shirt was made of a nubby textured fabric that was both elegant and rugged and molded perfectly to his broad shoulders. The same bolo tie that he'd been wearing the night of the reception was pushed against the base of his throat and she couldn't help thinking how the lime-green stone was the perfect hue against his dark skin.

Stifling a sigh, she picked up the menu and tried to focus on the main entrées. Across the table, Luke followed her example, but barely skimmed the contents before he placed it back on the tabletop.

"No need for me to bother with that. I want steak and french fries. I'm not a fancy eater."

Amused, she said, "Then you hardly needed to bother bringing me to this place. We could've gone to a pizza joint or hot-dog stand."

"I'm not that cheap."

She chuckled. "Cheap has nothing to do with it. I love pizza and hot dogs. Don't you?"

"Yes, I do." A dimple carved his cheek. "Next time I'll consider your cheap suggestions."

Next time? She started to ask him if he was thinking the two of them would go out again before they left the city, but just then, the waiter arrived with their wine. By the time he'd taken their orders and left them a second time, the right moment for the question had passed.

"I wasn't expecting this place to have a nice view of the river walk." With his wineglass in hand, he looked toward the window where rivulets of rain were beginning to stream down the glass. "Too bad it's started to rain again."

Her gaze followed his. "I wouldn't say that. I love any chance to see the rain. It's so rare where we live."

"Same way at Clovis. Rain could get mighty scarce at times. And there wasn't much in the way of large rivers or lakes. West Texas is very dry, too."

She turned her gaze back to him. "Do you ever go back to Texas to see friends or family?"

He nodded. "A few times a year to see my dad. I used to have an aunt and uncle and a few cousins there, too. But they moved away. What about you? Do you go down to Palm Springs often?"

"Only in the summer when my work schedule is light."

He sipped his wine, then placed the glass back on the table. Not for the first time, Prudence's attention was drawn to his hands. His fingers were long, the nails clipped short. He wore no rings. Yet oddly enough, it was easy for her to picture a yellow wedding band on his left ring finger.

The idea of Luke being married was ludicrous. He didn't want that sort of life for himself. Not any more than she wanted it for herself.

He asked, "Are your parents retired?"

She did her best to concentrate on his question. "Mom is technically retired, but she does so much substituting for other teachers that she might as well be working full-time."

"She's a teacher, too?"

Prudence nodded. "High school science and chemistry. She really should be working in a lab somewhere. She loves doing experiments with chemicals and that sort of thing, but she loves kids more."

"And your dad?"

Prudence smiled fondly. "Dad will probably never retire. He's in the computer business. Setting up computers for all kinds of businesses, repairing—that sort of thing."

He studied her thoughtfully. "Your parents must be wealthy."

"Why do you say that?"

His chuckle made her question seem inane.

"They live in Palm Springs," he reasoned. "I've never been there, but I've heard about the place. For years it's been a resort for the rich and famous."

"That's true. But normal folks like my parents live

there, too. Mom and Dad are financially secure, but they're hardly a part of the jet set. Neither one is the lounging-by-the-pool sort."

He smiled at her description. "Then you must take after your parents, because I can't see you whiling your days away in a bikini, sipping a cold drink through a bent straw. You're not the fun type. Remember?"

Prudence laughed. "Luke, I think you've been watching too many old movies."

His gaze slowly roamed over her face, and her heart began to bang against her ribs with slow, heavy thuds.

He said, "I don't watch movies. But if you like them, we could go to the theater after dinner."

She took another sip of wine, then licked her lips. "Uh, no. I'm not big on movies. I'm more into books. What are you into?"

"Bed."

It was a good thing Prudence had already swallowed the sip of wine; otherwise, she'd probably be spewing it all over the table.

"Excuse me?"

He chuckled. "Yes, you heard right. I said *bed*. With a job like mine, a body needs plenty of rest. Something I rarely have a chance to get."

She eased back in her chair and studied him thoughtfully. "There've been times that Kat has talked about how hard her husband and brothers-in-law work. They put in ridiculous hours. Especially

Chandler and his veterinarian job. I sometimes wonder what makes you ranchers want to do what you do. Is it really worth the exhaustion?"

He shrugged. "I can't speak for the Hollisters, only myself. But it's something that's hard to explain. I guess, to put it in simple form, it's in my blood. I wouldn't be happy doing anything else."

"How did you happen to get hired by the Hollisters? Was that something you'd been wanting for a while— to have a job on Three Rivers?"

Frowning, he shook his head. "Not at all. Oh, I'd heard of Three Rivers, all right. Especially the horses that came from there. But I never dreamed about working there. You know the old saying about a man needing to know his limitations—well, I definitely knew mine. And my dreams didn't include living on a ranch like Three Rivers."

"Then how did you get from the T Bar T to Three Rivers? Had you put out an ad hunting for a new job?"

"Lord, no! I was content where I was. The people I worked for at the T Bar T were good, fair employers. It was nothing about being dissatisfied. One day I got a phone call from Tag O'Brien. He wanted to know if I'd be willing to talk with Holt about becoming his assistant. You could've knocked me over with a feather."

"Tag. He's the foreman at Three Rivers, right? The one who married Emily-Ann?"

"Right. You see, Tag and I were acquaintances

from way back when we both lived in Texas—not that far from each other, actually. We'd kept in touch over the years, and he knew I'd been working with horses all this time. He told Holt I was the one for the job. When you boil it all down, I guess Tag is the reason I'm living and working on Three Rivers now."

"Wow. He must be quite a friend," she commented.

"We didn't pal around together all the time. But we were buddies—sort of kindred spirits, I guess you'd say. He lost his mother at a fairly young age, too. We could relate."

She glanced down at the red liquid in her glass. "I heard he lost a wife and unborn child years ago when he lived back in Texas."

A stark expression suddenly stole over his features. "Yeah, he had a rough go of it. He was the last person I expected to see get married again and have a baby. But it seems to be the best thing that could've ever happened to him. I'm glad it turned out that way."

He just wouldn't be glad to follow Taggart's path. Even though he hadn't spoken the words aloud, his expression and the tone of his words said it clearly. Well, she could understand his way of thinking. She'd been through enough hell with Gavin to ever want to try marriage again. So why was she sitting here having dinner with the man? Even more, why had she kissed him? Why did she want to kiss him again? And again?

Because it had been so long since she'd let herself feel like a woman, she answered the self-imposed questions. Since her divorce, Luke was the first man who'd made her want to be close to him, touch him. The heady sensations she experienced whenever she was near him were so strong, they pushed the pain of the past into the far recesses of her mind.

She sipped the wine and waited for the tightness in her throat to subside before she replied. "I'm glad for Kat, too. She went through some really bad things before she married Blake. Now the two of them have three children and are very happy."

A lukewarm smile touched his lips. "Some people are lucky. They get second chances. While others never have a chance at all. But that's life. Isn't it?"

During the reception, he'd told her that he'd come close to marriage once and now he didn't want to be responsible for a woman's happiness. What had happened to end it all? Had he simply gotten cold feet about being tied down to one woman? Or had his lady love given him the heave-ho?

None of that had anything to do with now, she firmly told herself. And this was hardly the time to let her mind dwell on him loving a woman in the past. Nor did she want to think about how much she'd been hurt when she'd blindly believed in Gavin. Luke wasn't her ex. Just like she wasn't the woman he'd nearly married.

This time with Luke would never happen again,

she thought. And she didn't want to waste a moment of it.

With that thought in mind, she put a cheery smile on her face. "What were the chances of the two of us crossing paths again? I'd say we were lucky."

Surprise pushed up one black brow, and then as his gaze met hers, a grin slowly spread across his face.

"Oh, yeah. Very lucky." He reached across the table and clinked his glass against hers. "Let's toast to crossing paths—again."

The rain had stopped when the two of them eventually left the restaurant. Ragged clouds were skidding off to the south, exposing a few twinkling stars between the breaks. Cool wind shook the limbs of the juniper that landscaped the restaurant entrance, and Luke couldn't help but notice how Prudence had wrapped her arms around herself to ward off the shivers.

"I was going to ask if you were too cold to explore some of the river walk. But I can see that you are. We'll go straight back to the hotel, where you can get comfortable."

She shook her head. "Oh, Luke, I'm not that much of a fair-weather girl. I'd love to see some of the river walk. I'll get warmed up after we start walking."

"I'm glad. Let's see if this might help." He wrapped an arm around her shoulders and snugged her close to his side. "Better?"

"Much."

It definitely felt much better for him, Luke thought, as he steered her toward the nearest crosswalk. She felt incredibly soft and feminine, and just being able to touch her made everything around him seem more vibrant, every sound more intense; the scents in the air seemed fresher and sweeter. How could that be? If the moon were shining tonight, he supposed he could blame the change in him on being struck by a moonbeam. But there was no moon, only the precious sight of Prudence's face smiling back at him.

On the opposite side of the street, they took a short path that opened to a wide walkway edging the river. "Let's go in this direction," he suggested. "We've already seen the scenery from here back to the hotel."

"Sounds good," she agreed. "I'd enjoy getting closer to the water."

At this particular area of the Truckee River, a concrete balustrade separated the walkway from the water. Luke and Prudence leaned against it and stared out at the meandering river and the lights of the city beyond it.

"This is pretty," Luke commented.

His mild description produced a chuckle from Prudence. "Oh, Luke, it's more than that. It's gorgeous! I'm so glad we came down here."

Her eyes were twinkling, and for the first time since he'd met her, she appeared totally relaxed and carefree. "You must've forgotten about being cold," he said with a teasing grin.

"You've been sheltering me from the wind," she reasoned. "I feel perfectly warm."

Luke could've told her that his temperature had skyrocketed the moment he'd hugged her to his side. Which didn't make a lick of sense. He was a grown man, not a teenage boy with raging hormones. Merely putting his arm around a woman shouldn't be turning his insides to a raging furnace. But it was. And he could no more put any separation between the two of them than he could climb up on the balustrade and jump into the river.

"Isn't Reno called the biggest little city in the world, or something like that?" she asked.

Relieved to have her voice interrupt his wandering thoughts, he said, "Yes. Somewhere in town there's a sign that says as much. I haven't seen it yet. I haven't had time to do any sightseeing. We could do that together—tomorrow evening—if you like. That is, if you don't mind riding around in a truck."

"I'd love it," she said. "But what about your horse trailer? You might not want the hassle of pulling it through city traffic. I'll spring for a rental if that would make sightseeing easier."

"Thanks for the offer. But there's really no need. I left the trailer at the ranch where I'm going to view the stallions. The owners kindly offered to store it for me until I'm ready to head back to Arizona."

She looked curiously up at him. "Are you going to negotiate the deal if the horses turn out to be what Holt wants?"

"In a way. But I won't do anything until he consents to the animals and the price. And nothing can be decided until the horses are all vet checked and guaranteed to be sound. All of that is supposed to happen tomorrow and I'll need to be present. Holt wants to make sure a veterinarian is actually at the ranch, giving the horses a legitimate going-over. Just having a signed paper suddenly appear saying all is well isn't good business."

"I see," she murmured. "Sounds like you'll be busy for most of the day."

"Yes, but I should be finished well before dark," he said. "When will your seminar be over?"

"Four. Unless some of the speakers get long-winded. I'm praying that doesn't happen," she said, then laughed. "I'm sure I sound ungrateful to you. But I've been to so many of these seminars that after a while, it's like we're having a meeting just to see when we're going to have our next meeting."

He let out a hearty laugh. "Oh, that's a good one, Prudence."

She laughed with him. "Well, I don't want to sound like I know too much to learn, but all schools are different. Each one has to be managed and run in a way that fits it."

"In other words, it's not a cookie-cutter thing."

"Not at all. And I've been with St. Francis Academy long enough now that I've pretty much learned what works and what doesn't."

He urged her away from the balustrade, and as

they began to stroll on down the riverside, he said, "I'm curious about one thing—the male teachers. Ever have a problem with them?"

The dim pools of light shed from the lampposts lining the sidewalk were enough for him to see her face and the wry twist to her lips.

"Only the athletic director. He accuses me of catering to the fine arts. It's ridiculous. I try to make sure all subjects and extracurricular activities get equal funding. And I try extra hard not to let—uh, the problems I had with my ex influence my decisions about the athletic department."

Her ex. He hadn't wanted to think of him again. But since she'd brought it up, Luke could hardly ignore the elephant in the room.

"Why?" he asked. "Was he one of those brawn over brains?"

She sighed. "He was a football player in college with offers to go pro. The game was his whole life until an injury ended it all."

"Oh. Was that what caused your marriage to end, too?"

"That and other things," she said with a grimace.

"I see," he replied, even though he didn't. Not completely. But that private part of her life needed to stay with her. Just like his private life needed to stay with him. The more a person shared, the more tangled everything got, and he didn't want to be tangled up with anyone. At least, not emotionally.

He drew in a deep breath of the chilly wind. "So,

you don't have male teachers lined up at your office door, waiting to hit you up for a date?"

She let out a dainty snort. "Only the athletic director. Once in a while he asks me for a date, even though he knows I'm going to say no. And there used to be a geography teacher at St. Francis that I had lunch with from time to time. But those weren't dates. He was a nice gentleman in his sixties. But he moved back to California. I do miss him. I like older men. They're easier to talk to."

"Ouch. That leaves me out," he said with a chuckle.

She slanted him a coy smile. "I'm finding you easy to talk to. And I like you, Luke."

Her simple words drew him to her in a way that rattled every ounce of common sense he possessed. "That's good to know," he said gently. "Because I like you, too."

Spotting an empty park bench a few feet ahead of them, Luke guided her to the seat, then used his hand to brush away the rainwater. After they were settled on the slatted iron bench, he curved his arm around her shoulders.

"Just to make sure you don't get cold," he explained.

Smiling, she snuggled closer to his side. "Just to make sure I stay warm."

He laughed, and then because he couldn't help himself, he gently touched his fingers to her face.

Her expression turned earnest, and then her green-blue gaze delved deeply into his.

"Prudence."

Her name was the only word he could manage to push past his tight throat. Something was choking him, filling his chest with unrelenting pressure. And he decided if he didn't kiss her soon he was going to die from longing.

She must have read his thoughts, or maybe she was feeling the same desperate need that was gripping him. Either way, something had caused her face to suddenly draw near his, her lips parting with sweet invitation.

With a hand on her shoulder, he drew her forward, until his lips were on hers, tasting, searching, drawing on their sweetness. He'd never felt anything so soft and perfect. He'd never had a kiss take hold of his senses and spin them off to another world.

Somewhere beyond the rushing noise in his ears, he heard her moan, and then her arms curled around his neck, her mouth opening beneath his. He dared to touch the tip of his tongue to hers, and she responded by pushing hers between his teeth and sliding it across the ribbed roof.

In spite of the cold wind slapping at his back, flames were heating his insides and licking the edges of his brain. And in that moment he realized he wanted more from Prudence than just a heated kiss. He wanted everything from her. Every part of her.

She was the first to break away, and as she turned

her head aside and drew in deep, ragged breaths, Luke could only think about fastening his mouth back over hers.

"I—I don't know what got into me, Luke. I—"

The remainder of her words stopped abruptly as his thumb and forefinger wrapped around her chin and pulled her face back to his.

"I don't understand. You sound like kissing me is asking for trouble."

"Like that, it is," she said hoarsely.

He grimaced. "You mean kissing me with real desire? That's trouble?"

She nodded as a single tear slipped from her eye. The sight of it did more than confuse Luke; it tore a hole right through his chest.

He wrapped his hand around hers. "Why do you think it's wrong for you to feel passion for a man? That doesn't make sense, Prudence."

She blew out a frustrated breath. "It's wrong for me to invite problems into my life—to start something that can't be finished."

Can't be finished. Her remark should scare him away. He should politely walk her back to the hotel, thank her for keeping him company through dinner and then tell her goodbye. But he couldn't do that. He wanted her too much.

He cradled her face in his hands, his gaze delving into hers. "It isn't wrong to let yourself be human. To let yourself feel like a woman."

"Okay, maybe instead of saying it's wrong, I

should've said scary. Because I—don't do this kind of thing, Luke. I don't just follow my feelings. I have to be sensible."

Smiling gently, he pushed his fingers into her windblown hair and guided it away from her face. "When I kissed you in the hotel room, Prudence, I was trying to tell you that I wanted you. That being your friend isn't enough. I want to be your lover—until this fire between us burns out."

Her features tightened as she continued to stare into his eyes. "What happens then?"

"Then we happily go our separate ways. No strings or promises. No bitter recriminations. Just 'thank you for the beautiful memories.' And they will be beautiful, Prudence. I promise."

"No strings. No ties. No broken hearts." With each word she spoke, her face inched closer to his. "I think I can handle that. After all, we're two sensible people."

"I like to think so." Grinning, he slipped a hand to the back of her head and drew it forward until her mouth was touching his.

In a matter of seconds, the kiss deepened and Luke realized there was no turning back for either of them.

When he finally pulled his head back from hers, he rose from the bench and pulled her along with him.

"I think we should head back to the hotel," he murmured. "Don't you?"

"Yes."

During the walk back to the hotel, the wind cooled his heated body somewhat, but it wasn't nearly enough to wipe the urge to make love to her from his mind. And the closer they got to the hotel, the more he began to ask himself questions. Was she really ready to welcome him into her bed? Could it be that, deep down, she wasn't ready at all? And tomorrow she'd resent him for using this time away from home to seduce her? Or did he have that backward and she was seducing him?

Hell, none of that mattered, Luke thought crossly. Tomorrow could take care of itself. Tonight, the two of them deserved to make each other happy.

His whirling thoughts were interrupted as her hand reached over and wrapped snugly around his. The gentle contact caused him to glance at her face, and the smile she gave him looked like it could last forever.

But he didn't want forever, Luke reminded himself. He only wanted a few hours in her arms.

Chapter Five

Throughout the walk back to the hotel, Prudence expected a slice of reality to hit her. With each step she took, she anticipated common sense to push into her brain and remind her that she was headed straight toward a heartache. But nothing of the sort struck her. Instead, she was convinced she was floating rather than walking, and the only thing keeping her from soaring up to the clouds was Luke's strong arm curled around her shoulders.

Inside the hotel, they stepped onto the elevator and rode up to the fourth floor without any words spoken. But as far as Prudence was concerned, conversation between them was no longer necessary or needed. Throughout the evening, she'd felt something drawing them closer together. A smart woman would probably recognize that "something" as lust, but Prudence wasn't about to allow her brain to interfere tonight.

Earlier, before they'd left for dinner, she'd turned on a small night-light near the head of the bed. Now, as they entered her room and she dealt with securing the door latch, Luke walked through the semidarkness until he reached the window.

"Would you like for me to shut the drapes?" Luke asked.

Moving away from the door, she glanced across the room to where he stood, silhouetted by the view beyond the wide expanse of glass. The sky had begun to clear and the stars were twinkling high above the city lights, but the celestial splendor faded against his tall image.

"It's a beautiful view and no one is going to see us here in the dark," she answered. "Let's leave the drapes as they are."

She removed her jacket and tossed it on the back of an armchair. "There's a coffee machine over by the desk. Would you like a cup?"

He crossed the room to where she stood and shrugged out of his jean jacket. After tossing it next to hers, he removed his hat and placed it on a low table next to the chair.

Moving closer, she watched him slide a hand through his black hair. Everything about him was masculine, and she inwardly shivered with anticipation of having him touch her, of having his hard body next to hers.

Breathing deeply, she said, "There's tea, also. If you don't want coffee."

He turned around, and as their eyes met, a perceptive little grin tilted his lips.

"No tea. But if you're in the mood to celebrate, I can have room service bring us a bottle of champagne."

She didn't understand this sudden change that had come over her. She'd gone for years without being close to a man. Now here she was with Luke, uninhibited and feeling more of a woman than she could ever remember. Had Reno put a spell on her, or had Luke's brown eyes and the touch of his hand sprinkled her with moondust?

"That's a nice offer, Luke," she told him, "but I can think of a better way to celebrate. Can't you?"

A sexy chuckle rolled out of him as he reached for her and Prudence stepped willingly into his arms.

"About a thousand or more ways," he murmured. "And they all start right here."

He lowered his head toward hers, and Prudence was so hungry for his kiss that she rose on tiptoes and met his mouth halfway.

He tasted like rain, wind and man. The potent combination had a euphoric effect on her senses, and in a matter of seconds, she was mindlessly wrapping her arms around his waist and pulling herself tight against him.

They remained standing in that same spot as he kissed her again and again. And with each kiss, the intensity of his searching lips deepened, until heat was racing through her body, scorching her skin and lighting a fire in the deepest part of her.

At some point she felt his hands moving urgently against her back, until his fingers latched around both hip bones and pulled her forward. The bulge in his jeans pressed against the vee between her thighs, and the ache inside her grew to an unbearable point.

Finally, when she could no longer breathe, she pulled her mouth from his and gasped. "I think we need to—uh—"

"Get undressed?" he asked hoarsely.

With her eyes still tightly shut, she licked her throbbing lips. "That is the natural progression of things," she whispered. "Unless you've changed your mind—about wanting me."

He laughed under his breath, and the sound painted a picture in her mind of a wolf, happily circling his mate.

"No chance of that happening. And getting out of our clothes—yeah, that's a mighty natural thing." He plucked at the fabric of her dress. "How do you get in and out of this thing?"

"It pulls on and off."

He reached for the hem, and she lifted her arms to allow the garment to pass over her head. After he'd tossed the dress aside, he turned back to her, and Prudence's heart thudded faster and faster as his gaze slipped downward to her pale blue bra edged with brown lace. And farther still, to the matching half-slip that stopped at the middle of her thighs.

Moving closer, he stroked his fingertips along the edge of her bra cups. "Your skin is like satin, Prudence. I don't want the calluses on my hands to snag it."

The gentleness on his face brought a lump of sweet emotion to her throat, and with moisture stinging her eyes, she slipped out of her bra and reached for his hands. And when she placed them upon her breasts, she practically wanted to weep from the pleasure of feeling his warm fingers curling into the plump flesh, the rough skin of his palm rasping against her nipples.

"Oh, Luke, I'm not a piece of fragile glass that might shatter. I want you to touch me—everywhere."

"Everywhere. Yes." He pressed his lips to the middle of her forehead. "I—just don't want to hurt you."

"The only way you could do that is to not make love to me," she whispered.

Groaning, he placed a forefinger beneath her chin and lifted her mouth up to his. After a long, hungry kiss that left her head spinning, he pushed the slip down her legs and followed it with her panties.

Once he'd discarded the last of her clothing, she stepped out of her heels and stood to one side while he removed his tie, then moved on to the buttons on his shirt. As she watched the fabric slowly part to reveal a portion of his chest, she managed to tamp down the urge to grab him and finish the job. But by the time his fingers made it to the lower half of the shirt, her patience snapped and she reached for his wrist.

"Let me do it." The little half grin she gave him was warm and wicked. "I'm good with buttons."

He turned his wrist over in order to give her better access to the two buttons fastening the cuff. "Show me, beautiful."

She quickly dealt with the remaining buttons and then took great pleasure in pushing the heavy fabric off his shoulders. When the shirt fell to the floor, she didn't bother picking it up. She was too busy gliding her palms across his chest and down his ribbed abdomen.

"How many crunches a day do you have to do to look like this?" she asked. "A hundred? Two hundred?"

He chuckled. "I've never done a crunch in my life. I've never been in a gym in my life. Try riding and tugging on contrary horses all day, and you'll get plenty of exercise."

"Hmm. Maybe I do need to start riding." She dipped her head and slowly pressed a row of light kisses to the middle of his abdomen. "I need more muscle."

"The hell you do." Clasping his hands around both sides of her waist, he urged her backward toward the bed. When her legs bumped into the mattress, he lifted her onto the bed, then stood gazing down at her. "You're exactly the way you should be," he said, his voice rough with desire. "Soft and smooth and all woman."

The shadows of the room couldn't hide the glitter in his eyes or the slow, purposeful movements of his hands as he dealt with his belt and jeans. Just watching him was enough to send a rush of goose bumps over her arms and legs, and she wondered if he had any idea that her heart was beating wildly for him, that her body was aching for him.

When he'd finally stripped down to a pair of black boxers, he stretched out next to her on the wide mattress. Prudence rolled eagerly toward him, and he snaked an arm around her waist and tugged until the front of her body was pressed tightly to his.

All at once, she was flooded with sensations. The heat of his skin sliding against hers, the hardness of his muscled body, the masculine scent of him swirling around her head and filling her nostrils.

Pushing her fingers into the hair at his temple, she whispered, "I can't believe we're here like this— together. It's like a dream."

He cupped a hand at the back of her head and drew it forward until his lips were hovering over hers. "It's real, Prudence. Very real."

His breath was warm against her lips and cheeks, and she instinctively closed her eyes against the erotic sensations sweeping over her.

"Show me."

* * *

Only too glad to comply, Luke settled his mouth over hers, and as he began to kiss her, he forgot everything. All he knew was that if he stayed here all night with his lips plundering hers, his hands roaming the soft curves of her body, it wouldn't be nearly long enough.

Her fingertips made looping trails up and down his arms, across his chest and abdomen, then up the side of his neck. The feathery contact ignited a fire deep in his gut and caused heat to radiate through his whole body.

When the need for air finally forced him to end the contact of their lips, he rolled her onto her back and gazed down at her breasts. Small, but perfectly rounded, and the nipples were the color of a pale pink rose and presently puckered into two hard buds.

"I knew you'd be this perfect," he whispered. "This beautiful."

"No, Luke." Her voice was slightly choked. "You don't have to say that sort of thing to please me."

Chuckling, he lowered his head and touched the tip of his tongue to one nipple. "I'm not trying to please you. Not with words. I'm stating a fact."

She groaned. "I'm small."

"To match the rest of you."

He pulled the tip of her breast into his mouth and rolled his tongue around the peak. Beyond the rushing noise in his ears, he heard her moan and felt her fingers dig into his back. And when his mouth moved to the other breast, her thighs opened and her legs wrapped around his.

She wanted him. Maybe as much as he wanted her. The realization was like an accelerant poured on a wildfire, and though he wanted to take his time and explore every precious inch of her, the incredible pressure in his body was telling him he didn't have time for such a luxury.

Forcing his mouth away from her breast, he moved back to her lips and kissed her deeply, before he finally broke the contact and slipped off the bed. "I think—uh—I'd better take off my boxers," he explained.

With her gaze hungrily watching him, he stepped out of the underwear. And then it suddenly dawned on him. He wasn't carrying any condoms in his wallet. Why in hell would he be? He hadn't had sex with a woman in ages. And he hadn't come to Reno expecting anything like this to happen.

Groaning, he turned back to Prudence, and the look on his face must have mirrored his despair, because she suddenly sat straight up in the middle of the bed.

"What's wrong?"

By now, his erection was throbbing painfully, and it was all he could do to answer her through clenched teeth. "I—uh—just now remembered I—don't have any condoms."

"If that's the problem, you need to quit worrying. I'm protected."

He stared at her in wonder. "You are? How?"

She wrapped a hand over his forearm and pulled him down next to her. "I've been on oral contraceptives for years. Not for this reason, but to keep my cycles regular. There's no need for you to worry. Unless you're concerned about problems other than pregnancy. But I promise you, Luke, I'm perfectly healthy. I haven't had sex with a man for thirteen years."

Amazed by her admission, he stared at her for a long moment. "Thirteen years! No!"

Even in the semidarkness, he could see hot color splash across her cheeks.

"Why do you think that's strange?" she asked. "After my divorce, there just hasn't been anyone I wanted to get *that* close to."

The ache in his loins was momentarily forgotten as he eased down beside her on the bed and gathered her hand in his. "That's the part I don't understand, Pru. All that time—surely there was a man you wanted."

Grimacing, she shook her head. "I imagine you're thinking I'm frigid."

Even though he tried his best to stop it, a short laugh burst out of him. "Sorry, Pru. But I see you as a firecracker. Not a cube of ice."

Her lower lip trembled as she attempted a smile. "Well, I haven't exactly been cold toward men. More like bitter and suspicious."

Luke studied her somber face and wondered what

she was trying to tell him. That her divorce had caused her to turn away from all men. Until tonight? Luke didn't want to think she'd put such importance on him. He didn't want to think she might be developing any sort of tender feelings for him. All he wanted was for her to like him. And maybe admire him, just a little. A bit of respect wouldn't hurt, either. But not love. No. He didn't want to go there.

He released a long breath. "And now?"

Her chuckle was full of provocative promises. "You're different, Luke. You have a melting effect on me."

Her casual response was exactly what he needed to hear, and with a hand on her shoulder, he urged her back against the mattress. "Melting, huh? I think I like that, Pru. Let's see if I can melt your last bit of ice away."

Her arms slipped around him and pulled until he was partially lying across her.

"The ice has already turned to water," she said. "And it's close to boiling."

He shifted around until he could angle his face close enough to press tiny kisses across her cheeks and the bridge of her nose. "Mmm. You're good for my ego. Too good."

With a hand against his jaw, she guided his mouth down to hers, and Luke was more than happy to kiss her. But when her tongue thrust between his teeth and her lower body shifted so that the vee between her thighs was pressed against his erection, it was a struggle to hang on to his control.

When he finally managed to disengage his mouth from hers, he pulled in a deep breath and said, "If you're worried about us having sex without a condom—I've never had unprotected sex with any woman."

"Does it look like I'm worried?"

He lifted his head back far enough to allow his gaze to slip over her face, and the desire he saw burning in her eyes nearly took his breath away. "No. Oh, Pru, you're beautiful. So beautiful."

She cradled his face with her hands, and with their gazes locked, he slipped his hand between her thighs and stroked the dampness waiting for him.

She moaned, her hips lifting toward his searching fingers. He slipped them inside and continued to stroke her slowly, gently, until she was writhing beneath him and his body was throbbing for release.

Finally, when he thought he could no longer bear the fiery ache gripping his loins, he started to withdraw his hand, but she grabbed his wrist and pleaded in a guttural voice.

"No! Luke, you—"

"Pru, I—have to. I—"

Before he could say more, her whole body suddenly went rigid, and then she was crying his name over and over like a spellbound chant.

Watching her, seeing the undulating waves of pleasure passing through her, was like nothing he'd ever experienced before. He was amazed that he'd given her that much and amazed even more that he'd somehow managed to contain himself through it all. But as soon as he felt her body go limp with relief, he parted her thighs and drove himself into her.

By then, he was totally mindless. All he knew was that he was finally inside her and the warmth of her body was surrounding him, cocooning him with sensations so full and rich he felt blinded by them.

Considering what she'd just experienced, he didn't expect her to immediately respond to his thrusts. But he was wrong. Her hips arched eagerly toward his; her arms wrapped tightly around his waist. After that, Luke was lost to her and all that mattered was their heated dance and the incredible pleasure that was swamping his body and mind.

Five minutes could've passed, or maybe it was an hour. He didn't know, nor did it matter. Suddenly, the rhythm of their union had grown to a frantic pace. His lungs were burning for oxygen and his heart felt like a sledgehammer pounding against his chest.

Certain he was going to die from the longing, he clutched Prudence close and continued to climb toward that special place where relief was waiting for the both of them.

Before Prudence ever opened her eyes, she realized she was drenched in sweat. Damp clumps of hair were plastered to one cheek, while the other cheek was pressed against the mattress. If a fire alarm suddenly sounded out in the hallway, she doubted she could move off the bed, much less find enough energy to dash from the room.

Peeking between the strands of hair, she turned her gaze on the view beyond the plate glass. The stars were still glittering against the night sky, and beneath them the lights of the city burned brightly. After what had just occurred between her and Luke, it was hard to imagine that the world around her hadn't changed.

Making love to Luke had been a cosmic, mind-shattering experience. What did it mean? That all these years without a man had left her sex-starved? Or did it mean there was a connection between them that could only be described as beautifully special?

Rolling onto her side, she cushioned her cheek on the palm of her hand and gazed across the short space to where his head rested on the edge of a pillow.

Hanks of black hair were scattered across his forehead, while his eyelids were half-lowered over his brown eyes. He looked as sweaty as she felt and his chest was still rising and falling at a rapid pace. He was the most beautiful specimen of a man she'd ever seen, and just looking at him filled her with renewed desire.

"What are you thinking?" she asked drowsily.

"I'm wondering if I'm still alive. Am I?"

She scooted toward him until her hand could rest comfortably against his back. "Feels like you're breathing."

"Hmm. I was afraid my lungs had quit working."

She smiled. "I thought everything about you worked spectacularly."

That brought his eyes wide open. "You don't know much about men, do you?"

Amused, she said, "I think you'd better explain that question."

"It means you shouldn't put me on a list of best lovers. I'm not very imaginative or, for that matter, skilled."

Her gaze slipped over his face as she tried to decide whether he was joking or serious.

She tossed the question he'd thrown at her back to him. "You don't know much about women, do you?"

"I'll admit I've not known that many."

She sighed again, only this time it was more from frustration. "Then you don't understand that when a man makes love to her, a woman isn't concerned about skilled techniques. At least, this woman isn't."

He rolled onto his side and propped up his head so that he could look down at her. "What do you want from him?"

"Honesty. And his actions to be guided by this." She tapped his chest. "Not by his equipment below."

His brows pulled together as he traced a finger over her cheek. "Sometimes that's—asking a lot from a man."

"I understand that. Why do you think it's been thirteen years since I've been in bed with one?"

His head moved slightly back and forth before

a half grin lifted a corner of his lips. "Not because you're frigid. I can attest to that."

His reply was all it took to make her laugh, and as she pressed her cheek against the middle of his chest, she realized she'd never felt this alive or sexy or wanted. And no matter what the consequences might be, she didn't want this night to end. Or this time in his arms to be the last.

The next afternoon, Luke stood beneath the eaves of a large horse barn and tried to drown out the loud noise of nickering and squealing by pressing the cell phone closer to his ear. "Hey, Holt, did you get the pics I sent?"

"Sure did. All were clear and close enough to give me good detail."

"And? What did you think of the three stallions?"

"To be honest, I liked all of them."

Luke made a mental fist pump. Anytime Luke's views on horses matched Holt's, it meant he was right on target. "I'm relieved. Because I liked all three, too. Especially the big bay. To be a stud, he's a sweetheart. Actually, all three have nice dispositions. The palomino is a bit unruly, but you can't blame him. The ranch's breeding season has started, and there are several mares stalled just down the barn from him."

"We can deal with a little unruly. And his gold color is an added plus. I'm not all that excited about the sorrel. He's a looker, all right. But I wish he was at least one hand taller. And I'm not wild about his cutting-horse breeding. The demand for them has gone down, while the request for roping horses has skyrocketed."

"Hmm. Do you want to know what I think?"

"That's what I hired you for."

Luke smiled to himself. When he first went to Three Rivers, he never dreamed that working with Holt would be like working with a brother. But, incredibly, it had turned out that way. And sometimes Luke had to pinch himself to remember his good fortune wasn't all a dream.

"Okay then, I think the sorrel will throw some dandy babies. And there are plenty of people who like short horses. Easier to get on and shorter the fall to the ground."

Holt laughed. "Yeah, but he's pricey. I have to explain these costs to Blake, you know. He's the man with the ink pen."

"I realize he's pricey. But I figure the stallion will make that back and more with his first round of foals. Besides, the horse division makes Three Rivers tons of money and Blake isn't blind. He knows that you're the reason for its success."

Holt laughed. "Okay, Luke, no need for you to spread it on. You've sold me on the little sorrel. Now, what about the vet checks?"

"The man has been here for the last four hours putting all three of them through the tests. I think he's about to wrap things up, though," Luke informed him. "He wants to go over all the X-rays at his clinic tomorrow before he puts his final stamp on the health papers."

"That's fine with me," Holt said. "As long as you don't mind having to stay another day in Reno."

Thank God for meticulous veterinarians, Luke thought. He'd have one more night with Prudence and a few more hours of paradise.

"Uh—I don't mind at all. Reno is beautiful. And there are plenty of—things to keep me occupied."

Holt chuckled knowingly. "Yeah. Hope you have luck at the casinos. Play a hand of blackjack for me. We'll split the winnings."

Luke started to inform him that he wouldn't be using the extra time in Reno to gamble. But he didn't want to give Holt any excuse to question him further. Not for any reason would he reveal that he'd incidentally run into Prudence. Or that he hadn't been able to keep his hands off her.

Turning the phone aside, he drew in a deep breath and let it out before he said, "Sure, Holt. I'll do that. And I'll call you tomorrow after I get the final results from the vet. Hopefully I'll be bringing all three back to Three Rivers."

At the same time Luke was inspecting the horses, Prudence was in a hotel convention room, sitting around a long, polished table with dozens of other teachers. At the front of the room, a man with a receding hairline and silver-rimmed glasses was speaking about the necessity of having fundraisers throughout the school year. The message was about as enlightening as watching a snail make its way across a lump of garden soil, and she was having to fight to keep her attention on his words.

To be fair to the poor guy behind the lectern, Prudence had been struggling to keep her mind off Luke and the incredible night she'd spent with him.

This morning, when the alarm had sounded, she'd expected to open her eyes and find herself still wrapped in Luke's warm arms. Instead, there had been a note propped on the pillow explaining that he'd had to be at the ranch early this morning to deal with the stallions and that he'd see her this evening.

She'd appreciated the fact that he'd left a note, yet she wished he would've woken her before he'd left her room. If for no other reason than to kiss her goodbye.

But then one kiss might have led to another, she thought dreamily. And half the morning might've been gone before either of them realized they were going to be late for their meetings.

Releasing a long sigh, she forced herself to stare at the speaker, but she was neither seeing nor hearing the man. Her mind was consumed with Luke and the way it had felt to have his lips plundering hers, his hands sliding over her bare skin, his manhood driving into her with hungry, powerful thrusts.

How had their relationship developed so rapidly? How had she gone from telling herself she was never going to see him again, to inviting him into her bed, to making love to him more than half the night? Moreover, why wasn't she feeling any regrets?

Because, for once, since her divorce all those years ago, she felt truly desirable and deep-down happy. Two things she'd believed she might never experience again. She didn't regret anything. She only wished the afternoon would speed up so that she could finally be with Luke again.

"Miss Keyes, since you are the administrator of a private school with tuitions, you might want to address the subject of fundraising from a different angle."

Had someone spoken her name?

From a far distance, she mentally shook herself and looked up to see every single person at the table staring straight at her.

Heat spilled into her cheeks and she glanced help-lessly at the older woman sitting next to her. "Uh, I'm terribly sorry. Did someone ask me a question?"

The woman gave her a conspiring wink and spoke under her breath. "Your thoughts on fundraising."

"Thank you. I guess my hearing isn't so good today."

The silver-haired lady smiled with understand-ing. "Mine never is when I come to Reno, sweetie."

Prudence cleared her throat, and for the next few minutes, she answered questions about raffles, bake sales and every other fund drive St. Francis Academy implemented throughout the year. But as soon as the conversation shifted from Prudence to a middle-aged man at the far end of the table, her focus splintered. Before she could stop herself, she was checking her wristwatch and wondering how much longer she'd be stuck at this meeting. And once she got back to the hotel, would Luke be there waiting for her?

You're not behaving like a school superintendent, Prudence. More like a school student. You're letting yourself be romanced by a man who doesn't even pretend to have a serious thought about you! What do you think is going to happen when you go back home to Wickenburg? Nothing, that's what. He'll go his way and you'll go yours. And this brief time with him won't mean anything.

Yes, it would mean something, Prudence silently argued with the taunting voice in her head. It meant that Gavin's betrayal hadn't robbed her of everything. She could still feel and want, and experience the passion that every woman deserved in her lifetime. And even if this special time with Luke only lasted a day or two, she couldn't regret it.

Chapter Six

Luke was sitting near the hotel lobby's fireplace when he glanced around to see Prudence stepping off the elevator. She was dressed in blue jeans, a white button-up shirt and cowboy boots. The top part of her hair was clasped at the crown of her head with a barrette while the rest of her honey-brown mane flowed loose against her back. Was this really Prudence?

Rising from the chair, he met her halfway across the lobby.

"What's wrong?" she asked the minute he took hold of her hand. "You're staring at me!"

Bending his head, he planted a kiss on her cheekbone. "I'm staring because you look so different. I didn't know you owned a pair of jeans or cowboy boots!"

Chuckling, she looped her arm through his. "Oh, I pretend at being a cowgirl once in a while. Especially when I have dinner with Kat and her family at Three Rivers. But that's not very often."

"You look—very sexy. I like."

The smile she gave him was sunny enough to heat the coldest heart, and Luke didn't have to glance around the room to see a few male gazes had followed her. The notion made him wonder for the umpteenth time how she'd avoided men for all these years. Even more, why had she taken a second look at him? Why had she melted in his arms and given him so much of herself? The questions shouldn't be nagging at him. None of it should even matter. But it did, damn it.

"Thanks. I thought since we were going to be out and about town this evening, I needed to be comfortable and warm," she added impishly. "Have you been waiting long?"

"No. Five minutes at the most."

She glanced at him from beneath a veil of dark lashes. "I thought you might change your mind and come up to my room to fetch me."

A wry grin slanted his lips as he urged her toward the entrance of the hotel. "We would've never stepped a foot out the door."

She laughed lightly. "You're probably right. And then I'd be in trouble with Kat. I promised her that

I'd look the city over and give her a report. She's thinking she'd like to get Blake up here on a little getaway vacation."

Luke shook his head. "I'm afraid she'll have her work cut out for her. I can't imagine Blake taking any kind of vacation. Does the man ever let up?"

"He gets away from the ranch once in a while. But only for Kat's sake. You know, when his dad died he had to take over management of Three Rivers. It was a huge responsibility and I think it's made him driven. The ranch has been in existence since around 1849. If the place faltered under his management, Blake would be letting his whole family down. Not to mention the Hollister legacy."

"I honestly don't think I could handle that sort of weight on my shoulders."

"Neither could I."

"Wrong, Pru. You have the weight of a whole school with hundreds of children on your shoulders."

"Not really. There's a board of directors that makes the major decisions regarding St. Francis."

He opened one of the glass doors and followed her onto the concrete portico covered by a green canvas awning. "I hope you don't mind walking a bit. I had to park my truck on down the street."

"Not at all. After being stuck in meetings all day, this feels wonderful."

Luke could've told her that it felt wonderful to have her at his side. That having her company gave him more pleasure than anything or anyone had ever given him. But what would be the point? Tomorrow would probably be the last time they'd be together like this. No. It would most likely be the last time they'd ever be together. The thought was disheartening, but he reasoned that parting on friendly terms would be much better than ripping each other apart later.

"I've come to a decision," he told her as he guided her from beneath the awning and on down the sidewalk.

"What sort of decision?"

"That you're going to choose where we eat dinner tonight."

Her eyes twinkled as she smiled up at him and said, "Really? Anything I want?"

"Absolutely. My treat, of course. Uh—no, I need to correct that. Holt's treat. He's paying for all the expenditures of this trip. It's business, you see."

She laughed. "Poor Holt. If he only knew that you're up here in Reno kicking up your heels."

"Ha! He thinks I'm going to be gambling in my spare time."

Another chuckle joined her last one. "You are, aren't you? Gambling that you're not wasting your whole evening on an old schoolteacher?"

He curved his arm around the back of her shoulders. "You're a funny girl, Pru. Has anyone ever told you that?"

"No one ever calls me *girl*. Or *funny*. And definitely not in the same sentence."

Laughing again, he squeezed her shoulders. "See, you are funny."

She glanced up at him, and the tender amusement he saw on her face plucked at something deep in his chest, and it was all he could do to keep from pulling her into his arms and kissing her right there on the sidewalk.

"Maybe you make me that way," she suggested. "And regarding dinner, I've decided I want a chili dog, fries and a cola. And after all that, if I'm not too full, I'll have an ice cream cone dipped in chocolate."

He made a sound of disapproval with his tongue. "Aw, what extravagance."

"Before we leave Reno, you're going to learn I'm high-maintenance," she joked.

No, he thought, he was going to learn how hard it was going to be to live without her.

Much later that night, after the fast food and a major tour of the city, Prudence lay in the curve of Luke's body, her cheek resting on his upper arm as she stared pensively at the star-filled sky beyond the hotel window.

Making love to Luke was like flying among those stars, she thought, and she knew with brutal certainty that no other man could ever make her feel like this. All day she'd been telling herself that having him for this short time was far better than no time at all. And yet each time she pictured him driving away

Sunday morning and her boarding a flight, she felt lost and bereft.

"You've gone quiet, Pru. Are you asleep?"

She loved that he'd started calling her *Pru*. Silly or not, the shortened name made her feel as though she was special to him.

"No. I'm looking at the stars and wondering why they appear brighter up here than at home. Is it because Reno is farther away from the equator than Wickenburg?"

"Nothing so scientific. They look different because you're seeing them with me," he teased.

"Awww, such cheese."

He nuzzled his nose against the back of her neck at the same time his hand made a raspy journey up and down her bare hip. "Mmm. I love cheese. Especially pepper jack."

Groaning, she shifted so that she was facing him. "I'm not surprised. It's obvious you have a hot streak in you."

He gently pushed his fingers into her hair, and Prudence imagined him stroking a horse, calming it with the low, steady sound of his voice. The notion led her mind to Three Rivers and how nice it would be to watch him at work in the training arena. But she didn't expect him to ever invite her to the ranch or share his work with her.

Over the last two days, it had become clear to her that Luke didn't want this time with her to extend beyond Sunday, the day both of them would be leaving Reno. So far, he hadn't suggested or even hinted that once the two of them were home in Arizona, they should get together for a meal or simply to keep in touch. But then, she hadn't made any suggestions to him, either.

"When I first met you at Maureen and Gil's reception, I thought you were cool—and a bit prim," he admitted.

Amused by that idea, she let out a low laugh. "Did you honestly think that?"

One corner of his lips cocked upward. "Maybe you don't realize it, Pru, but you have the aura of a princess."

She laughed again. "Only in your imagination. I'm not cool or prim. And I'm hardly a member of a monarchy."

"That's good. Otherwise, you wouldn't be fraternizing with a commoner like me."

Smiling smugly, she curled her arms around his neck and settled the front of her body next to his. "You called me a funny girl, but you're the funny one, Luke. There isn't one common thing about you."

His hand roamed slowly against her back. "You don't really know me, Pru. My brother and I grew up not having much more than the essentials. Dad worked hard to give us those. He scrimped and saved to help put us through college. Everything he's ever done was for his wife and two sons. I don't know what loving a child would be like. But I can't imagine being as giving and loving as Dad has always been."

She tilted her head back to study his face. "What about your mother? Did she help with the financial needs?"

He let out a long breath. "She tried. I couldn't recount all the different odd jobs she had when Colt and I were kids. Something would always happen and she'd either get fired or bored and move on to something else. She—uh—just wasn't a grounded person. Dad always said she lived in the present and was incapable of considering tomorrow."

"Oh. That must've caused a few problems."

"Yeah. More than a few. But the accident ended all of that."

"Did you love her?"

His brows arched upward as he regarded her question. "Of course I loved her. She was my mom and she was good to me and Colt. I only wish things could've been different for her—for all of us."

"I wish things had been different for all of you, too."

His lips twisted into a resigned slant. "Well, everyone has something from their past to bear. How a person stands up beneath the weight of it is what counts. Don't you think?"

Prudence had plenty of albatrosses she was carrying from the past, and for a long time she hadn't dealt with them in a wise way. Funny how meeting Luke and getting close to him had opened her eyes to her shortcomings.

"I do think so." With a playful smile, she added,

"And right now I think we should call room service. My hot-dog dinner has worn off."

Chuckling, he cupped a hand against the side of her face. "Forget room service. In a little while we'll get dressed and go get another hot-dog supper."

"A little while? Why not now?"

He lowered his mouth onto hers. "At this moment, my sweet little Pru, I have a different kind of hunger to feed."

Prudence sipped strong coffee from a thick red mug and forced herself to focus on the expenditure list on the computer screen. New choir robes for the music department, a food warmer for the serving line in the lunch room, updated computers for the science lab…

The list went on, but Prudence quit reading as her mind slipped back to early yesterday morning. Luke had insisted on driving her to the airport to catch her flight, and throughout the short trip, she'd thought he might tell her how much he'd enjoyed the past few days with her. A small part of her had even believed he might suggest they see each other again. But she'd been wrong. He'd remained unusually quiet, and not knowing how to deal with him or the awkward situation, Prudence had kept her thoughts to herself and prayed that she didn't do something foolish in front of him, like cry.

Thankfully, when he'd pulled to a stop near the terminal entrance, he hadn't prolonged the agony of parting. Instead, he'd kissed her deeply and wished her a safe trip home. There'd been no promises or suggestions of seeing her again, and she'd followed his example.

When she'd slipped out of his arms and walked away, a foolish lump had collected in her throat and tears had stung her eyes. But she'd forced those sentimental feelings aside, and throughout the flight home, she'd reminded herself that she was a mature and reasonable woman. The brief time she'd spent with Luke had been incredible, but it was over and she had to forget. She had to return to her real life.

A brief knock on the open door of her office jerked Prudence from her glum thoughts, and she glanced up to see Katherine entering with a stack of manila folders balanced in the crook of one arm. Tall and regal in a black pencil skirt and white shirt, the woman looked fresh and lovely. A marvel, considering it was Monday morning and she'd probably spent most of the weekend chasing after her three-year-old twins, along with seeing after a teenage son and very busy husband.

Prudence inclined her head toward the bundle in her arm. "What is all of that?"

Katherine shot her a hopeless look. "Pru, don't tell me you've forgotten. These are all those old files you wanted me to store on computer. I finally finished them. Now, do you want the paper files back in the cabinets? Or do you want them shredded?"

Prudence had to think hard before she finally

remembered asking Katherine to tackle the task. "Sorry, Kat. I had forgotten about those. Just shred the paper ones."

Still holding on to the folders, Katherine sat down in one of the heavy wooden chairs in front of Prudence's desk and let out a long sigh. "Why do people go crazy on Mondays? Ever since I walked into my office this morning, the phone has been ringing nonstop. I've put off everything I thought was unnecessary. The rest are waiting for your return calls. One is a teacher from the seminar in Reno. He was impressed with the way you deal with parent-teacher day here at St. Francis and wants to discuss something about it with you."

Prudence waved a dismissive hand. "I barely spoke on the matter."

"Apparently, what little you said hit a home run. Or maybe the man just wants a reason to talk?" Katherine asked with a coy wink.

Prudence came close to groaning out loud. If Katherine had any idea how she'd spent her free time, especially the nights, in Reno, she'd probably be shocked. Or would she?

She glanced at Katherine. "Nothing of the sort. That man is as serious as a judge."

Katherine let out a short, scoffing laugh. "Plenty of people used to describe Blake in just that way. But I can let you in on a little secret—even judges like beautiful women."

Beautiful. Each time Luke had called her that, she'd felt special and warm and wanted. Now it hurt to remember how his raspy voice had sounded when he murmured the word to her. The memories were too raw and real. Hopefully, after a bit of time had passed, she'd be able to look back and smile on their time together. But how much later? When she was too old to care whether she had a man in her life or babies of her own?

"Oh, for Pete's sake, there's nothing remarkable about my looks," she said a bit crossly. Then, easing back in the plush executive chair, she turned a skeptical gaze on her secretary.

"Uh—Kat—this question is probably going to sound crazy to you, but—did you choose the hotel where I stayed in Reno for a specific reason?"

"Certainly. It had great amenities, and judging by the pics on the website, it looked like the place had a quaint, Old Western feel to it. I thought you'd enjoy that sort of thing more than a sterile, modern place." A faint frown pulled her brows together. "Why? You didn't like the hotel?"

Sighing, Prudence wiped a palm against her forehead. She'd slept very little last night. In between fitful dozes, she'd thought about Luke, about what his future would bring. And how hers was already mapped out. Everything about her life revolved around this office and her work. The idea had never left her as sad as it did at this moment.

"Don't worry. Everything about the hotel was exceptional. You're a gem, Kat, for taking pains with my travel plans and making sure I'd be comfortable."

Katherine shrugged. "Then I don't get it. Why did you ask about the hotel?"

Biting down on her bottom lip, Prudence glanced beyond Katherine's shoulder to a wide window that overlooked a part of the school campus. The green grass was clipped to a perfect height, the sidewalk edged with blooming flowers. In the middle of the lawn, on a tall white pole, Arizona's state flag was flying beneath the nation's Stars and Stripes. The view had always filled Prudence with pride and a sense of fulfillment, but today she wasn't feeling like her normal self. Moreover, she was beginning to wonder if her life would ever go back to what it was before she'd met Luke.

"I, uh— Nothing. I was just curious, that's all."

"You're a lousy liar, Pru. When you're not being totally honest, your cheeks turn pink and your lips squish at the corners."

"Ha! I'll try to remember that the next time I'm trying to lie my way out of a speeding ticket."

Katherine let out a short laugh. "You've never gotten a speeding ticket in your entire life."

"There's always a first time," Prudence said dryly, then picked up a pencil and tapped the eraser against the mouse pad on her desk. "So, you're telling me that you didn't know anything about Holt buying horses up at Reno?"

The blank look on Katherine's face made Prudence wish she'd kept her mouth shut. But in the end, what did it matter if her friend knew that she and Luke had run into each other in Reno? It didn't. Because nothing would ever come of it.

"Why, no. Did you run into Holt up in Reno?" Katherine asked with a thoughtful frown.

Prudence let out a long breath. "I'm sorry, Kat. I guess my imagination got to running away with me. I was thinking that maybe you or Blake or Holt was trying to play Cupid or something. Because the whole thing was—just too much of a coincidence."

Katherine leaned forward. "Cupid? What are you talking about?"

Prudence started to reply when the phone on her desk rang. Katherine reached over and picked up the receiver.

"Ms. Keyes's office." After a brief pause, she handed the phone to Prudence and mouthed the words "Mr. Gaynor, from the board."

Three minutes later, Prudence hung up the phone and did her best to smile. "It's nice to get good news once in a while. He's found a contractor willing to do the gymnasium floor at a much lower price," she said, then with a wry shake of her head, added, "Kat, sometimes I feel like everything but a teacher. I re-

member a time when I loved being in the classroom—
actually teaching."

"I thought you always wanted to be a superintendent."

Shrugging, she rose and walked over to the window. "Not always. I mostly came to that decision
after my divorce." Hating the pensive sound to her
voice, she attempted to laugh. "I think you know
firsthand how those things tend to change a person's
plans. But don't get me wrong—I'm happy being a
superintendent."

"You don't seem too happy today."

Prudence glanced over at her friend. "You couldn't
be more wrong. I'm perfectly fine."

"Okay," Katherine said. "Then I want to go back
to our earlier conversation before the phone inter-
ruption. What is this thing about the hotel in Reno
and Holt buying horses?"

Prudence pursed her lips. "I shouldn't have said
anything. But it struck me this morning that you
might have known about Luke being in Reno. After
all, Blake would know about Holt's plans to send
Luke up there."

A blank look came over Katherine's face. "Luke
was in Reno while you were there?"

Damn, she should have kept her mouth shut! Katherine clearly hadn't known about Luke. Now she had
to give her some sort of explanation.

"Yes. He was staying at the same hotel. We, uh—bumped into each other in the lobby."

"Wow! That is a coincidence. Blake hadn't mentioned anything about the trip. You say he was up there to buy horses?"

Prudence nodded. "For Holt. Stallions for Three Rivers."

"Hmm. I'm surprised Holt trusted him with something so important. But on the other hand, he seems to always be praising his new assistant. And Holt doesn't often hand out praise for anyone."

"Apparently, the man is an expert on horses. But I wouldn't know about that."

Katherine studied her closely. "You did talk with him, didn't you?"

Fearful that she might look like a lovesick puppy or worse, she turned her face back toward the window. "Oh, yes. We talked. We even had dinner together."

There. That was enough, Prudence told herself. She'd admitted that she and Luke had spent a little time together. That was enough of a confession.

Behind her, Katherine remained quiet for so long that Prudence finally glanced over her shoulder. The clever smile on the other woman's face made the empty feeling inside Prudence widen to a deep, dark gorge.

In a sly tone, she said, "Dinner together. I'm shocked you agreed to go out with him. But I'm glad. Did you have a good time?"

A good time? A hysterical laugh came close to bursting out of Prudence and probably would have if she hadn't hurried over to the desk and gulped down several swigs of coffee.

"It was—enjoyable."

"That's all you have to say? Are you going to see each other again?"

Darn it, Prudence had gone into the brief affair with Luke knowing it was only for three short days. Now that the time had ended, she shouldn't be feeling lost or dejected. In Katherine's words, she'd had a good time. And that was more than she'd ever expected to have.

Unable to look Katherine in the eye, she fixed her gaze on a spot across the room. "No. We both agreed that wouldn't be wise."

"Really? Why? You two just didn't click?"

If they'd clicked any more, the hotel room would've probably ignited with flames, Prudence thought.

"We got along fine. But he's not wanting to start up anything serious. And you already know that I don't want a man in my life—especially on a permanent basis. The two of us seeing each other again would be—well, fruitless."

Groaning loudly, Katherine gazed hopelessly at the ceiling. "How totally ridiculous! I can't believe you've squandered such an opportunity, Pru. If the man asked you to dinner, you know he has to be interested. Even if he insists he doesn't want anything serious. Unless you just don't like him."

"I do like him. But I also respect his decisions about his private life. Besides, even if I did want to see him again, I'm not the type to push myself at a man. And anyway, he's eight years younger than me. We'd never be compatible."

Katherine sighed. "For your information, your age is an asset, not a liability. But I'll be good and not pester you any more about Luke Crawford. Just answer me one thing, though. Is he the reason you're a little glum today?"

Prudence straightened her shoulders. Ever since her divorce, she'd made a point to appear emotionally strong and perfectly capable of taking care of herself. She wasn't about to show a chink in her armor now.

"I'm not glum. I'm a bit tired. And the seminar was so boring I had to keep pinching myself to stay awake. I need a day or two to recuperate, that's all."

Katherine continued to study her. "While I'm sorry you're exhausted, I'm glad you're not having regrets over Luke Crawford."

Prudence scowled at her. "Regrets? What kind of crack is that?"

Katherine's eyes narrowed to calculating strips. "That was no crack. I meant exactly what I said! Do you think I'm blind or stupid? I saw the way Luke was dancing with you at the reception. I doubt I could've wedged a thread between the two of you.

Then you see him in Reno and didn't make the most of a great opportunity? All I can say is that you should have regrets!"

It wasn't like Katherine to have such an outburst, but it was hardly like Prudence to be lamenting over a man, either. And there was no way Prudence could tell her friend just exactly what had happened in Reno. Those nights with Luke were private and special and not to be shared with anyone.

"Listen to you," Prudence snapped. "I remember a time when you were going to throw away your chance to marry Blake—your chance to have a wonderful husband and father for Nick, not to mention a fabulous home and financial security. Talk about regrets. You would've been the poster child for the biggest regret on planet earth!"

Katherine jumped to her feet. "All right. I wasn't always the brightest when it came to love and marriage. But I managed to open my eyes before it was too late. I just hope you do."

With the files in hand, Katherine marched out of the office. Once her friend was out of sight, Prudence dropped her head in her hands, and for a moment, it was all she could do to keep the tears at bay.

She did have regrets, but not the kind that Katherine was thinking. She regretted that she couldn't have met Luke years ago. Long before Gavin had filled her with bitter mistrust. Maybe then she would've been brave enough to go after him, to convince him that they should give their relationship a chance to bloom. But she wasn't brave. At least, not brave enough to risk another broken heart.

Lifting her head, she took a moment to compose herself before she walked into Katherine's connecting office. The other woman was busy jamming the stacks of paper into the shredding machine and didn't hear the tap of Prudence's high heels against the hard tile.

"Turn that thing off," Prudence ordered. "And get your purse."

The sound of her voice caused Katherine to jump, and she looked around in surprise.

"What?"

"Shut off the shredder and get your purse. We're going to Conchita's for lunch."

Katherine flipped a switch and the shredder went quiet. "We both can't just leave. It's—"

Before she could finish, the noon bell rang and Prudence smiled at her. "See. Perfect timing. We'll have time for a quick sandwich. My treat. And Emily-Ann can show us some pics of baby Brody. Better yet, she might have him with her at the coffee shop."

Katherine shot her a guarded look. "Are you sure you want to go?"

She walked over to Katherine. "I'm sure I want to apologize for being so crabby. Forgive me?"

Laughing, Katherine gave her a light hug. "Are you serious? You never need to apologize to me.

We're like sisters. We can be cross at each other if we want to be. Right?"

Her spirits lifting, Prudence laughed with her. "Right."

Chapter Seven

The afternoon sun was blazing when Luke braked the truck and trailer rig to a halt outside the main Three Rivers horse barn and wearily climbed to the ground.

For the sake of the horses' welfare, he'd broken up the eleven-hour trip home and made a layover at Beatty, where there were comfortable and safe facilities to stall the animals. Yet even with the extra night, the drive had been tiring.

Come on, Luke. You know damn well the drive isn't the reason you have a ton of weight on your shoulders. Yeah, you've driven a few hundred miles, but it's your mind that's done all the traveling. If you're not reliving the moments you spent in Pru-

dence's bed, you're agonizing over the stiff look on her face when she walked away from you at the airport. You're a bastard, Luke. Furthermore, you deserve to feel like hell.

Wrong, he shot back at the condemning voice. He didn't deserve to feel this bruised and broken. He shouldn't be punished for being sensible. Just like Prudence had been sensible when she hadn't clung to him or suggested they see each other again. She was smart enough to recognize he wasn't a family man. And she didn't want a long-term affair any more than he did.

Yeah, sure, Luke. The way you feel right now, you'd beg, borrow or steal to spend one more night with Prudence.

"Hey, Luke! Welcome home!"

Relieved to hear Holt's voice calling out to him, rather than the one going off in his head, Luke turned to see the man rapidly striding toward him. Two grooms with lead ropes tossed over their shoulders followed a few feet behind.

Luke walked over to meet him. "Good to be home, Holt."

Holt offered his hand, and as Luke shook it, the other man also gave his upper arm an appreciative slap. The warm greeting was a balm to Luke's frayed nerves.

"No problems on the way back?" Holt asked.

"None. Before I left the Grayson Ranch, I loaded the water tank with the water the horses were accustomed to drinking. So no problems with them getting dehydrated. And they cleaned up all their feed before we left Beatty this morning. Otherwise, they've been quiet."

"Great. You know my opinion of pampered horses with finicky appetites."

Luke chuckled. "Yeah. Get them ready for the next sale."

"Let's have a look," Holt said eagerly and motioned for the two grooms to follow. "I've been driving Isabelle crazy all weekend with talk about these stallions. She said I'm like a kid waiting to open Christmas gifts and I would've been better off going on the trip with you."

If Holt had joined him on the trip, Luke thought, he certainly wouldn't be preoccupied with thoughts of Prudence right now. None of those nights with her would've happened. None of those memories would be rolling over and over in his mind.

Shoving at that thought, Luke said with a touch of humor, "Well, I hope you like your early Christmas gifts."

On the left side of the horse van, a door lowered to the ground to create a safe walking ramp. Luke opened it, then went inside to fetch the first stallion.

A few minutes later, the grooms had led two of the horses away to the barn, and Luke was leading the last stallion down the ramp, when a work truck pulling a long open cattle trailer braked to a stop a little ways across the ranch yard.

Maureen and Gil quickly spilled out of the truck cab and headed straight over to them. Luke noticed Maureen was walking close to her new husband's side, and the wide smile on the woman's face made it clear that the honeymoon was far from over.

Standing between Holt and Gil, Maureen focused her attention on Luke and the sorrel stallion. "Say, he's a handsome guy!"

"You talking about Luke or the horse, Mom?" Holt teased.

She chuckled. "Go ahead and put me on the spot. I don't have any problem saying Luke is as handsome as the stallion."

Holt playfully stuck an elbow in Gil's ribs. "Looks like you married a fickle woman, Gil."

Laughing, Gil gave his wife's waist a little squeeze. "Don't worry. I'll keep her on the straight and narrow. Besides, I know for a fact that Maureen likes older men."

"Ha! For all you know, Luke might like older women," Maureen joked with her husband.

There's a big gap between our ages.

Luke was suddenly remembering Prudence's remark the night of the reception. She'd implied the difference in their ages was more like a wide river than a narrow stream. But in Luke's opinion, the extra years she had on him only made her that much more attractive. Could be that Maureen was on target, he thought. Maybe he was drawn to older women.

One older woman with caramel-brown hair and sea-green eyes.

"Take him around in a circle, Luke," Holt said. "Let Mom and Gil see what Three Rivers money is buying."

Luke led the red stallion away from the trailer and walked him in the open area between the two parked trucks before returning to the group.

"He's only fourteen and a half hands, but stout," Holt commented. "Luke thinks his height will be an asset. What do you think?"

Maureen arched a brow at her son. "He's perfect. Luke is right on. Not everyone wants a horse that requires a ladder to get in the saddle."

Holt chuckled. "Hell, we don't sell horses to greenhorns who need help to mount. But I'm glad you like him." He gestured toward the barn. "We've already stalled the other two, if you want to go have a look."

Maureen glanced questioningly at Gil, who promptly checked his watch. "We need to be going, honey," he said. "The men are going to be waiting."

"You two headed somewhere?" Luke asked.

"Roundup on the northern Prescott range," Gil explained. "Snow is predicted to hit there in the next few days."

"And to make matters worse, we've had a few calves born on those slopes in the past few days," Maureen explained. "We're sending them all to Red Bluff. Blake doesn't have room for them here."

Luke nodded, while thinking Maureen was both

mentally and physically stronger than the average woman and the complete opposite of his late mother. He hated to imagine how Paula would've managed to exist if things had been reversed after the auto accident. If Mills had been killed and she'd lost her leg, she would've most likely ended up in a nursing home, unable to care for herself.

"You have plenty of help?" Holt asked her. "If you need us, Luke and I could saddle up and join you. Right, Luke?"

"Sure," Luke answered. "You can't get any better training for a horse than using him on a roundup."

"Thanks for the offer," Gil said. "But we'll manage. You two have your hands full as it is."

After the couple drove away, Luke and Holt took the stallion inside the horse barn and turned him over to the grooms. Once they saw that the animal was stalled and settled, the two men entered Holt's office. Unlike Blake's fancy office in a separate building next to the cattle barn, Holt's was inside the horse barn, in an old space that had once been used as a tack room. The planked wooden floor was worn smooth from years of footsteps, while the ceiling was open to two-by-six rafters. Blake often talked about ripping out the wood and replacing it with fire-safe cinder blocks, but Holt balked at the idea. He'd argued that he didn't want to do horse business in a concrete cellar. To compromise, Holt had agreed to having several high-tech fire alarms and sprinklers installed in and around the room.

"Sit down, Luke. Let's have some coffee," Holt invited. "Have you had lunch? I'll call the house and have Jazelle bring you something."

"Coffee will be plenty," Luke told him. "I had a big breakfast. Anyway, I need to go change my clothes and get to work. I've been away from the yearlings too long. They're going to forget me."

Holt fetched the coffee, and after handing Luke one of the cups, he carried his to the chair behind the wide desk. As he took a seat, he said, "You're kidding, right? I hardly expect you to go straight to work after the long drive you've just made."

"No. I'm serious. I've missed the horses. And I'm not that tired."

Peering at him over the rim of the thick white mug, Holt said, "Sorry, buddy, but you look all done in to me. I wanted you to hit the blackjack tables and enjoy yourself, but I didn't mean for you to go overboard and stay up all night."

"I didn't hit the blackjack tables," Luke retorted, then realized he should've probably kept that information to himself.

Holt's brows shot upward. "Three nights in Reno and no blackjack? What did you do with all your time?" he asked. Then a sly look came over his face. "Oh, sorry, Luke. I wasn't thinking about the ladies. All I can say is you must have had a hell of a time."

Luke felt a hot blush creep up his neck and onto his face. "No ladies, either. I just drove around town and saw a few sights, that's all. If I look tired, it's probably from the stress of worrying about you."

"Me?" Holt laughed. "I've never heard that one before."

Luke grimaced while wondering what Holt would think if he actually knew he'd spent the entire weekend with Prudence Keyes. No doubt he'd be shocked that Prudence had let herself be seduced into having a brief affair. She was first-class all the way. And he'd been wrong to take advantage of the situation. Or had he? She'd assured him that she had no regrets, and Luke had to believe she'd truly meant it.

"Nothing crazy about that," Luke reasoned. "I was concerned you wouldn't be pleased with the horses once I got them here. And worried something might happen to them on the trip home. You know how it is out on the road. Even when you try to drive as safely as possible, things can happen."

Holt shook his head. "Listen, Luke. I don't ever want you to worry about me or anything else. If I don't like a horse, I can always sell him. If you have an accident, that's just it—an accident. I have confidence in you. But I don't expect you to be perfect. I'm sure as hell not."

Luke let out a long breath. He'd been truthful about his worries over the stallions, he thought. But he couldn't be honest enough to confess to Holt that he'd gotten his emotions tangled up with a woman.

No. It wasn't his emotions that were tangled, he thought crossly. He was spellbound with a bad case of lust. In a few days he'd get over it and everything would be back to normal.

"Thanks, Holt. That takes a load off," he said, then quickly changed the subject. "Uh—when did Maureen and Gil get back from Hawaii? I thought they'd be gone longer."

Holt chuckled. "Mom said she was going to get soft lying around on the beach drinking pineapple juice. And all Gil wants is to make her happy."

Luke smiled. "And being back on the ranch and back in the saddle is what makes her happy."

"It hasn't taken you long to learn how each of us Hollisters work," Holt said with a grin.

"*Work* is the key word when it comes to you Hollisters, Holt."

Holt shrugged off his comment. "We play a bit, too. I mean, you were at that shindig of a wedding reception. Everyone was whooping and hollering and dancing far past midnight."

Oh, Lord, hardly two seconds had passed and the mention of the reception had put Luke's thoughts right back on Prudence. Would he ever get away from her and the memories they'd made together?

"Yeah. Your family doesn't hold back when it comes to parties," he said.

The phone on Holt's desk rang. "Excuse me, Luke. That's Flo. She must be having trouble with some horse papers or something."

While Holt spoke with the ranch secretary, Luke finished his coffee and carried the empty cup over to a table holding a coffee machine and a platter of pastries. He was about to step out of the office when Holt abruptly hung up the phone and called to him.

"Wait, Luke. Before you leave, I was going to ask you about your dad and brother. Are they doing okay?"

"Both of them are fine."

"Are you sure?"

Luke frowned. "Yes, I'm sure. I talked to both of them last night."

Leaving his coffee on the desk, Holt stood and joined Luke at the door. "Good," he said. "I'm glad to hear it."

A wry smirk twisted Luke's features. "I'm beginning to think you're worried about me now, instead of the other way around."

Holt let out a guilty chuckle. "Okay. I guess I am a little. You seem a bit distracted. I'm afraid you might be getting homesick. And I don't want to lose you. Not for any reason."

Luke let out another long breath. "You couldn't run me off Three Rivers with a shotgun, Holt. Now let's go have another look at those stallions."

Holt gave Luke's shoulder an affectionate slap. "Let's go, buddy."

"Pru, it won't be the same if you don't come home for Dad's birthday. Mom is planning a big dinner party."

Prudence shifted the cell phone to the opposite ear before she replied to her sister, Daisey. "I wish I could be there. But I can't possibly take off work now. I imagine Mom will invite plenty of their friends to liven up the party. And I'll make a point to call Dad and wish him a happy birthday."

Daisey let out a good-natured groan. "Okay, I'll explain the situation to Mom and Dad. They understand your job is demanding."

"And what about your job?" Prudence asked. "How's it going?"

Daisey paused, then said, "To be honest, I'm getting bored with it."

Prudence was dumbfounded. "What? You're the manager of a high-end retail shop in the ritziest section of Palm Springs. You wanted that job for ages! It was all you talked about. Now you say you're bored?"

"I know, I sound childish and foolish, but deep down, I'm just not happy, Pru. You remember that old song where the woman singing keeps asking is this all there is? Well, I keep asking myself that same question. I think about Mom and all she's done with her life, and Dad has helped so many people, too. And then there's you with all your accomplishments. You're making children's lives better every day. All I'm doing is making sure people are happy with their clothes! It's frivolous."

Prudence glanced at the clock on the wall of her office. Five more minutes and the bell would ring to announce the end of lunch hour. Katherine had gone to the cafeteria to enjoy the enchiladas the cooks were serving today, but Prudence had begged off and chosen to remain at her desk and eat half a cheese sandwich. She'd barely managed to choke it down when Daisey had called and was still talking after twenty-five minutes.

"You always were a fashionista, Daisey. And a person should like what they do for a living. You get to dress up every day for work and put those dozens and dozens of high heels you own to good use."

"Oh, for goodness' sake, Pru, I'm thirty years old. I'm past the dress-up stage. I need to do something more meaningful. Actually, I'm thinking about going back to college."

Glad her sister couldn't see her shaking her head, Prudence walked over to the window and gazed out at the school campus. For the first part of October, the weather had turned unusually cool, and today was even more so, with a stout wind and heavy gray clouds blocking out the sun. Most of the students who were slowly heading toward the entrance of the building were bundled in jackets and sweaters.

A little more than three weeks had passed since Prudence had said goodbye to Luke at the Reno airport. She'd neither seen nor heard from him, and that was exactly how she'd expected it to be. So why couldn't she get the man out of her mind? Why did the memories of their time together keep following her around, haunting her?

Daisey's voice practically shouted in her ear. "Pru? Have you fainted or something?"

Shaking herself back to the present, Prudence said, "Sorry. I'm still here. Uh—what kind of studies were you thinking about? Business classes?"

"No. Criminal law. I want to be a lawyer."

Prudence gasped. "Are you joking?"

"Don't be mean. Maybe it does sound fantastic to you. But I've been thinking about this for a long time. I'm not dumb. And I was always good at debating and negotiating. True, I'll probably be your age by the time I actually get a license to practice. But that's okay. Good things don't come fast or easy."

In Prudence's case, her sister's prophetic words couldn't have proved more accurate. The euphoric connection she'd had with Luke had come too easy and ended far too quickly.

"I do believe you're growing up. What's happened? Have you met a man?"

Daisey laughed. "A man? Who needs one of those?"

Prudence was thinking how to reply to that when the bell rang. The sound carried over the phone to Daisey and her sister quickly made a smooching sound.

"Kiss. Kiss. I'll talk to you later, sissy."

Prudence hung up and was returning to her desk when a knock sounded on the outer door to her office.

"Come in," she called.

The door opened, and Syd Lyons, the high school athletic director, stepped into the room. Somewhere in his midforties, the divorced man was a physical fitness fanatic, and every piece of clothing he wore was chosen to show off his muscle-bound body. Prudence knew for a fact that some of the single female teachers swooned whenever the man entered the room. As for Prudence, she despised his cocky attitude, but because he was good at his job, she'd tried to overlook his faults.

"May I speak with you for a minute or two, Ms. Keyes?"

"Certainly." She gestured to the chair in front of her desk. "What can I do for you?"

He sat down in the chair and directed a grin at her. "Go to dinner and a movie with me?"

She bit back a curse. The man had no idea how crass or repulsive he was to her and she would've enjoyed telling him so. But she was a professional, and as the superintendent, it was her job to take care of any problems that reached her desk.

"Mr. Lyons," she said stiffly. "If you're here to discuss a school matter, then speak up. Otherwise, I'm very busy."

His jaw clenched before he spoke in a clipped manner. "Very well. A problem has come up with Brad—uh, I mean Coach Wilson. He's having a fit about the band riding the bus with his players to away games. He says their presence is too much of a distraction for the athletes. He thinks the band should take a separate bus of their own."

Prudence folded her hands together atop her desk.

"In other words, the school should have to dole out extra traveling expenses because Coach Wilson can't keep his ballplayers under control. Sorry, but that's not going to happen. The basketball team will share with the band. And if the coach has any problem accepting that situation, he should come speak with me himself—rather than sending you."

Syd bristled, but Prudence hardly cared.

"I am the athletic director," he crisply pointed out. "I do handle most things that come under the heading of sports. And frankly, Ms. Keyes, Wilson had already decided he wouldn't be able to reason with you. That's why he sent me to plead his case."

"Well, you can tell him he made a mistake." She smiled, but there was no warmth behind the expression.

Rising to his feet, the man walked to the door, then paused to look at her. "Just in case you're not aware of the situation, every coach at St. Francis knows how you feel. You hate sports and everything it involves. If you could, you'd send us all packing and replace every sport with some namby-pamby artistic subject."

Prudence had often had clashes with Syd, but she hadn't known the rest of the coaches held this opinion of her. To say the least, the revelation stung.

"That isn't true," Prudence denied. "I understand as well as you that sports play a major part in a child's development. Physical strength, character building, fair play, perseverance. I could go on, but you hardly require a list. On the other hand, the arts are important, too. As superintendent, I have to find a happy balance between the two. Surely you coaches can understand that."

"*Happy?* I don't believe you're acquainted with the word, Ms. Keyes."

He stepped out the door and shut it behind him with a heavy thud. Prudence blew out a heavy breath and reached to switch her computer out of dozing mode when she heard the tap of heels against the tile.

Glancing up, she saw Katherine standing in the doorway that connected their offices. She was thoughtfully tapping a pencil against her palm.

"I believe he was a bit angry," Katherine said, stating the obvious.

"How much of that did you hear?"

"Enough to know the top of your head is probably ready to blow right about now."

Grimacing, Prudence said, "Then you heard him asking me for a date?"

"No!" Katherine walked into the room and sank into the seat that Syd had just vacated. "What did you tell him?"

"That I didn't appreciate his attitude."

"Good," Katherine said. "Besides, if you want a date, there's always Luke."

The mention of Luke's name filled her heart with bittersweet longing. She'd hoped and prayed that after a bit of time passed, her memories of him would dim. She'd thought she'd be able to look back on their sweet encounter as a joyous, special time. Instead, she wondered how she'd been so foolish to think she could snatch a taste of his lovemaking and then forget it.

"Luke? Why are you bringing him up after all this time?"

"Oh, come on, Pru. Why don't you break down and call the man? You know you'd like to. And what would it hurt? Really?"

It would set her determination to forget him back about a thousand years. "Look, Kat, I can admit that Luke is handsome and sexy and nice. But none of that makes him right for me. There's not a man out there who's right for me. I used to believe—"

When she didn't finish the sentence, Katherine prompted.

"You'd find someone you could trust. And love. Right?"

"Something like that." She left her chair and walked over to a table that held a coffee machine and a bowl of hard candy. "I've never told you exactly why I divorced, have I?"

Behind her, Katherine said, "No. And I haven't asked because that's your private business."

Prudence poured coffee into a foam cup and stirred in a spoonful of sugar. "You told me everything that happened with your failed marriage. Why should I deserve more privacy?"

"As your friend, I knew you'd tell me sooner or later."

Returning to her desk, Prudence eased one hip onto the corner and faced her friend. "I hate to admit it, Kat, but Syd's visit opened my eyes. He was right. I'm biased and I don't view the sports department as I should."

Katherine stared at her. "What are you talking about? You were right about the extra expenditures and the fact that Wilson can't keep a handle on his boys. You weren't out of line. Maybe your voice was a little snippy, but Syd deserved it."

Prudence grimaced. "That's all true. But I'm afraid that, deep down, I harbor resentment against the coaches because of Gavin. And that's very wrong."

"What does your ex have to do with sports?"

A heavy breath slipped out of her. "He was an athlete—a football player, and a good one. When we got married he was getting offers from pro teams."

Amazed, Katherine shook her head. "You sure didn't mention you were married to a professional football player."

"Not exactly. Gavin was in his last year of college when we got married. We hadn't even had our first anniversary when he suffered a career-ending injury. From then on, everything started going downhill. He quit college and went to work for a construction company. He tried and I tried, but I wasn't enough to fill the void—football was his whole life and he'd lost it. Our marriage technically ended when I learned he was having an affair with his boss's daughter. I'm not sure if he had affairs prior to her. Thinking back on it, he probably did and I just didn't see the signs. Or maybe I had my eyes closed to his faults because I loved him."

For long moments Katherine thoughtfully studied her, and then finally she said, "Sports didn't do that to you, Pru. I imagine Gavin would've been unfaithful no matter how things had played out."

Nodding, Prudence said, "It's taken me a long time to recognize his problems were deeper than a knee injury. But I think—well, a few minutes ago when Syd said the coaches at St. Francis knew I hated sports, it was like a slap in the face. I don't hate sports. I only resented what it had done to my marriage. But now—dear God, how stupid I've been. The only thing that ruined our marriage was Gavin. Not only that, he scarred my future and made me afraid to love again."

Her expression soft, Katherine stood and rested a hand on Prudence's shoulder. "You're being too hard on yourself, Pru. The only person you haven't been fair with is you."

"Maybe in your eyes, but not mine." She slipped off the desk and gave Katherine a light hug. "Thanks for listening. Now let's get back to work. I want you to print out the bus scheduling, along with the dates of the boys' basketball travel games."

"Coming right up," Katherine assured her. "But I'm not sure why you need them. Syd does all the game scheduling at the beginning of school. Nothing has changed since then."

"I'm going to make some changes," she told her. "And then I'm going to go have a talk with Coach Wilson."

"To give him a piece of your mind?" Katherine asked slyly.

"No. To give him the news that he doesn't have to share his bus anymore."

Katherine's expression suddenly turned calculating. "My, my, Pru. Something is turning you into a marshmallow."

Prudence shrugged. "They say old age either mellows you or makes you crotchety. Let's hope in my case it's not the latter."

Already on her way out of the room, Katherine paused to look back at her. "Old age, my foot. You haven't been the same since you returned from the Reno trip. Something happened to you up there. And I'm fairly sure it was Luke."

Prudence tried to laugh, but the sound was more like a cross between a chuckle and a whimper. "You're such a silly romantic, Kat. Luke had a steak and I had a pasta dish. I consumed too many calories, that's all. There was nothing earthshaking about the dinner. Just two acquaintances eating together."

Smiling cleverly, Katherine said, "Brush it off all you want, Pru. But you've started thinking of yourself as a woman again. And I think Luke is the reason."

Forcing a smile on her face, she shooed Katherine

toward the door. "Go get the schedule before this soft spot leaves me and I'm back to being Ms. Grinch."

With a backward wave of her hand, Katherine left the room and Prudence returned to her desk. But instead of focusing on the list of expenditures on the computer screen, her mind continued to dwell on her friend's remarks.

Katherine was right, of course. Ever since Prudence had divorced Gavin, she'd stopped thinking of herself as a woman. Instead, she was just a person, a schoolteacher and superintendent. Her job had been her whole focus, and any thoughts of being a wife and mother had been pushed to the back of her mind. But after making love to Luke, she was feeling like a woman again and thinking with a woman's heart.

Her dreams of having a family had never really died; they'd just been suspended for a long, long while. Now all those yearnings and wishes for a family of her own had burst to life again. And with them, the warning that her biological clock wasn't just ticking anymore—it was leaping forward. The image of her spending the rest of her life without a child of her own was not one she wanted to contemplate.

Yes, making love to Luke had forced Prudence to open her eyes to the future, she thought. And it was painfully obvious that he wasn't a family man. He wasn't even interested in spending another night in her bed, much less a lifetime with her.

They'd agreed to go their separate ways after Reno.

They'd agreed there would be no strings or regrets.
They were both being sensible.

But how was she supposed to forget him?

Chapter Eight

Steam rose from the gray filly's back as Luke lifted off the saddle and carried it toward the tack room. A freezing breeze wafted through the open doorway at the far end of the barn, and Luke yelled down the wide alleyway to where a groom was leading a horse to its stall.

"Kirk! Shut the door! It's too cold this morning for that much fresh air."

"Got it, Luke!" he called back.

Luke continued into the tack room and was in the process of swinging the heavy saddle onto a wooden rack when his cell phone rang.

Once he had the piece of riding equipment safely positioned, he took a moment to check the phone.

As soon as he saw the caller was Holt, he punched a button to return his call.

"Hey, Holt, you need me?" he asked as soon as Holt answered the phone.

"A little errand, that's all. What are you doing right now?"

"Just finished putting Violet through her workout and I have Rowdy waiting in the catch pen."

"Get one of the wranglers to turn him out in the paddock. I need for you to make a run into Wickenburg for me. Actually, Blake and I both do."

Luke frowned as he absently ran a hand over the seat of the saddle. Holt never sent Luke on any kind of errand. There were plenty of men working around the horse barn who were always ready and willing to be a gofer. And to pull Luke away from his training job was something Holt wouldn't do on a whim.

"Must be an important errand," Luke said.

"Important enough. I need several meds from Chandler's clinic. Some of which I'd rather you be handling than just one of the wranglers. Chandler has the list, and everything will be ready and waiting whenever you get there."

"Okay. No problem," Luke told him. "What about Blake?"

"Uh—Kat forgot some papers at the house that she needs at school today. Blake is expecting cattle buyers here at the ranch in the next hour or two, so he can't take them to her. When I told him that you might be going to town, he was hoping you'd help him out."

Luke's mind was suddenly racing like a dog viciously chasing its own tail. "Are you saying he wants me to go by St. Francis Academy and deliver the papers to Katherine?"

"That's right. I think they have something to do with school insurance. Whatever they are, she needs them."

Luke couldn't refuse to go. Not without making himself look like a self-centered jerk. "Okay. I'll finish with Violet and be by your office for the list."

"Uh, Luke, do you know where the school is?"

He should. He'd driven by the place on two different occasions this past week with the intentions of stopping by Prudence's office to speak with her. But both times, common sense had prevailed and he'd kept on driving.

This time would be different. He couldn't chicken out. He had to stop. Would he see Prudence while he was there? Did he really want to?

Damn, but you're turning into a liar, Luke. At this very moment you'd give your eyeteeth just so you could look at her face. Furthermore, you know it.

"Luke? Are you there?"

"Uh—yeah, I'm here. And I know where the school is."

"Good man. I'll see you in a few minutes."

Holt disconnected the call and Luke thoughtfully slipped the cell phone back into his shirt pocket.

What would it hurt if he did see Prudence again? For more than a month now, he'd been asking himself that same question over and over. And frankly, Luke was tired of trying to answer it. He was even more tired of trying to convince himself that keeping his distance from her was the best thing to do. Being with her made him happy. Wasn't a man entitled to some happiness in his life?

Suddenly whistling under his breath, he left the tack room to tend to Violet.

With fifteen minutes to go before the lunch-hour bell, Prudence was making her way through a stack of emails when she heard the outer door to Katherine's office open, followed by the muted sound of a man's voice. Since the secretary often acted as Prudence's go-between, it wasn't unusual for Katherine to negotiate with anyone from landscapers to food suppliers for the cafeteria.

Forcing her attention back to the computer screen, she clicked open another message and was reading through a memo about a parent-teacher meeting when she heard Katherine's light laugh. Seconds later there was a knock on the open door connecting the two women's offices.

Looking away from the computer screen, she saw Katherine's face peeping around the door frame. The sly grin on her face had Prudence frowning in wonder.

"If you're wanting to go on to lunch, that's fine

with me," Prudence said with a dismissive wave of her hand.

"I'm going to the cafeteria. It's meat-loaf day," Katherine said, while her smile grew ever more impish. "There's someone here to say hello to you."

Thinking that Blake had made one of his rare trips into town and had stopped by to see his wife, Prudence rose and walked around the desk. "So, you finally got Blake into town, did you? Then why are you bothering with meat loaf? Make him take you out to Jose's. It's okay with me if you take an extra hour. After this hectic week, you deserve it."

She walked over to the door to say hello to Blake, but when she looked into Katherine's office, she didn't see the Three Rivers Ranch manager. Instead, Luke was standing in the middle of the room. He was dressed from head to toe in worn denim, and a brown Stetson was crushed between his two hands. His hair had grown since she'd last seen him. The thick black waves edged over his collar and very nearly hid his right eyebrow. The expression on his tanned face was more like a man waiting to be called back to a dentist chair, instead of a friend wanting to say hello.

"Luke."

As his name slipped past her lips, he stepped tentatively forward.

"Hello, Pru."

Their gazes locked, and Prudence suddenly forgot that Katherine was standing a few feet behind her.

Even the walls of the office seemed to disappear at the sight of him.

"Did you—uh—"

"Luke kindly brought those insurance papers to me that I forgot and left on my desk at home," Katherine quickly interrupted. "He was just about to leave when I assured him you weren't that busy."

Prudence darted Katherine a glance before she turned back to Luke and tried to swallow away the nerves in her throat. "Kat's right. I'm never too busy to say hello to a friend."

She could feel his eyes wandering over her, weighing her appearance as though she'd changed since he'd last seen her. Well, he wouldn't be wrong. She had changed in so many ways. Maybe not outwardly, but definitely on the inside.

"I wouldn't want to interrupt your work."

"You're not," Prudence said.

Standing a few feet behind Prudence's shoulder, Katherine cleared her throat. "Uh—Pru, if you don't need me, I'm going to head on to the cafeteria before the bell rings and the hall is overrun with kiddos."

"Sure, Kat. Go on and have a nice lunch."

"Thanks, Luke, for bringing the papers by. You're a lifesaver," Katherine told him.

"No problem. Glad I could help," he told her.

Smiling at both of them, Katherine slipped out the door and carefully closed it behind her.

Prudence cleared her throat and tried to smile, but she could feel her lips quivering, her knees turning to sponge. What was that about? Why had one look at this man suddenly made her so emotional? Oh, God, this wasn't the way it was supposed to be, she thought.

"I have to confess, Luke, I'm very surprised to see you."

His expression sheepish, he moved another step closer. "I—uh, hadn't planned on this. But Blake asked me to do this for him. Did, uh, Katherine really need those papers?"

She arched both brows at him. "Why, yes, she did. Were you thinking someone is trying to throw us together?"

Ruddy color swept over his jaws. "Sort of. Guess that sounds crazy, doesn't it? No one knows we were together in Reno."

Not *that* together, she thought.

"I mentioned to Kat I saw you in Reno, but that's all I told her," she admitted. "You see, I'd been thinking the same thing. That Holt or Blake had told her you were going to be in Reno and that Katherine had deliberately booked me at the same hotel in hopes of pushing us together."

"Did she deliberately book your room there?"

"No. It was mere coincidence."

"Imagine that."

"Yes. Imagine that."

He heaved out a heavy breath. "Actually, I've driven by the school a couple of times and almost stopped to say hello."

Why did it feel like she couldn't breathe? Why did she simply want to walk over and lay her cheek against his chest? That wouldn't fix anything. It would only make her want him more.

"Almost," she repeated with a wan smile. "Guess the brakes on your truck momentarily quit working."

His lips hinted at a grin. "Yeah. Something like that."

Silence stretched for a few seconds, and Prudence wondered how long he was going to keep standing there with his hat in his hand before he announced he had to be on his way.

Drawing in a bracing breath, she asked, "So how was your drive back from Reno? Was Holt happy with the stallions?"

"Thankfully, the drive back was uneventful. And Holt was very pleased. And I—I've been fine. Working and learning what it's like to raise horses in the Arizona climate. What about you? I'm sure school is keeping you busy."

"Always." It just wasn't enough to keep her mind off him, she thought dismally. "Kat hasn't mentioned it, but I'm sure the Hollisters are getting ready for a huge Thanksgiving dinner next month. Will you be eating with them, or are you going to visit your dad and brother?"

He shook his head. "Not for a while. Maybe during the Christmas holiday. Will you be going to visit your family in Palm Springs for Thanksgiving?"

"No. I don't have enough time off to make the trip. You know how it is—work has to come first."

"Yeah, work. We always have that."

Too bad they couldn't have each other in between, Prudence thought. Being with Luke, even on a limited basis, would make all the work, all the stress and worries of everyday life, much easier to deal with. But more time spent with the man would mean the more her heart became all wrapped up in his smile, his kiss, the very sound of his voice.

He glanced at his watch, and even though Prudence knew what he was about to say, she couldn't tear her gaze off him. She wanted to drink in as much of his image as she could before he disappeared from her life again.

"Uh—I'd better be on my way," he said. "I have veterinary meds in the truck. I need to get them back to the ranch and under refrigeration."

"Yes, well, I need to eat lunch before the bell rings again," she told him, while thinking she probably wouldn't be able to choke down a bite of the sandwich she'd brought from home.

He suddenly closed the few steps separating them and Prudence felt the quiver in her lips spread downward to her hands. Not wanting him to guess just how close she was to breaking apart, she curled her fingers into fists and pressed her lips together.

"I've been thinking about you, Pru," he said gently.

His unexpected words brought tears to the backs

of her eyes. After all these days without seeing him, she'd decided he'd pushed her totally out of his mind.

She blinked and swallowed. "I've been thinking about you, too, Luke."

"Have you? Honestly?"

"I've tried not to," she admitted. "But I haven't been very successful."

"I've tried, too. But this morning when Holt asked me to deliver the papers to Katherine, I was glad for an excuse to see you."

She was wondering exactly how much she could read into his revelation when he spoke again.

"Actually, I was thinking—uh—it might be nice if we had dinner together again. That is—if you'd like to."

Stunned, she stared at him as questions darted through her brain. "Dinner? I thought—"

He reached for her hand, and her heart jerked with a mixture of apprehension and pleasure as he folded both his hands around hers. The softness in his eyes, the gentle way his fingers were holding on to hers, was crushing her resistance to a pile of dust.

"You thought the plan was for us not to see each other again—that we wanted to avoid strings. Hell, Pru, we're both grown, sensible adults. Having a meal together isn't going to wreck our lives. Do you think?"

Her spirits were suddenly floating in a clear blue sky. "No. Like you said, we're both sensible. And honestly—I'd love to have dinner."

His fingertips drew loops over the back of her hand. "And I love that you've said yes. How does tomorrow night sound to you?"

"I don't have anything scheduled." *Except stare at the walls and think about the two of us locked in a hot embrace*, she could've told him.

"Fine. I'll pick you up at your place—around seven," he said. "If that's okay with you."

"Seven is perfect," she agreed.

"Do you have a favorite restaurant here in town? I haven't really tried that many yet."

"Jose's," she said without hesitation. "There are several good places to eat, but Jose's is my favorite."

His smile deepened and Prudence would've loved to kiss the dimples bracketing his lips. But he wasn't here to be kissed and it would be just her luck that a staff member would suddenly walk in.

"Then Jose's it is." He levered the hat down on his head, and with his gaze glued to her face, he began to back himself toward the door. "See you tomorrow night."

Nodding, she smiled. "I'll be ready. Do you still have my phone number and address?"

"I do." He lifted a hand in farewell, then let himself out of the office.

After he'd closed the door behind him, Prudence walked back to her desk on shaky legs and practically collapsed into the executive chair.

She should've had the courage and strength to give him a firm no, she thought. She should've told him that she had no interest in jumping into an affair that would undoubtedly lead to nowhere. But where Luke was concerned, her resistance was about as puny as a little sparrow trying to fight off a hawk.

What are you whining about, Pru? Having an affair with Luke will give you a few memories to take out on a cold night when you've grown old and are wondering how love and family passed you by.

Shaking off the dismal voice in her head, she switched off the computer and headed out of the office. Maybe a few bites of meat loaf would help ease the queasiness she'd been experiencing ever since she rolled out of bed this morning.

The next evening, darkness had already fallen as Luke approached the town of Wickenburg. The spattering of lights stretched across the desert horizon and merged into the starlit sky.

Normally, Luke would've been soaking in the beauty of the night, but he was too busy pondering a slew of self-directed questions to notice much more than the oncoming traffic.

What was he doing, anyway? How could anything good come out of seeing Prudence again? He'd survived for more than a month without seeing her or talking to her. It hadn't necessarily been easy, but he'd managed to hold himself together. Then a five-minute visit in her office had caused a major breakdown in his struggle to maintain a cool distance from the woman.

Yesterday, when he'd taken hold of her hand, he'd

had to wage a war with himself to keep from kissing her. If it hadn't been for the fact that they'd been at her workplace, he would've done more than kiss her. He would've locked the door and made love to her on the desk or floor or anyplace they could manage. How did he think he was going to keep his hands off her tonight? Moreover, why the hell should he?

You know why, Luke. This thing you feel for Prudence is different. It's more than fantastic sex. She makes you feel needed and wanted. She makes you happy. And the more time you spend with her, the more you want. It's that simple.

Simple? There wasn't anything simple about it, he shot back at the inner voice. But for tonight, he was going to try to forget all the questions and doubts. Tonight, he was going to be just like any normal man spending time with a beautiful woman. And to hell with keeping his distance.

Five minutes later, he turned onto a quiet residential street and drove slowly until he spotted Prudence's house number posted on a small gate that led through a low adobe wall. Beyond it was a rambling stucco painted desert pink and trimmed with dark brown wood.

After parking his truck alongside the street curb, he walked through a small front yard landscaped with red yucca, agave and a single saguaro cactus that wasn't yet old enough to have an arm. A feat that he'd been told took at least fifty years.

A walkway of stepping-stones, neatly edged with

white rock, led to a ground-level porch furnished with lawn furniture made of bent willow and decorated with brightly colored cushions. A dim porch light illuminated a brown wooden door covered with an old-fashioned wooden screen door.

After punching the doorbell, he glanced over his shoulder to the houses across the street. In one driveway, a child-size basketball hoop had been erected at one end of the concrete pavement, while in the yard next to it, a tricycle and a gym set made it obvious that children lived there.

From what he could see, it was a quiet, family-type neighborhood. Just the sort that fit Prudence's lifestyle.

His thoughts were suddenly interrupted as both doors swung outward and Prudence stood on the threshold, smiling at him.

"Hi, Luke. You're right on time." She gestured for him to enter. "Did you have any problem finding the house?"

"Not at all." He stepped past her and into a short foyer. The space was lit only by a pair of dim baseboard lights, but it was enough to see she was wearing a blue-and-gold floral dress that clung to the upper part of her body and flared out at her hips. After their time together in Reno, he'd thought every curve of her body had been burned into his memory, but now as he watched her close the door behind them, he realized there was so much more to see and learn about this woman.

"Have you lived in this house very long?"

"Since I first moved to Wickenburg. I took one look at the house and knew it was what I wanted. It's rather old, but that gives it character." She motioned for him to follow her. "Come to the living room and have a seat while I finish getting ready."

As he trailed after her, the faint scent of flowers drifted to him, and he recognized it as the same perfume she'd worn in Reno. Yet it was the scent of her bare skin that had haunted him for days after he'd returned home to Three Rivers.

They entered a cozy living room where a table lamp pooled a circle of light on a pair of armchairs and a couch. He took a seat in one of the chairs, while she stood, waiting to make sure he'd made himself comfortable.

"Would you like something to drink?" she asked.

"No, thanks. I'm fine. Go ahead and do whatever you need to do."

"I won't be long." She started out of the room, then paused at the arched doorway to look back at him. "I'm happy you're here, Luke."

Everything inside him wanted to rise and go to her. But he knew that once he took her into his arms, the moment his lips touched hers, all thoughts of dinner would be forgotten. And not for anything did he want her to get the impression that all he wanted from her was sex.

"I'm happy, too," he said.

She smiled faintly, then disappeared into another part of the house.

Once she was out of sight, Luke glanced curiously around the room. In one corner, a small TV sat on an entertainment console. On the shelf below the TV was a satellite radio. Both were currently turned off, leaving the room quiet enough to hear the faint ticking of a sunburst clock hanging on the wall. The couch was done in soft brown leather, while the armchairs were a dull gold suede. Throw rugs in the same color scheme were scattered across the ceramic tile floor, while the low ceiling was supported by dark brown timbers. There were just enough books, papers, and other odds and ends scattered about to give the space a warm, lived-in feel.

For no reason that he could explain, thoughts of the old Crawford homeplace in Texas suddenly drifted through his mind. The house back there had been an old two-story farmhouse with clapboard siding and a porch that circled three sides. The furnishings had been modest, but his mother had kept everything spotlessly clean and in its place.

When Luke had been a very small boy, he hadn't understood why his mother had suffered a minor meltdown if a glass had been left on the cabinet counter or a fingerprint left on the handle of the refrigerator door. He'd thought all mothers were fussy about keeping their houses clean. It wasn't until he'd grown older that he'd learned Paula's bipolar condition had caused her to be an obsessive house cleaner. There'd been times he'd seen her cleaning the cracks around the baseboards with a toothbrush, and more often than not, the skin on her hands would be cracked around the knuckles and close to bleeding.

Luke's father, Mills, had tried to reason with her, not just about the housekeeping but about her compulsive behavior and unwarranted outbursts. Sometimes she would listen. Other times, she'd be defiant and determined to go by her maiden name, Weatherby, rather than Crawford. She was her own person, she would shout, and no one was going to change her.

Luke was rubbing a hand over his face, trying to push the sad memories from his mind, when he heard Prudence's footsteps entering the room.

"Sorry for the wait," she said. "I was trying to find a certain jacket. Then halfway through the closet I remembered it's at the dry cleaner's."

Rising from the chair, he noticed she was carrying a red clutch purse to match her high heels. A jacket of the same bright color was thrown across her arm. She looked incredible.

"It's going to be cold tonight," he said as he walked over to where she stood. "Maybe you should take a coat."

She laughed lightly. "Oh, no, I'm not going to waste more time digging through the closet for a coat. This jacket will be enough."

"Are you ready to go?"

"Ready," she answered. "And hungry. I hope you

are, too. Do you like Mexican food? Even if you don't, Jose's serves traditional things, too."

"No worries. Mexican food is probably my favorite."

She turned off the table lamp and the two of them walked out to the foyer. At the door, he reached for her jacket.

"Better put this on before we go out," he said. "Let me help you."

"Thank you," she said softly.

Standing slightly behind her, he held the jacket so she could slip her arms into the sleeves. Once he lifted the garment onto her shoulders, he allowed his hands to linger just long enough to soak up the warmth of her flesh.

She went very still, and then slowly she turned to face him. Her eyes were full of doubts and questions as she gazed up at him.

"Luke—don't you want to kiss me?"

The question was so far from what he'd expected, he couldn't stop a laugh from bubbling out of his throat.

"Oh, Pru! What do you think? I'm dying to kiss you."

"Then why haven't you?"

His lips twisted into a rueful grin. "Because I'm afraid that once I start kissing you I won't be able to stop. How would we eat with our lips locked together?"

Smiling, she stepped close enough to slip her arms around his waist. "I'll take that chance."

Realizing he couldn't disappoint her, or himself, Luke bent his head and placed his lips on hers.

The contact was just as sweet and powerful as he remembered, and as he made a lingering search of her lips, he knew this wasn't just a passing thing with Prudence. He couldn't imagine his life without her. But more important, was she picturing Luke in her future?

Lifting his mouth from hers, he opened his eyes, and the dreamy look he saw on her face made him want to kiss her all over again.

"I—uh—think we'd better go—to dinner," he whispered.

With a coy smile, she opened the door and reached for his hand. "Yes, let's go have our dinner. After all, we have all night, don't we?"

The implication of her question was enough to send hot desire shooting straight through him, and he hustled her out the door before he could change his mind.

Chapter Nine

Located on the southwest edge of town, Jose's sat off the main highway just enough to make it a peaceful spot in the desert. The restaurant was a sprawling hacienda style with stucco walls painted a pale turquoise and a red-tiled roof. A porch with arched supports ran the width of the building. Normally, strings of dried red peppers hung from the center of each arch, but with winter months coming, the peppers had been exchanged for colorful gourds. At one end of the porch, a bougainvillea with a few yellow-gold blossoms grew to the top of the roof, while a fat saguaro with two arms stood at the opposite end.

"This is a neat-looking place," Luke commented

as they stepped onto the porch. "I have a feeling it's been here for a long time."

"Since back in the 1950s, I think. From what I've been told, the place is family-owned and has been handed down through the years. By the way, this is where Chandler and Roslyn were having dinner when she went into labor with Evelyn."

"Was it the food or something Chandler said?" Luke joked.

Laughing, she poked a finger in his ribs. "Neither. I think little Evelyn decided it was time she made her appearance."

He reached to open the carved wooden door. "Let's hope nothing that dramatic happens tonight," he said.

Inside, a hostess promptly seated the two of them near a tall arched window overlooking the desert. There was no moon, but plenty of stars shone down on the Joshua trees and stands of cacti and chaparral. Prudence never tired of the view, and tonight with Luke sitting at the table with her, it was like she was seeing it all for the very first time.

While waiting for their meal to be prepared, they sipped on icy margaritas and munched on an appetizer of tortilla chips and guacamole. Prudence had worked her way through several chips before she realized she'd been talking nonstop.

"Sorry, Luke. You must think I've turned into a canary tonight. I haven't shut up since we've sat down."

He shook his head. "I've enjoyed listening. Is it always so busy at St. Francis?"

Once they'd been seated, Luke had removed his hat and placed it out of sight in an adjacent chair. The brown felt pulled low on his forehead gave him a rugged, sexy look, but without it, she was seeing the man who'd lain next to her in bed. The man who'd made passionate love to her.

She supposed she'd kept up the chatter as a way to keep her mind away from those burning memories, but it hadn't worked. Even when she turned her gaze away from his face and out to the desert, she continued to relive those moments in her mind.

"If I had two quiet days in a row at school, I'd probably go into shock," she told him. "But that's enough about me and St. Francis. Tell me what you've been doing out at the ranch."

He shrugged and Prudence got the impression he wasn't all that accustomed to talking about his work with a woman. Was that because he didn't want to let things get that personal? Or did he think women weren't interested in his kind of work?

"My days don't change that much," he told her. "Holt and I have a routine we stick to. The only thing that changes is the horses. And that's what keeps the job interesting. They're just like humans—each one has a different personality and we have to adapt our training methods to match the horse."

"Just like a teacher has to adapt to each student," she said. "Does Three Rivers have many horses?"

He dipped a chip into the guacamole. "Counting the working remuda and the broodmares, probably close to four hundred head. And the cattle number in the thousands. Maureen and Gil are back from their honeymoon. They've been busy moving cattle down from the Prescott range—to beat the early snows."

"Maureen went through some major grief. I hope she and Gil will have years of happiness together." She looked over at him. "Has anyone in the family filled you in on how her late husband was killed?"

With a solemn nod, he said, "Holt told me everything. He wanted me to get the straight facts about the incident instead of hearing gossip. Pretty sad that Joel Hollister was killed for trying to help a victim of abuse."

"Very sad," she agreed. "But justice was served and the killer is behind bars now. And his poor wife, Ginny Patterson, is trying to overcome the stigma of her husband's crime."

Luke said, "I understand that Maureen has helped Ginny get an apartment and a job."

Prudence said, "I believe Ginny is working as a waitress now at the Broken Spur café here in Wickenburg. And she finally managed to get the divorce she'd been seeking for years."

"Did you know Joel Hollister?" Luke asked curiously.

"No. I hadn't met any of the Hollisters personally until Katherine married into the family. By then, Mr. Hollister had already been dead a few years. Everyone says Chandler looks just like his late father, but that Joel's personality was more like Holt's."

"Hmm. I wish I could've spent time with the man," he said thoughtfully. "He and Maureen obviously raised six fine children and kept the ranch in profitable shape. Considering the size of his family and the ranch, that's quite a feat."

"From everything I've heard, he was a strong man with a big heart," Prudence said thoughtfully. "Now Maureen is married to Joel's brother. Just goes to show you that a person never knows what the future might hold."

His gaze leveled on her face, and as Prudence looked into his brown eyes, she couldn't stop herself from wondering if he was pondering his own future. Did he want her to be a part of it, or was tonight just another brief encounter he would soon forget?

Don't be thinking about the future, Pru. Not tonight. Two days ago, you believed you'd never see this man again, but here you are with him having dinner. Don't mess things up by worrying over what might be.

The bossy voice going on in her head was pushed to the side when Luke replied, "I certainly never expected to be living in Arizona. Or...meeting someone like you. Just like you probably weren't thinking you'd wind up in Wickenburg."

Laughing softly, Prudence picked up her frosty glass and sipped the tangy margarita. "I wasn't thinking about leaving Palm Springs or taking a superintendent position. None of that happened until… after my divorce."

His eyes narrowed marginally. "What were you doing before your divorce?"

"Teaching in the classroom. You see, I'd always planned to do several years of teaching and then go into administration later. After—" Shaking her head, she took another sip of the drink and hoped the tequila would help clear the tangled knots of emotion from her throat. "Sorry. I was going to say after I had babies and got them raised to school age. But the divorce ended those plans, so when I saw the open position for superintendent at St. Francis, I thought what the heck, why wait?"

His gaze dropped to the basket of chips positioned in the middle of the table. "At least you managed to realize part of your dreams. That's more than most people get."

The faint cynicism in his voice surprised her. The only time she'd heard him express sarcasm, he'd done it in a joking way. Tonight was different and it made her wonder if he'd had some dreams of his own shattered. He'd mentioned once that he'd considered marriage, but he'd never really explained what had caused that plan to end. Had he been cheated on, too? Or had he simply decided he wanted to remain free?

She lifted her chin to a proud angle. "I like to think I'm wiser now."

His lopsided grin was full of disbelief, but she could handle that reaction better than the bitterness she'd gotten from him a few seconds ago.

"You learned a lesson. Is that it?"

"Something like that," she answered. "Mistakes are opportunities to learn."

Lowering his eyelids to sexy slits, he reached across the table and curled the tips of his fingers around hers. "You're the teacher, Pru. Maybe there's a few things you could teach me."

How to love? Really love? No, she thought. He wasn't thinking along those lines. His mind was on the purely physical. And for tonight she had to be content with the fact that he wanted her in that way. But could she be satisfied with just sharing a bed with him from time to time?

She didn't want to think about that question tonight. But come tomorrow, she was going to have to face it head-on.

After Luke and Prudence finished their meal, they took a short drive out in the desert before heading back to her house.

During the whole time Prudence was in a talkative mood, but the moment they walked onto the front porch and she unlocked the door, she went silent and Luke wondered if she might have decided that she wanted him to leave.

What would he do if she did announce their evening was over? Try to change her mind? Try to show her that the fire she'd built in him up in Reno was still burning as brightly as when it first ignited?

"I think my lock needs a bit of graphite," she said

as she jiggled the key in the doorknob. "It's been giving me problems about sticking."

He was about to offer his help when the lock finally clicked. As she pushed open the door and stepped inside, she glanced over her shoulder at him.

"You are coming in, aren't you?" she asked.

His heart was suddenly pounding with relief and anticipation. "Only if you want me to."

Reaching for his hand, she pulled him into the house. Luke hardly gave her time to shut the door and lock it before he snaked an arm around her waist and pulled her into his arms.

Tilting her head back, she looked up at him. "Was there any question about that?" she asked softly. "I've missed you so much, Luke. Missed having your arms around me. I'm not too proud to admit that."

"Oh, Pru. Just having you close to me like this— it's all I've been thinking about."

A coy smile tilted the corners of her plush lips as he brought his forehead next to hers.

"Does this mean you want to forget coffee?" she asked.

He chuckled under his breath. "Were we going to have coffee?"

"I was going to offer." Her hands moved from his back to the front of his shirt. "But it can wait."

"And I can't—wait to have you," he whispered as he brought his lips down on hers.

Kissing her was like a drink of ice-cold water after a hot, tiring day. So good and so needed. He didn't think he'd ever get enough of kissing her. Her lips conveyed feelings that he hadn't known existed. Her kisses pulled emotions from him that he was only beginning to identify as something deep and powerful. Everything about their relationship was beginning to scare him. But his heart didn't have the strength to end it.

His lungs were screaming for oxygen when he finally lifted his mouth from hers, and by then, his senses were so scattered he hardly recognized they were still standing in the foyer, only a couple of steps away from the door.

"We—uh—didn't make it very far—did we?" His words were broken by ragged breaths that did very little to ease the spinning in his head.

Her eyelids fluttered open, and as she looked up at him, Luke was jolted by the moisture glazing her blue-green eyes.

"At least we made it off the porch and into the house," she said huskily. Then, blinking rapidly, she glanced away.

Confused by her emotional reaction, he tentatively stroked a hand over her hair. "Pru, what's wrong? Have I hurt you?"

"No. It's— I'm okay."

She looked and sounded far from okay, he decided. She was torn about something. "If you want me to leave, I will."

Her misty gaze returned to his face. "I don't want you to leave," she whispered.

Luke's throat was suddenly so tight that he had to strain to make his vocal cords work. "You're having doubts about this—us—being together."

"You're wrong, Luke. I'm being a little emotional, that's all. I thought we were finished and—well, I'm happy that you're here. Truly."

Before he could reply, she wrapped her hand around his and led him out of the foyer. And like a helpless lamb, all Luke could do was follow willingly to wherever she wanted to take him.

At the end of a short hallway, they entered a door on the left, where the faint light slanting through the blinds outlined a double-size bed covered with a puffy white comforter.

Delicate lingerie was draped over the bed's footboard, along with a ruby-red dress. On the floor in front of a long dresser were two pairs of high heels lying next to their empty boxes.

"I have things scattered everywhere in here," she told him. "Just pretend you don't see the mess."

The sight of the cluttered room chased away the doubts swirling about in Luke's mind, and he quickly wrapped his arms around her waist and tugged her tight against him. "I'm glad it's messy. Makes you look normal."

She laughed under her breath. "Normal. Instead of?"

"Obsessive," he said.

"Mmm. The only thing I'm obsessive about is you."

She began to undo the snaps on his Western shirt, and as the folds of fabric parted, he thrust his hands into her hair and lifted the silky strands up to his face. The scent of it took him back to Reno, as did the soft touch of her hands roaming over his chest.

All these weeks since he'd been back on Three Rivers, a part of him had stayed behind in that hotel room, reliving the pleasures of her body, the tenderness of her sighs. Now he didn't have to go back there, he thought. She was standing right here in his arms and the whole night stretched before them.

Rising on the tips of her toes, she offered her mouth up to his, and he gladly accepted the invitation by fastening his lips over hers and wrapping her in the tight circle of his arms. By the time their tongues began to mate and her hands were marking heated trails across his back, Luke was forced to set her aside.

"I, uh, think our clothes are getting in the way, don't you?" he asked.

Purring deep in her throat, she reached for the zipper on her dress. "I say let's get out of them."

Once their clothing and footwear were piled in a heap on the floor, Luke lifted her onto the bed, then stretched out next to her.

The comforter was made of down, and as their weight sank deeply into the cloudlike softness, the scent of her, along with the warmth of her body, quickly enveloped his senses.

She immediately rolled into his arms and draped

a leg over his thighs. "I confess," she whispered against his cheek. "I've dreamed of having you here in my bed—my arms. Now it's a reality and oh so much better than a dream."

With a finger beneath her chin, he tilted her face so that their lips were practically touching. "I'll tell you what I've decided, sweet Pru. We've been crazy to stay away from each other all these days. We've wasted so much time—precious time that we could've been together, like this."

"Together," she whispered. "Is that what you really want?"

"I can't imagine wanting anything more."

Groaning, she closed her eyes and slipped an arm around his neck. "Kiss me, Luke. Love me until I can't think about anything but you."

With his lips on hers and his tongue delving deep into her mouth, he placed a hand at the base of her spine and drew her hips toward his throbbing member.

Another sultry groan sounded deep in her throat as she placed a hand on his shoulder and pushed him flat against the mattress. Then, with their lips still locked in a heated union, she quickly straddled him and lowered her hips until his manhood had slipped deep inside her.

Intense pleasure rocketed through every cell of his body, and when she began to move against him, his senses quickly floated away to a faraway place.

The space was soft and warm and filled with a million tiny stars that rained over him like a squall of golden sparks. And suddenly he couldn't hold back. All he could do was hang on to her while spasms of relief racked his body.

When his senses finally returned, he realized her damp body was still draped over his and her cheek was nestled against the hollow of his shoulder. Beneath his hand, her back rose and fell with each deep breath she took. And in that moment, as he relished her warmth and the beat of her heart thumping rapidly against his chest, he realized something profound had shifted things around in his heart and his mind. He wasn't the same Luke that had walked into this house a few hours ago, and the fact scared the hell right out of him.

He was trying to force the deep thoughts away when her head shifted and she pressed a kiss beneath his jawbone.

"Mmm. You taste salty," she murmured. "And even better than one of Jose's tortilla chips."

Bending his head, he nuzzled his lips against her temple. "Am I in danger of being eaten?"

Her soft chuckle fanned her breath over the side of his face. "Maybe. Are you worried?"

He'd never been so worried in his life. But he wasn't about to let her know that a passel of fears and doubts were swirling around in his head. Nor was he going to allow the upheaval in his heart to overshadow this night with her.

"I'm as tough as boot leather," he said in a teasing tone. "You'd break a tooth trying to chew me."

"It might be fun to try."

Sliding his fingers through her hair, he rested his cheek against the top of her head. "I didn't intend for that to happen, Pru."

She tilted her head back in order to see his face, and as he gazed into her eyes, his chest began to swell until the thickness traveled all the way to his throat.

"That? You mean us having sex?"

She called it *sex*. And, normally, Luke would have labeled the union of their bodies as just that—sex. But in the deepest recesses of his heart, he recognized it had been far more than physical for him. Yet he couldn't admit such a thing to Prudence. She didn't want strings. And he didn't want to scare her by hinting that he was beginning to think of her as more than an enjoyable date. Hell, he didn't want to scare himself.

"Mmm. Sorry I caused it to end too soon. But— oh, honey, you shipwreck my self-control."

"It wasn't too soon. It was perfect." A tender smile curved her lips as she touched her fingers to his cheek. "And where you're concerned, I don't have any self-control. Put a fudge brownie in front of me and I can push it aside. But you—I just want to pull you closer."

A veil of lashes suddenly hid her eyes and Luke could only wonder what she was thinking. Not about this very moment, but about tomorrow and the next day and the next. A month from now, even a year from now, would she still be wanting to pull him closer? Or would she be out searching for that right man? The one to give her children and a home together?

Since when have you started worrying about the future with a woman? Don't be a sap, Luke. Grab what pleasure you can from Prudence and move on before things get sticky. Before you get trapped into living your life for her and not yourself.

The sound of Prudence's soft sigh interrupted the taunting voice inside him, and he looked down to see that her eyes were searching his face.

"Is something wrong, Luke? You look like you're somewhere else."

Groaning, he rolled them both over until she was lying flat on her back beneath him. "I'm right here with you, Pru. Right where I want to be."

She murmured, "I hope Holt isn't expecting you to be at the horse barn very early in the morning."

"Five o'clock," he said, then lowered his lips to hers. "But we have hours until then. Let's not waste them. What do you say?"

Her lips formed a smile against his. "Seconds,

minutes, hours. No amount of time I spend with you is wasted."

Luke held her words to his heart as he lost himself in her kiss.

Chapter Ten

At seven forty-five the next morning, Prudence was sipping sweet, creamy coffee from a red mug when Katherine entered her office with a handful of folders.

"Good morning," she said cheerfully. "The top folder has the estimates you wanted on the maintenance for the bus fleet—excluding fuel costs, of course. The next one is a list of the topics the board members intend to discuss at their next meeting. Which will be two weeks from today. The third folder is a cafeteria order for the Thanksgiving food. This year we've had to use a different supplier, so the cost has gone up, naturally. And last but not least, Mrs. Morgan wants you to call her. She's so furious over her son being punished for having cigarettes in his backpack that she's threatening to pull him out of school."

"That's just what the boy needs," Prudence said, not bothering to hide her sarcasm. "Mrs. Morgan needs to take her gripe up with the principal. Whatever discipline Mr. Granger handed out, I fully back."

"Maybe you should make that clear to Mrs. Morgan," Katherine suggested.

"I will. As soon as I get a bit more of this coffee down."

Katherine placed the folders on Prudence's desk and sank into the chair in front of it. "Now we have that bit of business out of the way, we have at least five minutes to visit. So how was your date last night with Luke?"

Prudence lowered the cup and stared suspiciously at her friend. "I didn't tell you I was going on a date with Luke."

"No. You kept that little tidbit to yourself. Blake happened to meet Luke on the ranch road last night. He told Blake that he was taking you to dinner. But I should've guessed before. You seemed awfully smiley after he left the office the other day."

"Smiley? Really?"

"Yes. You actually looked happy. Which is more than I can say for you this morning. What happened? Did you two wind up in a sparring match or something? Or are you worried about something here at school?"

Prudence drew in a deep breath and let it out. "Heaven knows, there's always something to worry about here at school. As for Luke and I—we had a lovely dinner at Jose's. And a nice time afterward."

Katherine frowned. "That's all? *Nice?* I was hoping you were going to say *terrific* or *fabulous*!"

Prudence hoped her face didn't appear as red as it felt. "Look, Kat, the man is one sexy cowboy. And, yes, he does make my heart go pitter-patter. But that's as far as I can let it go. Actually, I was sitting here thinking that I'm—"

"What? That look on your face is scaring me, Pru. It's the one you used to have before you decided to be a woman again. Please don't go back to being that Prudence again. It isn't fair to you. Or to Luke."

An insidious pain suddenly snaked a path between her breasts. "You don't understand, Kat. That's the person I've had to be to survive—to keep from being hurt again. And I'm afraid—I've let my guard down with Luke. I've let him move into my heart, and if I don't do something quick, I'm going to be in for a huge letdown."

Frowning, Katherine shook her head. "Why a letdown? For some reason you're assuming that Luke is going to turn his back on you. I hope you have a good reason for thinking such a thing."

Prudence gripped the coffee mug and wondered why this morning when she'd woken to nothing but a short note Luke had left on the nightstand, she'd had the horrible feeling that her life, the life she'd worked so hard to make for herself here in Wickenburg, was sliding down a slippery slope.

"Kat, even if I had the courage to fall in love again, I'm not blind or stupid. Luke is a confirmed bachelor. He's made his mind up that he doesn't want the headache or the heartache of a wife or family. And don't ask me why he thinks that way. I have no idea. And I don't intend to ask. If I have to dig and pry or beg him to be a different man just for me, then it would never work."

Her eyes felt like she'd just walked through a sandstorm. But what could she expect after only a couple of hours of sleep? Prudence didn't have to look in a mirror to know she appeared wrung out. She'd carefully tried to camouflage the bags beneath her eyes, but she figured Katherine had already spotted them.

"Listen, Pru. You've heard this all before, but for your sake, I have to say it again. You know the hell I went through during my first marriage. And after I came back to Wickenburg and ran into Blake again, I was scared to death to get involved with him. I mean, first of all, he's one of the wealthiest ranchers in Arizona and I grew up with nothing—just an alcoholic father and a mother who grew too bitter to love anyone. I didn't have much more than that whenever we started dating. And Blake didn't want to get married. Remember? But *you* were certain the two of us belonged together. If you were so certain

Blake would come around to having a family, why don't you believe that Luke might?"

"I honestly can't answer that question, Kat. Except that—he keeps his feelings to himself. And last night—well, I felt like something was wrong, that he was someplace else." Sighing, she rose and walked over to the coffeepot to refill her mug. "Look, Kat, I'm eight years older than Luke. And I imagine he's been thinking about that gap. Even if he wanted to make a long-term go of it, I doubt I could hold on to him."

"Why not? What has your age got to do with that?"

Prudence shot her a bored look. "Don't be daft. You can't escape gravity's pull. In ten years, I'll be nearing fifty. I won't look like I do now. Not that my looks are special, but at least they're still youthful. Sooner or later, Luke is going to realize he doesn't want to be saddled with an older woman."

Katherine actually laughed, then stood and started out of the room. "I'll be right back," she called over her shoulder.

Prudence was still standing in the same spot, sipping her coffee, when a moment later, Katherine returned carrying a fancy gold-plated powder compact.

"Sorry, Kat, more powder isn't going to help my face today. I didn't get enough sleep."

"Hmm. Wonder why?" Katherine asked sarcastically. "Because Luke was too busy telling you all the reasons he doesn't want to be a husband?"

She opened the compact and held it in front of Prudence's face. "Take a good look," she ordered. "That isn't what Luke sees when he looks at you."

"No. His gaze usually doesn't remain on my face. It travels downward," Prudence said wryly.

"That only proves he's a man," Katherine retorted, then shook her head. "He sees your beauty, yes. But he also sees your kindness and your huge heart, among all that intelligence and— Well, I could go on and on. But you get the picture, don't you?"

Prudence got the picture, all right. Katherine was a romantic through and through. Blake adored her. Their love was unshakable. Of course Katherine was going to believe that Luke would eventually change into a family man. But Prudence wasn't that romantic or that much of a fool to let her beliefs go that far.

Pushing the powder compact and Katherine's hand aside, Prudence walked over to her desk. "Kat, besides being too romantic, you're a cockeyed optimist. But don't worry about me. This thing with Luke—I'm not going to let it get out of hand. What will be, will be."

Frowning, Katherine asked, "What does that mean?"

Thankfully, at that moment the first bell of the day rang, along with the telephone in the adjoining room. Both gave Prudence a good excuse to shoo Katherine out of the office. "Get out of here. I hear your phone ringing."

"You hear the bell," Katherine insisted.

"I hear both. We'll talk about me—later."

Realizing her phone was actually ringing, Katherine hurried toward the door while tossing over her shoulder, "You can bet we'll talk later."

Once her friend was totally out of view, Prudence grimly reached for her purse and fished out her cell phone.

She was going to do something she should've done weeks ago.

Luke stroked a hand down the filly's blazed face and smiled when she nudged him for more of the same.

"Blue Girl, you're beautiful, smart and willing to please. I think I'm going to tell Holt I want you for myself. He'll probably want an arm and a leg for you. But that's okay. You'll be worth it."

The filly gave his shoulder a nudge and Luke gave her a few more affectionate pats on the neck before he began the task of unsaddling her.

He was loosening the girth when he felt the cell phone in his shirt pocket buzz. Thinking it might be Prudence, he leaned against the hitching rail and pulled out the phone. But the caller wasn't Prudence; it was his brother, Colt.

Slipping off his glove, he swiped the screen and jammed the instrument to his ear. "What has you up so early this morning? An earthquake?" Luke teased.

Colt chuckled. "Ha! Eight thirty in the morning is the middle of the day for you and me. I've stopped for a cup of coffee, and for some damn reason you popped into my mind."

"You have room up there for me with all those women you date?"

Colt snorted. "I haven't been out with a woman in at least four days."

Luke grinned. "Wow, four days. That's an eon for you. What's wrong? Losing your touch?"

There was a short pause, and then Colt said, "Maybe that's it. Or maybe I'm getting bored with too many giggles and conversations about—nothing."

"How do you have a conversation about nothing?"

"You basically listen about hairdressers, nail technicians or the latest diet fad."

Luke started to laugh, but something in his brother's voice stopped him. "What's the matter, Colt? Don't you appreciate those topics?"

Colt muttered a curse word. "Something a little deeper would be a nice change," he answered. "But I didn't call to talk about my dates, or lack of them."

"Why did you call? You don't have enough horses to keep you busy?"

"Too many and too little help," he said flatly. "I mainly wanted to hear my big brother's voice. I guess I'm missing you more than I thought I would."

It wasn't like Colt to be sentimental. Normally, his younger brother was happy-go-lucky. "You could fly out for a visit," Luke suggested. "Thanksgiving is coming up."

"I promised Dad I'd spend the day with him,"

Colt said. "Lenore Whitley invited him to have dinner with her, but he turned her down."

"Lenore? Are you talking about the widow with the ranch south of Canyon?"

"That's the one. She'd be a nice catch for Dad, but you know him. He'll never get over Mom."

A melancholy feeling suddenly settled on Luke's shoulder. "Because he loved her so much? Or because of the…heck he went through to try to keep her happy?"

The line went silent for a moment, and then Colt finally said, "Both reasons, I'm thinking."

"Yeah. Both reasons." Luke's gaze drifted to the opposite end of the barn, where Holt appeared to be giving instructions to a pair of grooms. Only this morning his boss had confided that he and Isabelle were trying for another baby. Normally, that sort of thing would've drifted in one of Luke's ears and out the other, but not this time. Instead, Luke had been wondering if he had the makings to be a father. And how would it feel to have a child with a woman he loved?

Clearing his throat, Luke added, "I'm glad you'll be with Dad."

"Heck, spending the day with Dad will be a hell of a lot more enjoyable than listening to a step-by-step procedure of getting highlights in your hair," Colt said dryly. Then he added, "I'd better get back to work. But before I go, tell me how you've been. Still liking Three Rivers?"

"It's a horseman's paradise. I almost feel guilty for taking a salary."

Colt remarked, "I guess I'd be an idiot to ask if you've found a woman you can't live without."

Luke had found a woman. But after he'd vowed for years to remain single, did he honestly want to tie himself to Prudence? To keep her in his life?

You fool! Why can't you be honest with yourself and admit that you sure as heck don't want to let her go?

"Yeah, you'd be an idiot to ask," he said flatly, while thinking he didn't want to mention Prudence to his brother. Colt would pepper him with all kinds of questions. Many of which he wasn't ready to answer.

Colt let out a heavy breath, and Luke got the impression his brother wanted to say more about something. But after a moment of silence stretched between them, he finally told him he had to get back to work and ended the call with a simple goodbye.

Luke made sure the connection was ended and was about to slip the phone back into his pocket when he noticed a text message had come in while he'd been talking.

Spotting Prudence's name, he quickly opened the message and read:

Are you going to be home tonight? I need to drive out and talk to you.

Talk? She was going to drive all the way out here to the ranch to talk when all she had to do was call?

Telling himself not to look a gift horse in the mouth, he tapped out a reply: Okay. I should be home by seven.

Prudence was so late getting away from work that evening, she didn't have time to go home and change out of the leather skirt and silk shirt she'd worn to school. Luke had texted that he'd be home by seven and she didn't want to be late. She needed to get this talk over with as quickly and painlessly as possible.

How she was dressed or the fact that her makeup had faded to nonexistence didn't matter, she thought, as she steered her car over the dirt road leading to Luke's house. She no longer wanted him to look at her with desire. She didn't want him to touch her, kiss her, melt her with his lovemaking. She'd behaved like a reckless fool. She'd allowed herself to become attached when she had vowed never to feel that way again. But the starry-eyed blindness she'd been suffering had finally lifted and she was bound and determined to pull her heart back to safety.

When Prudence finally parked her car and walked up to the front porch of Luke's house, the night had turned cold and cloudy. To match her mood, Prudence thought dismally, as she stood beneath the circle of light shed by a porch lamp hanging over the carved wooden door.

As she waited for Luke to answer her knock,

she glanced across the length of the porch and was surprised to see pots of bright yellow and copper-colored chrysanthemums lining the edge of the wooden planked floor, while at the far end, a group of red-and-white motel furniture invited a person to sit and gaze at the distant buttes. The homey images didn't fit a rough, tough cowboy who shied away from family life, but she was finished with hoping and wishing that he'd show her a different side of himself.

Her deep thoughts were interrupted by the rattle of the doorknob, and she looked around just in time to see Luke pushing open the door.

"Hello, Pru." Not giving her time to reciprocate the greeting, he reached for her hand and pulled her across the threshold and straight into his arms. "This is a surprise."

"Luke, I—"

He didn't allow her to finish. Instead, his lips covered hers in a hot, searching kiss that practically sucked the air from her lungs.

"Mmm. What a way to start the evening," he murmured when he finally lifted his head. "I think I could get used to this."

Dear God, what was she doing? He was the best thing that had ever happened to her. Why wasn't she willing to claw and fight any and every which way she could to keep the two of them together?

"Hello, Luke," she said quietly. "I'm sorry about barging in on you like this."

"Are you crazy? I'm so glad you're here." He stepped around her to shut the door, then took her by the hand. "Come on. Let's go to the kitchen. I've made coffee. Have you eaten yet? I have chicken and dumplings that Reeva made. I don't know if you're familiar with the Hollisters' cook, but everything she makes melts in your mouth."

The happiness she heard in his voice tempted her to give in and simply throw her arms around him. To tell him that she'd driven out to the ranch because she couldn't wait another minute to be with him. But one night would turn into another night and another. And each hour she spent with him chipped away at her resolve to have more in her life than a hot affair with a sexy young cowboy.

"Yes," she finally replied. "I've eaten a few of Reeva's meals. She should have her own cooking show."

Luke laughed. "Reeva on camera might not work. The few times I've been around her, I've noticed she blurts out whatever is on her mind. With a few colorful words thrown in."

Prudence tried to laugh, but the sound lodged against the giant lump of emotions in her throat.

"Uh—I'm really not hungry, Luke," she said. "You go ahead and have your supper. Coffee will be enough for me."

With his hand still wrapped around hers, he urged her away from the door and through a large living area.

"You must've eaten a huge meal in the school cafeteria today," he said as they passed through a hall-way and entered another room. "You always have an appetite."

"No. I didn't overindulge. I'm just not hungry to-night."

The hollow sound to her voice must have caught his attention because he paused to level a quizzical look at her.

"Okay, Pru, what's wrong? You don't look or sound like yourself."

Prudence doubted she'd ever be the same woman who'd danced in his arms at Maureen's wedding reception, or the uninhibited woman who'd given herself so freely to him in Reno. But that Prudence hadn't been playing it safe.

She swallowed hard as the backs of her eyes began to burn. "I guess I'm not myself tonight," she admit-ted. "I have a lot on my mind—that's why I'm here."

The gentle smile on his face disappeared. "Come sit down," he urged. "Tell me what's bothering you."

He guided her over to a long rust-colored couch, and as she sank into the leather cushion, she recog-nized they were in a cozy den with a wall of win-dows facing the river that traveled a crooked trail behind the house.

He took a seat on the cushion next to her, all the while his anxious gaze never leaving her face. "Something is off with you. Your face is white and you don't want to eat. I—"

"I have something I need to say," she interrupted,

fearful a few words from him would break her resolve. "I...don't want us to see each other anymore."

The expression on his face was that of a person
who'd just been told an inane joke. "If you're trying
to be funny, Pru, you're failing."

She drew in a deep, bracing breath. "There's nothing amusing about what I'm trying to say. I feel like
we made a mistake last night, Luke. After Reno, we
should've never gotten together again. I think you
know that as well as I."

His head jerked from side to side. "A mistake?
That's not the way it felt to me! And you were hardly
behaving as though you believed it was wrong!"

Her face flaming, she turned her gaze toward the
row of windows on the opposite side of the room.
"You don't understand, Luke. I've enjoyed every
minute I've spent with you. And if we continued
on, I'd still feel that way. But this morning...when I
woke up and found your note—"

He reached over and wrapped his hand around
hers. "I had to go to work, Pru! You, of all people,
should understand I can't shirk my job. And you were
sleeping so peacefully I didn't want to wake you."

Shaking her head, she said, "None of that has anything to do with my decision. You have to take care
of your job. Just like I have to take care of mine. This
is about my future—your future. We want different
things in our lives. I respect your feelings about staying single. And I certainly don't want to try to change

you into someone you're not. But I'm eight years older than you, Luke. This just isn't going to work."

His expression changed into a stoic mask as he released his hold on her hand and stared across the room. "I see. Well, it's not like we, uh, made a commitment to each other or anything. You knew I wasn't looking for anything serious. I guess—" He looked back at her. "I was hoping that we could've spent more time together before you decided to… end things. But I feel lucky that you've given me this much."

He was being open-minded and understanding. She should be feeling immense relief. Instead, her heart was breaking, and tears were threatening to spill onto her cheeks.

"I feel lucky, too, Luke. You came into my life and showed me that it was time to let myself be a woman again. If not for you and the special time we spent together in Reno, I might still be living in the past, too bitter to think about loving another man."

Not waiting to hear any reply he might have, she rose from the couch and tried to face him with a smile. But her whole face felt as though it was cracking like dried clay. She couldn't let him see that she was falling apart, she thought frantically. Not now, or ever.

"I… Goodbye, Luke. I hope…you'll always remember me as a friend."

She practically ran from the room and was crossing the hallway when he caught up to her. Wrapping a hand around her upper arm, he turned her to face him.

"You're going to leave—just like this?" he asked.

Damn it, why couldn't he let her go? Did he want to see her cry and crumble right at his feet? "There's nothing else for me to say or do, Luke."

He pulled her into his arms and kissed her for long, long moments. When he finally set her back from him, he murmured, "That's the way I'll remember you, Pru. Always."

Pressing the back of her hand to her burning mouth, she shook her head, then turned and raced out of the house.

Somehow Prudence managed to hold herself together while she started the car and headed it out of Luke's driveway and onto the ranch road. But once she could no longer see the lights of his house in her rearview mirror, tears began to burn the backs of her eyes. Only this time, she didn't allow the drops of heartache to fall. Instead, she swallowed hard and told herself she was doing what was best for the both of them.

At one end of the training arena, Luke handed the reins of the horse he'd just ridden to one of the young wranglers who'd been assisting him since the day had begun nearly twelve hours ago.

"Let Lumpy out in the north paddock, then fetch the little buckskin from the holding pen, Jim. I want to ride him before I quit for the day."

Jim cast Luke a worried look. "It's almost dark now, Luke, and you've put in a long day. Don't you think the buckskin can wait until morning?"

"In case you haven't noticed, the arena has plenty of lights. If you want to quit for the day, that's fine," Luke snapped at him. "I'll go get the horse myself."

"You can get mad if you want," Jim shot back at him. "But if you ask me, you're going a little overboard."

"I don't remember asking for your opinion about my work hours," Luke retorted.

His jaw clamped tight, the cowboy muttered, "From now on, I don't give a damn if you fall over from exhaustion. I'll saddle the buckskin."

Luke was watching Jim stalk off toward the holding pen when Holt walked up and stood next to him.

"You two having trouble?"

"Nothing I can't handle," Luke said flatly. Then, with a rueful shake of his head, he glanced at Holt. "Sorry. I sound like a jerk. And I just treated Jim like a doormat. I'm going to have to apologize to him and hope he accepts it."

"You've been working way too hard, Luke. You need to understand that I don't expect this much out of you. Neither does anyone else in the family. In fact, we're all getting a little concerned about you."

Luke arched a skeptical brow at him. "About me? Why? I'm fine. Am I making a mess of my job or something?"

Holt grimaced. "Not at all. You're doing wonders

with the horses. We admire your work. We're worried about you personally, that's all."

Luke's gaze dropped to the toes of his dusty boots. "I didn't realize I've been putting off bad vibes until Jim called me out just now."

"Maybe you should tell me what's wrong. Has something been going on with your brother or father?"

"No. Thank God, they're fine," Luke answered.

"Then it must be something about Prudence that's troubling you."

Luke tried not to stiffen at Holt's suggestion. "I don't want to talk about Prudence. She's out of my life. Which is the way it should be."

A moment of silence passed before Holt thoughtfully repeated, "Out of your life. Guess you pushed her out—because you didn't want a serious kind of girl like her."

The pain that Luke had been carrying around in the middle of his chest suddenly grew to an agonizing ache. Nearly two weeks had passed since Prudence had told him goodbye, and time hadn't lessened the loss he was feeling. Everything she'd said to him had been playing over and over in his mind. Everything about that last kiss he'd planted on her lips had continued to haunt him.

"Prudence deserves more than I can give her. Stepping out of the way was the only way to fix things."

"As far as you're concerned, it doesn't appear to me like anything is fixed. You look like hell. Mom wants to send you to the family doctor. She thinks you're physically ill. I'll be sure to tell her that it's your head that has the problem."

Luke grimaced. "You couldn't be more right, Holt. My head got all mixed up when I first met Prudence. I was thinking we could get involved without getting attached. I was wrong. But I'll get past it. I just need a little more time to forget."

"I'm guessing you thought she'd go along with just having an affair—or something like it," Holt said frankly. "I can't say that I blame you. I mean, what man doesn't want to have his fun without the added responsibilities?"

Luke didn't miss the sarcasm in Holt's voice and he realized he deserved every bit of disdain the man could dish out. "I never made promises to Prudence. We only had a brief relationship. It was nothing serious."

"If it wasn't serious, then why do you look like your world has ended? I'm certainly not an expert when it comes to human nature. I can read horses a hell of a lot better than I can a person. But even I can see you're unhappy."

"Damn it, Holt. I miss Prudence," he gruffly admitted. "I guess I'm having a few regrets, but I'll get over it."

"Okay. If you think playing the field and being a bachelor means more to you than Prudence, then you don't have a thing to worry about. You'll stop missing her—eventually." He gave Luke's shoulder an affectionate slap. "I'm heading home for the night. Gabby has promised to bring Carter his favorite dish of meatballs tonight. She spoils her grandson rotten. It'll be a good thing when the baby gets here."

Luke looked at him. "The baby?"

Holt's grin spread from ear to ear. "Didn't I tell you? Isabelle is pregnant. She should arrive smack in the middle of this coming summer."

Luke was truly happy for Holt. Yet at the same time, he felt like a kid who'd been forgotten at Christmas. Which was a stupid reaction. He didn't want to be a father or a husband. Especially since he'd seen for himself how Prudence could instantly go from hot to cold. One night, she'd been loving and passionate. The next night, she'd flatly announced that the two of them were over. The whole horrible scene was like watching his mother's moods swing from happy to sad in the matter of a few seconds. And yet, deep down, he knew that Prudence wasn't like his mother in that sense. Nor would she ever be.

Shoving the dismal thoughts aside, Luke did his best to sound cheerful. "Congratulations, Holt. You've already learned the baby is going to be a girl?"

Holt chuckled, and it was easy to see the news of the coming baby had put the man on top of the world.

"No. But I like to tease Isabelle. She wants another boy. She has a penchant for rascals," he added with another laugh. "Explains why she married me."

"Lucky you."

"Yeah, lucky me. See you in the morning, Luke."

Holt strode off to the back end of the arena, and as Luke watched the man pass through a small gate, the outdoor lights flickered on and flooded the perfectly harrowed ground where Luke was standing.

Hell, he was bone tired. Riding the buckskin should've waited until the morning. But he'd already made a big enough jerk of himself. He wasn't about to tell Jim to take the horse back to the paddock.

"Here he is, Luke. I put the high-back saddle on him. Since it's getting cold, I thought he might be feeling frisky." The cowboy handed the reins of the buckskin out to Luke. "Will you be needing me for anything else?"

With a rueful shake of his head, Luke tossed the split reins over his forearm. "No. Except that before you leave I want to apologize. You should've knocked me flat a while ago. I've been acting like a first-class jackass."

The young cowboy awkwardly scuffed the toe of his boot against the loose dirt. "Aw, forget it, Luke. We all have bad days."

Every day since Prudence had said goodbye had been a bad day for Luke. But from his standpoint, there was nothing he could do about it, except move forward and remind himself not to make the same mistake again.

"Thanks, Jim. Me flying off the handle had nothing to do with you. You're always nothing but the best. I've been…going through a rough patch, that's all."

The cowboy thoughtfully lifted his hat and raked a hand over a mass of thick blond hair. "We all have them, Luke. Try not to be so hard on yourself. Tomorrow will be better."

Jim turned and walked out of the arena, while Luke wearily mounted the buckskin. As he nudged the horse into a trot, then methodically put the gelding through a series of stops, spins and a loping circle eight, Jim's remark came back to him.

Try not to be so hard on yourself.

Hell, Luke deserved every minute of the misery he was feeling. From the very first moment he'd looked at her, he'd known they were a mismatch, but he hadn't been able to resist her. And then slowly and surely, he'd decided he didn't want to resist. No matter the consequences, he wanted to be with her and a part of her life.

The night he'd taken Prudence to Jose's for dinner and they'd gone back to her house and her bed, he'd been a heartbeat away from telling her that he didn't want their relationship to end after one or two more nights together. He'd very nearly admitted that he wanted the two of them to always be together. But something had held him back.

Maybe the image of his father limping slightly on his prosthetic leg, or his mother yelling obscenities and throwing objects around the room. Luke couldn't be sure what had held the words inside him.

And now, after Prudence's sudden about-face, he was glad those words had remained buried somewhere deep inside him.

At least now she'd never know that he'd made the foolish mistake of falling in love with her.

Chapter Eleven

For Prudence, Friday mornings always seemed to be more hectic than Mondays. Everything that needed to get done during the week seemed to culminate on that last day to demand her attention. This Friday was no different. She'd been at work for an hour and a half, and most of that time she'd spent on the phone or dealing with staff problems. Normally, Prudence thrived on her work, but this morning she was struggling to remain physically upright.

"Pru, you can argue and fuss all you want to, but I'm making you a doctor's appointment. If you're suffering from a stomach virus, you need to know it. And you certainly don't need to be here at school spreading it through the staff or students."

Prudence let out a resigned sigh. "Okay. I give up. I'm tired of feeling like this. Go ahead and see if a doctor can work me in this morning. I have an afternoon meeting with the PA system technicians, remember? I don't want to miss them."

"You're more important than new speakers being installed in the auditorium. You look awful, Pru. I'm betting you've lost ten pounds."

"No. Only five pounds. But I'll get it back as soon as this nausea subsides," Prudence assured the other woman.

A frown of concern marred the brunette's face as she picked up the phone on Prudence's desk and punched in the number of the medical clinic located only a couple of blocks down from St. Francis Academy.

While she dealt with the clinic receptionist, Prudence leaned back in the executive chair and closed her gritty eyes. It was very unusual for her to be ill. In fact, she couldn't remember the last time she'd had so much as a simple cold. But something had her feeling swamped with fatigue, and the thought of food made her want to run straight to the nearest bathroom. True, she'd been upset over the breakup with Luke, but she didn't think the stress of a broken heart was enough to ruin her digestive system.

Or maybe it was, damn it! Since that night three weeks ago when she'd told Luke goodbye, everything seemed to be falling apart.

Katherine hung up the phone and handed her a

small slip of paper with an appointment time scribbled on it. "Okay. Nine thirty with Dr. Whitaker. That means you have fifteen minutes to get to the clinic and register. Can you drive yourself? Or would you like for Selby to take you?"

Selby had been the head custodian at St. Francis for more than forty years and was always happy to do any task that was asked of him. "I don't need Selby to chauffeur me to the clinic. I can make it."

Rising to her feet, she reached for the white woolen coat she'd hung on a hall tree in the corner of the room. Katherine was instantly at her side to help her get into the garment and button the row of buttons down the center of the front.

"There. At least I won't have to worry about you being cold." Katherine finished fastening the button at Prudence's throat before she stepped back and a look of concern slid over her face. "I could get Elaine to watch my office while I go with you to the clinic."

"Principal Granger has enough problems without you distracting his secretary. Now quit worrying about me. I'll be back as soon as my appointment is over. In the meantime, if anything super urgent comes up, text me."

"I wouldn't text you if the whole school caught on fire," Katherine informed her. "Now get out of here."

As usual, the clinic lobby was jammed with waiting patients, and as Prudence took a seat in one of the plastic chairs, she expected to remain there for at least an hour or more before she was summoned back to an examination room. But, surprisingly, only ten minutes passed before a nurse called her name and ushered her down a hallway to a large alcove where she promptly took Prudence's vital signs, along with weighing her and taking notes on her symptoms.

Once the older woman was finished with those tasks, she directed Prudence on down the hallway to a lab room.

"Do I really need a blood test, Nurse?" Prudence asked. "I haven't been fasting."

The nurse cast her an understanding smile. "From what you've told me, there's nothing in your stomach anyway. But don't worry. A blood test will most likely give the doctor the clues he needs to diagnose your problem."

Once she was finished at the lab, Prudence was taken to an examining room, where she waited and waited some more for the doctor to appear. After more than an hour, a rap on the door announced his arrival, and a tall doctor wearing a stiff white lab coat strode in as though he didn't have a minute to waste.

The matronly nurse following him took one look at Prudence and frowned. "I'm sorry, Doctor. The patient should've already been undressed."

Uneasy with the way the situation was progressing, Prudence glanced from the nurse to the doctor, who was already on his way out of the room.

"Undressed?" Prudence practically screeched.

"Is that necessary for a stomach virus? I need to get back to school!"

"Relax, Ms. Keyes. As soon as you get out of your clothes, put on this gown. Open to the front." The nurse handed the white paper garment to Prudence. "I promise you'll be out of here and on your way before you know it."

Thirty minutes later, Prudence had to admit the nurse was partially right. She was out of the clinic, but she wasn't on her way back to school. Rather, she was sitting behind the steering wheel of her parked car, her hand gently cradling the lower part of her stomach.

She didn't have a stomach virus! She was going to have a baby.

When the doctor had announced she was pregnant, she'd been totally stunned. She'd been on oral birth control during the time she'd spent with Luke. The thought of getting pregnant hadn't crossed her mind. Although the idea should've registered with her before now. The doctor explained that even oral contraceptives weren't totally foolproof. Looking back on it, she should've realized the repulsion toward food and the bouts of fatigue meant she was in the early weeks of pregnancy.

Eight or nine weeks wasn't so early, she mentally corrected herself. The timing meant she'd gotten pregnant in Reno. The magical time she'd spent with Luke in Nevada had created a baby—their baby.

Oh, Lord, what was he going to think? How was

she going to find the strength to face him with the news? No doubt he was going to be upset with her. He was a man who didn't want to be tied down with a wife or children. She was hardly going to suggest he marry her. Even so, that wouldn't take away the fact that he was going to be a father.

And what about her parents and sister, all of whom considered Prudence to be so conservative? She couldn't imagine how they were going to take the news.

Forget about Luke and your family, Prudence! Just think how the St. Francis school board is going to react when they hear that you're having a child out of wedlock! Along with academics and sports, the school is based on moral and spiritual learning. How is it going to look for their superintendent to be pregnant without a man at her side?

Ignoring the condemning voice in her head, Prudence started the engine, and while she made the short drive back to St. Francis, doubts and questions darted at her from every direction. And yet they were far outweighed by the joy that fizzed and popped inside her like the glasses of champagne she and Luke had shared at Maureen's reception.

True, the situation wasn't ideal, she thought. But right at this moment, she wasn't going to let anything stymie her excitement. She'd wanted children for so long and now she was finally on her way to becoming a mother. Whether Luke would be happy or bit-

ter about the news, Prudence could only guess. As
for her, it was a dream come true.

An hour later, sitting on a small couch along one
wall in Prudence's office, Katherine continued to
look at her with wry amazement.

"Apparently, what happens in Reno doesn't always
stay in Reno," she said with a coy grin.

Prudence groaned. "It's all your fault, you know. If
you hadn't booked me at that damn hotel, I would've
never seen Luke again. Unless it was from a safe
distance. Like a mile away and through a binocu-
lar lens."

She hadn't planned to tell Katherine about the
baby. Not until she'd had a chance to see Luke and
tell him face-to-face. But as soon as Prudence had returned to her office, her friend had taken one look at
her stunned expression and mouthed the word "pregnant."

Her eyes twinkling, Katherine exclaimed, "Oh,
Pru, I'm so happy for you! You're going to make a
wonderful mother."

"I intend to do my best. But what about Luke? I'm
not even sure he'll want to be a part of the baby's life."

Katherine scowled. "Luke isn't that kind of a man.
He's going to be happy about the baby. I just know
it. And what a coincidence—I don't think I've told
you yet, but Isabelle and Holt are expecting another
baby. I think it's due the last part of June."

"How incredible. That's when the doctor said mine should be arriving."

"Hmm. Horse trainers who work together will have babies together. This is like Joe and Connor all over again! But it's nice. I know Holt will think so. He's gotten pretty close to Luke."

Prudence's eyes flew wide. "You won't tell Blake or anyone else about me being pregnant, will you? I need time to speak with him before the news spreads around your family."

Katherine reached over and patted the back of Prudence's hand. "You know me better than that. Not a peep from these lips until you give me the word. Cross my heart."

Prudence heaved out a long breath, then leaned her head against the back of the couch. "Oh, Kat, I don't… I expect Luke is going to be unhappy about this. And it's all my fault. I assured him that I was protected with the pill. Now he's going to think I'm lying."

Katherine's mouth fell open, and then she actually laughed. "Your fault? Are you kidding? Anytime a man has sex with a woman, there's a chance of creating a baby. Luke would have to be pretty dumb not to know that old score."

"Yes, I'm sure he's aware of the fact. And the doctor told me that the only birth control that's foolproof is abstinence. Still, this pregnancy makes me look conniving—or worse." She wiped a hand across her furrowed brow. "Oh, well, I suppose the why or how doesn't matter. It's not like I expect anything out of the man. But our son or daughter deserves his love."

Katherine leveled a pointed look at her. "When are you going to tell Luke? Soon?"

Prudence scooted to the edge of the couch and pushed her tumbled hair off her face. "If he's going to be home, I'll see him tonight. There's no use in putting off the inevitable."

"You're right. And everything is going to be… great, Pru. You just wait and see."

The phone in Katherine's office began to ring, and the woman gave Prudence's hand another encouraging pat before she hurried to answer it.

Luke's watch read half past five that evening when he steered his truck onto Prudence's driveway and parked behind her little economy car. Darkness had already fallen and the cool spell that had arrived earlier this morning had dipped the temperature even lower.

Flipping up the Sherpa collar on his denim jacket, he climbed out of the warm truck cab and hurriedly strode to the porch. Prudence must've been watching for him, because the door opened before he had a chance to knock.

"Come in, Luke," she said. "I hope you didn't drive all the way into town just to meet with me. I was going to come out to your place."

He stepped past her and into the house. "I realize you said in your text that you'd drive out to the ranch. But I had personal business in town at the bank. And Holt wanted me to pick up a few things at the farm and ranch store. There was no need for you to drive all that way."

She bolted the door behind him and then gestured for him to precede her into the living area.

"I appreciate you coming by. What I have to say is important. Otherwise, I wouldn't be bothering you."

Bothering him? She'd been doing that ever since he'd looked over his shoulder at the wedding and spotted her lovely face, he thought.

"I'm sure you wouldn't," he said flatly.

She darted a glance in his direction and Luke sensed that her nerves were rattled. Why? Had she changed her mind about the two of them? Had she decided that her decision to end things between them was wrong?

"Have a seat. Would you like something to drink?" she asked.

"No, thanks. I'm fine. I just had coffee at the Broken Spur." He took off his jacket and hung it and his brown hat on the back of an armchair before he took a seat on the couch.

She sat down on the couch a short distance away from him, then drew in a deep, bracing breath, and as Luke allowed his eyes to travel over her, he realized she looked almost ill. Her face was extremely pale and there were dark smudges beneath her eyes. Was something wrong with her health and she wanted him to know about it?

Resting her folded hands on her lap, she said, "I'm sure you're wondering why I wanted to see you."

"I'll admit I was surprised to hear from you."

"Well, like I said, it's important and…something you need to know about."

"Really? I honestly can't imagine why I'd need to know anything about you. You cut the ties between us—what few there were," he added bitterly, then shook his head. "Sorry, Pru. I promised myself I wasn't going to be angry or hateful or— Well, you made your choice. That's all I'm going to say. I'll live with it."

She closed her eyes and pinched the bridge of her nose, and for one awful moment, Luke thought she was going to cry. But then she dropped her hand away from her face and gave him a wan smile.

"Yes, I made my choice. And I'm pregnant."

He was so busy trying to figure out her motive for this meeting tonight that he very nearly missed the word *pregnant*. Then, like a jagged bolt of lightning crashing onto a mesa top, it struck him.

"You? Pregnant? You're going to have a baby?"

"I just found out this morning. At the doctor's office."

The questions swirling in his head were far outweighed by the tender feelings prodding at the protective wall around his heart.

"Pru, I— This is incredible!"

Her lips compressed into a thin line. "I'm sure you're thinking I purposely planned this."

Luke hardly heard what she was saying. All he wanted was to pull her into his arms and hold her until the wondrous feelings inside him flowed into her.

"No," he said. "The thought never entered my mind."

Her shoulders drooped. With relief, he supposed. Or was that outright misery weighing her down? Just because he was happy about this turn of events didn't mean she was jumping for joy. Actually, she looked like a woman who was about to burst into tears.

Dropping her head, she said, "I was being truthful when I told you I was on the pill. This morning the doctor explained that in spite of me taking oral birth control, there are a number of medical reasons why I ended up getting pregnant." She shrugged. "I could name them off to you, but I happen to think the reason was heavenly intervention."

He scooted closer to her. "I happen to agree with you. But, Pru, I have to know—are you unhappy about having my baby?"

Her head flew up and her eyes grew misty as they rapidly scanned his face. "Do you really want to hear the truth?"

"I wouldn't expect anything less from you."

Her smile was nothing more than a weak quiver to her lips. "I'm super happy. Considering the circumstances, I doubt most people would make much sense of that. But I've told you before how much I wanted children." She flattened a hand against her lower abdomen. "And this baby is already loved. Very much."

Something inside him was melting, pouring through him like soft, warm rain. This beautiful woman was carrying his child, *loving* his child. If God chose this moment to rip everything else away from Luke, he would still be a blessed man.

"I'm glad. Very glad," he said.

Her expression was impossible to read as she looked aside and wiped a hand over her eyes.

"Are you?" she asked in a strained voice.

"Why wouldn't I be glad?"

Grimacing, she turned her gaze back to his face. "You've made it perfectly clear that you never intended to be a family man. But there's no need for you to worry, Luke. Yes, you'll be a father, but you'll still be a free-roaming maverick. And that's the way it should be—the way I want it."

He felt his jaw drop as he struggled to digest the meaning of her words. "I'm not exactly sure as to what you're trying to say, but I'll be exact. I want you to marry me. I want us to be parents to our child together. That probably sounds old-fashioned to you, but it's the way I think and feel."

Jumping to her feet, she turned her back to him. "That is old-fashioned of you, Luke. And I—I'm trying to be a progressive woman. One who isn't afraid to take care of herself and her child. Rest assured that I'll always want you to be a part of the baby's life. But marriage is…out of the question."

Like a cold, hard wind, her words slammed him. "Why? A guy who rides horses for a living isn't good enough for you?"

"Don't be stupid," she muttered. "Your occupation has nothing to do with this."

"Then what does? You don't love me? Well, I don't expect you to." *But it sure would be nice*, he thought. The realization stopped him short.

Since when had he started thinking in those terms? Days ago? Weeks ago? The timing no longer mattered, he thought. He wanted her to love and need him. But she didn't, and the fact was like a knife to his heart.

With her back still to him, she said, "Listen, Luke, I've already made the mistake of marrying a man who had no business being a husband. I'm not about to put myself through that kind of hell again. You don't want to be tied to a woman. You'd be miserable, and your unhappiness would spread to me."

"Okay, I admit that I had it in my head to remain single. But a man can change, can't he?"

The sound she made was a mixture of a groan and a cynical snort. "Overnight? No, Luke. It wouldn't work."

Standing, he reached for her hand and enfolded it between the two of his. "Object all you want, Pru, but this baby binds us together—for the rest of our lives."

She kept her face averted from his. "Yes, but we don't have to be married to parent our child."

"The hell you say. That's pathetic. I don't care

what society has evolved into. And maybe being single parents works for some folks. But that's not the way I want my son or daughter to be raised!"

She whirled to face him and the look in her eyes was stark, almost angry. "And I'm not going to be tied to a husband who doesn't love me! A man who married me just so we'll be living under the same roof. What the hell kind of marriage is that?"

"Pru, I— You make it sound horrible. It wouldn't be that way. I—"

Her eyes were sparking fire as she interrupted his next words. "Luke, don't you dare start spouting that you love me! That you've loved me from the first moment you saw me. But, of course, you didn't recognize your feelings until tonight."

"I wasn't going to say any such thing," he shot back at her. But he'd been thinking it, damn it, and that was just as bad.

"Good. Because you'd be wasting your breath and my time. I wouldn't believe you if you got down on your knees and groveled!"

Oh, God, he supposed he deserved this irony. The only time in his life that he'd ever really loved a woman and he'd missed his chance to tell her. Anything he could say now would come across as phony and placating. There was no use in trying.

"I'm finished making a fool of myself," he said flatly. "If you change your mind about things, you know where to find me."

He walked out of her house. But not out of her life,

he thought. Now, with their baby on the way, walking out of her life could never happen.

Cold food settled better on a queasy stomach. That was what Prudence's mother, Bonita, used to say when her young daughters suffered a tummy ache. Following that advice, Prudence had brought a turkey and cheese on rye and stored it in the lounge refrigerator until the lunch bell had sounded a few minutes ago. But now that she had the sandwich lying on her desk in front of her, she had yet to take a bite.

A knock had Prudence glancing up to see Katherine standing in the doorway.

"Hey, I'm on my way to the cafeteria," she said. "Feel like coming with me?"

Prudence pointed to the sandwich. "I brought my lunch today. But I haven't gotten the nerve to take a bite yet."

Katherine marched into the room and jabbed a finger at the sandwich. "If you don't intend to eat the sandwich, I'm going to drag you to the cafeteria. The baby needs nourishment and your stomach will be much happier with something in it."

Since Katherine had learned that Prudence was pregnant, the woman had been hovering over her like a proud mother hen. Apparently, her friend hadn't stopped to think that Prudence would most likely have to resign her position as superintendent. St. Francis was a faith-based school. The board couldn't possibly allow a single pregnant woman to remain in charge. But she didn't have the heart to bring up this sad fact to Katherine right now.

Sighing, Prudence picked up one of the triangles. "Okay. I'll eat. For the baby."

"Good. And while I'm gone, you'd better not throw it in the trash and tell me you've eaten it."

Prudence smiled wanly. "You're so suspicious."

Laughing, Katherine headed out of the room. "You're so right."

Minutes later, she'd managed to finish most of the sandwich, along with a bottle of milk, when her cell phone rang.

Glancing at the screen, she saw the caller was Daisey. Prudence wasn't exactly ready to talk to her sister about the baby, but she supposed there was no point in putting it off any longer. At least when the bell rang, she'd have an excuse to hurriedly end the call.

"Hi, sis. How are things in Palm Springs?" she asked, doing her best to sound cheerful.

"Okay. Just the same routine over and over."

Prudence frowned at the blah note in her sister's voice. Usually Daisey was upbeat and planning something exciting with her friends.

"Sorry it's so rough living in paradise," Prudence teased. "You should come up here and see how normal folks live."

"Hmm. You know, I've been thinking about doing just that. Do you have sheets on your spare bed?"

"No, but that can quickly be remedied," Prudence told her. And then, before she could think on the matter too much, she added, "Actually, I'm glad you called. I have a bit of news for you."

"News? Oh, please tell me that you've decided to fly down for Thanksgiving. Mom and Dad would be thrilled. And we could go out on the town and kick up our heels."

"I'm not really up to traveling or kicking up my heels," Prudence said. "I've been under the weather with my stomach. Thanksgiving dinner is probably going to consist of a few crackers and a glass of milk."

"Oh, Pru! I know exactly what's wrong—that stressful job of yours has finally given you an ulcer?"

"I love my job. And it's nothing as serious as an ulcer."

She swiveled her chair so that she was staring at the small cart that held the coffee machine. This past week, Katherine had decorated the table with a paper turkey and set out mugs with orange pumpkins and fall leaves painted around the rims, along with several pumpkin spice creamers. The holiday at Three Rivers would be a big affair with tables and tables of food and plenty of family and guests to enjoy it. Would Luke be taking in the Hollisters' revelry? Probably so. She couldn't imagine Maureen allowing Holt's assistant to sit home alone.

The heavy sadness in her chest forced her to close her eyes and swallow before she could go on. "Actually, you might think it's serious. I happen to think it's wonderful."

"What's wonderful about not being able to eat?"

The perplexed sound in Daisey's voice put a smile on Prudence's face. "I can't eat because I'm pregnant. The doctor has given me something for the nausea. And he seems to think it will ease up soon when I get into my third month."

A long stretch of silence passed and then Daisey let out a loud shriek. "Pru! Is this for real? You're not playing a joke on me?"

Daisey would find it hard to believe that Prudence, the stuffed shirt of the family, had gotten pregnant out of wedlock.

"How often do I play jokes?" Prudence asked dryly.

"Oh, that's right. You don't joke around," Daisey replied. "Okay, sister—don't keep me in suspense. Who's the lucky daddy?"

The image of Luke's handsome face appeared in her mind's eye. "He's a horse trainer for Three Rivers. He's Holt Hollister's assistant."

"A cowboy? You're blowing me away, Pru! What are you doing with a cowboy?"

Prudence rolled her eyes. "That should be obvious, Daisey."

Laughing, Daisey said, "I mean other than creating a baby. I didn't know you went for the cowboy type. But actually, since your divorce, you haven't really gone for any type."

Ignoring that comment, Prudence said, "You've been to Wickenburg before. You know it's mostly a cowboy ranching town. That's the kind of men you meet around here."

"Oh, pooh. I was there and I remember all kinds of men on the staff at St. Francis and there were plenty of businessmen downtown. This horse trainer must really be special to have turned your head. Where did you meet him? This is exciting! I want to hear everything!"

"I don't have time to tell you *everything*. The bell is going to ring in about five minutes and I have a teleconference soon after that."

"Oh, shoot," she complained. "Then I'll call you back tonight to hear all the details. In the meantime, when is the wedding?"

Prudence closed her eyes and tried to ignore the pain crushing the middle of her chest. "There isn't going to be a wedding."

The phone went silent, and then Daisey practically shouted, "No wedding! What kind of jerk is this man?"

"You're going way off base, sis. Luke wants to get married. I'm the one who refused."

"Prudence! Have you lost your mind? And don't start giving me some spew about you being an independent woman or Gavin's infidelity has put you off marriage. I won't believe it! If you cared enough about this man to go to bed with him, that means you love him. And that's all that matters."

Prudence inwardly groaned. "You don't understand, sis. There are other issues."

"I don't care if the man is a pauper and has buck teeth. If you love him, there are no other issues. Got it?"

Tears sprang to Prudence's eyes, and she was grateful when the bell out in the hallway rang loudly.

"I have to go, Daisey. My lunch break is over. We'll talk about this later."

But no amount of talk was going to change things, Prudence thought sadly. She was carrying the child of a man who didn't love her. It was that painfully simple.

Cold wind was whooshing through the ranch yard, picking up clouds of dust as it traveled rapidly southward. About the time Luke was wishing he'd taken the time to pull on a jacket, rain began to spatter the ground and pepper down on his denim shirt and black hat. Directly behind his right shoulder, a young sorrel gelding danced impatiently against the lead rope.

Bending his head against the wind and rain, he quickly opened the wooden gate, and after slipping the halter off the horse's head, he allowed him into a small paddock with his buddies.

Given his freedom, the sorrel whinnied and took off in a run to the back of the pasture where a small herd of ten horses were gathered beneath the overhang of a barn. No doubt the animals were trying to figure out exactly what was falling from the sky. Most of them had probably only seen rain four or five times in their young lives. Luke hadn't seen any rain on Three Rivers since he'd moved here. In fact, the only rain he'd seen in the past few months was when he and Prudence had been in Reno.

The memory caused a heavy weight to spread through his chest, but he determinedly ignored the pain and continued walking back to the horse barn. He was getting fairly good at pushing through the heartache, at pretending all was well, Luke thought, when in reality he'd never been this dispirited in his entire life.

"Hey, Luke! Holt wants to see you in his office."

Luke glanced around to see Randy, one of the older wranglers, striding quickly toward him. The man had donned an oiled duster, and the long tails flapped against his tall yellow boots as he walked. Rain was already dripping off the brim of his hat.

"I'm headed that way right now," Luke told him. "Have the men started feeding yet?"

"Inside the horse barn. Uh—did you want the hay for the outside horses to be spread beneath the loafing sheds tonight? I think this rain is supposed to set in for a while."

"Probably a good idea, Randy. Get Lester and some of the guys to help you move the hay mangers. And make sure the gate on the back side of the little barn is open so the yearlings can shelter. It's already turning cold this evening."

"Right, Luke. I'll see to it."

Luke thanked him and strode on to the back of the main horse barn.

Inside the cavernous building, the ranch hands were busy toting feed and hay to the stalled horses and water buckets were being cleaned and filled, while the odd pieces of tack that had been left throughout the barn were being carried to the tack room.

Luke was making his way down the alleyway between the rows of stalls when he spotted Taggart emerging from the old tack room where Holt's office was located.

The ranch foreman was about to head off in a different direction when he spotted Luke and walked over to greet him.

"Hey, Luke. How's it going?"

Taggart had found himself a real home here on Three Rivers, Luke thought. After going through some tragic years back in Texas, the man had finally found the happiness he deserved. Not only did the Hollisters admire his work, they'd taken him into the bosom of their family. Luke was glad for his friend. Glad, too, that the man now had a loving wife and child to make his life complete. Luke only wished he could've been more like Taggart. He'd grabbed his chance for happiness and held on tight. Whereas Luke hadn't realized what he'd had until he'd lost it.

"Okay," Luke answered. "What about yourself?"

"Busy as ever. Blake and I are still trying to figure out where to put the last of the Prescott herds. The ranges here on Three Rivers are already full."

"What about Red Bluff?" Luke asked. "Holt tells me the southern ranch has good grazing during the winter."

"True, but Matthew has been building the herds down there. Although he says he has some room on the new property they've added to the ranch, trouble is, they still don't have it all fenced yet. He believes they'll wind up the fencing by mid-December. Emily-Ann is keeping her fingers crossed for that plan. She wants to go visit Camille during the holiday. They've been the best of friends for years."

"Maybe that will work out for everyone," Luke said. He didn't want to think about Christmas this year. Obviously, Prudence would be spending the holiday with someone other than him.

"How's your dad and brother doing? You going to spend Thanksgiving with them?"

Luke shook his head. "No. I have too much to do around here with the horses. And my family isn't expecting me anyway."

Taggart nodded that he understood, then grinned. "Well, you're always welcome at our house. Emily-Ann is actually learning how to cook something other than sandwiches," he joked. "And Reeva will make sure none of us go hungry on the big day."

"I imagine you're right about that," he said with more enthusiasm than he felt. "Well, Holt is waiting to see me. I'd better go find out what he wants before he heads home. See you later, Tag." He started off, then looked back at his friend. "Oh, in case you didn't know, it's raining outside. You ought to get your slicker."

Taggart laughed. "Not me, buddy. It's been too long since I felt some rain on my back."

The foreman strode off in the opposite direction and Luke hurried on to Holt's office.

When he entered the room, the horse trainer was sitting at his desk, impatiently flipping through a stack of papers.

"I hate technology, Luke. Why can't we go back to the way things used to be when everything was written down on paper?"

Luke walked over to his desk and rested a hip on the corner. "What's wrong? Lost something important?"

"I can't find a damn thing. Flo tells me she's put all the foaling data for this past spring on computer file. I sure as hell can't find any of them. I've resorted to searching through my personal paperwork. Trouble is, I can't decipher half of what I've scribbled down."

Flo, a redheaded woman in her sixties, was actually Blake's private secretary. She worked in a connecting office to the ranch manager's office that was located between the cattle barns and the main horse barn. Along with handling the enormous amount of paperwork for Blake, Flo also helped Holt with the paperwork that went with breeding and selling horses.

"Since I've had a chance to be around Flo a bit, I think she'd be more than glad to help you find what you're looking for. She's always super kind to me."

Holt laughed. "Oh, sure. Why wouldn't she be sweet to you? You never ask her for anything. And you're young and good-looking. She's a cream puff for guys like you."

Luke would've normally laughed at Holt's comment, but this evening, all he could manage was a grunt.

"Well, I've heard that Matthew Waggoner is her real pet," Luke said. "But Flo rarely gets to see him since he and your sister live down on Red Bluff."

Holt laughed. "She loves humble men. That's why she's always yelling at me." He pushed the papers aside and looked up at Luke. "I'll search for the list of breeding dates later. Right now, I have an invitation to run past you."

Luke tried not to stiffen. He didn't want anyone feeling sorry for him just because it was going to be Thanksgiving in a couple of days and he didn't have anyone to help him celebrate the holiday.

"Um, thanks, Holt, but I don't want to intrude on you or any of your family for the holiday. If that's what you meant by *invitation*."

Folding his arms against his chest, Holt leveled a pointed look at him. "Don't be assuming things you don't know about. And you sure as hell don't need to be feeling sorry for yourself."

Luke grimaced. He didn't know why, but Holt had an uncanny knack for reading his thoughts. Especially thoughts he'd rather keep to himself.

"This is fatigue you see on my face, not self-pity. And I never was big on holidays. I mean, I realize you Hollisters thrive on them, but you're a big family. You have a lot to be thankful for and plenty to celebrate."

"Don't you figure you have plenty to be thankful for, too? You're a strong, healthy guy able to walk around on two legs and ride horses all day long. You like your job and your home, or so you say."

"I am thankful, Holt. It's just different for me."

Holt thoughtfully narrowed his eyes as he studied Luke's face. "Is there anything you want to tell me?"

Luke's gaze dropped to the toes of his dusty boots. "No. You couldn't help me with this problem anyway."

"You're talking about Prudence now," he said.

He wiped a hand over his face. "I haven't talked to anyone about this, Holt. But Prudence is pregnant. She told me nearly two weeks ago and since then— well, she refuses to marry me."

There was a pause, and then Holt said, "I'm sorry, Luke, but I do know. Not because I've been prying into your business, but Katherine has been so upset about Prudence, she had to talk to Blake about it. He thought you might've already confided in me."

Luke used his forefinger to draw imaginary circles on the top of Luke's desk. "I've been kind of messed up, Holt. I don't know what to think or say. I tried to reason with Prudence, but she won't see things my way. It's making me damn crazy. I can tell you that much."

Leaning back in the desk chair, Holt studied Luke's sober expression. "Well, I don't know if this has crossed your mind yet, but Prudence is in a pickle."

Unease shot through Luke. "Why? Is anything wrong with her or the baby?"

He'd texted her a few days ago to inquire about her and the baby's health. She'd shot back a curt We're fine, and that was all she'd said. Luke realized that at some point soon the two of them were going to have to have a serious discussion about the coming baby and how they planned to co-parent him or her. But he'd been trying to give her time to adjust to the idea of becoming a mother. Just like he'd been trying to absorb the idea of becoming a father.

"No. She's not having physical problems. It's something else—her job. From what Katherine says, she's planning to turn in her resignation."

Luke was so stunned he stood straight up and stared in wonder at the other man. "Resign? She loves her job! Why would she resign? Most women work and have babies. She can hire childcare. I'll help her pay for the expense."

"You're not thinking, Luke. St. Francis is a private school with strict moral codes. What kind of message would it say for the superintendent to be pregnant out of wedlock?"

He let out a long breath, then lifted his hat and raked both hands through his hair. "Oh, damn, Holt. I wasn't thinking in those terms. I guess I've been too busy agonizing over why she won't marry me. And now—it doesn't make sense! Marrying me would fix everything. She wouldn't have to lose her job."

"Maybe you need to have another long talk with her. Make her see reason," Holt suggested.

Luke grimaced. "Nothing I can say now will get through to her. She'd only think I was lying if I told her I loved her."

"Hmm. Have you tried?"

"No. She practically screamed at me not to bother."

"Oh. You must've really burned her up."

"I don't know about that. I just know I wasted my chances with her. I was too busy thinking I didn't want to end up like Dad."

"What's wrong with your father?"

"Nothing. Except that he'll be walking around on a prosthetic leg for the rest of his life."

Holt stroked a thumb and forefinger over his chin. "I'm sure there's some sort of connection there, but I'm not getting it. What does your father's leg have to do with Prudence marrying you?"

Luke grimaced. "I'm not sure any of it would make sense to you. But my parents' marriage was always a roller-coaster ride. Mom was bipolar and

Dad wore himself out trying to deal with her. In the end, she caused the wreck that killed her and caused Dad to lose his leg."

Holt frowned. "How so?"

"They were traveling home from an outing with friends. She flew into a rage—I think because Dad spilled food on his shirt. In her mind that was criminal. Anyway, she jerked the steering wheel out of his hands and caused the truck to crash and overturn."

Holt shook his head. "I'm sorry, Luke. For her and for your father's loss. But your mother being bipolar—that's no reason to run from love or marriage. If that's what you've been doing."

"Why the hell not? Dad bent over backward trying to make the woman he loved happy. In the end, I'm not sure it ever really registered with her."

"Prudence isn't mentally unstable."

"I've always understood that. But I kept thinking she's a woman. And if we were married she would lean on me. She'd need me in ways that… Well, I wasn't sure I could be the man she needed. And maybe I'd never be enough to make her happy. Maybe I'd always be like Dad, wearing myself out trying to please her. But then—when I found out about the baby—I didn't care about any of that. Now I just want us to be together. Be parents to our baby together."

"Because you love her?"

"More than anything."

Holt smiled. "Then you need to tell her so. And don't leave anything off."

"I'm not sure she'll see me or hear me out."

"You'll figure out how to go about it. But in the meantime, I have an invitation for you. Mom is having a dinner party tomorrow night and wants you to be there. Other than eating, I'm not sure what she has planned for the evening. She's keeping it a secret."

Luke was hardly in the mood for a party. But being antisocial, especially with the Hollisters, was not an acceptable way for him to behave. "I don't understand why your mother would want me at her party. I'm just an employee."

Holt laughed. "Tag used to say the same thing. But after a while he learned that we think of him as family. As we do you. The sooner you get that into your head, the better, Luke. And I'll tell you another thing. Whenever you have a problem, we want to help—any way we can."

Yes, the Hollisters were always ready to offer a helping hand, but in Luke's case, they couldn't do anything to help him. Prudence's mind was closed off to marrying him.

"Okay, Holt. I'll be there and I'll do my best to put on my happy face. What time is this dinner?"

"Six thirty. When you get there, go to the back of the house. We'll all be gathered in the den."

Luke eased off the corner of the desk. "All right. Was there anything else you needed to tell me? Otherwise, I should go help the guys with the chores. It's raining and I wanted everything fed under shelter."

"Raining? I wondered why you had splotches on your shirt. Whoopee! We might get a little green grass for Christmas." Rising from the chair, he came around the desk and gave Luke's shoulder a fond shake. "See, we always have something to be thankful for, Luke. And you and I are especially blessed right now. We're going to have babies at the same time. What could be better than that?"

What could be better? That Prudence wouldn't be resigning her job. Instead, she'd be telling him that she wanted to be his wife. That she wanted the three of them to be a real family. For always.

Chapter Twelve

The loud whistle of the teakettle was accompanied by clouds of steam billowing from the spout. Prudence switched off the burner and carefully poured boiling water into a mug holding a bag of Earl Grey tea.

With the weather turning cold and wet, she wanted something warm and soothing before she crawled into bed for the night. God only knew she'd had a hectic day at school trying to get all the loose ends tied together before the extended holiday. And then Katherine had really upended her nerves with an invitation to Three Rivers tomorrow night. She didn't want to spend the evening at the ranch. If Luke was there, she might take one look at his handsome face and start thinking being married to him, under any circumstances, would be better than the misery she was going through now.

She was stirring cream and sugar into the tea when the doorbell rang. Who could that be? Surely not Luke come to argue his case for marriage again, she thought bitterly. The day he'd left, he'd had a final look on his face. One that said he was all finished dealing with an obstinate woman.

Tightening the belt of her robe, she hurried out to the door and peered out the peephole.

"Daisey!" Her sister's name came out with a gasp of surprise.

"Pru! Hurry and open the door. I'm freezing out here!"

Prudence fumbled with the lock, and as soon as the door opened, Daisey leaped over the threshold and grabbed her in a tight hug.

"Oh, Pru, it's so good to finally see you!" The petite brunette stepped back and bestowed her older sister with a loving smile. "Don't be annoyed with me, sis. I had to come."

Dazed, Prudence shook her head. "I'm not annoyed. More like stunned. How did you get here?"

"I flew to Phoenix and hired a rental car at the airport." She grimaced. "I thought you said it never rained up here. It's darn wet outside. I'm sure my hair has turned into a curly mop."

Prudence stepped around her sister and locked the door before she came to stand in front of Daisey.

At thirty, she looked far closer to twenty. Her ebony hair rippled in waves down her back and her smooth complexion was the perfect example of peaches and cream. Instead of green-blue eyes like her sister's, Daisey had rich brown eyes that flashed fire whenever her temper was riled.

"You look beautiful. And I'm happy you're here." Grabbing Daisey by the upper arm, Prudence led her into the living room. "Take off your wet jacket. I was just in the kitchen making tea. Come have some with me."

"Mmm. Sounds good. I can't remember the last time I've felt this cold!" She removed a faux fur jacket and tossed it over the back of the couch before she followed Prudence to the kitchen.

Prudence forced out a little laugh. "Probably when you went snow skiing at Lake Tahoe."

"I didn't have time to get cold there. Not with that flirty ski instructor always trying to wrap his arms around me. I was never so glad to get back to Palm Springs in my life!"

"Naturally. It's much more pleasant to have a flirty lifeguard at the pool put the make on you. I know how your mind works," Prudence said wryly. "Or at least, I thought I did. I have no idea what you're doing here. You haven't come to talk me into going to Palm Springs with you, have you?"

Daisey frowned at her. "Why, no! Why would I want to do such a thing?"

"Hmm. Could be you think I need to be around

family now—so the three of you can take care of me and the baby. I'm sure before you left you discussed it with our parents."

Inside the kitchen, Prudence fetched another mug for her sister while Daisey took a seat at the small dining table.

As Daisey pulled off her damp ankle boots, she said, "Pru, you should be ashamed for thinking I'd tell our parents about something as private as the baby. Before you've had a chance to do it yourself!"

Prudence added a tea bag and water to the mug and carried it over to the table before returning to the cabinet for a tiny pitcher of cream and a sugar bowl.

"You haven't said anything to them about the baby?" Prudence asked as she sank into the chair next to Daisey's.

"No. I only told them I wanted to come spend a few days with you while St. Francis is out for the holiday."

"Oh." Prudence sipped her tea and was relieved that her stomach welcomed the warm liquid. "I'm sorry I jumped to conclusions. To be honest, I've been putting off talking with Mom and Dad. Like a fool, I've been thinking I needed to get things more settled in my mind."

Frowning, Daisey dipped the tea bag up and down in the mug. "Settled in your mind? What's there to settle? You're going to have a baby. Or were you thinking that you might have something else to tell them? Like a wedding date?"

Bending her head, Prudence absently smoothed her robe across her lap. "In the beginning, I was hoping a wedding might happen. If things had been right. But they weren't right. Now I'm certain that Luke and I will both be better off like this."

"Is that so? And what about the baby? You think your son will be better off? What's he going to do whenever he needs his dad around?"

"The baby might be a girl," Prudence protested, even though she knew that meant no difference. A little girl needed a dad just as much as a boy. "And anyway, I've made it clear to Luke that he'll always be welcome in his child's life."

"That's big of you," Daisey said with sarcasm.

Prudence groaned. "Please, sis, you just got here. Do we have to discuss Luke and the baby? I've had a rough day. And I'd much rather hear what you've been doing."

Daisey removed the tea bag and thoughtfully stirred in cream and sugar. "Nothing I've been doing compares to your news. And I'm sorry you don't want to talk about the baby or Luke. Avoiding the subject isn't going to fix anything."

Prudence let out a long breath. "There's nothing to fix."

"So you say. But I'll tell you one thing. I'm not leaving here until you and Luke have this all straightened out."

"Sounds like you're planning to stay on permanently here in Wickenburg. They have some high-end boutiques in Phoenix. Maybe you can find a job at one of them and commute back and forth."

"Very funny, sis," Daisey told her. "Only I'm not laughing."

"Neither am I. On second thought, you might try putting a boutique of your own here in Wickenburg that caters to the Western crowd. Lots of silver and turquoise, fancy boots and leather clothing. You could make a success of it. Oh, I forgot. You're planning on going back to college for a law degree. Well, there's a fine one in Phoenix or Prescott."

"Quit trying to distract me. It won't work. Since we talked on the phone, I've been thinking about you constantly. Actually, I've been crying because—" The remainder of Daisey's words broke off as tears suddenly flooded her eyes.

Prudence was so overcome by her sister's emotional display, she leaned over and hugged her tightly.

"Daisey, honey. You shouldn't be crying. Don't you understand how happy I am to be having a baby? I'm thirty-nine years old. I thought it would never happen. I'm so very blessed and you should see it that way, too."

Daisey sniffed and wiped at the tears beneath her eyes. "I do, Pru. Really, I do. But you deserve more. You went through pure hell with Gavin. You deserve to have it all now. The baby, the wedding, the husband who loves you."

Prudence shook her head. "Have you forgotten the wedding our parents gave me? It was over-the-top. A show that had little to do with vows of love. I should've never agreed to any of it. But I was young and all my friends thought I was so lucky to have such a fairy-tale ceremony. And Mom was having such fun planning it all." She rubbed her fingers against her forehead. "It's no wonder I hate to attend weddings nowadays. That one was such a farce."

Daisey sipped her tea. "Not really, sis. I think Gavin loved you—in the very beginning."

Prudence grimaced. "He loved me as long as everything in his life was going his way. That's not love. That's caring for someone when it's convenient and easy."

"I guess so," Daisey said thoughtfully, then turned a tentative smile on her sister. "What do you have planned for Thanksgiving? Are we cooking a turkey?"

Prudence chuckled. "I'm thinking you and I will head out to a restaurant. We can stay here in Wickenburg or drive off to Prescott or Phoenix. I'll let you choose."

"Sounds fun. As long as I can have cranberry sauce with the berries in it. That's all I ask."

"I promise you'll get your cranberry sauce. Even if I have to make it myself," Prudence said. Then, suddenly remembering Katherine's invitation, she added, "Actually, I do have a party to go to tomorrow night. But if you'd rather not go, I can beg off."

"What kind of party? The staff at St. Francis is getting together?"

"No. It's a dinner party at Three Rivers Ranch. My secretary, Kat, is insisting I go. She says her mother-in-law, Maureen, has something special planned."

"Three Rivers Ranch," Daisey thoughtfully repeated. "Isn't that where your guy works?"

"He's not *my* guy," Prudence stiffly reminded her. "But, yes, Luke works there. He also lives on the ranch. In a house about two or three miles from the main ranch house."

Daisey's brows arched with interest. "Oh. I hope he'll be attending the party. I want to see this man who fathered my little niece or nephew."

Daisey's taste in men usually went to the preppy, intellectual sort. Still, she'd have to be blind or half-dead not to think Luke was a gorgeous hunk of man. Not that his looks made the situation any less awful, Prudence thought.

"Kat didn't say anything about Luke being invited. But if he's there, I don't intend to let him ruin my evening. And I don't want you making any waves by confronting the man."

Daisey groaned. "Oh, Pru, I'd never do anything so…uncouth. I'll be on my best behavior. Uh, but are you sure the Hollisters won't mind if I go as your guest?"

"I'll call Kat in the morning and check it out with her. I'm positive she and her family will welcome you."

A coy smile spread across Daisey's face. "This

is going to be fun. I've never been on a real ranch before. Just that dude thing Dad took us to when we were little girls. Remember? He rented a horse for each of us, but I was so scared I ran off crying."

Prudence chuckled. "How could I forget? I never saw Dad so annoyed with you. But don't worry—getting on a horse won't be required of you tomorrow night. Just smile and be yourself, and everyone will love you as much as I do."

Daisey leaned back in her chair and continued to study her sister. "I shouldn't bring this up. Not tonight. But I just have to know what you plan to do about your job. Women having babies outside of marriage is a normal thing now. But I doubt St. Francis has such progressive views."

Prudence let out a heavy breath. "When the board learns about my pregnancy, they can't allow me to stay on."

"But that's so cut-and-dried," Daisey argued. "Surely they could make an exception in your case."

Prudence shook her head. "St. Francis was founded on spiritual and moral values. I can't ask them to break the rules for me. I wouldn't want them to." With a heavy sigh, she rose from the chair and carried her cup over to the sink. Then, standing sideways, she stretched the material of the blue robe across her tummy. "Look, in two or three more weeks, this little bulge is going to become very obvious. I might get by for another month by letting people think I've gained weight. But that will only give me a short reprieve.

No, I've decided the only thing to do is hand in my resignation. I'll be able to keep my same health insurance. Even though the premium will cost more. But that won't be a huge issue. And I can find another job. If not as a superintendent, then a teacher's position."

"Have you told Katherine about this?"

Prudence nodded glumly. "I have. And to say she's very unhappy with me would be putting it mildly."

"Oh, Pru, no! You love your job. It's been your life for thirteen years. And you don't have to tell me that the students love you. I— You're jumping the gun. You don't know what might happen in the next two or three weeks. You and Luke might settle your differences."

There were no differences, Prudence thought. Luke wanted a marriage of convenience for the sake of the baby. Prudence wanted a marriage based on love.

"Don't worry, Daisey. I can find another job. I'll have to commute. Or I might even have to move from Wickenburg, but it will all work out."

Daisey looked horrified. "Katherine has been your secretary for years. What is this going to do to her job? I mean, I get that she'll work for the person who takes your place. But you two are like sisters. It won't be the same for her or you!"

Prudence didn't want to think about Katherine or how this would affect her friend. Now that Nick was a teenager and the twins were in nursery school,

Katherine had returned to work full-time. The two women were like a tag team. Prudence considered her a second sister.

"I don't want to talk about this any more tonight. Let's go to the guest bedroom and you can help me put linens on the bed," Prudence told her.

Daisey looked as though she wanted to say more, but thankfully, she must have realized that Prudence needed a break from the questions and worries about her future.

Smiling, Daisey rose to her feet. "Lead the way, dear sister."

Even before Luke opened the French doors leading into the den of the Three Rivers Ranch house, he heard Christmas music playing, interspersed with voices and laughter. Obviously, everyone was in a merry mood this evening, Luke thought, as he plastered a smile on his face and stepped into the busy room. Maybe he could fake his way through. At least, until dinner was over and he could find a decent excuse to slip away and go home to his empty house by the river.

Sure, Luke. Go sit in the dark and think about the utter mess you've made of your life. Think about the dozens and dozens of missed chances you had to make things right with Prudence, but you were too big a coward to grab them.

"Luke, would you like something to drink? If you

don't see anything on the tray that grabs your fancy, come over to the bar and I'll fix you something else."

Luke looked around to see that Jazelle, the Three Rivers housekeeper, had walked up to him carrying a large silver tray loaded with an assortment of drinks. The young, very pregnant blonde was wearing a red sparkly dress and a headband with reindeer antlers adorned with jingle bells that tinkled every time she moved her head. Any other time, Luke would've enjoyed teasing her about the antlers, but tonight he could barely summon a smile.

"A plain soda will do me, Jazelle. And by the way, couldn't you get the night off tonight, to enjoy the party?"

Laughing, she handed him a glass filled with ice and cola. "Oh, I didn't want off. As long as Reeva is working, I'm working, too. Besides, this way, I get to visit with everyone." She inclined her head toward the opposite end of the den. "Blake and Tag are sitting over there, if you'd like to join them. And if you want to shed your jacket, just leave it at the bar. I'll hang it up in the hall closet for you."

"Thanks. I'll do that," he told her.

The housekeeper moved on, and after taking a long sip of the cola, Luke started to head over to the two men. He'd taken one step when far across the room a flash of bright color caught the corner of his eye, and he paused to glance toward the fireplace and the group of people gathered around the roaring fire.

Prudence!

Seeing her here tonight shouldn't surprise him. After all, she'd been a friend of the Hollisters for years. But the sight of her stopped him in his tracks, and for a moment, all he could do was stand and stare.

She was wearing a Christmas green dress that draped across her breasts and tied snugly at the waist, her caramel-brown hair looped into messy curls and fastened atop her head with rows of rhinestone pins. The updo showed off the elegant line of her neck and the emerald necklace resting in the cleft between her breasts.

He was wondering why she had to look so achingly beautiful when his attention was drawn to the woman standing next to Prudence. Her hair was much darker, but she was the same size as Prudence and her features were similar. This had to be her younger sister, Daisey, he decided.

Any other time, Luke would've enjoyed meeting Prudence's sister, but with everything between them strained to the breaking point, he needed to keep his distance from both women.

The thought had barely had time to enter his head when Prudence suddenly glanced in his direction and their gazes momentarily locked. Except for two bright pink dots on her cheeks, she looked incredibly pale, her features stretched to taut lines.

This wasn't the Prudence he'd fallen in love with, he thought. This was some sad, miserable woman he barely recognized. Was that what having his baby was doing to her? For one instant, he started to cross the room to her and lead her away to some quiet nook where he could try to talk reason with her. But this was Maureen's party. He didn't want to do anything that might cause a scene.

"Hey, Luke," Taggart called out to him. "Over here with me and Blake. We have plenty of room."

Grateful for the distraction, Luke purposely looked away from Prudence and went to join the men.

"Are you kidding me? That's your baby's daddy?" Daisey whispered in a shocked voice next to Prudence's ear. "He's incredible. A walking hunk of gorgeous."

Prudence tried not to blush as she stared into the glass of orange juice she'd been sipping. "Daisey, please! Someone is going to hear you."

"Well, so what? Most of your friends here on the ranch already know that you're pregnant. And frankly, sis, now that I see Luke Crawford for myself, I'm beginning to question your sanity."

Prudence frowned at her sister. "What is that supposed to mean?"

"If that man proposed to you and you turned him down, then your brain has clearly collapsed."

"Looks hardly make a marriage, Daisey."

Daisey continued to gaze across the room to where Luke had taken a seat on the couch between Blake and Taggart. "I'll say one thing, sis. I can't blame you for falling into bed with him. He'd be impossible to resist."

"He was. But I can resist him now."

"Can you? I don't know. The way you're looking at him… Gosh, Pru, just go over there and tell him you want to talk. Better yet, take me over there and introduce me. That'll give you an opening to talk to the man."

Prudence turned her face toward the fire. "I don't want us to create a spectacle right now. Luke and I have things to discuss about the baby, and we'll do that eventually, just not tonight, okay?"

Daisey looked as though she wanted to continue to argue, but at that moment, Jazelle announced that dinner was served, and everyone in the den began to file down the hallway to the formal dining room that was large enough to easily seat the twenty-plus people in attendance tonight.

It was a huge relief to Prudence when she discovered that she and Daisey were sitting some distance down the table from Luke, who was seated between Taggart and Holt. Directly across from Prudence, Vivian's teenage daughter, Hannah, and Katherine's teenage son, Nick, were sitting together and chattering nonstop.

The pair had been inseparable friends, and cousins by marriage, ever since Blake and Katherine had married a few years ago. Now that Vivian had married Sawyer Whitehorse and moved to the Yavapai reservation north of here, the two young people didn't get to spend nearly as much time together as they used to. But they made up for lost time whenever they were together.

"Mom says Daisey wants to learn how to ride a horse," Nick said as everyone began to dig into tossed salads. "Hannah and I can teach her. We'd be glad to, wouldn't we, Hannah?"

"Oh, sure!" Hannah replied. "Mom is going to let me stay here on the ranch for a week while school is out for the holiday. Nick and I will be saddling up and going out every day."

Daisey smiled at the teenagers. "Well, that sounds like a nice offer. But I'm not sure I'd be very good teaching material. I have two left feet and terrible hand-eye coordination."

Prudence said, "Now, Daisey, you're making excuses. The kids have kindly offered."

Hannah giggled. "We know how to deal with greenhorns."

Daisey looked helplessly at Prudence. "Greenhorns? Am I one of those?"

Nick laughed and Hannah giggled again.

"My sister is from Palm Springs. She doesn't know about livestock or ranching life," Prudence explained to the young people.

"Oh, then we'll take extra good care of her," Hannah promised.

As the teenagers continued to ply Daisey with questions, Prudence pretended a keen interest in her salad, but actually, it was all she could do to keep her eyes off Luke's end of the table.

Daisey was right. He was an incredible hunk of man, and tonight, dressed in a pale yellow shirt and brown Western-cut trousers that showed off his long legs and lean hips, he looked as though he'd be just as confident in a boardroom as he was on the back of a horse.

Since that night she'd told him about the baby, she'd thought many times of calling him. Truth being, she'd been so upset that evening that she'd missed hearing half of what he'd been trying to say. Maybe some of it had made sense. She didn't know anymore. The only thing she was certain about now was that her heart was breaking and everything inside her wanted to go to him and lay her cheek upon his chest. She wanted to tell him that it didn't matter if he couldn't love her. Maybe years from now, there would be something in his heart for her. All that really mattered was that they were together.

The emotional thoughts clogged her throat, and as she reached for her water glass, she felt Luke staring at her. This time when she looked at him, she didn't try to hide her misery or her longing. And to her surprise, he didn't look away.

Maureen suddenly stood and tapped her spoon against her wine goblet. "Okay, everyone, here comes the prime rib," the matriarch announced. "The best beef that Three Rivers has to offer, and Reeva has made some delicious side dishes to go with it. I want everyone to eat up and enjoy. Afterward, Gil and I have an announcement we'd like to make."

"Announcement?" Holt bellowed the question. "What the hell, Mom? Don't tell me you and Gil are going off on another honeymoon. You haven't ended the first one yet!"

Everyone around the table laughed, except for Prudence and Luke. He was too busy staring at her and she was too busy trying to figure out how they'd let such a cold wall ever come between them.

"Listen, buster," Maureen joked, "if Gil and I decide we want to take off on a second honeymoon to the arctic circle, we will."

Holt laughed, while Chandler teased, "If you two head up there, Mom, you'll need heavier clothing than what you took to Hawaii."

Laughing, Maureen eased back into her chair. "You don't need to worry about that, son. Gil and I know how to keep each other warm."

Vivian let out a good-natured groan. "Oooh, Mom, you're awful."

Chuckling along with his wife, Gil wrapped an arm around Maureen's shoulders. "Actually, after Thanksgiving tomorrow, we're going to drive down to Red Bluff to spend some time with Camille and Matthew," he told everyone. "So you men better eat up. You're going to have to take over our workload for a while."

"But that's not the announcement," Maureen added slyly. "You'll have to wait for it."

* * *

Luke couldn't remember if he'd eaten any of the prime rib, scalloped potatoes or snow peas. One minute he'd been pushing the food around on his plate, and the next minute everyone was leaving the table and filing back into the den.

"Aren't we going to have dessert, Mom?" Chandler asked. "When I walked through the kitchen, I saw Reeva setting out a row of pecan pies."

"In due time," Maureen promised, then motioned for everyone to gather around her and Gil in front of the fireplace. "This won't take long and then Jazelle will serve dessert and coffee."

As family members and close friends assembled in a loose group in front of Gil and Maureen, Luke chose to stand at the back of the crowd, directly behind Taggart and his wife, Emily-Ann. A few steps to his right, Daisey was standing with her arm wrapped in a supporting circle around the back of Prudence's waist.

No doubt, the younger Keyes sister was thinking Luke had to be a first-class jerk for getting Prudence pregnant, then leaving her to deal with the consequences on her own. But it wasn't that way. He wanted her to be his wife. He wanted them to be a real family. But what was it going to take for Prudence to recognize his feelings?

Maureen began to speak, and Luke forced his attention to the fireplace hearth where she and Gil were standing close together.

"I don't have to remind any of you that the journey Gil and I have taken to finally become husband and wife has been anything but easy. The years directly after Joel died were the hardest I'd ever had to face. I never thought I'd lose my will to move forward, but I came darn close. I even questioned my ability to help you children keep this ranch viable." She looked at Gil and smiled. "But then Gil began to quietly remind me that Joel had left behind an incredible legacy for me and you children and I had a responsibility to keep the spokes rolling. And of course, Gil was right."

She drew in a deep breath and continued, "I realize that all of you believe Gil and I fell in love gradually these past few years. For me, that's true. But not for Gil. He was in love with me years ago, even before Joel and I were married."

Shocked glances were exchanged while questions rumbled through the group. Maureen quickly held up a hand to ward off any interruptions.

"Don't start jumping to conclusions. You have to hear the whole story to understand," Maureen insisted. "You see, I met Joel and Gil at the same time when they were both very young men, helping their father, Axel, build Three Rivers into an even bigger cattle empire. I liked Gil very much, but I fell in love with Joel straightaway and he with me. Back then, I hadn't known that Gil held any kind of feelings for me. I didn't find that out until later, after Joel and I had married and returned from our honeymoon. We were shocked to learn that Gil had left the ranch and moved to Phoenix. Axel had been tight-lipped about the whole ordeal. He'd only said that Gil wanted to pursue other interests. But in truth, Gil had left because he'd never wanted to cause a problem or come between me and Joel. You see, he'd loved his brother so much that he'd been willing to give up his part of Three Rivers to ensure our happiness. Gil sacrificed so much for me and Joel." Turning to Gil, she reached for both his hands, and the look she gave him was glowing with boundless love. "Now it's my deepest desire to make him happy, and I hope you children feel the same way."

For a moment, the room was so quiet Luke could hear himself breathing. Everyone was exchanging looks of amazement until Vivian finally rushed forward and kissed her mother and then Gil.

"Mom, this is the most wonderful holiday message we could've ever received!" Vivian exclaimed. "Now that Gil is back on Three Rivers where he belongs, our family is whole again. And if Dad is looking down on us now, I know he's saying the same thing."

Blake, Holt, Chandler and Joseph all followed their sister's example, and as the family hugged and celebrated together, Luke suddenly realized what it meant to love and be loved. Not just with physical passion, but with feelings so deep that they transcended years of trials and tribulations, of doubts and pain. Luke now understood why his father had remained at his wife's side through all the ups and downs. He'd loved her in spite of her shortcomings.

Somewhere in the bottom of his heart, hope tried to flicker to life, and he glanced over to see if Prudence had been as affected as he'd been by Maureen's story. To his surprise, she was walking slowly toward him, and even from a distance, he could see tears were making glittery tracks down both cheeks.

Meeting her halfway, he curled a hand around her upper arm and brought his lips close to her ear. "We need to talk, Pru. Let's go find a quiet spot."

Nodding, she gave him a wobbly smile. "Yes. I have plenty of things I need to say to you."

They walked through the French doors that opened out to the back patio. Someone had built a huge fire in the firepit, and Luke led Prudence over to a low rock bench where the heat of the flames chased away the chill of the night.

"I didn't know you were going to be here tonight," Luke said. "But I should've known Kat and Blake would invite you."

"If you'd known, would you have stayed away?" she asked.

"No. Are you sorry you came?"

"No. I— Oh, Luke, I've been miserable without you. And a few minutes ago, when Maureen was talking about Gil and how he'd loved her for all those years, I could only think that—" Pausing, she shook her head. "That's the way I feel about you. I'll always love you. No matter what. No matter how you feel about me. I need to be with you. Our baby needs you. I don't know why it's taken me this long to figure things out."

Amazed by what she was saying, he took her by the shoulders and pulled her toward him. "Do you really mean that, Pru? You honestly love me?"

She touched her fingertips to his cheek. "I think I loved you from that very first dance at Maureen and Gil's wedding reception. I was just too afraid to acknowledge my feelings. Afraid I was getting myself into another bad situation."

Groaning with disbelief, he pulled her tight against him and pressed his cheek against the top of her hair. "You afraid? Oh, Pru, I've been a crazy, blind fool. All this time, I didn't want to give in to the fact that I loved you. I didn't want to believe that I needed you in my life. For years I watched my father go through misery trying to make Mom happy. And the hell of it, I'm not sure she ever realized or cared how much he gave up for her. You see, she was bipolar, and most of the time she couldn't recognize the problems she was creating for herself and others."

"Oh, Luke. That's not the way all women think or behave."

"No. I understood Mom's situation was different. And I never set out being worried about getting tangled up in the same sort of problem as my dad. I mentioned to you once that I'd considered marriage. Well, that was during my college years. I started dating a girl who seemed like a perfect match for me.

Then out of the blue, she started to change. I never knew what person I was going to be dealing with. It was like I was seeing a younger version of my mom and I couldn't get out of the relationship fast enough. After her, I promised myself I'd keep my distance from all women. But then I met you and all my intentions fell apart."

"And now do you believe you can trust me to have a normal personality?"

He laughed and she frowned.

"Is that a funny question?" she asked.

"Not really. I'm laughing because I can see now how stupid my thinking has been all these years. Truth is, Pru, I was never worried about you having wild mood swings or being capable of functioning normally. I was more worried about myself and being the husband that you needed and wanted. It just took me a while to face up to that truth." He pressed kisses across her forehead. "When I heard Maureen talking about Gil's quiet, undying love for her, I knew that's the way it would always be with me—loving you no matter what."

She tenderly cradled the side of his face with her hand. "And me loving you—no matter what," she whispered softly.

Joy poured through him as he covered her lips with his and kissed her with a longing he could no longer suppress.

"You know what I think?" she asked, when he finally eased his lips from hers. "That the Hollisters were doing a little manipulating and nudging tonight when they invited us both to be here."

"I wanted to tell Holt I didn't want to be here. But I didn't. He and his family have been too good to me. Now I'm just happy that I showed up and that Maureen shared her and Gil's story with us all."

Slipping her arms around him, she hugged him close. "Mmm. How could a man love a woman so much that he could willingly give up a fortune in order for her to be happy?"

"I don't know, my darling Pru. I only know that I don't have much to give up, but I'd toss it all for you and our baby—and the babies we'll hopefully have after this one. You do want a big family, don't you?"

"A big family. Oh, yes!"

She kissed him and then he urged her up from the bench. "Let's go tell your sister and everyone that we're getting married—as soon as we can get the license!"

She let out a breathless laugh. "That soon?"

Grinning, he splayed a hand over the lower part of her stomach. "By the time the St. Francis school board realizes you're pregnant, you'll be a married woman. But if you have your heart set on a big wedding, I won't stand in your way."

Laughing, she grabbed his hand and squeezed it. "Are you kidding? I hate weddings! Daisey will have to have the next big wedding for the Keyes family. You and I are going to have a quiet ceremony. With only a preacher and smiles on our faces."

"You won't have to worry about the smile," Luke said as he urged her toward the house. "You've just put a permanent one on my face."

Epilogue

Birds were singing and the hot June sun was filtering through the shade trees as Luke carried his newborn son in one arm, while his other arm was securely wrapped around the back of Prudence's waist as they crossed the front porch of their little ranch house by the river.

"Are you okay, Pru?" Luke asked anxiously. "Do you feel strong enough to make it inside?"

Laughing softly, she glanced up at him. "Don't worry, darling. I feel wonderful. It's so great to be home—with our son," she added as her gaze dropped lovingly to the bundle cradled carefully in the crook of his arm.

"I really think you should've stayed in the hospital one more day," Luke said. "Just to make sure you're both okay."

"Nonsense. I gave birth yesterday morning, more than twenty-four hours ago. Since then, the doctor pronounced us both healthy as horses. And you should know what that means."

She moved ahead of him and opened the front door. As soon as they stepped inside, they were greeted with the scent of lasagna and freshly baked Italian bread.

"Oh, wow, someone has been here," Prudence exclaimed as she sniffed the delicious aroma. "I wonder who?"

Luke chuckled. "As if you didn't know. I'll be surprised if Kat and Blake aren't over here before the evening is over. Tag and Emily-Ann, too."

"I'd feel bad if they didn't show up," Prudence said. "And they've all had babies, so they know to keep a careful distance from little J.J."

They had named their son Jameson Jerome after both of their fathers, but Prudence had already nicknamed the baby J.J.

"All had babies," Luke repeated with a laugh. "That's an understatement. Jazelle and Connor's daughter, Madison, arrived two days after Thanksgiving."

"That's right. And then a week later, Tessa delivered Joe another son they named Gilbert. After Gil," Prudence said happily. "Now we've had our baby and

Isabelle is due any day. I'd say the ranch is prospering, wouldn't you?"

Luke smiled at her. "Between all the babies, the new foals and calves, the ranch is brimming over."

Grabbing hold of his free arm, she turned him toward the kitchen. "Let's go see what they brought us."

Inside the kitchen, they found a huge casserole dish of lasagna with a loaf of Italian bread next to it and a note that read, "Love, Reeva." Across the room on the large pine table stood a massive bouquet of blue and yellow flowers with a floating balloon announcing the baby was a boy.

"How beautiful!" Prudence pulled out the card and read, "'Congratulations from the Hollister family and all your friends.'"

"And look at this," Luke said, pointing to the huge blue basket sitting next to the flowers. "Someone was thinking of my sweet tooth."

"Oh, my! Emily-Ann has sent enough pastries from Conchita's to last a week!" Prudence exclaimed. "How am I ever going to repay all these kindnesses?"

"When the time comes, you can make sure their children get a good education," Luke said with a chuckle. Then, taking her by the upper arm, he ushered her in the direction of the bedroom. "Come on. You and little J.J. are going to lie down. I don't want you overdoing it."

Inside their bedroom, Prudence kicked off her shoes and obediently reclined on the bed with a pair of pillows propped behind her head. Directly across the hallway, the small guest bedroom had been transformed into a nursery, but for now they planned for the baby to sleep in a bassinet next to their bed.

"Don't put J.J. in the bassinet yet," she told Luke. "Put him right here next to me."

"Yes, Mommy." Grinning, he placed the baby at Prudence's side, then sat down on the edge of the bed next to them.

Pushing the corners of the receiving blanket away from the baby's face, Prudence gazed down at her new son. "I can't keep my eyes off him. He's so handsome. Just like his daddy."

"Are you trying to feed my ego? Or do you honestly think he looks like me?" Luke asked, as his gaze made a loving inspection of his son's face. "He does have lots of dark hair. And his eyes look like they might be brown."

"He has your mouth and dimples, too," Prudence added. "And he's very loud when he's hungry. I expect by the time he's two years old he'll be wearing a hat and a pair of spurs."

Luke chuckled. "That's right. Three Rivers is always going to need good horse trainers."

"You don't think he's going to be a superintendent like his mother?" she asked slyly.

Chuckling again, Luke shook his head. "Not this boy. Maybe the next one will be a girl and she'll be the studious sort like you."

He kissed her on the forehead and Prudence sighed with contentment.

"We married the day after Thanksgiving and since then I didn't think you could make me any happier," Luke said. "But you have. Giving me a son has put me on top of a cloud. I doubt I'll ever come back to earth."

Prudence's heart was overflowing with love as she scanned her husband's dear features. It didn't seem possible, but over the past months their love had grown even stronger and their life together was everything and more they imagined it might be.

"You'll come down off that cloud whenever he starts crying with a dirty diaper," she teased, then followed that with a kiss on his cheek. "Oh, Luke, you've made me so very happy, too. We have a beautiful home here on the ranch. We both have jobs we love and—"

He interrupted, "Only now you have a thirty-minute commute to St. Francis every morning to get to that job."

"That's nothing. Kat and I make the drive together. Gives us plenty of time to catch up on the daily gossip."

Grinning, he touched a finger to the tip of her nose. "I should've known you girls wouldn't waste the time," he said. Then he added on a serious note, "You do really like living here on the ranch, don't you?"

"Are you kidding? It's so beautiful here and I'm

surrounded by my friends." She looked down at the baby. "And, most of all, this will be the perfect place to raise J.J. and his brothers and sisters."

"Speaking of siblings, when are Daisey and your parents coming up to see the baby?" Luke asked.

"When I talked to my parents this morning, they said they plan to be here in a couple of weeks. But Daisey is another matter. She might show up any-time. If that happens, I hope you don't mind."

He nuzzled his cheek against hers. "Why would I mind? Your family is mine, too. And anyway, you might be seeing another Crawford around here pretty soon."

Prudence shot him a coy smile. "Luke, I'll need a few weeks to recuperate, and then it will take nine months to get another little Crawford here."

He chuckled. "That will be well and good when-ever you feel ready for another baby, darling. But I'm not talking about our own little Crawford. I meant my brother, Colt. Blake and Holt are trying to talk him into taking the position of horse barn manager here at Three Rivers."

She looked at him with interest. "Oh, I didn't know the job had come open."

"Mick's already put in his notice. He didn't want to leave, but his family over in California needs him right now," Luke explained.

"Do you think Colt will take the job?"

"I'm keeping my fingers crossed that he will. It

would be great to have my brother working close by. And I know he'd like the ranch."

Prudence slanted him a calculating smile. "Hmm. Wouldn't it be wonderful if Colt was lucky enough to move to Three Rivers and find the love of his life? The way you did?"

Drawing his face down to hers, Luke whispered against her lips. "No man could ever be that lucky."

* * * * *

COMING SOON!

We really hope you enjoyed reading this book.
If you're looking for more romance, be sure to
head to the shops when new books are
available on

Thursday 10th June

To see which titles are coming soon, please visit

millsandboon.co.uk/nextmonth

LET'S TALK
Romance

For exclusive extracts, competitions
and special offers, find us online:

- facebook.com/millsandboon
- @MillsandBoon
- @MillsandBoonUK

Get in touch on 01413 063232

For all the latest titles coming soon, visit
millsandboon.co.uk/nextmonth

MILLS & BOON

HISTORICAL

Awaken the romance of the past

Escape with historical heroes from time gone by. Whether your passion is for wicked Regency Rakes, muscled Viking warriors or rugged Highlanders, indulge your fantasies and awaken the romance of the past.

MILLS & BOON

HEROES

At Your Service

Experience all the excitement of a
gripping thriller, with an intense romance
at its heart. Resourceful, true-to-life
women and strong, fearless men face
danger and desire - a killer combination!

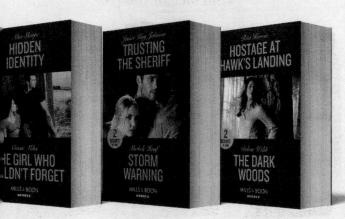

MILLS & BOON
MEDICAL
Pulse-Racing Passion

Set your pulse racing with dedicated, delectable doctors in the high-pressure world of medicine, where emotions run high and passion, comfort and love are the best medicine.